KT-446-606

Barbara Parker was born in South Carolina and has taken separate university degrees in History, Law and Fine Arts. For a while she was a prosecutor in the criminal courts in Miami, and eventually entered the private practice of law. Her writing career began when she produced a short story for her six-year-old son, and her first novel, *Running Mates*, appeared in 1991. *Suspicion of Innocence* is her second novel, and she has completed a sequel. The author now lives in Fort Lauderdale, Florida.

Suspicion of Innocence

Barbara Parker

Copyright © 1994 Barbara Jeanne Parker

Published by arrangement with Dutton Signet,
a division of Penguin Books USA Inc.

The right of Barbara Parker to be identified as the Author of
the Work has been asserted by her in accordance with the
Copyright, Designs and Patents Act 1988.

First published in Great Britain in 1994
by HEADLINE BOOK PUBLISHING

First published in paperback in 1994
by HEADLINE BOOK PUBLISHING

A HEADLINE FEATURE paperback

10 9 8 7 6 5 4 3

All rights reserved. No part of this publication may be
reproduced, stored in a retrieval system, or transmitted,
in any form or by any means without the prior written
permission of the publisher, nor be otherwise circulated
in any form of binding or cover other than that in which
it is published and without a similar condition being
imposed on the subsequent purchaser.

All characters in this publication are fictitious
and any resemblance to real persons, living or dead,
is purely coincidental.

ISBN 0 7472 4384 0

Typeset by CBS, Felixstowe, Suffolk

Printed and bound in Great Britain by
Mackays of Chatham PLC, Chatham, Kent

HEADLINE BOOK PUBLISHING
A division of Hodder Headline PLC
338 Euston Road
London NW1 3BH

With love
to Jeanne and Bill,
who are always with me when I write

Acknowledgements

Without the generous advice, inspiration, and wit of many friends, both old and new, this book would not have been nearly as much fun.

Special thanks to my editor, Audrey LaFehr, who took me into hardcover; and to Les Standiford, Director of the Creative Writing Program, Florida International University, who gently insists on real characters for commercial fiction.

For guiding me through criminal law and procedure, I am grateful to Sergeant David W. Rivers, Metro-Dade Homicide Bureau, who could make you confess to anything; and to Lance R. Stelzer, Esq., who could get you acquitted of anything. Karen H. Curtis, partner at Shutts & Bowen (Miami), is the kind of civil-practice attorney I'd like to be in my next life; and senior Circuit Court Judge Harold G. Featherstone still knows his probate.

I received lessons in history from Ronnie Jimmie, Miccosukee tribe of Indians; the Historical Museum of Southern Florida; W.S. Steele, Florida historian and archaeologist; and Robert S. Carr, Archaeological and Historical Conservancy (who wants to remind us that there really are nothing but old bones in burial mounds, so please don't go poking around in them).

Thank you, Warren Lee, for the stories about growing up moderately rich and wild in Miami. *Cariños a mis amigos cubanos*, Miriam Cabrera Mier and Carlos Maza for insights into Cuban-American culture. And for details I couldn't have done without: Ann Ciccarino, Carl Donato, Ray King, Patricia M. Kolski, and fellow FIU MFA's Christine Kling and Elizabeth Pittenger.

Finally, for her astute reading of the manuscript and some nifty turns in the plot, a hug to my sister Laura.

Prologue

Jimmy Panther pushed forward on the stick. The airboat shot over an open path through the water, then skidded around a fallen palmetto palm. Everyone leaned left, then right. The sawgrass was a green blur. Marie back at the gift shop would have his ass if she could see this. But she was the one who had sold these people the tickets, knowing he didn't like to go out this early, especially on Mondays. Jimmy intended to make this a fast trip, a couple miles into the Everglades and out again.

The four tourists sat in the square bow, kids clamped between their parents' knees as if they might otherwise jump out at forty miles an hour. The man held his sun visor on and the woman's blonde hair whirled around her head. Jimmy sat behind them, six feet off the water above a 327-cubic-inch Chevy engine. The noise from the propeller was deafening. Would be deafening, if he didn't have his ear protectors on. He'd given the passengers cotton balls. White tufts came out of their ears.

The girl twisted sideways far enough to look around her father's arm. She smiled, pigtails flying. He could tell she wanted him to smile back, so he did.

Jimmy wore a baseball cap to keep his hair out of his eyes. Marie had once told him a bandanna would look more authentic. He had laughed. How about a Tonto headband with a turkey feather in it? She did

1

insist on a Miccosukee jacket, though, and he obliged. He wore one his aunt had made, a long-sleeved, blousy patchwork of red and yellow and blue, stitched into geometric patterns and accented with rows of white rickrack.

He cut a sharp turn, leaning hard on the stick, and the airboat skipped sideways, sending out a wave that rolled over the sawgrass. The kids squealed and ducked down. The man and the woman hugged them into their chests.

These particular people in the airboat, he guessed they were from Sweden, the way their voices slid up and down. Probably taking a day trip off one of the cruise ships at the Port of Miami. Their noses and cheeks were already red. They weren't made for this latitude. The locals he took out were mostly younger, usually with a kid or two. The old people liked to take the bigger airboats up at Holiday Park where they could all sit together, a dozen or more behind a Plexiglas windscreen, with a roof to keep the sun off. The Cubans liked the airboat. They'd pay him extra to stay out longer. The blacks hardly ever showed up, for some reason.

Jimmy eased back on the throttle. The boat slowed, nosing down heavier into the water. The water was shallower here, and he didn't want to drag the aluminum bottom on a rock. He maneuvered into deeper water and hit the gas. The boat skimmed over the water, saw grass clattering against the hull. A few minutes later they broke into open prairie, and he ran the boat in a wide arc across the flat, unbroken surface.

Jimmy had seen the Everglades from the air a few times, a shimmering mirror, sky and clouds so perfectly reflected you could be looking up, not down. Dark curving areas where the land came out of the water far enough to be called dry. Straight gray lines where the roads went through, a glimmer of canal alongside. Nearer Miami you could see long scars where the ATVs kicked up dirt. You could see where the city was closing in. The land was drained and cleared in neat rectangles, scraped down to white rock that wouldn't dig, wouldn't move unless it was blasted out.

Nearing a line of trees, he cut the engine. The noise lifted off him like a thick hood. He dropped his ear protectors on a hook welded to the seat. The woman stood up and stretched, laughing and grabbing the man's shoulders when the boat rocked. She was about thirty, wearing shorts and a yellow 'Bayside Marketplace' T-shirt. She pulled the cotton out of her ears. The man did the same, then took off his visor, wiped his brow on his shirt sleeve. He smiled at Jimmy. 'It is warm today.'

Jimmy shrugged. Only the first week in March. These people should come back in August.

The boat drifted past a clump of water lilies. A plum-colored, red-beaked bird the size of a pigeon picked its way across the lily pads.

'What is the bird?' the woman said.

Jimmy pronounced it slowly. 'Purple gallinule.'

The husband clicked his camera. The bird vanished into the bushes before he could take another shot.

Jimmy swept his arm in a wide circle, going into his Indian guide routine.

'This land was formed many thousands of years ago. Early man came down through the peninsula, made his home here. Hunted deer and fished. They lived on islands, like that one.' He pointed to one of the hardwood hammocks a few hundred yards off, a clump of green rising out of the water.

'They had camps out there. You could go out on that hammock, maybe, and find where the early people lived, the Tequesta. You might find tools made from

3

shells or pieces of pottery. There's still some land like that, untouched.'

Four pairs of blue eyes were looking at him sitting up there over the engine. They smiled and nodded, didn't have a clue. Then the man turned toward the trees and took some pictures through his telephoto.

It was nearly nine-thirty. He ought to take them back. They would probably go to the snack bar, have some fry bread and frogs' legs for breakfast, being adventurous. He never ate it himself. Marie had it for the tourists, like the other stuff in the gift shop. Marie carried cypress wood spears, moccasins with hard soles made by the North Carolina Cherokees, rubber alligators, a line of souvenir T-shirts, postcards. Even a paperweight that when you shook it made snow over Miami. Probably the most true-to-life Miami souvenir in the gift shop, he had told Marie. But she didn't get it.

Jimmy swung himself down off the seat to stretch his legs. A breeze came up, bending the tops of the trees, blurring the image of the clouds in the water. The airboat drifted, sawgrass scraping the sides. The girl reached out for a long blade of it, testing the serrated edge.

'Careful. You'll get cut.'

With a wooden pole, Jimmy pushed them to where the grass was shorter, sparser, barely reaching past the sides of the boat. Beyond a clump of cattails was a county park, too small to attract many people.

The man was watching the water. 'There are alligators here?'

Alligators. They all wanted to see alligators.

Jimmy nodded, reached into a box under the rear passenger seat for the loaf of stale white bread he kept there. 'Look over that way. They like to hide in that pond, under the bushes.'

4

He untwisted the top of the bag, then sent a slice of bread spinning. It bobbed up and down, minnows snapping at it.

The girl leaned over the brownish water, the tips of her pigtails just breaking the surface. Her mother pulled her back by her shirt.

'I'll let you know if I see one.' Jimmy tapped the girl on the shoulder and jerked his thumb toward the pilot's seat. 'Sit up there.' After a second, the girl climbed up. Her brother followed, laughing.

The woman looked alarmed, said something in Swedish.

'No, it's okay,' Jimmy said. 'They're all right.' The kids sat side by side on the padded seat, holding on to the metal arms, playing with the stick. 'Just don't turn the key.'

Jimmy poled through the water, pushing against the weight in the boat. He saw the man's camera pointed at him, the lens opening, closing. The Indian guide on his airboat. He'd be in the same album with the gallinule. Jimmy tossed another piece of bread out ahead of them.

The man swung the camera toward the water now, ready for that long, dark shape gliding out of the shadows under the mangroves. That silvery path in the water, moving closer.

This was what the tourists came out here for. Slitted eyes just above the surface. A hiss, a flash of teeth. Pulling your hand back, laughing because the son-of-a-bitch had come *this close*.

Too bad they didn't speak more English. He would tell them about the lady down in the National Park. Leaned out a little too far with her camera, leather shoes slipping on the metal bottom of the boat before her old man could catch her. They pulled her back in, but the gators had done some damage.

5

Jimmy sent another slice of bread spinning. None of the tourists were talking now. A dragonfly hung over the cattails.

Then the boat rocked a little. The girl was standing up on the seat. She was steadying herself on the propeller cage, looking toward the break in the cattails, not saying anything. The water tapped against the sides of the boat. The girl squinted in the sun, looking toward the shore. Just looking, quiet now, not moving.

The boy stood up beside her, asked her something.

Whatever it was she said back, their parents' heads turned in the same direction. The woman stood on her toes, her hand shading her eyes. Jimmy stuck the pole in, leaned on it hard, pushing them closer.

He could see it now, too, about twenty feet ahead. The end of the nature walk, the heavy wood weathered to gray above the shallow water. Somebody had spilled a can of rusty-colored paint, maybe. The streaks had run down the two-by-twelve and one of the pilings. And there was what looked like a bundle of clothes just off the end. Bumping up against the pitted white rock, moving in the waves the airboat had pushed to shore.

Jimmy stared. The water ticked on the sides of the boat. He heard the buzz of flies. The knowledge came to him slowly, like a picture turning right side up.

The man pulled at the sleeve of his jacket. 'Go now. We are going back.'

Jimmy jerked his arm away. The airboat drifted sideways into the cattails. A flock of blackbirds exploded upward, screeching.

It was a woman. He could see a shoulder now, an arm. Pale, mottled skin. A red tank top. Blonde hair drifted around her head. Her body rolled face up. The nose and lips were gone.

She was small, almost like a girl.

Jimmy Panther clamped his teeth together against a rush of nausea.

He knew her.

Chapter One

Shortly past one o'clock in the afternoon, Gail Connor pushed open the heavy brass door of the Hartwell Building and turned west. At midday Miami shimmered – white clouds dancing across the glass skin of skyscrapers, narrow streets bathed in light. Squinting, Gail reached into her jacket pocket for her sunglasses.

At one-thirty she would argue a motion at the courthouse. She was in no mood to be nice to opposing counsel. If their latest skirmish was any indication, he would stumble through his argument and stare at his file as if somebody had stuck a copy of *Playboy* inside. Gail didn't like to beat up on other attorneys – that kind of attitude could come back at you – but today she felt like nailing him to the wall. This case should have been settled already. Either that or have gone to trial.

A gust of cool air washed over her face and neck. The doors to a shoe shop were wide open, the air conditioner pumping out onto the sidewalk. A clerk in a silky gold shirt and pleated pants stood near an outdoor bargain table of high heels. His skimpy mustache and smooth cheeks put him under twenty. Gail saw his eyes fix on her face, slide down her body, then climb up again, his head swiveling to follow her.

He spoke as she went by. *Oye, mamacita.* As if she were his type – five-nine, hair permed at collar length, marching down Flagler Street in a navy blue suit.

Tightly gripping the handle of her briefcase, she cut around a pack of Japanese tourists, then between two missionaries: dark-haired women in white dresses and high, pointed caps, offering religious tracts in Spanish. The pushcart vendors were out, and the smell of ripe fruit sweetened the air – peaches, grapes, mangoes, and strange tropical fruit she could not name and had never tasted.

At Miami Avenue, a 'Don't Walk' sign flashed on. She checked her watch again. One-ten. Not bad.

Five minutes would get her to the judge's chambers on the twelfth floor, where she would sign in with the bailiff. Like the other thirty-some judges in the civil division, Judge Arlen Coakley would schedule as many as two dozen cases on motion calendar, heard in the order in which the attorneys picked up the files. With any luck at all, her case would be first or second in line. George Sanchez was Latin – second-generation Cuban, to be exact – but as punctual as a Yankee banker. He might not be there when she signed in, but he would be ready when the case was called.

The light changed, and the crowd surged into the intersection.

The Dade County Courthouse occupied its own city block, wide steps leading to a slate terrace all around, Greek columns front and back. Gray blocks of granite rose twenty-three stories, ending at a stepped pyramid bristling with antennas. Turkey vultures roosted on top, a local joke: the spirits of deceased attorneys. They sat, shoulders hunched, then flapped away to catch the updrafts. Approximating tourist season, they arrived in November from somewhere in Ohio, then vanished before summer.

Gail pushed through the revolving door into the tiled lobby that echoed with voices. She laid her briefcase on the conveyor belt to be X-rayed, then stood in line to walk through the metal detector – routine in Miami courts.

The crowd was thinner on the twelfth floor, with only a handful of attorneys outside Judge Coakley's chambers at the end of the corridor. She knew some of them by sight. Her watch said one-sixteen. She would not be first, but close enough.

'Gail Connor.' The husky female voice came from the open waiting area across from the elevators. Gail looked around and saw Charlene Marks, a gray-haired woman in a red and white polka-dot dress.

'Hi, Charlene.'

'Would you believe, I was going to call you this afternoon.' Charlene dumped her file on a wooden chair.

A young blonde was sitting in the next chair, winding a Kleenex through her fingers. She wore a white leather dress with puffy feathers at the neck, and fringed white boots. A divorce client, Gail was certain. Charlene specialized, particularly in the rich or wacky.

The client could fit both categories. She looked up, her forehead creasing. 'Wait. What if they call us? Where are you going?'

'Right out there in the hall, okay?' Charlene patted her shoulder. 'Two minutes.'

Gail glanced toward Judge Coakley's door as Charlene lit a cigarette. Discreetly, because smoking was prohibited.

'I've got a case you can have, if you're interested.'

'I'm always interested,' Gail said. 'But give me a second. I need to check in with Eddie.'

The bailiff sat just inside the door. He glanced up from a folded newspaper when she leaned against his desk. 'Which case are you, Ms Connor?'

'*Darden v. Pedrosa Development*,' Gail said. She pointed at the computer printout in front of him. 'It's there, at the bottom of page one.'

Eddie clicked his ball point. 'Sanchez is outside?'

'No, not yet, but—'

'Can't write you down till you've got a team.'

'Come on, Eddie. He'll be here.'

'Sorry. New rule.' Eddie made a small check by Gail's name, then looked up. 'Go ahead and take the file if you want to.' There were two stacks of them on his desk.

Gail opened her mouth to argue, but another lawyer was already giving Eddie his own case number. She left the Darden file – heavy with pleadings, orders, and motions – where it was.

The clock on the secretary's desk said one-nineteen. Gail begged a couple of aspirin from her and took a paper cup of water from the cooler.

'What's the matter with you?' Charlene Marks asked when Gail returned.

'Eddie won't give me a number until the other attorney gets here.'

'Who's the other attorney?'

'George Sanchez.'

'Don't know him.' Charlene exhaled blue smoke out to one side. 'Maybe he's operating on Cuban time.'

'He's doing this on purpose, I know it.' Gail watched as pairs lined up outside the door.

'So if he doesn't show, you win by default.'

'No, I won't. He'll probably put another motion on the calendar to set aside the order on this motion, because he was mugged on the way to the courthouse.'

Charlene laughed out loud, then lowered her voice and pointed with her cigarette. 'That girl back there. My client.'

'The urban cowgirl?'

'Be nice. Does the name Marcanetti ring a bell?'

After a second Gail said, 'No kidding.'

The Miami Dolphins had just cut Dennis Marcanetti after his third drunk driving conviction. This time he had launched his Corvette into Biscayne Bay, making a perfect arc over a fishing boat carrying the Canadian consul. Marcanetti was said to be at Jackson Memorial with both legs in traction. Gail hoped Charlene had Marcanetti's signature on the divorce settlement before he took the ride.

Charlene said, 'Missy's got a problem with some business partners.'

Gail glanced over Charlene's shoulder. The soon-to-be-ex-Mrs Marcanetti was nervously swinging her foot, the fringe on her boot dancing up and down. 'I'll bet Missy's her real name.'

'Good guess,' Charlene said. 'Anyway, she and Dennis and another couple invested in this boutique on South Beach.' Charlene took a last drag off her cigarette and bent to stub it out in a stick-dry potted palm. She was grinning. 'Post-industrial chic, is how she described it.'

'The kind of place where they charge a hundred dollars for a bra made out of metal kitchen strainers?'

'Oh, so you shop there. Dennis gave Missy his share of the boutique as a part of the settlement, but the other two are trying to take over. I'm not up on commercial litigation, or I'd take the case myself.'

'How's the business going?' asked Gail. 'Profitable?'

Charlene rocked her hand back and forth. 'They serve wine. And the clientele is darling. The guys like the leather pants with the buns cut out.'

Gail dragged her eyes away from Missy, who was thumbing idly through a copy of *The Florida Bar Journal*, probably trying to find the pictures. 'I don't know. It sounds like something a smaller firm should handle.'

She glanced around when the elevator bell dinged. A clerk pushing a basket of files got out, a female

13

lawyer Gail had gone to law school with, and a tall Hispanic attorney about forty in an eight-hundred-dollar suit, carrying a shiny briefcase made of some kind of endangered reptile. He looked around as if to get his bearings. Still no George Sanchez, damn him.

She said to Charlene, 'We try to stick to bigger corporate accounts, unless the client can stand the fees.'

'Jesus. Don't you ever take a case for fun?' Charlene pretended to shudder. 'Poor you, in that big firm. I've got my own office and my own hours and if I want to screw off for an afternoon or two I can damn well do it.'

Then she looked past Gail's shoulder, her finely penciled eyebrows lifting. Gail turned. It was the man with the briefcase.

Charlene reached for his hand. '¿Cómo andas, mi amor?'

'Bien, bien. ¿Y tú?' He bent to brush his lips across Charlene's cheek when she turned it up to him.

'What brings you to these parts?' she said. 'This ain't criminal court.'

He did a slow smile, lines bracketing a curvy mouth. Lots of white teeth. 'I am here under duress, but your presence makes it a pleasure.'

Gail wanted to roll her eyes.

Charlene laughed and pulled him closer. '¡Cabrón!'

He glanced at Gail, acknowledging she existed. A subtle aroma of something expensive clung to his skin. She gave him a perfunctory smile.

'Gail, this is Tony Quintana,' Charlene said. 'He defended a couple of my naughtier clients last year.'

The dark brown eyes moved quickly over her face, taking inventory. No matter how good the manners, Gail was certain the sexuality could never be bleached out of a Latin male. She couldn't complain.

14

They were exquisite creatures to look at.

Gail stuck out her hand before he could go for her cheek. 'How do you do.'

Charlene said, 'My friend Gail Connor, of Hartwell Black and Robineau.'

His look was still polite, but something else slipped into place. He released her hand. 'Ah, Ms Connor. I think I'm looking for you.'

Gail could have kicked herself for being so slow. *That* Quintana. 'I assume George Sanchez can't make it.'

'Unfortunately, no. A conflict came up, and he asked me to take care of this matter for him.' Quintana's Spanish accent was barely there. He smiled, the charm back in place. 'George hoped we might work something out.'

'Oh? How optimistic of him.'

'Surely this isn't a case worth fighting over. Certainly not worth the time a firm such as yours will have in it.'

Gail would have bet money that Anthony Luis Quintana, Esq., had ordered George not to come, that he had been hiding out in the men's room to make sure the Darden case would be dead last on the motion calendar. 'I can tell you, Mr Quintana, attorney's fees are *not* an issue.'

'No?' He gave a slight shrug. 'But in your motion, you ask that my client pay your fees.'

'Correct. Due to your delays in—'

'Mine?'

'Your firm's. Your client's.'

He innocently raised his brows. 'But I am here. On time.'

Gail smiled back at him. 'Just go check in with the bailiff, why don't you?'

When he had gone, she muttered to Charlene. 'God. He ought to be flogged.'

15

Charlene's mouth twisted into a grin. She said, 'Gotta go. It's time to water Missy. Call me.'

They took their places in the back of the narrow room, Quintana by the door, his briefcase on the floor by his feet, Gail standing by the windows. Judge Coakley's big desk occupied the far end. Perpendicular to it was a long conference table, six chairs on either side. They were all taken, opposing attorneys facing each other. The judge rocked back and forth in his brown leather chair, the springs squeaking softly. Gail doubted he would oil them even if handed a can of WD-40. In chambers, he wore a short-sleeved shirt and tie, leaving his robe on a wooden hanger behind the door. Bushy eyebrows jutted over pale gray eyes. His hair, once auburn, had dimmed to rusty white.

'Good afternoon, ladies and gentlemen,' he said. 'I'm covering a hearing at three for Judge Potter, so let's not waste any time.'

Thank God, thought Gail. She leaned her briefcase against the wall and crossed her arms, looking toward the window, seeing nothing but blue sky at this height. The glass was cloudy with grime. A black shadow flapped slowly past, then swooped upward. She idly studied the photos, many turning yellow, that hung around the room. One picture showed the judge with Governor LeRoy Collins outside the state capitol in Tallahassee. Behind him half a dozen other men, among them Gail's grandfather, John B. Strickland, lined up across the steps. All men, all white, all in suits with thin lapels and skinny ties.

Rotating her shoulders, Gail dug her fingers into the muscles of her neck, barely listening to the drone of voices. Her skull felt like it was going to crack off right at eyebrow level. She knew the cause: She had lain awake until nearly three a.m. reliving her mother's birthday party Saturday night. It could have been

16

scripted by Tennessee Williams and badly overacted by the cast of a small-town dinner theater. Her mother pretending she wasn't really fifty-seven. Her sister Renee as the drunken little bitch, falling out of her tank top. And Gail's husband, Dave, playing the brooding son-in-law, making an ass of himself. Gail couldn't decide where she fit in, except as a reluctant audience, a witness to this tedious melodrama.

She noticed that across the judge's chambers Anthony Quintana was frowning into the pages of the thick court file on *Darden v. Pedrosa*. What was he doing, some last-minute cramming? She doubted he knew what he was getting into, a shoving match between two sets of clients – builder and home buyers – who were approximately tied for the jerk-of-the-year award.

Gail represented the buyers. When Nancy and Bill Darden had seen an ad in the *Miami Herald* for a subdivision called Cotswold Estates they had no idea that the builder would be Cuban. Nancy asked, 'Isn't that some kind of fraud?' They had signed the contract because the houses were 'so cute,' and because the subdivision was within five minutes of the new medical office where Bill worked, in the far reaches of West Kendall, where the Everglades still sent its feral creatures scurrying across clipped and watered lawns.

The concrete pad was poured, the drywall up, a hole for the swimming pool dug. But the roof didn't suit the Dardens. 'It's so spindly,' Nancy whined. 'I took some photos. Here, you can see for yourself. My God, if we have another hurricane, it will just blow right off.' The molding around the doors wasn't the heavy oak they had seen in the model, but white pine. The supervisor at Pedrosa insisted oak would cost them more. Bill said put it in, then made a stink on the next construction payment. So the builder installed cheaper kitchen fixtures. When Nancy saw the aluminum sink, she told the plumber she wanted stainless steel. He nodded, but spoke no English and installed porcelain at three hundred and fifty dollars. The schedule stretched out, and out, irate demands coming from both sides.

Bill Darden told Gail, 'They're trying to take us, I know they are. Damn Cubans.' And this while Gail's secretary, Miriam Ruiz, was handing them copies of the documents.

'I don't care so much about the money,' Bill said. 'Although of course three hundred thousand dollars is a fair amount to lose.' He took Nancy's hand. The slender, tanned hand with the gold and diamond tennis bracelet encircling the wrist. 'Nan doesn't want the house anymore. If they're going to be like that, God knows what it would be like to live there.'

Gail had sued for breach of contract, rescission, and delay. The other side had promptly countersued. Motions had flown back and forth. For the past two months Gail had tried to get the company's relevant financial records and take the depositions of its owners. All she had been given was excuses.

Gail wondered what lunacy made Ferrer & Quintana hang on so tightly. Latin machismo? Fat fees?

Whatever they got, it would be more than Gail expected to bring in. Nancy was the daughter of US Senator Douglas Hartwell, whose granddaddy had founded the firm. Not exactly kosher to waive payment of fees, but the other partners chalked it up to good community relations. Gail, doggedly working her way up to partner, had to smile and enter the hours on her time sheet in red.

She heard two soft clicks. Anthony Quintana had taken his office file out of his briefcase. She recognized the nervous doodles George had made on its cover. Quintana calmly began to flip through its pages,

18

marking this or that with a gold pen.

Anthony Luis Quintana was taller than the average Cuban, nearly six feet. His medium brown hair was swept straight back, thick and gleaming. He was a bit too flashy for a motion calendar in civil court, Gail decided. The jacket of his forest green suit was unbuttoned, showing an abstract print silk tie that must have cost more than dinner at the *Chez Vendôme*. And the shoes. Polished and tasseled, low cut. He wore patterned socks, darker green, with maroon squiggles in the weave.

As he closed the file, Quintana glanced up and saw her looking at him. Gail smiled coolly and let her eyes drift to the pair next in front of the judge.

Ralph Matthews, a black lawyer representing a downtown bank, sat opposite a young attorney who was apparently going down for the count.

Judge Coakley spoke with a mixture of incredulity and amusement. 'Mr Aguilar, what do you want this court to do? Do you want this court to issue a restraining order against a federally chartered bank? Do you want me personally to go down the street and tell them not to open their doors?'

'Your honor, what we're seeking—'

'I know what you're seeking, Mr Aguilar.'

Gail noticed the botched pronunciation: *Ag-will-ar* instead of, properly, *Ag-ee-lar*.

'This action is filed in state court because the relief demanded—'

'You're in here because you know good and damn well you can't get to trial inside of eighteen months in federal court, they're so stacked up with drug cases over there.'

Eyes politely fixed somewhere above his opponent's head, the bank's attorney sat, chin on tented fingers, waiting.

The judge extended a hand to him, palm up. 'Mr Matthews, do you have an order on this?'

The attorney pulled it out of the file. 'Yes, judge.'

Judge Coakley lifted a pen from a scuffed, gold-plated desk holder. 'I got no jurisdiction, Mr Aguilar. What you ought to do is run over to federal court and file this case where it belongs.'

The judge handed the signed order back to Matthews. 'As for state court, well, I've just got to say – Bye-bye.' He waggled his fingers. 'Next case, please.'

Matthews stood up. 'Thank you, judge. I'll make sure Mr Aguilar gets a conformed copy.'

'You do that. Next case.'

It was two-twenty-five when Gail took her place opposite Quintana at the end of the table, waiting their turns to slide down the line. The springs in Coakley's chair squeaked in a slow, steady rhythm. Eek-eek-eek. Like baby rats, Gail thought. The noise went right up her spine into her throbbing head.

She shifted in her chair.

Quintana was drumming his long fingers on his file. He wore a ring on his right hand. Gold with a diagonal row of diamonds. Not quite heavy enough to be tacky, she decided. Her eyes climbed up his sleeve, across his shoulder. He was watching something out the window. He had eyelashes like curls off a chunk of hard chocolate. A mouth you'd like to get your teeth on. Just a couple of notches this side of excessive, she decided. The kind of man her sister would go for. Yes. Renee's type exactly.

Gail leaned her forehead on her fingers and rubbed. Unbidden, unwanted, like photos thrust in front of her, scenes from her mother's birthday party intruded into her mind.

Click. Renee at the front door, arms flung out. Ta-daaaaaah! Gail hadn't seen her in months, until Saturday night. She suspected the only reason Renee showed up was to ask their mother for another loan. Renee had brazenly pretended Irene's present was still being engraved.

Click. Irene pulling Renee into the living room, showing her off to all her friends as if she had just come back from missionary work in Belize. *Click.* Renee, buzzed on Southern Comfort, talking Dave into playing the piano, though he hadn't played for years. Renee singing, 'The Way We Were,' the song that got her into the finals of the Miss Miami pageant ten years ago. Renee muffing the words halfway through, then falling into Dave's lap, both of them laughing, the piano bench going over, a tangle of arms and legs, Renee flashing her panties. He had kissed her cheek, still laughing, and helped her up.

Gail and Dave had argued again about it last night. No shouts. Just a cool exchange, leading to a colder silence. Gail took her pillow to the sofa. He must have seen her lying there this morning, but left her to wake up late, the weave of upholstery fabric on her cheek as red as a slap.

Gail pulled back her cuff far enough to see her watch. As soon as this was over, she would have to call Miriam. No way to make it back in time for the deposition at three.

When the attorney to her right moved along the line, Gail slid down another chair.

Quintana clasped his hands loosely on his legal pad. Gail could tell the writing on it was in Spanish. He must have done it to keep her from knowing what was there. Her own Spanish was barely conversational. She noticed his neat manicure, the nails buffed to a soft patina. Another ring on the left hand – gold with dark green stones. A thin watch with a black lizard strap was just visible under a spotlessly white cuff. And on his

21

right wrist – she would have been surprised not to see it – a gold link bracelet that could never have been mistaken for a woman's. He probably had a chain around his neck, too, with a religious medallion on it. The patron saint of Cuba, whoever that was, tangled in black chest hair.

On the left cuff she managed to decipher the initials upside down: *ALQP*, stitched in tiny red letters. Gail's curiosity about the P following the Q was cut short when she had to move to the next chair. She glanced up and Quintana was looking at her again. He leaned back in his chair and dropped his hands into his lap.

Finally, gratefully, she moved down to the final seat, and heard Judge Coakley say, 'Well, looks like you folks are all she wrote.'

'Gail Connor, with Hartwell Black, for the plaintiffs.'

'How you doing, Gail?'

Quintana's eyes lingered on her as he handed the judge the court file. He hadn't missed the familiarity. 'Anthony Luis Quintana, your honor. Ferrer and Quintana, for the defendant.'

'Good afternoon, Mr Quintana.' Gail noticed the twangy mispronunciation. *Kwintana*.

'That's *Keentahna*, judge,' he said, smiling.

'What? Okay. Sorry. I guess I ought to learn *español*.' Judge Coakley settled back, springs squeaking. 'Keentahna.' He opened the court file. 'Motion to suppress. Tell me about it.'

Startled, Gail sat up straight in her chair, staring across the table.

'Pedrosa Development is moving to suppress the plaintiff's request for production of certain financial records on the grounds—'

'Hold it.' Gail nearly laughed out loud. 'What motion to suppress? We've received no such motion.'

Quintana frowned at his copy. 'No? The certificate

of service is dated two weeks ago. It's in the court file.'

'Impossible.' She looked at the judge, but he lifted the top sheet in his file.

'Says it's a motion to suppress.' He chuckled. 'The post office strikes again.'

'Apparently,' said Gail. 'But I don't have it. And Mr Quintana's motion isn't on the computer list outside. His motion can be heard as soon as he properly sets it.'

Quintana bounced his gold pen lightly in his palm. 'Surely Ms Connor would not take up the court's time at another hearing, when we can dispose of this matter now.'

'We have had no opportunity to prepare for this motion, judge.'

Coakley was thumbing through the court file. 'Then what are you here on, Ms Connor? I don't see anything from your office.'

She felt her stomach tighten. 'A motion for sanctions on two matters, judge. First, fees. Second, along with the documents we want, we've attempted to take the depositions of Ernesto and Carlos Pedrosa for over two months, and—'

'Judge—' Quintana broke in. 'Ernesto Pedrosa has nothing to do with this case. He owns the company, yes, but in name only. Plaintiffs' counsel is aware of this.'

'I prefer to hear about it at his deposition,' Gail said. Her eyes were on the judge, who was still looking through documents.

'Here it is,' he said, pressing open the file.

'Such blanket production of the company's financial records is beyond the bounds of discovery,' Quintana said. 'The Florida Rules of Civil Procedure—'

'Don't quote the rules to me.' Coakley looked pained. 'This case just keeps coming back and coming back. Can't you settle it?'

'We've offered a reasonable settlement, your honor. The plaintiffs—'

Gail quickly broke in. 'What counsel would call "reasonable" is nothing less than total capitulation.' She noticed the judge look at his watch, and forced herself back on track. 'As we are here on my motion, I'd like to explain to the court—'

'No.' Coakley flipped the file shut. 'This is what I'm going to do. Mr Quintana, I'm ruling that your clients don't have to turn over the records on the list. It's too long. And Ms Connor, you go ahead and set the depositions. Both Pedrosas. I don't care if it's at two a.m. at the Orange Bowl, they have to show up. If they don't show up, come back and I'll make them pay whatever you think is fair. Are we clear on that, folks?'

Quintana looked pleased. 'Yes, judge.'

'And when Ernesto and Carlos arrive, they can bring all the records along and Ms Connor can look at them and decide what she needs.'

His smile faded. 'All the records? My clients cannot bring every piece of financial data—'

The judge stood up and walked across the room. He lifted his black robe off its hanger on the back of the door. 'I'm not going to listen to any more of this right now. She knows what records she needs.'

Gail put her file back into her briefcase, giddy with relief. 'Shall I draw the order on that?'

Anthony Quintana held the elevator door, his gold bracelet catching the light. He turned to Gail as he punched the button for the lobby. They were the only occupants. 'I'd like to see the order before you send it to be signed.'

'Yes. You probably should.' Gail added, 'I may have to call you so we can get it straight, just what his order was.'

24

Quintana smiled, the lines deepening around his mouth. She wished she knew the name of his cologne. She would buy Dave a bottle. 'Welcome to the civil division,' she said. 'Are you going to handle this case for George from here on in?'

'Why not? I know my way around juries.'

'A jury? On this case?'

'We did ask for one in our counterclaim.'

'Waive it.'

He shook his head slowly. 'And trust my clients' fate to Judge Coakley?'

'You've got to be kidding. We won't get a jury trial within our lifetimes. You have no intention of going to a jury on this.'

The elevator door opened. 'So settle,' he said, letting her go out first.

'It's a matter of principle for the Dardens,' Gail said. 'They don't want to pay for something they didn't get.'

'Easy to say, when you pay nothing for your principles.'

'What do you mean?'

'I've met Douglas Hartwell and I know who his daughter is.' Quintana looked out onto Flagler Street through the glass doors of the courthouse. 'I would venture a guess,' he said, 'that the resources of Hartwell Black are . . . fully committed.'

'So settle, Mr Quintana.'

'It isn't that simple.'

She waited, watching him smile.

'Pedrosa Development is owned by my grandfather, Ernesto Pedrosa. Carlos is my cousin.'

'So that's it. I knew you couldn't be so obsessive for no reason. You're not getting paid either. This is ridiculous, you know.'

'I know.' He sighed. 'Let me buy you a cup of coffee. We'll see what we can do about it.'

25

Gail looked at him, trying to figure this out. She doubted he was coming on to her, not that her wedding ring would stop him. Maybe he truly had nothing better to do than spend an hour dawdling over coffee, which she could not for a moment imagine. Or maybe he was sincerely trying to get the case off square one.

His eyebrows arched. 'I must have said something funny.'

'No, not at all,' she said. 'I wouldn't mind a cup of coffee, but at the moment I have to get back to my office.' She allowed herself another smile. 'Perhaps next time.'

He nodded, a single inclination of his head. 'I look forward to it.'

She watched him go through the revolving door, then trot gracefully down the granite steps, the sun glinting off his sleek brown hair.

Ah, yes, she mused. The letter P embroidered on his cuff. Pedrosa, if Ernesto Pedrosa were his maternal grandfather. Spanish names were confusing that way. Anthony Luis Quintana Pedrosa. His mother's surname at the end.

She dropped a quarter into a pay phone by the elevators and dialed.

'Hartwell Black and Robineau.'

'Hi, Gwen. This is Gail. I'm on my way back. Could you—'

'Hold on. Miriam wants to talk to you.'

'No, just tell her—' Too late. Annoyed, Gail listened to several bars of canned Mozart.

A click, then Miriam's voice. 'Gail, your mother called a little while ago. She wants you to call her back.'

'Fine, as soon as I get there. Have the three o'clock people shown up?'

'Not yet. I think you ought to call her. She sounded kind of funny.'

26

Something in Miriam's voice sent a chill skidding across Gail's shoulders. She hung up and dialed her mother's number.

The telephone rang six times before someone picked it up. 'Hello.'

Gail didn't recognize the woman's voice. 'Connor residence?'

'Yes.'

'This is Gail Connor. Let me speak to Irene, please.'

There was a hesitation. 'Just a moment.' The silence thickened, as if a palm had been placed over the mouthpiece.

Gail pressed the receiver closer to her ear. A faint buzz came over the line, then the hand must have been removed.

'Honey?' It was her mother's voice now, nearly a whisper. 'Can you come? Please?'

'What is it? What's wrong?' The sounds of the courthouse lobby echoed dimly in the background. 'Mother, what happened?'

'She's killed herself . . . Oh, Gail . . . my baby's gone.'

Gail would later remember the emotions that raced through her mind, one close upon another, in those seconds after she learned her sister was dead. There was an instant disbelief in which she closed her eyes and replayed her mother's words. Killed herself. Gone.

Then came a strange burst of anger. Renee had actually done this thing, selfishly not caring about the pain she would inflict.

Then a flash of spite: Renee had gotten exactly what she deserved. And then Gail was aware of her mother's grief.

She heard her sobbing over the phone, and she knew that the tears wouldn't stop easily, because they were for Renee, as they had always been for Renee. Gail would try to comfort her, but there would be more tears. More than if Gail had been the one . . .

Irene couldn't relate more than the barest details: a park near the Everglades; they found her this morning. Her wrists. A sergeant from the Metro-Dade Police came by the house, a nice man, very kind.

After a glance at her watch, Gail assured her mother that she would be home as soon as she could, please not to worry. Yes, yes, she would come. She would take care of everything.

All this while another part of her mind was frantically trying to figure out who would cover her appointment at three; how in hell she could reschedule every blessed court appearance for the rest of the week; how to pick up Karen from the sitter.

Then she hung up and turned around, leaning unsteadily against the edge of the phone booth, catching her breath. Someone across the lobby laughed. A soda clunked out of the machine near the revolving door.

Finally Gail felt the shame of knowing that her first reaction had not been sorrow.

She had felt all this, but never surprise. Not that. Renee had been heading toward self-destruction for years, and now, she had arrived.

Chapter Two

'Poor thing. Such a shock.'

The woman glanced past Gail's shoulder across the visitation room. Irene Connor sat on one of the long sofas, a small figure in black. Her sister Patsy was beside her; more people gathered in groups around the room.

'She's lucky to have you, Gail,' the woman whispered. 'Someone has to be strong. My brother Kenny died last year, you know. Cancer. A blessing, really, but our father fell apart. Just devastated. I was the only one who could manage.'

Gail had no idea who this person was. She forced herself to smile. 'We're so glad you could come.' Pretending to see someone else in the crowd, she excused herself and slipped away. They had been here since five, in this dimly lit visitation room with its cold, sweet florist's-shop smell. Gail supposed some of the flowers were from Renee's friends, but she wouldn't have recognized the names. There were the expected arrangements from family friends and out-of-town relations. But she knew most of the flowers weren't for Renee at all. They were for her mother. Irene Strickland Connor, a piece of local history, granddaughter of one of Miami's pioneer families. Even the mayor had sent a wreath.

It had been years since Gail had seen some of the people who had shown up. They had taken Irene's hand, dredging their memories or imaginations for something nice to say about Renee. Then they had walked between the rows of chairs to the recessed niche where the casket lay, gleaming wood and brass. More flowers. A crucifix on a mahogany stand had been placed behind it, and at each end candles flickered in tall, red glass holders. Gail had seen the puzzlement on their faces. They had probably expected to see Renee herself, returned to virginal innocence with paint and glue. Blonde hair laid in perfect curls on a satin pillow; lips set into a sad little smile. They might have expected to look at the bouquet of lilies and find that it didn't quite hide the black sutures on her wrists.

No one had asked Gail why the casket was closed. Maybe they knew.

Now she busied herself straightening a box of Kleenex on a table. Her watch seemed to have stopped at six-thirty. She wondered if she ought to call again to check on Karen. They had left her at Irene's with a neighbor's teenage daughter.

Gail glanced up at a movement at the door. Ben Strickland, Irene's favorite cousin, was coming in. He smoothed his white hair, looking around as if lost. When Gail crossed the room he held out his arms. 'Hey, honey. You okay?'

'Fine. I suppose.' Gail let herself lean against him for a moment. She rested her forehead on his shoulder, then pulled away. 'Ben, would you do me a favor?'

'Sure. Anything.'

'I'd like you to handle Renee's estate.' Ben had retired early from the circuit court bench six months ago, joining a small law firm on Flagler Street.

'You want me to be the attorney? Gail, honey, I wasn't in the probate division. I figured Irene would ask you.'

'We haven't discussed it. And I don't do probate either, you know.'

'That's true. But you've got people in your law firm who could guide you through it.' He saw her shake her head. 'What's the matter? You don't want to?'

Gail looked across the room at Irene. 'You know how she and I were about Renee. We agreed a long time ago that we'd be better off not talking about her.'

'Damn shame you girls didn't get along.'

'Well. Too late now. I'd feel strange getting involved, and I don't think Mother would really want me to.'

Ben thought about it. 'I'd have to get one of the other attorneys in my office to write up the paperwork.' His gaze moved to the casket. 'My God, my God,' he said softly. As Gail watched, his lips trembled. Then he laughed a little, embarrassed, and took a breath. 'I'm sorry. I didn't think I was going to get this way. Lord have mercy. All right, I'll talk to her about it, if you want.'

She squeezed his arm. 'Thanks, Ben.'

Irene was walking a friend away from the casket, their arms linked. Her sister Patsy laughed at something, and Irene gave half a smile. Irene was still pretty, a petite redhead with clear blue eyes. Today her eyes were swollen. Today she moved as though something inside her was broken.

When she saw Ben she put her arms around him. They stood silently for a while, her head under his chin. Her words were muffled against his shoulder. 'Oh, Ben. Why did she do this? Would somebody just tell me why?'

He awkwardly patted her back. 'Shhh. I don't know. I don't know.' He turned her toward the first row of chairs. 'Come on. Sit down for a while.'

Her lips pressed tightly together, Gail glared at the

31

casket. Renee could have had the decency to leave a note. *Dear Mom, Life is just too hard. Besides, I'm pregnant and I don't know who the father is. Forgive me. It isn't your fault.*

Gail had been the one to identify the body at the morgue – what was left of it. The one to hear the ME say that Renee was nearly two months pregnant. Not that this would have bothered Renee unduly. She was hardly a blushing Catholic schoolgirl. Even so, Gail didn't intend to tell her mother about the baby.

She grabbed a water pitcher from a nearby table and shook it. Empty. When she peered into the funeral director's office, his young assistant came out, hands clasped in front of him. Owen Finney wore a dark suit and a striped tie five years out of fashion.

'Yes, ma'am?'

She gave him the pitcher. 'I wonder if we could get some more ice water.'

'Certainly,' he said quietly, as if she had handed him a dead kitten. 'I'll take care of it. And more paper cups?'

'Thank you.'

'No problem.'

On her way back through the lobby Gail spotted Dave in an armchair in the corner, his eyes focused on the turquoise carpet. Above his head hung a mediocre landscape painting of snow-topped mountains. An odd choice for Florida. Gail supposed the shafts of light parting the clouds were meant to be inspirational.

She stood beside his chair. 'Dave?'

He glanced up.

'Doesn't it look a little odd, your sitting out here? You should be with the rest of the family.'

'Oh, my. Whatever will Aunt Patsy say?'

Gail sat in the other chair. 'Don't, Dave.'

'Sorry.' Her hand lay on the small table between them, and Dave entwined their fingers. He said, 'How's Irene?'

'Glued together with Patsy's Valiums.'

He nodded. 'I was thinking we ought to go get Karen.'

'A nine-year-old has no business at a funeral.'

'I went to my first funeral when I was five.' He withdrew his hand.

'We'll be finished in an hour, so what's the point?'

The front door swung open and two people came through it. The woman – in her mid-twenties, with a frizzy ponytail – wore spike heels and a knit dress that showed a rounded stomach. At least the dress was black, so Gail couldn't immediately assume she had wandered into the funeral home by mistake. Her legs were tan and muscled.

Her companion, a heavily built Hispanic, wore a royal blue suit with the sleeves rolled up, no tie. He had a mustache and a strand of hair which curled past his collar like a little black tail.

Glancing at a small sign with Renee's name on it, the woman pointed to the left. Long silver earrings swung against her neck. 'She's over this way, Julio.' They signed the guest registry and disappeared down the corridor.

'Good lord,' Gail said. 'What was that?'

'Some of Renee's friends, I would imagine.'

'A pregnant exotic dancer and a pimp. Lovely.'

'Christ, Gail. You're at her funeral.'

Gail leaned her forehead into her open palm. 'I'm sorry. Don't let me get like this in front of Irene. I don't know why I do it.'

'Because you hated Renee's guts.'

She raised her head. 'That's a rotten thing to say.'

Dave shrugged, then stood up. 'Well, I guess we

33

ought to go put in an appearance.' He waited. 'Are you coming or not?'

'In a minute.'

'Jesus. You're the one who wanted us both in there.'

Gail drummed her fingers on the arm of the chair, then got up and followed him back inside. He went off to talk to Ben. She found her mother in the first row of chairs with Patsy. Irene took Gail's hand as she sat down. 'Patsy says she can stay another few days.'

Patsy nodded. 'I told Kyle to go on home tomorrow. I'm gonna take a flight back to Tampa on Wednesday.' She settled into the chair on the other side of Irene. 'I need somebody to run me out to the airport, though.'

Gail hoped Patsy wouldn't ask her to do it. The mountain of work waiting for her at the office made her pulse race every time she thought of it. She had relied on the telephone and fax machine this week, but it wasn't enough. The senior partner in her department was beginning to wonder if he should temporarily shift some of her cases to other attorneys.

Patsy leaned back to look around Irene's head. 'I can't stand taxis, and I'm not letting Irene drive anywhere, the shape she's in. I swear, people over here drive like they're on drugs . . .'

Her voice trailed off as her eyes focused on something behind Gail. Gail turned to see. The other people in the room were watching, too, their conversations fading.

It was an Indian. He looked like an Indian, at any rate. He wore a patchwork jacket stitched in rows of colors – tiny squares and triangles of red, yellow, and blue. Half a dozen strands of beads hung around his neck.

The Indian waked slowly along the aisle, his eyes straight ahead of him. His long hair, black with silver shot through it, was tied back in a leather thong.

He stood at the casket for more than a minute

34

before he turned and looked at Irene. She smiled up at him. 'Why, Jimmy.'

He stood silently in front of her, then put his hand on her shoulder. 'Mrs Connor, my heart is full of sadness for you.'

'That's sweet.'

'Renee's body is lying over there in the coffin, but her spirit is with the Mother of the Earth.'

Gail exchanged a look with Patsy. Where had he learned this routine, old Westerns? The stoic Indian, not a hint of a smile, talking about death and spirits in a rumbly bass voice. Everyone within earshot stood transfixed.

Irene said, 'Do you know my other daughter Gail?'

The Indian's eyes shifted. He gave a polite nod. 'Glad to meet you.'

'Gail, this is Jimmy Panther. Remember I told you about him? From the Historical Museum?'

'Oh, yes. How do you do.'

'And my sister Patsy. She's from Tampa.'

After a second, Patsy smiled. 'Hi. I like the jacket. What kind of . . . Seminole, right?'

'Miccosukee,' he said, and shook her hand when she held it out.

Jimmy Panther reached under his hair to take off one of the strands of beads he wore. It tinkled softly. Bells. He opened Irene's palm and held the strand over it, tiny white shells. From the bottom hung three funnel-shaped silver bells.

'These were made by my grandmother. Like the ones that Coacachee – known as Wildcat – brought back from the spirit world after he was called by his dead sister.'

They clicked together and caught the light as he let them drop into Irene's palm. She looked at them, uncomprehending.

35

'The white represents purity and peace. The bells are the voice of the dead person. They help you remember her.'

Irene picked them up. The bells rang softly.

He said, 'When Renee visits you in your mind, you must welcome her. And don't cry over her. That would make her spirit sad.'

'I'll try,' Irene whispered.

Patsy stifled a sob and pressed a Kleenex to her nose.

Jimmy Panther nodded. 'We all have a time to die. We're lucky if we can choose our place. Renee liked the Everglades. It is a good place to die, if your time has come.'

Irene stood up and put her arms around his neck, still clutching the beads. 'Thank you,' she said, and he let her kiss his cheek. Jimmy Panther placed his hands momentarily on her shoulders, then silently turned and crossed the room, everyone watching until he had gone.

Gail wandered far enough into the lobby to see the front door close behind him. She hadn't known he and Renee were friends. They could well have met at the Historical Museum, when Renee was working there as a volunteer. What Gail did know was that Irene had already donated more money than she should have to Jimmy Panther's Miccosukee history center. As far as Gail had heard, the center was still no more than a pile of concrete blocks out on the Tamiami Trail, the highway heading west across the Everglades.

Irene didn't need anyone playing on her sympathy, Gail thought. Particularly not Jimmy Panther, with his beads and his bullshit about Renee's spirit.

A brown pickup truck turned out of the parking lot. For an instant, flashing from window to window, Gail saw the Indian at the wheel, patchwork jacket off, his elbow resting on the edge of the door. He wore a short-

36

sleeved blue shirt. There was a gun rack in the back window.

Gail turned around just as Dave came into the lobby.

He pulled his car keys out of his pocket, then studied them in his hand. 'I'm going to get Karen.'

'Dave, we already decided.'

'*You* decided.' He headed for the door. 'I'll be back in time for the services. It'll be good for her.'

Gail followed through the door, across the slate terrace, then down the steps. 'Do you want her to remember Renee like this? In a funeral home, in a casket? She can't even see her.'

'Does it matter?'

'Are you that bored?'

He whirled to face her. 'I'm not *bored*, Gail.'

Gail leaned against the side of their Buick. Under her dark suit she felt hot, prickly. The sky was still a bright, cloudless blue, the wind rattling the fronds of the palm trees in the parking lot. She pushed her hair off her forehead.

Dave sorted through the keys on the ring. 'Karen liked Renee, you know.'

'Damn it, that isn't the reason I left her home.'

He unlocked the door and waited for her to get out of the way. 'Do you mind?'

They looked coldly at each other for a moment, then Gail moved aside. 'You be responsible for her while she's here.'

Dave got in. He turned the ignition and the backup lights went on. The Buick shot into reverse at the same time as a silver Mercedes coupe cornered at the street and sped across the lot.

'Dave!'

Both cars slammed on their brakes, the Mercedes skidding on a patch of loose dirt. The Buick bounced, its horn blasting. Gail saw Dave look angrily over his shoulder and raise his middle finger.

The other driver's dark tinted window slid down. She could see him now, a bearded man in gold-rimmed sunglasses. He leaned out the window and screamed something in Spanish. But Dave was already halfway to the street. The Mercedes backed into a parking space and the window slid up.

The car's chrome grille bore a gold Mercedes emblem the size of a dinner plate. On each headlight there was a tiny gold-colored windshield wiper. The door opened.

The driver tucked his tie into the front of his dark blue jacket. He was young – thirty, not much more than that – and a bit pudgy. His hair was thinning on top, but his beard was thick, closely trimmed to his face.

He closed his door, catching sight of Gail at the same time, and grinned at her. Behind him, the headlights flashed. There was a high-pitched chirp from under the hood. He spun the key chain around his finger and turned toward the front of the building.

A drug dealer. Or an auto thief particularly careful about his own property. But then, most of the luxury cars in Miami had alarms. At every clap of thunder they would go off like so many frightened children.

In the lobby Gail checked the guest registry. No name had been added to those of the women from her mother's parish who had come in just before him.

'Ms Connor?'

She looked up.

It was Owen Finney. He whispered, 'I have a message for you.'

'Oh?'

'Yes. Father Donnelly called to say he might be late.' Something in Gail's face made him add, 'He took a wrong turn off the expressway. He'll be here, for sure.'

She checked her watch. Not quite seven. 'All right. Thanks.' She should have been grateful that a priest was coming at all. It had been damned hard to find one.

Gail had spoken first to Father Hagen at Irene's parish, which her mother attended now and then. He was a thin, hollow-eyed man, his theology drier than his handshake. He offered his sympathy, but doubted he could in good conscience appear at the services. Gail knew it wasn't Renee's suicide that bothered him. He was still ticked off that Renee, at seventeen, had told him to kiss her sweet white ass. Irene had never heard about this.

Gail said yes, she understood, but it was Irene who needed him, not Renee. For fully more than two minutes, Father Hagen mulled it over, his eyes fixed on the ceiling. Finally he told her he could put her in contact with a Father Eamon Donnelly. Father Donnelly was Irish, retired from a country parish, and recruited by the Archdiocese of Miami.

Father Hagen explained: The church had a crisis on its hands, what with the older priests dying off, and so many Latin American Catholics immigrating in. And then there were the Haitians – Heaven only knew what the Archbishop was going to do without priests who could speak Creole. Luckily Father Eamon Donnelly had picked up some Spanish in Madrid. He had consequently been sent down to Homestead, to minister to the migrant workers in the tomato fields.

Father Hagen apologized when he handed Gail the telephone number, but Gail caught the flicker of satisfaction in his eyes.

The next day Father Donnelly said of course he would come. Naturally a donation to the poor was customary. Two hundred dollars, cash preferred. After a moment of stunned silence, Gail said she would arrange it. He asked about Renee; Gail gave him Irene's number.

What a joke, she thought now. A Catholic funeral for an atheist. Flowers from people who would never have spoken to Renee on the street.

As she began to turn away from the window, Gail caught sight of a sporty gray Cadillac turning into the driveway and disappearing past the side of the building. The funeral director's door was open and there was a window behind his desk that faced the parking lot. She went in far enough to look through it. The driver had seemed familiar.

The car stopped in a space next to a cluster of palm trees. Its brake lights went off. The door opened, and a man's foot in a low-cut black shoe appeared, planted on the ground for a moment before the rest of him got out.

It was Anthony Quintana. Gail had thought so, but couldn't imagine what he was doing here. He started walking toward the building, then stopped. Gail automatically tensed before she realized he was looking at someone who had come around the corner.

She saw a beard and a blue suit. The drug dealer – if that's what he was – said something to Quintana. They spoke, standing at some distance, not a smile from either of them. Then the younger man headed for his car, and Quintana came toward the funeral home, so close to the window she could see the subdued pattern in his tie. No splashy colors today. His suit was charcoal gray, conservatively cut.

Possibly the bearded man was one of his criminal defendants. But why was Anthony Quintana here? Much as the idea intrigued her, Gail doubted he had come because of her. Courtesy did not extend that far. Had he known Renee?

She heard footsteps behind her. It was the funeral

40

director himself – thin, balding, his eyebrows lifting. 'May I help you?'

Gail murmured an apology and left his office.

She went back to the visitation room and looked past a group of women from the country club. Anthony Quintana was standing at the casket, head bowed, one hand on the kneeler. The diamond ring was gone. Today he wore a different one – silver with black stones.

He finally turned around and she met him at the last row of chairs. 'Thank you for coming, Mr Quintana.'

'Please, call me Anthony.' He took her hand. 'I was very sorry to hear about your sister.' he said. 'We will all miss her.'

'You knew Renee?'

'Yes. From the title company.' When Gail looked at him blankly, he said. 'My law firm owns a title company. Renee worked there in the closing department. I thought you knew.'

'No, I—' She tried to remember precisely what she had heard from Irene or Ben. 'I knew Renee had a job for a title company, but I didn't know where.' Gail began to walk with him back across the room. 'You didn't mention Renee the other day when we met.'

'Should I have?'

Gail considered. 'No, I suppose not.'

He said, 'Would you introduce me to your mother? I'd like to offer her my sympathy.' Anthony Quintana's manners were impeccable, even courtly.

Irene didn't recognize his name, but brightened when he spoke of Renee.

He said quietly, 'She will be missed, I tell you this sincerely. Her sense of humor. Her compassion for other people's troubles.' He reached into his jacket pocket. 'She left this on her desk.' he said. 'There were other things, but nothing so personal.'

'Oh, my.' Irene unfolded it, a gold-colored photo

41

frame with two hinged sections. She studied each one.

There was a photograph of a Caribbean harbor, Renee in the foreground in the stern of a fishing boat. The other made Gail hold out her hand. 'Mother, may I see it?'

Irene gave it to her, then turned to talk to Anthony Quintana.

Gail held the frames closer to the lamp. She saw two little girls flying up in a backyard swing, both in shorts and sneakers. The smaller one was sitting down, legs straight out. The other girl stood up, leaning back, holding onto the chains.

Gail remembered the chirp of rusty metal, the sun in her face, the lurch of her stomach as they reached the zenith and fell back, the earth rushing toward them. Renee was laughing, a giggle that wouldn't stop. A shadow cut across the grass – whoever took the picture. A man. Their father, probably. The colors were faded now. One corner was torn.

Gail stood there with the frame in her hands, until her mother tugged it away.

Irene said, 'Thank you so much, Mr Quintana. You were very kind to bring this.'

'Not at all.'

Gail walked with him to the door.

'Call me Monday, if you think of it,' he said. 'Maybe we can work on settling that case.'

'Oh, yes. That.' Gail shook her head. 'I'm afraid I haven't drawn the order yet.'

He looked at her for a long moment, then said, 'The photograph upset you.'

'No. Well, perhaps a little. I haven't seen it in years.'

'You looked so much alike,' he said. 'Your hair was the same color then.'

'I was the taller one, of course.' She laughed. 'We were so skinny, weren't we? That was our backyard.'

'Yes.' Then he added. 'Renee told me.'

'She did? You knew her well?'

'We met about a year ago.'

'Ms Connor?' Owen Finney had come up behind her, his hands clasped. He said softly, 'Father Donnelly is here. He asked to speak to you.'

Gail glanced back at Anthony Quintana. 'I'm sorry. I have to go.'

'We'll talk next week,' he said.

She followed Owen to a room further along the corridor, a small office. Father Donnelly – Gail assumed the elderly man in the notched collar must be the priest – was hanging his coat on the back of a chair at the other end of the room. A white robe on a hanger lay across the desk.

He turned when she came in, smiled at her, and nodded. 'Missus Connor, is it?' He was a short, balding man with broken veins on his cheeks.

She hesitated. Mrs Metzger, actually, but she didn't use Dave's last name. 'Yes,' she said.

He met her across the room and took both her hands. He was breathing quickly and his face was flushed. A wisp of gray hair, wet with perspiration, angled across his broad forehead. She noticed his cheek where his razor had missed, leaving a patch of white stubble.

'God comfort you in your time of sorrow,' he said, and squeezed her hands.

'Thank you.' She glanced again at the robe. It wasn't necessary. It was too ceremonial for a funeral home. She had expected only the black suit and a simple stole around his shoulders.

He patted a tissue across his forehead. 'Please forgive my tardiness, Missus Connor. I lost my way. And the traffic!' His accent sounded even thicker to her now than it had over the telephone yesterday. Pure brogue.

43

Gail reached into her pocket for the envelope containing the money he had asked for.

'Oh,' he said. He took the envelope as if he had no idea what it was, then dropped it into the pocket of his coat. 'I am sorry to bother you with such things.'

Gail said, 'Have the director let us know when you're ready to begin.' She turned to go.

'No, wait a bit. Wait a bit.' The priest stuck his thumbs under his suspenders, which made two lines down his shirt, curving over his belly. 'This is a difficult thing, your sister. Unfortunate. But I'm glad to help. She had her burdens, didn't she? As do we all. I ask, shall she be shut out of heaven because she couldn't carry them, and stumbled?'

The late afternoon sun was hitting the small, high window. Gail could see the shadow of steel mesh behind the curtains.

'Father Donnelly . . . is there something you wanted to talk to me about?'

'Sit down, if you like. I'll be only a minute or two.' He lifted his white robe off its hanger. 'When I was in Ireland, I had a parish. A small parish, and I knew each family well. It was in Clonmel. Did I tell you?'

'Yes,' Gail said. 'You did.'

He nodded, sliding his arms into the wide sleeves, one, then another. The robe belled out, catching a puff of air, then settled over his black trousers. 'I have no parish of my own now,' he said, 'but still I like to know the loved ones I pray for. I have done so many I could read the service with my eyes closed, and be thinking about my supper. But that's not right, is it?' He zipped the robe to his neck.

Gail frowned slightly. 'I thought Mother told you about Renee.'

'She did, bless her, but—' Father Donnelly's cheeks colored and he smiled sheepishly. 'When I spoke to

44

your mother, I wrote it down, what she told me, on a little piece of paper. And I seem to have lost it.'

He thrust his hand through a slit in his robe into his pants pocket. 'Now could I have . . .' He sighed. 'Oh, well. Doesn't matter. Tell me about her. I'll remember what you say. She was . . . a young woman, was she not?'

After a pause, Gail shrugged. 'She was twenty-nine. Never married. No children. I'm her only sister. Our father died when we were very young.'

Through the open door Gail could hear music begin to filter down the corridor from the visitation room. Strings and a flute. She looked at the priest. 'What exactly do you want to know about her?'

'Tell me . . . who she was,' he said. 'Her work. What she liked to do.' He slid a narrow purple stole off its hanger and lightly kissed the cross embroidered on the center of it, murmuring words she could not hear.

Gail felt suddenly closed in, as if the room had grown too small. As if she had intruded into preparations for a rite of death that had nothing to do with her. Father Donnelly lifted the stole and put it carefully around his neck, smoothing the satin fabric, aligning the edges.

He glanced at her. 'What was she like?'

'What was she like . . .' The seconds seemed to stretch out. Gail's mind was reaching for something, anything. Did he want details he could sprinkle through his prayers, or did he want the truth? Her lips would not move.

And yet to say nothing was untenable. As if her silence would be weighed and judged.

'Renee had a beautiful voice. Or at least she did at one time. She could have sung professionally. But she . . . well, her lifestyle wasn't exactly conducive to sustained effort, you might say.'

45

Gail's smile faded as Father Donnelly continued to look at her. He prompted, 'And her work?'

'She . . . she worked in a real estate title company,' Gail said, aware of how banal it sounded, how unreal. 'I don't know whether she liked it or not.'

He waited, not moving, standing quietly in his robe.

Her mouth was dry. 'I don't know what to tell you. I don't.'

The funeral director tapped at the open door. 'Excuse me. Everything is ready.'

Gail nodded. 'Yes. I'm coming.'

She looked back at Father Donnelly. His hands rested lightly on his chest, thumb and forefinger holding the edges of his stole. The nails were ridged, the skin like parchment. An old man's hands, she thought, and then noticed their peculiar grace.

Gail said, 'Renee was expecting a child.'

'I see.'

'My mother doesn't know. I don't want to tell her.'

'Renee confided in you, did she?'

'No. No, I found out from the coroner. She didn't— We weren't . . . close.'

He nodded slowly.

'We used to be. As children, I mean. Then something happened between us as we grew older. I don't know why.'

Father Donnelly picked up his liturgy from the desk – a thin, black book, its corners soft and frayed, showing cardboard underneath the binding.

Gail's throat felt tight. 'I thought sometimes we should start over, you know. For our mother's sake. But . . . we never did.'

Turning the pages, he found the right place in his book, then closed it on his thumb.

'I think,' he finally said, 'that in our last hour, we are all forgiven.' He looked up, smiling at her. 'Go take your place. I shall say . . . Renee Michelle, beloved daughter and sister. It's enough.'

When Gail returned to the visitation room, everyone had moved to the rows of chairs facing the casket. Ben's arm was around her mother's shoulders. Dave had come back with Karen. Her hair was brushed into a ponytail and tied with a ribbon. Gail sat between Karen and her mother.

There was a soft buzz over the sound system, then 'Ave Maria' came through the speakers, a clear soprano voice singing in Latin, soaring, resonant.

Karen pulled on Gail's arm. 'Mommy.'

'Shh.'

'Mommy, come here.'

Gail turned to her, whispering. 'What is it?'

'Is Renee in there?'

Gail nodded.

'Why can't we see her?'

'Because . . . We can't. I'll explain later.'

Karen sat quietly, her feet crossed at the ankle, swinging back and forth a little. Gail glanced at Dave. His eyes were shiny with tears, the muscle in his jaw tensing into a hard knot. It occurred to her she ought to reach across Karen's lap to take his hand, but this reversal of sympathy was too strange.

They were all trapped in a surreal play, she thought. All of them playing parts. The casket was a painted prop. An urge to laugh ran through her, and she clenched her hands together. The soprano on the tape was reaching for the last high notes now, and making them easily, her voice rich and liquid, pouring into the room like a kind of light.

'Mommy.' In the momentary silence Karen was tilting her head up to speak. 'Why did she kill herself?'

Gail gave Karen a look hard enough to make the girl

face front again, but then put her arm around her shoulders.

As if from a distance she heard Father Donnelly begin the liturgy, but Karen's question repeated itself in her mind.

Why? The reasons were there, if you looked. Depression, anger. A woman hitting thirty, with nothing to show for it. Too many burdens, as the priest had said. Not hard to understand, if you knew Renee.

Gail gradually became aware that Father Donnelly was leading the room in prayer. She smiled at the Irish accent. He said, 'We pray that God may free our sister Renee Michelle from punishment and darkness.'

The people around her gave the response, a murmured chorus. *'Hear us, Lord, and have mercy.'*

Gail could not speak.

'We pray that in his mercy God may forgive all her sins.'

'Hear us, Lord, and have mercy.'

'We pray that God may give her peace and light forever.'

'Hear us, Lord, and have mercy.'

Gail's eyes fixed on the casket, the candles at either end flickering in their red glass holders.

When her father had died, it must have been June because the poinciana in the park across the street was in full bloom. Blood-red blossoms made an arching canopy. Renee had run across the street, legs pumping, hair streaming out behind her. Irene screamed for her to stop. But Renee was already in the park, grabbing handfuls of blossoms from the lowest branch. Ben carried her back across the street, kissed her, then lifted her up to let the red flowers fall into their father's casket. At thirteen, Gail had looked sullenly on, wishing she had been the one to think of it.

Chapter Three

Whenever it was that the sky brightened from gray to blue outside her fourteenth-floor window, Gail didn't notice. She was paying more attention to her work than to the view. She had laid out her papers and case files in neat stacks on her desk, to be attended to in order of importance. She held a microcassette recorder in one hand and flipped through the pages with the other.

'Miriam, on *Ewing v. Southeast*, send copies of the complaint and answer to Dan Mursten with a note, 'At your request enclosed find, etc. If you plan to file as an intervenor please contact me before doing so.'

Gail reached for her time log. She wrote down the case name and number and the activity code – LTR Dan Mursten. In the space for time she entered point-three. Three-tenths of an hour, eighteen minutes, which reflected the amount of time she would have spent if she had sat back in her chair for a review of the file, then dictated the entire letter, word for word. No attorney in his right mind would have done it that way. Only, perhaps, the naive, the senile, or anybody not under pressure to make forty billable hours a week at one hundred seventy-five dollars per hour. Forty hours which did not include staff meetings, reading legal publications, reviewing documents sent back down from word processing, fielding phone calls from potential clients, going to the bathroom, or having normal conversations with other human beings in the office.

No one who expected to make partner at Hartwell Black and Robineau would stop at forty hours. The truly creative might log fifteen billable hours from eight in the morning to five in the afternoon, five days a week, and grab another ten or so on the weekends. If you couldn't cut it, you would be gone. Sooner or later, they would make it known to you: find another job.

For three mornings in a row, determined to make up for time lost the week before, Gail had arrived while the city was still dark, checking in with the sleepy guard in the lobby. She had ridden up in an empty elevator, then let herself in with her key.

Hartwell Black and Robineau took up the two top floors of a granite block building dating from the thirties. The main reception room on the fourteenth could have been lifted from an English manor house: deep leather furniture, landscape paintings, a polished staircase curving to the upper floor. On the hour, a grandfather clock melodiously chimed. The firm employed a butler, an elderly man in white gloves who would direct important clients through the maze of hallways, or push a tea cart to the partners' meetings.

Despite the impressive facade of the public areas, only the partners possessed offices of any considerable size. Others made do in a warren of rooms and cubicles, most of them crammed with outdated furniture. Gail's office held her desk and chair, a credenza behind it, a bookcase, and two chairs for clients. She had bought all these herself, in blonde wood, brightened with plants and framed prints of tropical flowers.

Gail ripped the duplicate time slip off the log and stuck it in the file – the last that absolutely had to be done today to avoid the pits of hell yawning open at her feet. By Friday she might be completely back on schedule. The file went into a cardboard box on the floor by her desk.

She pulled a stack of correspondence, memos, and messages directly in front of her. For a moment she gazed down at the cards on top of the pile. Sympathy cards.

Yesterday she had thought of taking them home, of writing thank-you notes to the senders, many of whom had also sent flowers to the funeral. Last night at the doorway to her office, turning off the light, she had noticed them, and had left them on her desk. There were sixteen cards, envelopes neatly paper-clipped to show return address. *In the time of your sorrow . . . God's guiding hand . . . With sincere sympathy for your loss . . .* Pastel-colored sunsets, open garden gates leading who knew where, Jesus Christ holding a lamb.

Now she sat looking at them as if they had been left there by mistake. Last night Irene had called her at home, not for anything in particular, and mentioned Renee. Surprisingly, Gail couldn't remember what Renee looked like, an odd fact she had not passed on to her mother.

She pressed the button on her recorder. The tape spun slowly. 'Miriam, about these sympathy cards. My personal stationery's around somewhere. See if you can run a thank-you note through your PC, something simple. And use the person's first name. At the end just put "sincerely." I'll sign them.'

Gail set the cards aside.

Of the telephone messages the first six went into the trash can under her desk; those matters had already been handled. The next was a message from Nancy Darden, stapled to the four that she had already left. Gail could almost hear her, that put-out tone, those whiny syllables. Nancy would have said to Miriam, 'Her sister died? Oh, to baaa-a-d. Well, what is Ms Connor doing about our caaa-a-se?'

Ms Connor was taking care of it, thank you. Ms

51

Connor planned to have a settlement proposal by week's end.

Click. 'Miriam, give Nancy Darden a call and tell her the order went out Monday to the opposing attorney for review . . .' Gail hit the stop button. No good. She'd have to call Nancy Darden herself, who would get her nose out of joint if she had to discuss the case with a mere secretary. Gail hadn't called Anthony Quintana yet because she wanted to go over the entire file first. Perhaps she would do that over lunch, then call Nancy in the afternoon. She rewound the tape and cancelled the instructions.

The next two messages were also stapled together. A Sergeant Frank Britton of the Metro-Dade Police had called twice yesterday. Gail didn't know any Frank Britton. None of her cases had that name listed as a witness.

'Oh, yes,' she said, remembering. She had made a contribution a few years ago to the Police Benevolent League or the Police Athletic League or something like that, and they kept coming back, worse than Jehovah's Witnesses. She routinely sent a check, like warding off evil, getting that PBA reflective sticker for the rear bumper of her car. The form letter had come in recently, stamped envelope included.

'Miriam. This message from Britton at Metro-Dade. I think he's collecting for the PBA. Call him and see what I gave last year. If he doesn't know, tell him I'll send fifty bucks. And do a personal check.'

Gail pressed rewind. The tape chittered. She hit play until she found the right spot. 'Call him and say I'll send twenty-five dollars.' The way things were going with Metzger Marine, she shouldn't be so free with money.

Dave's company was in trouble. *Their* company, actually. Dave had bought if five years ago, a complete

52

line of powerboat parts, with a marina and shop attached. But it had sucked up their savings and added a second mortgage to their house, and now a new set of creditors was getting impatient.

Leaning back in her chair, Gail pressed her fingers to her chest and rubbed. The cup of high-octane from the coffee room half an hour ago was making her heart jump. A little tickle, then a thud. Same thing last night. She had felt it lying down in bed.

On Sunday Dave had complained about missing his usual doubles match because Gail, who planned to work, had forgotten to get a sitter for Karen. The blame in his voice had rankled. He said, 'Jesus Christ. How the hell long is this supposed to go on?'

Gail blew up. 'Ask me that when I don't have to carry the load around here. When you spend more time at work than you do on the tennis courts, ask me that.' She had slammed the door behind her. Later she called from the office, feeling guilty. There had been long silences on the phone, neither of them knowing what to say.

Her family was becoming entries on her time sheet: order and pick up pizza, point-four; look over daughter's homework, point-five; lovemaking with husband, point-three. Lately there seemed to be more pizza than lovemaking.

Gail set the rest of the messages beside her telephone. She would return the calls starting at nine, an hour from now. It took her just under two minutes to review four final bills to be sent to corporate clients. It took five minutes to flip through a memorandum of law prepared by one of the law clerks and another fifteen to dictate changes.

Next was an interoffice memo from Stanley Birken, a partner in the banking division. He had spent the weekend in Palm Beach at the polo matches. The owner of a string of ponies, one *Señor* Osvaldo Hoffman de Armas of Asunción, Paraguay, brother-in-law to the president, had expressed interest in raising venture capital for expansion in South Florida. If any of the members of the firm would wish to attend a cocktail party at Stanley and Margot Birken's home on Grove Isle next Tuesday evening . . .

Gail dropped it into the trash. A high-tone Tupperware party.

'Good morning, Ms Connor!' A voice sang out from the corridor.

Gail swiveled her chair toward the door and smiled.

It was Miriam, her face still flushed from what must have been her usual fast walk from the Metrorail station. Gail had seen her one morning practically skipping along the street, long brown hair bouncing on her shoulders.

Gail said, '*Buenos días* to you, *chica*,' in the purposefully thick American accent that usually made Miriam laugh.

This morning it didn't. Miriam looked at her with almost motherly concern. 'Were you here early again?'

'No, I spent the night.' Gail put the box of files and papers on her desk and ejected the cassette into it.

'*Tú eres loca*.' Miriam came in to take the box. There was a policy about not speaking Spanish in the office, which she selectively ignored.

Gail rummaged in her desk for another tape. When she glanced up, Miriam was still there. Her eyes had grown moist. They were large brown eyes, outlined in black pencil. 'You are so brave,' Miriam said. 'If I lost my sister, I wouldn't know what I would do. She's my best friend.'

Such young, uncomplicated goodness. Miriam was married to a twenty-two-year-old paramedic for Hialeah Fire Rescue. Their wedding picture was on her desk, along with snapshots of their baby. Miriam's mother kept the baby during the day. Her father owned a shoe store. Traditional Cubans, they still chaperoned Miriam's younger sister Naomi. Miriam called her mother at least twice a day.

'I'm all right,' Gail said. 'Thanks.'

'Can I bring you another cup of coffee?'

'Better not. I've already had two.' Miriam picked up the box of files.

Gail said, 'Wait. Did you see that temporary girl around this morning?'

'Cindy? We came up in the elevator.'

'Who's she working for this week?'

'Bob Wilcox, I think.'

'I'll arrange to have her help you out this afternoon.' Wilcox was one of the new babies. One good thing about being higher on the ladder: In an emergency, Gail could raid his cookie jar and he couldn't do much about it.

More than once Gail had thanked God, Allah, or whatever other divine benefactor had blessed her with Miriam Ruiz. The girl was more on the ball at twenty-one than most of the firm's established secretaries. Unfortunately, whoever thought up the pay structure rewarded longevity, not brains. To keep things fair, Gail quietly gave Miriam cash on the side.

Miriam scurried out the door with the file box, on her way to her glass-fronted cubicle across the hall.

A tap came on Gail's open door.

'Good morning.' It was Lawrence Black, her supervising partner. He was only thirty-eight, but already graying, with a high forehead and long, thin face. The original founding Black had been his grandfather. Larry was lucky to have the name, Gail thought. Most of the family's intellectual currency had been spent before it got to him.

She wondered what he wanted. He rarely dropped in unless he had something to bitch about. Conferences were usually held in his office upstairs.

'Hi, Larry. Sit down.'

He took one of the client chairs, putting his coffee mug on the corner of her desk. The mug had an Orange Bowl Committee logo on the side. She doubted Larry had been inside a courtroom in years. He didn't have to. He and the other fifteen partners of the firm went out and hustled business.

'I've not had a chance to come down and ask how you are,' he said. 'Is there anything I can do?'

She shook her head, smiling. 'No, I'm fine. Thank you.'

'Deedee asked me to tell you she has extra snapshots of the school musical. The girls look great. I'll bring you duplicates of the ones with Karen, if you like.'

Their daughters were in the same third grade at Biscayne Academy, which had put on *Winnie the Pooh* last month.

Gail said, 'Yes, I'd like to have copies.' She restrained an impulse to look at her watch.

Larry took a sip from his coffee mug, then held it in his lap. 'I had a little chat with Jack Warner yesterday.'

'Did you?' Warner supervised the litigation department.

'He noticed we're showing a lot of hours on that case for Doug Hartwell's girl.'

So that's what this was about. Gail lined up the cassette recorder with the edge of the desk. 'I sent you a memo last week, Larry.' Which he had obviously forgotten. 'I could give a copy to Jack.' That would be the fastest thing to do. But perhaps not the smartest. She had learned a long time ago that partners rarely seemed pressed for time. A grand illusion, no doubt, but so was half the practice of law. 'Better still, I'll drop

56

by his office sometime this afternoon and bring him up to date.'

'Excellent.' Larry nodded, then stood up. 'Well, duty calls. Another damnable staff meeting.'

Gail walked with him to the door.

He glanced at someone passing by, lifting a hand in greeting, then looked back at Gail. 'I'm having lunch with Jack in the partners' room upstairs at noon. Why don't you join us?'

On the penthouse floor, connected to a four-star continental restaurant, the firm had a private dining room, one area for lowly associates and another, grander space for partners and their guests.

She smiled. 'Certainly.'

When he had gone she closed the door and leaned against it, grinning to herself.

Three gold-framed oil portraits hung in the main lobby – the men who had founded Hartwell Black & Robineau in the twenties, when the land boom hit Miami. The firm had survived the boom, the bust, hurricanes, depression, and immigration from both north and south that had turned Miami from a sleepy tourist town to the unofficial capital of the Caribbean. Flashier, bigger law firms had formed, died, and reformed, clustered in the sleek glass towers lining Flagler Street or Brickell Avenue, but nobody could match Hartwell Black for longevity or tradition.

She had been with the firm for eight years, ever since the summer before her final year of law school, hired as a clerk against stiff competition. They hadn't mentioned Judge Ben Strickland, but of course they knew. Gail was an honorary member of the club. Since then, she had worked damned hard, and had the clients and the cases to show for it.

There were eleven women attorneys out of sixty-seven, not a bad ratio for a crusty old firm like this one.

But only two women partners. Gail intended to be the third.

Back at her desk, she dropped the new tape into her recorder, ready for the stack of legal pleadings which had arrived since Friday. Miriam had already assured her that none of them was vital enough to warrant a same-day reply. Gail worked her way through four of them, then stared at the next.

'I do not believe this. The absolute balls—'

It was a motion for recusal on *Darden v. Pedrosa Development*, asking that Judge Arlen Coakley disqualify himself and send the case to another division. George Sanchez's signature appeared at the end for Ferrer & Quintana.

Disbelieving, Gail scanned the motion. '. . . the close business and personal relationship between not only the court and plaintiffs in this case but between the court and said plaintiffs' attorney, prejudicing thereby the rights of the defendants to a fair, just, and equitable result in this matter.' She recognized the overblown prose – definitely George. Accompanying the motion was a notice requesting that the court set a special hearing. That alone could take anywhere from three to six weeks.

Of course she knew the judge, but he wouldn't do her any special favors. And it wouldn't make a damn bit of difference to Coakley that he was an old friend of Senator Hartwell. The motion was only going to piss him off.

Then again . . . Coakley might throw the case out of his division if he was that pissed.

'Damn.' Gail tossed her pen on the desk. George had written the motion, but was he devious enough to have thought of it?

She picked up the phone and dialed. Anthony Quintana had talked about settlement. He had come to the funeral with that little double-photo frame for Irene. How nice of him. Now this.

After two rings a female voice answered – a bilingual answering machine. Gail waited, tapping her nails on the arm of her chair.

'This is the law firm of Ferrer and Quintana. *Esta es la oficina de Ferrer y Quintana.* You may leave a message at the tone. *Deje su mensaje al sonido electrónico. Gracias.'* Beep.

'This is Gail Connor, Hartwell Black. Please have Mr Quintana call me as soon as he gets in.' She recited the number, then let the receiver down sharply, glancing at her watch. Eight-fifty.

After dutifully writing point-two in her log, Gail paper-clipped the duplicate time slip to the pleading. As if the firm were going to collect a dime.

'Ms Connor?' Miriam knocked, then opened the door. 'There's somebody in the lobby to see you,' she said.

'I don't have any appointments scheduled this morning.'

'I know, but Gwen said there's an Indian named Panther, or something like that—'

'*Jimmy* Panther?'

'*¡Imagínate!* And Gwen says he told her it's important.'

'No.' Gail laughed tiredly. 'Tell him to write me a letter. Or come back next week.'

'He says it's about your sister.'

'Oh, lord.' Gail let her breath out. 'I suppose he wants . . . I have no idea what he wants.'

'Well, if it's about your sister . . .'

She rolled her eyes. 'All right. Bring him in. Five minutes, I mean it.'

Without the dim lights and flickering candles of the

59

funeral home, Jimmy Panther could not pull off his role as mystical shaman quite so neatly. But still, when Miriam showed him into the office, Gail noticed two paralegals walking slowly past her door, watching.

He was dressed in blue work pants and a beige short-sleeved shirt that showed dark, muscled forearms. There was only one strand of beads around his neck, green glass ones with an amulet of some kind that clacked softly when he walked.

Gail automatically extended her hand. 'Good morning, Mr Panther.' The name felt strange coming off her tongue. 'Sit down.'

'Thanks.' When he let go of her hand she saw the bone handle of a knife at his side. His belt ran through the sheath. She couldn't see the blade, only a bit of shiny steel before it disappeared into eight or nine inches of hard brown leather.

He glanced down, then up again, smiling slowly, showing slightly crooked teeth. 'Miami is a dangerous place. Somebody grabbed me one time in the parking lot outside the Historical Museum.'

'Really. I hate to think what you did to him.'

'That was before I carried this.' Jimmy Panther sat in the chair closer to the window and rested his elbow on the ledge. 'I haven't had any trouble lately.'

Miriam still hovered. 'Mr Panther, can I get you a cup of coffee? Some tea? A Danish?'

'I'll pass on the Danish. Tea would be great. Some artificial sweetener. I'm trying to watch my weight.' He shifted his long ponytail from between his back and the chair.

Miriam turned to Gail.

'Nothing for me. And Miriam. Would you close the door, please?'

Jimmy Panther was looking around the office, vaguely

oriental eyes traveling over the books and files and furniture.

He turned them on Gail. 'Renee said you were a lawyer. What kind of law do you do?'

'Commercial litigation. Some real estate. Whatever they hand me.'

He leaned to his left to look through the window, which faced north. Gail knew what he would see: air conditioning fans on the silver-painted roofs of run-down stores and offices, the downtown college, the federal courthouse, and to the east a small slice of Biscayne Bay, as much as could be seen from this angle. The partners had a better view, all the way to the Atlantic.

Jimmy Panther pushed lightly on the bottom of the metal frame. 'Doesn't open.'

Gail said. 'Mr Panther. You wanted to see me about Renee?'

'You can call me Jimmy, okay? First, I'm sorry about what happened. I liked Renee. We got to be good friends. I never thought she'd do something like that. I'm glad it was me that found her, though, not a stranger.'

Gail had to let this sink in. '*You* found her?'

'I run an airboat off the Trail. I went out early that day with some tourists.' He let a second or two go by, as if wondering how much more Gail might want to know. Then he said, 'Renee liked the boat. I took her out a few times, down around Shark Valley.'

'I see.'

He nodded. 'We met at the Museum. I did lectures on Indian life. She supervised the kids' tours. She was good with the kids.'

'Renee?'

'Yeah. We talked a lot about history. She was really into it. I guess because your family has been here a while.' He smiled again, his black eyes pushed into

61

slits. 'I had to tell her, my family was here longer.'

There was a soft knock on the door, then Miriam came in with a styrofoam cup. She set it down on a napkin, along with a blue packet and a stir stick.

'Thanks a lot,' he said.

Behind his back, Miriam raised her eyebrows at Gail before she pulled the door closed.

Jimmy Panther poured the sweetener in, then dropped the corner he had torn off inside the little bag, and folded it neatly. His hands were heavy with calluses and nicked with scars.

Gail rocked back and forth in her chair.

'Anyway,' he said. 'Why I'm here. I called your mother yesterday and she said I should talk to you.'

'Mr Panther. Before you even ask. If this is about a contribution in Renee's name—'

'No.' He looked surprised. 'No, it's not. Renee had something of mine and I need to get it back.'

'Oh?'

'I lent Renee this mask my grandmother made.'

'A mask?'

'Right. Made out of clay.'

'By the same grandmother who made the beads?'

'Yes. She had a kiln outside in the chickee. Used to make ashtrays and ceramic alligators and stuff for the tourists.' Jimmy paused, then said, 'Renee liked the mask, so I let her borrow it. It's in the shape of a deer head.' He spread his hands about eight inches apart. 'About so tall. Reddish color. It has lines carved around the eyes, big ears. You might have seen it at her apartment.'

Renee had owned a condominium in Coconut Grove on a shady street where the buildings were half hidden behind oaks and banyan trees. Gail had been there only once, to find something for Renee to wear in her casket.

'No,' Gail said. 'I don't remember anything like that. But I could have missed it.'

'Your mother said you hadn't cleared Renee's things out yet. I could meet you over there.' He blew across the surface of the tea, then took a swallow.

'Well, I doubt that I'll be going again personally,' Gail said. 'Forgive me for asking, but do you have some proof it's yours?'

'Only what I tell you.' Jimmy Panther's eyes showed no readable emotion. He said, 'My grandmother is dead now, and I don't have much of hers left.'

Gail continued to look at him.

Panther said, 'Irene told me she didn't mind if I looked around, but I should talk to you first.'

'She said that?'

'Yes.' He smiled. 'I told her it's like a piece of the old woman's spirit is wandering, and needs to come back home. And anyway, Renee promised to bring the mask back to me last week. Then this happened.' He drank his tea.

Gail pushed a lock of hair behind her ear, glancing away to hide her annoyance. She had no reason not to give Jimmy Panther the deer mask. Maybe his grandmother had made it.

'Why did you lend it to Renee?'

'She thought Indian masks might go good in the shops in the Grove, so she took it around to a few places, like a sample. We don't have many ways to make money, except with our hands.' Jimmy Panther paused. 'I'm telling you this in confidence. I don't want the idea to get out.'

'I won't tell a soul, trust me.' After a moment, Gail nodded. 'All right. As far as I know, my mother is going over to Renee's condo next weekend. I might go along, I'm not sure. Either way, we'll look for the mask.'

'I appreciate it.'

'Please do one thing, though. Call me if you have any further questions. My mother shouldn't be disturbed.'

He put his empty cup on the window ledge, then pulled a piece of paper out of his shirt pocket and gave it to her. 'You can leave a message at this number. It's the gift shop where I park the boat.'

Gail walked Jimmy Panther to the corridor, and Miriam took him back to the lobby.

The Indians had a few tourist shops along the two-lane highway, but Gail didn't know what they did to earn a living. She had seen the trailers and shabby concrete block houses on the Tamiami Trail – US 41 – near the Miccosukee Reservation. Further east, toward the city, at the intersection of Krome Avenue, in the middle of a flat nowhere, the tribe had leased out some land for a bingo hall, a building as big as a football field. Gail had been there out of curiosity. It was managed by people with Italian names, and the staff wore black vests and ruffled shirts. Not an Indian in sight, except the occasional one at a bingo table, marking the numbers off just like the tourists or the older people bussed in from their retirement communities.

The idea of Renee on an airboat, or hobnobbing with a Miccosukee Indian, was incredible.

Gail sat down again with her cassette recorder and a stack of correspondence to answer. She had almost finished when the intercom buzzed. She marked her place and picked up the phone.

'Yes, Miriam?'

'Anthony Quintana said you called him?'

'Indeed I did.' Gail lifted papers to find the motion for recusal. 'By the way, if you've got the Darden file out there, bring it in, will you?'

Before lunch – before Jack Warner looked at her over his prime rib and Caesar salad – this had to be straightened out. Gail hit the button and leaned back in her chair. 'Mr Quintana. Guess what I found on my desk this morning.'

'Hmm. I don't know. What?'

'A motion for recusal.'

'Ah. George told me he mailed it Monday. Apparently he didn't call you.' The soft voice had a tone of surprise that Gail didn't buy for a second.

'No, he didn't. Who's handling this case, you or George?'

Quintana let a couple seconds go by. 'You asked to speak to me, and here I am.'

Miriam came in with the file and left again.

Gail spoke slowly. 'Mr Quintana, I'm going to assume this is your case, all right? I don't know how they do things over in criminal court, but I can tell you this: Judge Coakley doesn't like attorneys playing around with the system. Fair warning. Don't make me bring this up on an emergency basis.'

'Are you asking that I withdraw the motion? Until there is a settlement, the case proceeds. We both know how this works.'

'If you prefer.' Gail twisted the phone cord around her fist, imagining it was his silk tie. 'You've no doubt had a chance to review the order I drafted. A courier can take the original to the judge this afternoon. And as long as we're on the subject, we may as well discuss a date and time for me to depose Ernesto and Carlos Pedrosa.'

She thought she heard him sigh. 'Listen, Ms Connor – No, I won't be formal with you. Listen, Gail. We could drown ourselves in paper and procedure. But now we are speaking to each other – not face to face, but speaking nonetheless. I had hoped we could leave the adversarial relationship for the courtroom.'

The man was smooth, she had to give him that

65

much. 'I'm not hard to get along with,' she said. 'But motions out of nowhere set my teeth on edge.'

'As I can understand. All right, then. Let's talk about it this afternoon. Allow me to buy you that cup of coffee you declined before. I have a deposition to attend in your building, so it would be convenient.'

Gail noticed the way he pronounced deposition: with a soft *s*, not the hard English *z*. She ran her thumb down the plastic index tabs sticking out of the Darden file. 'I'll be honest with you. My clients aren't in a mood to be generous.'

Anthony Quintana chuckled. 'We must both beware of our clients. What time?'

'I need to speak to the Dardens first. May I call you early next week?'

'Of course. Until then.'

Gail hung up, then frowned at the thick file on her desk, with the motion on top still creased from mailing. She knew when she was being pushed. Most attorneys who tried it went for a full tackle. Nothing personal, of course, and afterward everybody shook hands and had a drink together. Those were the rules. But Quintana was playing another game: Get her unbalanced. Smile. Try charm instead of cold demands. If she doesn't play along, then get tough.

Just try it, *amigo*, Gail muttered to herself. She reached for her time log. Point-four. If she could only send a bill in this case, the Dardens would be on their knees to settle.

She opened a foreclosure file, then swore softly when the intercom buzzed. She picked it up.

Miriam said, 'It's that Britton guy from Metro-Dade. He's outside.'

'Who?'

'The police officer you wanted me to call, remember?'

'He's here?'

66

'Uh-huh. I don't think he's collecting for the PBA.'

Typical plainclothes cop, Gail thought as Miriam closed the door behind him. Muted blue plaid jacket, a dark tie, short brown hair, gold-framed glasses. A late-thirties guy going slightly heavy around the middle. He could have been an appliance salesman for Sears. Until he handed her a white card with a gold shield on it. Metro-Dade Police Department.

'Ms Connor, I'm Frank Britton. How are you this morning?'

She took his hand, extended across her desk. 'Sit down, Sergeant. What's this about?'

He had a pleasant face. She had seen faces like that before, on expert witnesses about to testify. Settling into the witness chair, straightening the front of his jacket a little, getting comfortable.

Gail put the card on her desk. 'This says Homicide Bureau.'

'Yes, ma'am. I'm investigating your sister's death.'

She sat down in her chair. 'I don't understand.'

'You might know this, being an attorney, Ms Connor. The Homicide Bureau looks into suicides, just like any other death by unnatural causes.' Britton's delivery was polite, his accent from somewhere in north Florida, that down-home drawl uncommon in Miami.

He said, 'Now, we did a preliminary investigation at the scene last Monday, after we got the report. Search of the area and so on. We did her apartment the same morning, but—'

'Is that routine?'

'Absolutely. We look to see if anybody's in there. You never know. There could be somebody injured or deceased. And if she had a roommate, we'd want to notify that person.' He paused to make sure Gail understood, then said, 'I want to go back and do it again. Your mother said to call you.'

'Did she? Why? I mean, she is the personal representative.'

'She didn't mention it. I thought you'd probably be handling your sister's affairs.'

'No. And my mother didn't mention this . . . investigation to me.'

'Maybe she forgot,' he said. 'It happens. People don't like to think about death.'

'But Renee killed herself. Isn't that what the death certificate says?'

'No, ma'am. It's still pending. We're not going to release the certificate until I can look into it further, and I usually start with the decedent's place of residence. Last time we had the landlord let us in. If we go back, we're going to need a search warrant unless we have a family member along.'

Gail said, 'I don't see the point. Renee was found in a county park with her wrists slashed.'

'Yes, ma'am, a policeman comes in, starts asking questions, when everybody is trying to get over the loved one's death. I realize it can be a shock.'

Half smiling, Gail looked down at his card, aligning it with the edge of her desk. 'This is unreal. Do you do this with all suicides?'

'Lord, no. We don't have that kind of manpower. It's a judgment call, usually after somebody asks us to look into it.'

'Meaning my mother.'

Behind the glasses, his pale blue eyes showed sympathy. 'You can kind of see her point. There was no note, for one thing, or a terminal illness. Most people who do themselves in are depressed. Your mother didn't think Renee was in that frame of mind.'

'Did she tell you Renee tried to kill herself before? With a razor blade?'

'When was that?'

'About four years ago.'

'Huh.' Britton said. 'Well, we still need to check it out. When can you come let us in?'

'Look, Sergeant, I don't mean to be difficult, but I really don't have the time for this.'

The light reflected in his glasses. 'Then we'll have to get a warrant. Or ask Mrs Connor to go with us.'

Gail let a few seconds go by. 'All right. I can meet you Saturday morning.'

'Friday's better.'

'Fine. Five o'clock. It's the best I can do.'

After Britton left, Gail told Miriam to hold all her calls. She sat at her desk with both feet curled under her.

Irene might have gone so far as to call the sheriff of Dade County. And if he didn't know who Irene Strickland Connor was, then she would have referred him to the Mayor of Miami. They might not pay attention to every distraught mother, but they had to this one.

A few years ago Gail had come by Irene's for lunch and had found her at the kitchen table thumbing through a brochure for burglar bars. This in a walled neighborhood with a guard house and security patrols. Gail had been mystified until she remembered Irene was due for minor surgery the next week. Irene had come out of the hospital; the bars had never been installed.

Gail berated herself for having let three days go by since she had last seen her mother. But the days were a blur; she could barely remember any of them.

She got up and crossed to the window ledge, where Jimmy Panther had left his teacup. She picked it up. He had said Renee promised to bring the clay deer mask to him last week. That could show something about her state of mind, if he was telling the truth. If Jimmy Panther could say what he wanted. And Renee had a history of forgotten promises.

Gail tossed the cup into her trash basket.

Chapter Four

Irene Strickland Connor lived in a subdivision a few miles north of downtown called Belle Mar whose homes ranged from twenties Mediterranean to ultramodern glass and soaring wood. At the main entrance, Gail put on her blinker and turned from Biscayne Boulevard onto Seagrape Lane. The smaller street, bordered with royal palms and flowering hibiscus, divided at a tiny guardhouse. Ten years ago, nervous about civil disturbances and immigration, the residents had put up an eight-foot-high security wall.

'Open the gate, sweetie,' Gail said to Karen. The girl sat in the passenger seat of the Buick with a gate opener pointed at the striped barrier across the road. She pressed a button and the wooden arm swung upward.

Karen closed her geography book, which she had been reading on her lap.

'Did you finish the chapter?'

'Almost.' Karen leaned over to put the book in her book bag.

'Almost?' Gail slowed over a speed bump. 'You won't keep your A's that way. You can finish it while I'm talking to your grandma, all right?'

Ben had called her at work that afternoon. He had prepared the estate papers for Irene's signature and wanted Gail to notarize them. He had insisted: *No, no, I don't want to hear you're too busy. Bring Dave. We'll all have dinner together. Besides, Irene says she hasn't seen you all week.* Trust Irene for melodrama. Gail had seen her three days ago.

Seagrape Lane meandered past Banyan, Bottlebrush, and Jacaranda and finally ended in a circle. Gail pulled into Irene's driveway, tires crunching on acorns from the overhanging oak tree. The house was a rambling one-story with a facade of old brick and a white tile roof darkened with mildew. An orange cat sprawled on the porch, licking its paws. A tabby watched them from a window ledge.

At the front door Gail used her own key, letting herself into the foyer. Karen followed, her school bag bumping past the screen door, which banged shut behind them. The painted metal decoration on it – a flamingo – rattled on loosened rivets.

'Irene! It's us!'

After a second, a muffled voice called out, 'In the kitchen.'

Gail found her pulling plastic containers and foil-wrapped plates from the refrigerator.

'You're early,' Irene said. She set a casserole on the table, the glass lid clanking. 'I was going to have dinner all ready for you, and here you are.' Her voice was husky enough to make Gail wonder how much she had had to drink.

Karen dropped her book bag in a chair. 'Hey, Grandma.'

Leaving the refrigerator door wide open, Irene held out her arms. 'Come here, precious.' She enveloped the girl in a hug. 'My goodness, you're so *big*.'

Karen's face was buried for a moment in Irene's flowered blouse. Gail noticed the rest of her outfit – parrot-green slacks and gold leather sandals studded with rhinestones. A scarf ran through her red curls, a perky bow tied behind one ear.

72

Gail wasn't sure if the clothes meant Irene had cheered up or if she was going slightly dotty. She went to push the refrigerator door shut.

'Are you hungry, baby?' Irene asked, straightening Karen's T-shirt over her jeans.

Karen made a face. 'I am not a baby.'

'Well, *no*. I'm so sorry.' She spread her hand over her bosom. Gail saw she was wearing the white beads Jimmy Panther had given her at the funeral.

Karen petted the gray cat curled up on a kitchen chair. 'But I am hungry. Definitely.'

Gail said, 'We'll eat as soon as Ben gets here. Why don't you go out on the patio and finish your homework?'

'Oh, let the child eat, Gail. She doesn't have to wait for Ben.'

Gail found an apple in the fruit basket and gave it to Karen. 'Go on. I want to talk to your grandmother.' Karen shot Gail a look, sighed pointedly, then dropped the apple into her bag. There were tables and chairs by the pool where she could study, if she weren't distracted by the view. Boats were crisscrossing Biscayne Bay, most of them heading back to their marinas at this hour. The distant grumble of engines wove through the chirps of mockingbirds in Irene's backyard.

'Stay on the porch,' Gail added. The cat shot through the sliding glass door as she closed it.

Irene picked up her cigarette from a heavy crystal ashtray and eyed the table. 'I thought we'd finish off this stuff so I can give the dishes back.'

Gail recognized plates and casseroles that neighbors had brought last week, but the contents had dwindled. A few slices of roast beef, drying at the edges. Meat loaf reduced to a corner of a square pan. Remnants and scraps of green beans, potatoes au gratin, creamed corn, pickled mushrooms, lasagna, half a key lime pie –

73

and more dishes she couldn't see into.

'Where's Dave?'

'He's home,' Gail said, 'getting some papers ready for the accountant tomorrow.' This was true, but Gail had also told him she needed Irene to herself.

Irene took a last drag on her cigarette and crushed it out. 'Let's eat in the dining room on the good china. We can have some wine.' She laughed. 'What goes with Jell-O?'

After a second, Gail said, 'Mother, we need to talk.'

'Oooh, that sounds serious.' Irene picked up a short glass with a few ice cubes at the bottom, glanced at the contents, then pulled a quart bottle of Smirnoff out of a lower cabinet. 'What can I fix you?'

'Nothing, thanks.'

'You're no fun,' Irene said. She held her glass under the ice dispenser. It made a little grinding noise and spat out cubes.

Gail said, 'A homicide detective came by my office today, a Sergeant Britton with Metro-Dade. They want to search Renee's condo.'

Irene unscrewed the cap on the vodka and poured. 'Yes. I hope it's okay if I volunteered you.'

She had thought Irene might explain, or even laugh. *Oh, it all sounds so silly now.* But she only took a lime out of the refrigerator and plopped it on the cutting board. She severed it neatly, the bow in her hair bobbing, a sharp smell of citrus drifting across the kitchen.

Finally Gail said, 'Why did you ask them to do this?'

Irene squeezed the lime into her glass, then with a little flourish let it drop. 'Who knows? They might find something.'

'Renee killed herself. Why would you tell them she didn't?'

'I just said it bothered me. It doesn't matter now,

does it? Let them have their little look. What's the harm?'

'You could have talked to me first,' Gail said.

'You were busy.'

'Come on, Irene. When have I ever not talked to you?' There was no answer. Gail said, 'They can go through the apartment with a microscope and tweezers, I don't care. But calling them at all is truly bizarre.'

Irene stirred her drink. 'I didn't tell you because you would have tried to talk me out of it. You have to have a logical reason for everything. I just knew . . . I *felt* . . . that she would not have done this.'

'But she *did*. Look at how she was. She never finished college. She wound up at a part-time job behind a desk, something she swore she'd never do. She was never able to keep a man. She had a drug problem. She drank. And this after she grew up believing she could have anything she wanted.'

Irene yanked open a drawer. The silverware inside clanged. 'I suppose next you're going to tell me it was all my fault. I spoiled her.'

Gail felt the full weight of her own fatigue. 'I wish – for once – you would see things as they really are.'

Irene turned around with a handful of forks and knives. 'Here, you can put these in the dining room for me.' When Gail didn't immediately take them, Irene dropped them on the table. 'The place mats are in the buffet.'

'I know where you keep things.' Gail watched her take down plates and saucers, stacking them on the counter, reaching into the cabinet again.

Irene spoke over the clatter. 'Fine. I don't see things. I didn't know my own daughter. You never made the effort to treat her like your sister. If you had, you'd know Renee wasn't what you think.'

Gail's voice rose, lifted on a rush of anger. 'Really?

The medical examiner told me she was nearly two months pregnant when she died.'

Irene turned around, three wineglasses in her hands. She set them down slowly, one by one. 'You . . . had no right – *no right* – not to tell me this before.'

There was a long silence. Finally, painfully, Gail nodded. 'Mom, I'm sorry. I should have.'

Irene picked up a dish towel and wiped a smudge off one of the glasses. 'I don't suppose you know who the father is. Was.'

'No.'

She dropped the dish towel on the counter, then pressed her fingers to her eyes. She made a single, muffled cry. Gail stood up quickly and put her arms around her. In the flat sandals, Irene felt as fragile as a child.

'I tried so hard with Renee. I did.'

Gail hugged her close.

'I can't think about this anymore.' She pushed Gail away and crossed the kitchen for a napkin to blow her nose.

Gail followed. 'Mother, let me help with Renee's estate. You shouldn't take it all on yourself. If you don't want to go through her things right now, I'll just have them packed and stored.'

'No, you don't have to bother.'

'I want to.'

The doorbell rang, and Irene glanced toward the living room. 'Oh, lord. That's Ben and look at me.' She dabbed underneath her eyes. 'Am I all right?'

'You're fine.' Gail straightened Irene's bow.

'You haven't said anything to him about the police, have you?'

'No.'

'Well, don't. I'll sound like some hysterical female.' She went to let him in.

76

Gail stood in the middle of the kitchen, listening to Irene's cry of delight at the front door, as though Ben's visit were an unexpected surprise. She listened to their voices growing closer, then pushed open the sliding glass door and told Karen to come wash her hands for dinner. Karen furtively slid a half-assembled Lego moon vehicle into her book bag, then followed Gail back to the kitchen.

Ben saw her and ruffled her hair. 'Hey, Little Bit.'

'Hi, Ben.' Karen hugged his waist.

He carried a zippered leather folder and wore a pullover golf shirt which had faded to dull blue. He looked down at the food on the table, then grinned at Gail.

'What's this? Irene, are you opening a cafeteria?'

'Oh, hush.' Laughing, she took a short glass from the cabinet and filled it with ice cubes. Ben was accustomed to a sip of Wild Turkey before dinner.

Gail turned Karen toward the hall. 'Go wash your hands, sweetie.' There was a guest bathroom around the corner.

'Where's Dave?' Ben asked.

'He couldn't come. He had some work to do.'

'You should have given him the night off.' When Gail only shrugged and smiled, Ben held up his folder. 'All right. Grab your notary stamp. We might as well get this taken care of, if we can find room on the table.' He sat down, stacking a plate of diced tomatoes on the roast beef. 'Irene, come over here, darlin'.'

Irene put his drink down on a cocktail napkin and watched him unzip the folder. 'Not now,' she said.

Ben looked up.

She went to rummage for candles in a cabinet drawer. 'Dinner first. Dinner, then business. You all just serve yourselves whatever you want, and we'll pop it in the microwave.'

Gail exchanged a look with Ben, then put her inked stamp and the heavy silver-colored seal back into her purse.

'All right, then.' Ben tasted his bourbon. 'Later. Say, what about eating on the back porch? We'll have a picnic.'

Irene turned around with long yellow candles in her hand. 'I thought the dining room would be nice. Karen likes the chandelier.'

'No, no. You sit in there and all you can hear is that damn clock ticking. Let's go outside.'

'Well, all right, if you'd rather.' She laid the candles back in the drawer.

Gail started to protest but went to look for Karen instead. Ben would only laugh and say he didn't need a lecture from somebody who didn't even use her husband's last name.

Karen wasn't in the bathroom around the corner from the kitchen, but one of the embroidered blue hand towels was askew on the rod. Gail followed the hallway that connected the kitchen with the other end of the house. She passed the door that led to the den – once her father's study. Then the hallway opened into a larger area where Irene had hung framed family pictures. A tall cabinet held porcelain birds so realistic that when she was a small child Gail had tossed one into the air to see if it could fly.

The door to her mother's room was half open. Gail looked inside. The satin comforter had slipped to the floor and Irene's clothes were tossed carelessly over the bed, shoes at odd angles next to it. On the nightstand were the two photos in the folding frame that Anthony Quintana had given her. The television was on, but the sound was off.

Her own room was closed. What had once been her

room, now a guest bedroom with a pull-out sofa. At the last bedroom Gail leaned against the open door with her arms crossed. 'There you are,' she said.

Karen looked up from where she sat at the mirrored dresser, and her reflection grinned guiltily. She held up one hand. 'See? I painted my fingernails.' They were neon pink, garish on her small fingers. The bottle was open, the brush sticking out of it.

It didn't surprise Gail that Karen had found nail polish rattling around in Renee's dresser. The drawers were full of odds and ends: hair clips, cheap jewelry, a curling iron, a broken Walkman. Renee had moved in and out so many times, before leaving for good, that Irene had never cleaned out her room. The bookcase was still crammed with romance novels and fashion magazines. If Gail opened the closet she would find cardboard boxes of Renee's old clothes, labeled whimsically in black marker. *Aerobx. Shuz. Brrr – winter*. And if she pulled aside the curtains she would see that the window had never been fixed, not since Renee broke the crank handle so she could sneak in and out at night. Gail had never told Irene about it, waiting to see if Renee would get caught. She never did.

'Put the top back on the polish,' Gail said, still at the door. 'Dinner's ready.'

'I'll look stupid with only one hand painted,' Karen said. She screwed the top on, holding the fingers of her left hand out stiffly so she wouldn't smudge them. 'Can I take it home?'

'No, you can't.' Gail motioned for Karen to come out of the room.

Karen swung her sneakered feet back and forth. 'Who gets all this stuff?'

'What do you mean?'

'Renee's stuff.'

'I don't know.'

79

'Can I have it?' Karen asked.

'Certainly not,' Gail said. 'Come on. They're waiting for us.'

'Why not?'

'Karen. Out,' Gail ordered. 'And you have to clean that off your nails before you go to school tomorrow.'

Then Gail remembered, though she hadn't thought of it for years, the Saturday Irene had asked her to take Renee shopping for school clothes. Renee's birthday had been the week before and Ben had asked her what she wanted. She had put her arms around his neck and pouted. *Something to wear, please please please Ben, my clothes suck, Momma doesn't have any money and I look like a freak at school.* He gave her five hundred dollars and Renee insisted on going all the way to Dadeland Mall, clear across town. At fourteen years old, with five hundred dollars in the pocket of her jeans, the first thing Renee did was have fingernails put on. Long, red acrylic nails, fifty dollars, glued over her own ragged ones. Gail paced back and forth, grumbling. Then Renee walked casually from boutique to boutique. Everything was just so gross, she said. Gail screamed at her to hurry. Finally Renee found a store she liked, with exposed air conditioning ducts and salesgirls dressed in black. Weird clanging music came from somewhere. Renee stood away from the racks and pointed with her long red fingernails. *That one and that one. No, not that.* The salesgirls followed along, the clothes piling up on their arms. Renee didn't go to the fitting rooms, afraid to muss her nails. She never wore half the clothes she bought, or bothered to return them.

Gail closed the door to Renee's room and followed Karen down the hall. Karen's long brown hair swung against her narrow back. She walked with a little bounce, then a skip. Even at nine years old, Gail thought, she knew who she was. Gail caught up and hugged her. 'I'll ask if you can have the nail polish, okay?'

'Thanks,' Karen said. 'Can I have the jewelry, too?'

Gail laughed. 'I don't care. Ask your grandma.'

They carried their plates out to the patio and sat around a glass-topped table on the other side of the swimming pool. Across the bay, the buildings on Miami Beach had turned pink in the setting sun. Beyond them a line of puffy clouds drifted above the horizon, their tops still brilliant white.

Irene tapped Karen on the shoulder. 'You see that little island out there?'

Karen turned around in her chair. 'Which one?'

She pointed. 'With the tree broken off at the top. See? A pelican just landed on it.' When Karen nodded, Irene said, 'When I was a girl we used to row out there and have picnics. Grandpa would take our dinghy down to the boat ramp and we'd get in and away we'd go. A whole boat full of cousins. You remember that, don't you, Ben?'

Ben pushed his plate away and reached for his cigarettes. 'Good days, Irene. Gone and never to be repeated.'

Karen said, 'Daddy takes me on our boat.'

'I bet he does, Little Bit.' Ben pulled a cigarette out of its pack and held up his battered Zippo lighter with one hand so Karen could see. A quick snap of his thumb and forefinger and Gail caught the scent of lighter fluid. He had showed her how to do it when she was a little girl, the flint and wheel and sudden burst of heat and color.

A breeze came off the bay, and Irene's bow fluttered. She laughed a little and lifted her drink. 'Ben, remember that time we all got kicked out of the Olympia Theater? We were in the balcony and you had a squirt gun and shot some poor man right on his bald spot.'

Karen bounced in her chair. 'That's funny.'

Gail began to clear the table, stacking plates and silverware on a tray. 'I never heard this story,' she said.

Irene burst into laughter, her shoulders shaking. 'He was so wicked. I could tell you things.'

A smile played around the corners of Ben's mouth, but he only continued to gaze out at the bay, his elbow on the table, snapping the lid of his lighter open and shut with one hand. His wrists were thick, the hair on his arms going white.

Out of nowhere, he said, 'I'm going to sell the ranch.'

Irene blinked. 'What?'

He tossed the lighter onto the table. 'Hell, Irene, might as well. I pay more than it's worth to feed the dogs out there and keep the fence up.'

Gail hadn't been out to Ben's property in several years, two thousand or more acres of woods and marshy grass southwest of the city. The Stricklands had owned it before there were paved roads to get to it. To call it a ranch was to stretch the truth: Back in the forties a few head of cattle had grazed during the dry season. Ben and his friends used to hunt wild boar or pheasant and even stock the land with deer and turkey from farther up the state. They had paid no attention to hunting season. The county sheriff had been a member of Ben's exclusive club.

Gail sat down again. 'When did you decide this?'

'Been thinking about it for a while.' He smoked the cigarette. 'You hear traffic over on Krome Avenue, or draglines and power saws. People dump old tires and refrigerators along the access road. Used to be, you couldn't hear a thing except birds and frogs. Maybe an alligator or two by the canal.' He smiled at Karen. 'You know how they go? Whomp, whomp, whomp.' She laughed at the guttural sound he made in his throat.

Irene said, 'Oh, Ben, this really is too bad.'

He waved the thought away. 'I'll make some money off it. Some Cuban builder thinks he's stealing it from me. You know him, Gail. Or anyway, he knows who you are. Pedrosa.'

She laughed. 'You're kidding. Carlos Pedrosa?'

'He says he has a case with you.'

'Against me is more accurate. I'm suing to get a down payment back for Doug Hartwell's daughter.'

Irene got up and stacked the rest of the dishes on the tray. 'You two finish talking,' she said.

Gail was still watching Ben. 'How much does he want to steal it for?'

'Not all of it. Three or four hundred acres, eight hundred per. I told him fifteen. He wants an option for now.'

Gail scooted the chair closer to the table. 'What's he going to do with it? It's mostly wetlands. He'll hang himself in red tape with all the environmental regulations.'

'Then I guess you don't know the Pedrosas.' Ben tapped his cigarette over the ashtray. 'The old man has a few friends on the Metro Commission and the zoning board, both.'

'Who, Ernesto?' Gail leaned forward on her crossed arms, intrigued, remembering what Anthony Quintana had told her at the courthouse. Ernesto Pedrosa. Not only Carlos's grandfather, but Anthony's as well.

'Mommy, can I go feed the fish?' Karen's heels were rhythmically kicking the legs of the chair.

Gail reluctantly broke away from her conversation. 'Sure, honey. See if your grandma has some stale bread.'

'Plenty of it,' Irene said, coming back outside with another Wild Turkey on the rocks for Ben. 'We'll make some doughballs.'

Karen ran across the lawn toward the seawall, the screen door closing behind her. The sun had set now, and the sky was losing its brilliance. A six-inch gray lizard skittered up the screen, then stopped abruptly, its red throat flap extending, retracting. It disappeared into a tangle of ferns.

Gail turned back to Ben. 'Tell me about Ernesto Pedrosa.'

Ben blew a stream of smoke upward. 'He's a big deal in the Cuban community. Pedrosa has – or used to have – connections to anti-Castro terrorist groups. Back in the early seventies he avoided a federal indictment for bombing a Miami radio station because the CIA was secretly funding him. That's what I heard. He can get things done, if you know what I mean.'

'Not precisely.'

'Come on, where've you been? Latinos move up here and think they can operate on payoffs and favoritism just like they did back home.'

She laughed. 'Since when hasn't Miami had political corruption? It's the local pastime.'

'And Miami's gone straight to hell, as far as I'm concerned.' Ben put down his drink. 'Say, you want to handle the negotiations with Carlos for me?'

Gail was glad the topic had veered in another direction. She hated arguing with Ben. 'I can't negotiate with Carlos. We're supposed to be tooth and nail on the Darden case.'

Ben squinted at her, the cigarette briefly to his lips. 'That lawsuit doesn't have anything to do with the property.'

She shrugged. 'Maybe. I'll pass it by Larry Black.' Gail knew one of the lawyers in the firm Ben had just joined could represent him. She also knew how much he valued family connections. He would give the case to her if he could, even indirectly.

'Let me know,' he said. 'I'll send over what I've got so far.'

She tilted her glass and finished off the iced tea in it, now warm and diluted. 'How did you connect with Carlos Pedrosa, by the way?'

Ben got up, extending his arms, stretching the muscles in his shoulders. He glanced at his watch. 'Renee introduced us. She found out he wanted to buy some property and gave him my phone number. He ran a lot of his real estate closings through that title company she worked for.'

Gail nodded. And Anthony Quintana's firm owned the title company. 'You don't know the other grandson, do you? Anthony Luis Quintana? He's a criminal attorney.'

'I don't believe I do.' Ben's attention shifted across the porch. 'Irene!' She had reached the back door with a plastic bag of bread in her hand. Ben said, 'It's nearly eight o'clock and I need to get on home. How about signing those papers for me, darlin'?'

Irene glanced at Karen, who was doing cartwheels in the grass. 'I don't know.'

'You don't know what?'

'If I want to sign them. Let Gail do it.'

Ben looked at Gail, who could only look blankly back at him. He walked around the table. 'Irene, what are you talking about?'

She lifted the screen door latch. 'I've thought about it, and I've decided. Gail can be the personal representative.'

Ben looked at Gail again, frowning this time. 'I'll have to prepare a whole new set of papers.'

Gail spread her hands, palms up.

'All right,' he said. 'I can't file the estate yet anyhow. We don't have the death certificate. I don't know what the problem is. Some screwup.'

A screwup named Frank Britton, Gail thought. She said, 'What do you want me to do?'

He rubbed his fingers across his cheek, thinking. 'I'll get the papers redone, bring them to your office. You want to take a look at what I've got so far? See if there's anything you can add.'

Ben went in and got his folder, turning on the porch light as he came out again. 'Irene told me pretty much everything over the phone,' he said. 'I've put a summary of Renee's property on the petition for administration. We can file the inventory later.' Ben pulled on the heavy zipper. 'Maybe you could go by her apartment, make a list of what's there.'

Gail nodded. 'Yes, I could do that.'

'Just generally. Don't get specific unless there's something of particular value.' He withdrew three or four sheets of paper – legal forms, she saw – and laid them on the table. 'Bring me the check-books and savings account records, things like that. I can fill in the total before I file these.'

Gail looked down at the petition when Ben slid it across to her. *In re: Estate of Renee Michelle Connor, Deceased.* Age 29. Beneficiary: Irene Strickland Connor. Real property: Unit 202, Cocobay Condominium . . . Personal property of the estate: one 1991 Toyota Celica, clothing and jewelry, various household goods, various bank accounts . . .

Gail turned the paper over, then back again. 'Her trust isn't listed. I know she couldn't have spent it all.'

'No,' Ben said. 'She couldn't touch it, not before she was thirty. Just like your share.'

'Then where is it? I mean, why isn't it on here?' Gail hesitated before admitting, 'This shows how much I know about probate.'

'The trust passes outside the estate. It wasn't really hers until she reached thirty,' Ben said. 'Naturally she received the interest it paid out while she lived, but the principal goes straight to you. Don't worry. It's all there.'

Gail had to stare at him while she repeated this odd bit of information in her head, and then aloud. 'Straight to me?'

His brows knitted. 'I thought you knew this.'

'Knew what?' Gail asked. 'I already received my share. The other half goes to Irene. Doesn't it?'

'You never read a copy of the trust?'

Gail numbly shook her head. 'I might have. If I did, it didn't sink in.'

'Well, that's how your granddad wanted it. If one of you girls passed away, the other would get the whole thing.'

'My God.' The absurdity of it made her laugh. 'Three years ago I got over two hundred thousand dollars.'

Ben nodded.

Sobering, Gail sat there for a minute, watching Irene and Karen throwing doughballs into the bay. She said quietly, 'Does Mother know about this?'

'We discussed it last week.' When Gail didn't reply, Ben added, 'She's not resentful. She knows you and Dave are having trouble at the marina.'

Irene's words, Gail was almost certain, had been murmured in a tone of quiet martyrdom. All the money spent and lent and lost must be forgotten. That Irene had said nothing to Gail meant that she resented it a great deal. A gift like this – terrible and wonderful at the same time – could only cause problems.

She continued to sit on the patio in the gathering dusk until Irene and Karen came back across the yard with the empty bread wrappers.

Chapter Five

Gail waited until Karen was asleep before she came out to the garage to speak to Dave. If there was going to be an argument, she didn't want Karen to hear it.

Dave had said he would be stringing a couple of his tennis racquets. From the kitchen door she could see him bending over his stringing machine, a racquet clamped down tight. He poked the string through another hole and back again, the muscle flexing in his right forearm, which was noticeably bigger than the left.

In the late seventies, Dave had been second on the University of Florida tennis team, but he didn't have the drive – the desire, whatever it took – to make it on the pro circuit. After the last season, he had zipped his racquet into its cover. He hadn't so much as stepped on a court until two years ago, and then he had thrown himself back into the game like a man rediscovering his first sweetheart.

Often when he came home his hair would be plastered to his forehead, his legs trembling. One day last August he had showed her how much he sweated: He took off his briefs in the bathroom and wrung them out over the sink. The sun had turned his hair the color of hemp. Squint lines fanned out from his eyes, which seemed to have faded to a paler blue against his tan. His weight had dropped from one-ninety to a lean, hard one-sixty-five. The time he ripped a muscle in his abdomen she asked him why he did this. He told her that on a tennis court, unlike life, there are clear lines. The ball is either in, or it is out.

In college she had liked to watch him play, liked the power and speed. Then it had been a game. Now, if provoked, he could scream at his opponent, hitting balls directly at his head. Gail would get embarrassed for him when he lost, and he would know it, walking away from her attempts at sympathy. She didn't go to tournaments anymore unless invited.

Gail closed the kitchen door and crossed the garage in her bare feet. She dusted off a stepladder and sat down on it, facing him. Dave glanced up. He was dressed in his work clothes – khaki pants, a white knit shirt with 'Metzger Marine – Custom Outfitters' printed on the pocket. There was a little drawing of a fishing boat on stylized waves.

He said, 'So do you want to tell me what's so bad about getting two hundred thousand dollars?' He pulled the string tight and clamped it down. 'It's not like we couldn't use it.'

'I know that,' she said, 'but this is different. Renee probably thought the money would go to Irene – if she thought about it at all.'

'Come on.' Dave turned the tension knob. 'Irene gets everything else, doesn't she? Renee's condo?'

'Yes, with a huge mortgage attached. Ben and Irene and I talked before I left, and she said she didn't want a dime of the money, that her father wrote the trust the way he did for a reason, and she would abide by his wishes.'

'Good for Irene.'

'Oh, Dave, it was so phony. Granddad thought my father was a failure. Irene thinks he left the money to Renee and me rather than to her because he wanted to rub her nose in it. She sat there tonight sipping her

90

fourth vodka and tonic, trying to look noble. She hardly spoke to me, as if I had something to do with it. As if I were glad. You know how she can frost up.'

Dave swung the stringer around, continuing the cross strings. 'I'd be glad. I am glad, in fact. Two hundred thousand dollars' worth of glad.'

Gail rested her elbows on her knees. 'We didn't need this to come between us. We already had Renee to argue about. Now this. I had hoped we could finally establish some kind of normal mother-daughter relationship, if that isn't too much to ask.'

Dave looked across the machine at Gail. 'Don't feel so guilty about your mother. I'll bet she's got all kinds of money tucked away, with those investments your dad made. She hasn't worked in thirty years.'

'She works very hard, and you know it.'

'What, that charity stuff?' Dave wove the string in and out across the throat of the racquet. 'So when is all this going to happen?' He pulled back on the tension lever and the machine creaked.

'Ben says I need to give the bank a certified copy of the death certificate. That's another thing that happened today. I found out the police won't release the death certificate until they do another search of Renee's apartment. I'm supposed to meet them there on Friday.'

'What are they going to do that for?'

'It's so useless. Mother asked them to. She's a wreck, more than I imagined. I don't know what she's thinking. Anyway, they'll go in and poke around. The paperwork on the trust could be done within a week or so after that.'

Dave ran the end of the string back and forth through his fingers. 'Look, Gail, I'm sorry we're getting the money this way. But it happened. If Irene doesn't want to take it – I mean, what can we do? We need it worse than she does.'

Gail looked at him for a while, then said, 'I thought about this on the way home. Renee owed her money. Irene ought to get that back, no matter what. I have no idea how much Renee wheedled out of her. Thousands. Tens of thousands.'

'Wheedled?'

'Exactly. All that money she got, it wasn't a gift. Renee would say, "Oh, Mom, I'll pay you back in a few weeks, I swear." And in a few weeks maybe she would, maybe not. But sooner or later she'd be back for more. Where do you think she got the down payment for that condo? Not from her earnings. She could hardly hold a job.'

'Come on, Gail. The girl had problems.'

'Oh, poor Renee.' Gail stood up abruptly, dusting off the seat of her pants. 'That's one reason Renee came to Irene's birthday party, in case you didn't know – to borrow more money.'

'Is that why you and Renee were screaming at each other in the back bedroom?'

'We weren't screaming,' Gail said. 'I told her it was time she grew up and tried to solve her own problems for a change.'

'I'm sure she appreciated the advice.' Dave unclamped his tennis racquet from the machine and bounced the heel of his hand on the restrung head, not looking at her.

Gail watched him zip the racquet into a cover, then pick up another one, sleek black graphite, its strings slashed in an X, ready to be removed. She said, 'The other thing I've decided. I'll pay off our charge card debts and the second mortgage, but I don't want to put any more money into the business the way it is.'

Dave turned around. 'Excuse me?'

'I said the way it is. I've put in nearly a hundred

thousand dollars already, and where is it? We're up to our necks in debt.'

'Whoa. Whoa.' Dave held up his hand. 'You and I talked about this already. We said we needed somebody to invest in the marina. Okay, now we can do it ourselves. Atlantic Marine has a high-lift truck they want to get rid of. We could go vertical, rent space to the smaller boats.'

'Really. How simple. What do we use for a storage shed?'

'We build one. There's not a decent dry storage marina within two miles of here.'

'Dave—'

'No, listen. I've been thinking this out—'

'You listen.' She faced him across the stringing machine. 'No more. We don't need to buy a high-lift truck, we need to do better at what we've already got. The accounts receivable are a joke.'

His face was turning red. 'I just love it when you play corporate lawyer with me. I beat my brains out down there, and you know all about it.'

Gail said coolly, 'I'm not going to throw my money down a hole.'

'Your money?'

'Yes, it is.'

Dave rummaged through his tool tray. 'As long as you're going to pay Irene back, why don't you pay me back, too? I lent Renee some money.'

There was a long silence. Then Gail said, 'When?'

'Last winter. She didn't want to ask Irene again. She sure as hell couldn't ask you.'

'How much?'

He shrugged. 'Five thousand.'

'Five thousand *dollars*?'

'About that. I've got it written down somewhere.'

'For *what*?'

Dave studied the blades of his wire cutters, then wiped them on a towel. 'Stuff for her house. Furniture. Whatever.'

'You were in Renee's house.' It wasn't a question but a blank statement of surprise.

'Sure.' He began cutting the slashed strings out of the tennis racquet. 'Was I supposed to ask permission?' The cutters made a steady clipping sound.

Gail stared at him, remembering how Renee had fallen into his lap at Irene's party; how he had kissed her, laughing. How he had wept at her funeral.

'Were you sleeping with my sister?'

Dave looked up from the racquet.

'Were you?' Gail's voice was rising.

His mouth worked into a little smile. He went back to the strings. 'I knew you were jealous, but really, sweetheart. This is ridiculous.'

She snatched the tennis racquet out of his hands. 'Tell me the truth.'

'Give me that, dammit.'

'I want the truth.'

'I should have fucked her. I don't get much from you.'

Gail slung the racquet across the garage. It skidded on the hood of her car, then ricocheted off the wall with a sharp snap.

'Goddamn you!' Dave spun her around, grabbed her upper arms, and pushed her into the stringing machine. She cried out as the hard edge of it dug into her back. They stood motionless, breathing hard. Then the fury on his face dissolved.

'Oh, Gail. I'm sorry.' He dropped his forehead to her shoulder. 'Christ, I'm sorry.'

She put her arms around his waist, felt the hard muscle in his back. 'I didn't sleep with her,' he said. 'I wouldn't do that.' His ragged breath came through the

94

fabric of her shirt. He said, 'I'm sorry about the money, but she needed it. I was family. Who else was she going to go to?'

'You could have told me.'

'No. You would have flipped out,' he said. 'For nothing, like you just did. I never cheated on you. Not once. And Renee – I liked Renee. When is it a crime to like somebody? I felt sorry for her.'

'She used you, Dave. Can't you see that?'

He pulled back. 'Okay. She made mistakes. You've never made a wrong step in your life, have you? I didn't sleep with her. We had lunch a few times. That's all.'

'Lunch?' This was like opening a familiar door and seeing a room she had never known existed. 'Where?'

'Restaurants. Where do you think, a hotel? It wasn't like that. We had lunch. Usually on Monday unless one of us was busy. Nothing fancy, no roses and violins. I went to her house a couple times, maybe with some deli sandwiches. Sometimes we'd just sit at a table at Peacock Park. It wasn't a *date*, for God's sake.'

'When was the first time?'

'I don't know. We ran into each other at the boat show at Dinner Key Marina, when I had that customized Excalibur on display.'

'Almost two years ago.'

Dave didn't speak for a while. Finally he said, 'Yeah. She was a mess back then. On cocaine, drinking pretty heavy. I talked to her about it. Came down really hard. Maybe it did some good. I don't know anymore, with what happened.'

'What did you talk about?'

'Nothing in particular. I'd tell her about the business. What I wanted to do, that kind of thing. We'd kid around, tell each other jokes we'd picked up lately. I sent her a birthday card once. And I said if she needed anything, ask.'

'Did she tell you she was pregnant?'

'Oh, no.' He shook his head. 'Was she? I didn't know.'

Gail heard a car in the neighbor's driveway, heard doors slam, a teenager's laughter.

Dave said, 'It wasn't mine, if that's what you're thinking. We had this agreement. No sex. I mean it. I suppose that sounds weird to you, but that's how it was. Sex would have ruined it.'

Gail stood silently, then let out her breath, a long sigh that ended in a weary laugh. She folded her arms across her chest, studied the concrete floor.

'What?' he asked. 'Don't you believe me?'

'Yes. I think I do.'

'So what's the matter?' He reached out to touch her shoulder and she shrugged off his hand. 'Gail?'

'Leave me alone. Please.'

'What are you going to do, stay out here all night?'

She turned away, watched the box fan whirring at the window. After a while she heard the kitchen door close.

Fourteen years ago Gail had brought Dave home for spring break. She was nineteen, a sophomore. He was about to graduate, thinking of going on for his MBA, not putting much faith in the market for tennis jocks. Irene didn't mind having him as a houseguest – she knew his parents – but of course he and Gail would have separate bedrooms. Gail was just as glad. She wasn't sure if she wanted to marry Dave or not. He hadn't asked her yet, but she knew he was going to.

Renee was fifteen, Renee with her blonde hair pinned up on one side of her head in a pink butterfly clip, her faded jeans so soft and tight they showed her crotch. Renee said Dave was a riot, and laughed at his jokes, and told him she wanted to learn how to play tennis.

She made sly remarks about balls and holding the handle of a racquet. Over dinner in the formal dining room on Sunday, Gail saw how his eyes kept going to Renee.

That night Gail sneaked into his room and by morning they were engaged.

Chapter Six

Renee had lived in Coconut Grove on a narrow street canopied with banyan trees. Gail didn't much like the Grove anymore, except as a place to take out-of-town visitors, who always asked to see it. It had become trendy and self-conscious, a singles street party with too many rich drunks and too many sports cars with the top down, everybody trolling for instant thrills. The tops went up if the cars wandered into the black Grove, with its rundown beer parlors, laundromats with wire mesh over the windows, and sway-backed wooden houses.

On a Friday afternoon shortly past five o'clock Gail zoomed down Bayshore Drive, then north at the Grand Bay Hotel. A few more turns this way and that, and she braked hard at Cocobay Condominium. It was easy to miss behind the bougainvillaea-draped wall. Before she could pull into the driveway, two skaters glided past on the edge of the street, a young man and woman, both in lime-green skates and kneepads, moving at the same pace on long, tanned legs. A flock of parrots whirred overhead, screeching.

Renee's townhouse was in a Mediterranean-style building with decorative awnings. At the end of the parking lot Gail saw a white and green van: Metro-Dade Crime Scene Investigation. A sedan with a blue light on the dash was in Renee's space. Gail parked beside it and got out.

On the front patio Frank Britton and two other men – one black with a mustache, the other ruddy and blond – watched her come up the walkway. Britton was in a brown jacket. The others wore open-collared sport shirts and badges clipped to their belts.

'I'm a little late,' she said, glancing at her watch.

'That's okay. Friday traffic's a bear.' Britton gestured toward the other men. 'Officers Thomas and Wooten with the investigation unit.'

'How do you do.' Gail smiled automatically, then put down her briefcase so she could reach inside her purse. She withdrew Renee's key ring: five keys and a gold 'R'.

'Hang on a second,' Britton said. 'Let me show you something.' He pointed to a strip of red tape about eight inches long and two inches wide running diagonally at eye level from the door to the jamb. It was ripped at the crack.

He said, 'I put this here the day your sister was found. Somebody's been inside.'

Gail walked closer to the tape. There was a date on it – March 8 – and what could have been a case number, then the initials FJB scrawled in pen. She remembered. 'Yes, I came by a couple days before the funeral to get a dress for her to wear. I'm sure it's all right. The keys haven't been out of my possession since then.'

'Ms Connor, you should have called us.' Britton's tone was gently chastising. 'The tape is right there on the door. It says, "Evidence. Do Not Open."'

Gail looked at him. 'Well, I didn't see it. I came at night and frankly all I wanted to do was go in and out as quickly as possible. I went straight upstairs. I doubt if I spent more than five minutes.'

'You haven't been in here since then?'

'No.'

100

'And you only took a dress.'

'Yes, Sergeant. A dress. Pale blue linen, to be precise. And shoes to match.'

'Okay.' He nodded toward the door. 'Go ahead and open it up.'

There were two locks on the door, one in the brass doorknob, the other on a deadbolt. Gail pushed the door open and stood back. Thomas and Wooten entered first, each carrying a satchel. Britton gestured for her to go in.

One of the technicians flipped a switch, and light from recessed fixtures fell in pools in the dim entrance hall. Mexican tile led straight ahead to a living area, kitchen through a door to the right, two bedrooms upstairs. A stagnant odor came from somewhere. The air was heavy and still. Gail shivered, even in the heat.

The blond officer – Wooten – said, 'Let's get that AC going.' He went to find the thermostat. The other man glanced up the stairs. He was chewing a piece of gum between his front teeth, the muscle in his jaw moving.

Britton said, 'Why don't you guys take the kitchen first?'

Their motions were smooth and precise, not wasting any time. Gail imagined they wanted to finish up and go have a beer. She followed Britton further inside.

A glass-topped table and six chairs marked the dining area. At the other end of the room a white L-shaped sofa faced an entertainment center, its oak shelves crammed with electronic equipment and a color TV. A pink neon telephone glowed on an end table. Renee had tacked up unframed travel posters – the Rockies, Paris, Jamaica.

Gail lifted the hair off the back of her neck. A breeze was blowing from the vent. She set her briefcase on the dining table. 'How long do you think this will take?'

101

'Not too long.' Britton hung his jacket over the back of a chair. Gail had expected to see a gun in a holster, but there was only a tan striped shirt and brown belt. He pulled out a chair for her. 'Have a seat. You can tell me about your sister while you're waiting.'

Gail pulled a pen and legal pad out of her briefcase and began to jot down a list of the contents of the room, as Ben had instructed her to do. She said to Britton, 'I don't know how much help I can be to you. Renee and I hadn't seen each other regularly for years.'

Britton crossed to the entertainment center and began opening drawers. 'How come? You and Renee didn't get along, or what?'

'I suppose you could say that.' When he glanced at her, she gave a little shrug. 'It happens.'

He pulled out the drawer under the television. Compact discs, tossed carelessly inside. Videotapes. Gail could read the titles of a few of them. Foreign erotica. Oddly, she felt embarrassed, as if Britton were poking through Renee's lingerie.

Britton closed the drawer and opened another one. 'Do you know any of her friends?'

'No, I'm sorry, I don't. She worked at a title company. Vista, I think it was called, in Coral Gables. Someone there might help you.'

As she scanned the room, Gail looked for the deer mask Jimmy Panther had described. It wasn't in here. Under the coffee table she noticed a pair of shoes that lay where they had been kicked off, turquoise leather flats with bows. Renee's feet had been small, white, and high-arched. Gail remembered Renee sitting in the backyard by the seawall in her bikini, painting her toenails, cotton balls holding her toes apart.

Britton was walking slowly from one end of the shelves to the other, tilting his head to read the titles of a few popular novels. The light filtering through the vertical blinds reflected off his glasses.

'Your mother said she didn't think Renee was particularly depressed.' Britton glanced at Gail.

'My mother has a hard time accepting what happened, Sergeant. That's why she asked you to do this.' Gail put her pen into her jacket pocket and sat down, crossing her legs.

Britton moved aside a parched fern, then slid it back into place. Gail made a note to herself to put the plants out on the patio before she left so they could get the rain.

He said, 'I can understand how she feels. Losing a child in that way. She's a fine woman, your mother. I'm sorry either of you had to go through this.'

'Thank you,' Gail said, wondering how he maintained such innocent blue eyes in his line of work. She smiled at him.

Britton lifted an open, upside-down issue of *Cosmopolitan* on the coffee table. 'I spoke to her this morning, as a matter of fact. She called me, said never mind going through Renee's place, sorry for the bother. She says you asked her to call.'

'Well, not directly, but I did suggest it.'

'How come?'

'Because all this is so useless.'

'Well, let me worry about that.' He smiled back at her.

Gail said, 'I don't mean to sound unappreciative. I know you have to do your job.'

From the kitchen she heard the low rumble of male voices. A laugh. A scrap of conversation about the NBA playoffs. Drawers opened and closed.

She stood up. 'Sergeant Britton. As long as I'm here, I need to make a list of Renee's possessions and pick up her financial records.'

Britton looked around.

She said, 'I'm the personal representative of her estate.'

'I thought you said your mom was the PR.'

'Did I? Well, we thought it would be better if I handled it.' Gail picked up her briefcase from the table. 'I'll just be upstairs.'

'I'd rather you stay down here, if you don't mind.'

'Actually, I do mind.' Gail checked her watch. 'I have a daughter waiting for me at home.'

'Ms Connor.' Something in his tone made her turn around. He said, 'Stay here. Please.'

'I certainly won't take anything without giving you an opportunity to review it first.'

He nodded. 'Yes, ma'am. I intend to do that.'

After a few seconds, she put her briefcase back on the table.

Britton walked to the kitchen door and leaned in, holding on to the frame. 'Y'all about done in there?'

Gail could see the black officer hold up a plastic bag with a short glass inside. 'We're going to print a few of these at the lab. We dusted the counter and appliances. Nothing in the garbage.'

'All right.'

The two technicians came out with their satchels, then moved quickly up the stairs. Gail followed Britton into the kitchen. He opened the refrigerator.

'Sergeant, if we could go over the records now, then I could leave. You can keep the keys and lock the door when you finish.'

He turned around. 'I know you're a busy lady, but you're going to have to bear with us.' He gestured toward a small table under the window.

Gail sat down. A cup half full of soup, now obscured by mold, had been left on a plate with a few scraps of potato chips. She pushed it aside. Footsteps thumped overhead, muffled voices. Britton pulled open one drawer after another, the utensils inside rattling. The cabinets were light gray Formica, smudged around the handles. Gail wondered at the traces of black powder, then realized they marked where Thomas and Wooten had lifted fingerprints.

She wrote down on her legal pad: kitchen table, four chairs, various appliances, a clock radio, pots and pans, etc.

When Britton opened the refrigerator, Gail could see inside it. The usual bottles and jars of condiments in the door. On the shelves, Chinese food cartons, several bottles of opened wine, left-overs in plastic bags, a box of granola. He picked up a clear-wrapped package with two thick steaks inside and tilted it toward the light.

'You could have them, but they're probably spoiled,' Gail said.

Britton laughed. 'No, I was checking the expiration date.' He showed her the sticker. 'The tenth. Figure back a few days, she could have bought them the seventh.'

'Is that important?'

'Not really.' He tossed the package back inside and shut the door.

Gail said, 'I suppose you want to know why Renee would spend over twelve dollars for filet mignons the same day she decided to kill herself.' When Britton glanced around, she continued, 'Renee was impetuous. She rarely thought ahead.'

Britton regarded Gail closely, then said, 'She bought two. Filets don't keep and she was no bigger than a minute. Do you know who the other one was for?'

Why yes, Gail thought, perhaps she was planning to have my husband in for lunch on Monday. She said, 'I have no idea.'

'You don't know who her boyfriend was? According

to the autopsy, she was at least a couple months pregnant.'

Britton's delivery was so flat Gail thought he might be probing to see whether this was news to her.

'So I heard,' she said. 'I really don't know who she was dating.'

'Was Renee the type to keep a diary?'

'She never did as a teenager.'

Britton didn't say anything for a moment, just continued to lean against the kitchen counter, arms spread out on either side of him, the light making miniature windows in his glasses.

There was an odd pattern in the grease spattered above the stove, and Gail realized she had seen it before. She had, after all, come into this kitchen on her way to get a dress for Renee, her curiosity roused by the stale odor of garbage and the sound of rap music coming softly from the radio on the counter. She had glanced around, finding a perverse satisfaction in the mess, then had turned off the radio.

Gail stood up. 'May I look under the cabinets? There's a piece of Indian pottery I have to find while I'm here. A friend of hers lent it to her and he'd like to have it back.'

'Sure, go ahead.' Britton moved aside while Gail opened the doors. 'I thought you didn't know any of her friends.'

'This one contacted me.' Gail bent to look under the sink. 'His name is Jimmy Panther. A Miccosukee Indian.' She checked the other cabinets. Nothing remotely resembling a deer mask.

'How well did he know her?' Britton asked.

'You'd have to ask him that. In fact, you probably have his name in your reports somewhere. He's the one who found her body.'

'Is that right?' Britton gestured toward the kitchen

door. 'You want to take a look for those records now?'

She preceded him up the stairs. Nearing the top she heard voices coming from Renee's bedroom. Her steps slowed. She felt like a trespasser. She walked further down the hall and stood at the open door.

Gail had come at night the last – the only – time before, not seeing much but her way to the walk-in closet. Fleeting impressions, unwillingly registered. A lace bra and panties on the floor. A satin teddy thrown over a chair. Mirrors. Unmade bed, too many pillows. Pink and black. The smell of perfume. Irises in a tall, cut-glass vase.

She could see now that the water in the vase had turned green and cloudy. A dank odor filled the room. Thomas was bending over Renee's dresser with a soft brush, whisking away powder.

His back to the door, Wooten had made a little pile of things on the bed, pulling them out of the open drawer of a nightstand. He wore latex gloves. A length of black silk rope coiled across the sheets patterned with pink and purple orchids. Jars and tubes lay among the flowers. An open book of photographs – the color of flesh.

Wooten opened the next drawer. Gail couldn't see what he took out, then heard him laugh. 'Hey, look at the size of this thing. Girl knew how to have a good time.'

Thomas looked around, then toward the door, his grin fading. Wooten turned and saw Gail standing there. He moved the plastic phallus out of her sight, embarrassed.

'Sorry,' he said.

Gail lowered her eyes and backed out of the door.

Britton spoke quietly. 'Never mind those guys. They don't mean anything.'

'I'm not offended,' Gail said, following him toward

the other room. 'Nothing you find here would surprise me.'

She regretted her response. In the same instant she had attempted both to assure him that she was no prude and to disassociate herself from Renee – a combination of cowardice and disloyalty. Then Gail wondered why she cared what he thought.

They entered a smaller bedroom with a daybed and odd bits of furniture. Gail recognized a chintz-covered armchair that had been their grandmother's. A desk and chair were by the window, a bookcase opposite. She made a note of all these on her legal pad. Britton turned on the desk lamp and started going through the drawers.

Gail crossed the room to the closet. Inside she found clothes jammed on the rod, shoe boxes underneath. On the shelf overhead, a cardboard box about a foot square. She set it on one corner of the daybed and noticed a shipping label. A novelty company in California had sent the box to Trail Indian Gifts, at a post office box in Miami. Gail pulled back the plastic bubble wrap inside and lifted out the face of a deer.

'What'd you find?' Britton was behind her when she turned around with it. 'Funny-looking thing,' he said. 'Is this what that Indian wanted you to look for?'

'I imagine so.' Gail showed him the long, triangular mask. Large ears – one of them was chipped – flared outward. The gently slanting eyes were outlined with delicate curving lines. A bas-relief crescent decorated the forehead. The remnants of paint – perhaps once it had been red – flaked from the surface.

Gail said, 'I'd like to take it with me, if you have no objection.'

'I can't think of any.'

While she put it back into the box, Britton returned to the desk, opening and closing drawers. 'Lot of stuff here,' he said. 'Tell you what. You jot down the information you need. Banks, charge account numbers, whatever. That would save some time. I'll go through all this at headquarters and deliver it when I'm done, how's that?'

She set the box on the daybed. 'You're in charge.'

Britton picked up an unlined tablet from the desk, held it to the light at an angle, then put it to one side. He noticed her looking at him. 'The lab boys can tell what's been written here, four or five sheets up.'

Gail smiled. 'I can't believe you're doing all this.'

'Here, sit down.' Britton pulled the desk chair out for her, then dragged the armchair over for himself. He sat on the edge of it, his pant leg riding up far enough to show the tip of a black holster strapped to his ankle. He opened the top drawer and took out a double handful of loose papers.

She raised her eyes from the gun.

Britton was shuffling through a stack of charge slips. 'Like I said in your office the other day, we wouldn't bother, except that your mother seemed concerned. Normally in a suicide you're going to have an upset relative. Oftentimes people just need something to hang their emotional hat on. So they ask you to check it out, make sure it wasn't something else.'

'This is a lot of trouble to go through to make my mother feel better.' Gail took the checkbook he handed her and flipped it open. Checks were entered but the remaining balance wasn't figured. Renee's record-keeping was as chaotic as her housekeeping. She wrote down the name of the bank and the account number.

Britton held the second drawer on his lap, poking through loose bank statements. 'A couple other things bothered me,' he said. 'In the parking lot. Her purse was on the seat with the car door locked. Would you leave your purse like that?'

'Sometimes,' Gail said.

'So does my wife. I tell her don't do that in Miami, but she does anyway.' He turned over papers. 'She says what's the big deal, I'll be right back.' He shoved the second drawer shut and opened the last. 'The razor blade bothered me, too. We found it about eight feet off the end of the boardwalk in a foot of water. The bottom's pretty soft there, the officer just got lucky.' He looked at Gail, explaining. 'We always try to find the instrument, see if it matches up with the wound.'

Gail nodded, trying not to show a reaction. Before this, she hadn't thought about the scene at all. It had seemed enough that Renee was found dead. No gruesome details required.

Britton went on. 'It had to be the one. Brand new, no rust. No prints, either, but that's not surprising. The thing is, though, if you kill yourself, you don't throw it eight feet away.'

'You don't?' Gail maintained an expression of rapt interest even as the skin on her neck tightened.

'No, you drop it where you are.' Britton made the motion with his right hand, opening his fingers. 'This is what you do.'

It was all a game to him, Gail thought. A jigsaw puzzle to be put together, even if he already knew how it would come out. She began writing down credit card numbers. 'Sergeant Britton. Have you ever, in – How many years as a homicide detective?'

'Eight. Have I ever seen a wrist slashing turn into something besides a suicide?'

'Have you?' She lifted her brows.

He nodded. 'Yes, ma'am. It can happen. There was this one case, guy tried to make us think his wife did herself in. Problem was, the cuts were made in the wrong direction.' Britton held out his left wrist and drew a finger across it right to left. 'That's just not

110

going to happen unless you use an electric meat slicer or something.'

Gail felt her breath stop.

'And people who kill themselves that way make the first cuts shallow, like they're seeing if that was enough, or if they have to go deeper. One guy I saw had over fifty little cuts on his wrists. But your sister. No hesitation marks that the ME could find. One or two cuts, all the way to the bone, both wrists.'

Gail closed her eyes.

'I'm sorry.' Britton put his hand on her arm. 'I should've known better.'

She took a deep breath, nodding. She pushed the papers aside. 'I don't need to do this now. The estate can't be filed until we get the death certificate.'

Britton seemed apologetic. 'I can get you a preliminary certificate, how's that? It'll show cause of death, but not manner of death. I have to leave that open for the time being.'

Gail managed a smile. 'I don't understand the difference.'

'Renee died of exsanguination – she bled to death. That's the cause.' As if gauging Gail's ability to hear anymore of this, he continued slowly. 'There are many ways to die, but only four manners of death. Natural, such as dying of cancer. Or you could die in an accident. Or there's suicide. Or homicide.'

'I see.'

He gently took the papers from her. 'You didn't get a letter in the mail from Renee, did you? Didn't find a note, anything like that, when you were here, that we might have missed?'

'No, I only came in long enough to get the dress, as I told you. I didn't want to stay any longer.'

'I can understand that. You didn't lend the keys to anyone else?'

'No.'

'Do you know anyone who might have wanted to harm your sister?'

'No, I don't.'

He leaned forward, elbows on his knees. 'Did she own any property besides the condo here?'

Gail shook her head.

'Did she have a will?'

'I don't think so.'

'No, most young people don't,' he said.

'Didn't you discuss all this with my mother?'

'Sure, but I might have missed something. Sorry I have to put you through this. I know you'd rather be home with the family.'

Gail started to cap her pen, missed, and leaned over to pick up the cap from the floor. 'Do you know that I don't even have a will?' She laughed a little. 'Me, a lawyer.'

He smiled at her. 'Did Renee have a life insurance policy?'

'No. She had no one to leave anything to.'

'You think maybe she was depressed about the baby? You know, unmarried and so forth.'

'I doubt it.'

'How come?'

'Renee had already had two abortions, the first when she was sixteen. She asked me to go with her. I used my savings.'

'And the other one?'

'It was . . . Renee was twenty-five.' Renee had asked her for help again; Gail had refused. 'She tried to commit suicide the first time a few months later. We . . . my mother and I had her committed to a psychiatric hospital.'

'How long was she in?'

'A few weeks. She was an outpatient for several months after that.'

The technicians were talking in the bathroom. One of them flushed the toilet. The medicine cabinet opened, its hinges squeaking.

Gail pushed her hair off her forehead.

'Are you okay?'

'Yes.' She laughed. 'Actually, no. We argued the last time I saw her. We really had it out. That keeps going through my mind.'

He patted her hand. 'No, people don't decide these things as a result of one argument.'

'Sergeant, we're finished.' It was the black technician at the door. 'You got anything else?'

'No, let's just take these papers. You can bag them up as is. I want to give Ms Connor a receipt.'

Gail stood up. 'I'll be in the bathroom. If that's permitted.'

'Sure.'

She closed the door behind her and pulled off a few sheets of toilet paper to wipe her nose. She hadn't wept, thank God. She hated losing control in front of strangers. A glance in the mirror told her nothing was out of place. She fluffed her hair.

Not wanting to go back into the guest room, Gail wandered down the hall to Renee's bedroom. If anyone asked, she had a purpose: making a quick inventory of furniture and clothing.

The pile of things on the bed had vanished, probably shoved back into the nightstand, a concession to the relatives' sense of propriety.

Slowly Gail let her gaze go around the room again, both fascinated and repulsed. The colors and textures raised an expectation of uninhibited, guiltless sex. Over the mussed bed, with its pouffy pillows strewn about, hung a huge print of a Georgia O'Keeffe painting: an open orchid with soft, ruffled edges.

The sun had moved further west, streaming through

the mini-blinds on the double window, making a pattern of slanting stripes on the deep pink carpet. The cut-glass vase on the dresser threw shards of light into the room.

Gail sat down at the dresser and turned the vase. Rainbows moved across the walls.

A few months before their father died, Gail was in Renee's room reading while Renee played with her Barbie dolls. Rather, both book and dolls lay untouched on the floor. The adults were arguing. They could hear their mother's sharp voice, their father's angry responses. A door slammed, opened, slammed again. Renee's eyes widened. She hugged her knees, rocking back and forth, a flush of excitement on her face.

Then from the living room came a crash, an explosion of glass, then another and another. The front door slammed, and their father's car roared out of the driveway.

They tiptoed into the living room. Irene stood in the middle of it. The crystal from her étagère – bowls, vases, paperweights – was smashed against the fireplace. Gail ran weeping to her mother. Renee crunched across the carpet in her sandals. Diamonds, she said. Diamonds everywhere.

Gail turned the vase on the dresser and watched the light bounce off the greenish water. Renee had seen light dancing on the ceiling, filling the room with tiny rainbows. Gail had been afraid, but not of broken glass. Her father had come home past midnight that night, and she could hear the bedroom door opening, closing, then muffled voices, finally her mother's husky laughter. Gail had held her pillow over her ears.

There was a knock at the open door. Britton came in, put a Metro-Dade property receipt on the dresser. 'We're done in here, if you want to leave with us and lock up.'

She stood up. 'I'd like to stay for a while.'

'No problem.' He watched her for a second, then said, 'I'll give you a call about getting Renee's stuff back to you.'

After they had gone, Gail crossed the room and closed the mini-blinds. She would stay long enough to straighten up a little, before Irene could see all this. She would clean out the nightstand and empty the rotting irises from the vase on the dresser.

Chapter Seven

Paul Robineau, the managing partner, had set up a catered buffet lunch in the main conference room on Wednesday for all attorneys of the firm. Those who arrived first found places at the long mahogany table. Others, including Gail, took chairs along the walls and had to balance their plates on their knees.

The announced topic was attorney-paralegal interaction in billing procedures. The real agenda, Gail quickly saw, was to explain why the firm couldn't buy a new computer system. More to the point, to explain why the budget committee was honing its scalpel. The year had not been good to Hartwell Black & Robineau. That law firms in general were suffering failed to lighten anyone's mood. Gail saw only grim faces in the sea of suits.

Picking at the crust on her miniature quiche, she wondered what all the food had cost.

Gail shifted her plate on her lap, ignoring the drone of the supervising paralegal. She mentally reviewed her schedule for the rest of the day. Some documents to go over, phone calls to make, a deposition transcript to review. And Anthony Quintana. He would show up at two o'clock to discuss the Darden case. Gail wondered what to say to him. Maybe she should throw herself on his tasseled Italian shoes and beg.

When the meeting was over she pushed back her

chair and headed for the door, where the butler and a woman in a starched apron waited to tidy up. Through the crowd streaming out of the room she noticed Lawrence Black's secretary signal to her.

Gail joined her across the corridor.

'Mr Black asked if you could come upstairs a moment. He's about to leave for the airport, so you'll have to hurry.'

On her way up the back stairs Gail fell into step behind Maxine Canady, once an editor of the *Harvard Law Review* and now a full partner and specialist in taxation. Maxine had not been at the meeting. She had the clout to play hooky if she wanted to. Maxine was dressed in a severe suit and black pumps, just the attire for discussing the IRS.

Maxine glanced over one padded shoulder, smiled, then paused to let Gail catch up. 'I was just thinking about you,' she said. 'Louis and I have decided to trade in our boat.'

'That leaky old thing? I should hope so.' Gail had seen their boat – a forty-foot Bertram yacht, fully air conditioned.

Maxine laughed. 'Well, Lou wants something he can take down to the Islands next winter with the kids. Not my idea of heaven, to go bouncing around the Caribbean, even if I had the time, but he has his heart set on it.'

'Men,' Gail said.

'Do you suppose Dave could give him some advice? We'd like a good used boat if we can find one. We really can't afford anything new.'

Poor Maxine, thought Gail. Falling on hard times. She said, 'I'll ask Dave to give you a call. Maybe what you want to do is outfit your Bertram for longer distances.'

'There's a thought.' They reached the top of the

stairs. Maxine said, 'Come by next week, we'll have lunch.'

Gail watched Maxine turn the corner into her office. Well, well. Lunch with Maxine Canady. Maxine Canady did not usually invite rank-and-file associates to lunch. Gail's mood lifted a notch.

She knocked at Larry's open door and went in.

Larry had a stunning office, twenty feet square, thickly carpeted, and decorated with polished antiques. There were a couple of Cubist paintings by minor but respectable French artists, which the firm – Larry's grandfather, Reginald Black, to be accurate – had purchased back in the forties. By the windows Larry kept a brass telescope on a stand. He could watch the cruise ships heading out from the Port of Miami. All of this had been in place long before he made partner, as if the designation were only a formality – which, given his bloodlines, it probably was.

Larry himself stood by his desk, snapping shut his briefcase. He glanced around.

'Gail. Just in time. I have a flight to Tallahassee, but I wanted to speak to you first. Close the door, would you?'

'What's up?' Gail asked.

He motioned her toward the striped settee under the windows and sat beside her. 'I ran into Doug Hartwell last night.'

'Did you?' She knew immediately where this conversation was going: Nancy Darden, Hartwell's daughter.

'Yes, Doug flew down from DC for a congressional fundraiser. A group of us from the firm went. Big party at the Hyatt Regency afterwards.'

Gail smiled. 'How exciting.'

Larry casually crossed his legs. 'Doug says Nancy's a little concerned about her case. He asked if I'd see what's going on.' Larry's gray eyes told Gail there was hot water somewhere, but he would be damned if he'd be the one to fall into it.

She spoke slowly. 'Do I understand that Nancy Darden has gone over my head to speak to her *father*?'

'I know.' Larry lifted a long, thin hand off his knee. 'I mentioned to Doug that you've had some family obligations to attend to recently, after losing your sister.'

'My sister's death has not affected my job one iota,' Gail said. 'If Nancy Darden is concerned about her case, the least she could do is speak to me directly.'

'I'm not yelling at you. I want you to understand where the conflict lies.'

'You know the real problem as well as I do. Senator Hartwell's darling daughter doesn't have to pay two cents in legal fees. She sends me in to get bloodied while she watches from the hill with her parasol and box lunch.'

Larry pursed his lips. Gail wondered why she had bothered making a joke. The man had no sense of humor.

She started again. 'As I explained to you and Jack Warner over lunch last week, the other side has been putting up roadblocks for months. I managed to set a date for taking depositions, but the case may be settled first.'

His high forehead puckered into a frown. She continued. 'Nancy and I have been playing telephone tag for days. I got in touch with Bill Darden at his medical office this morning – finally – and he told me to go ahead and see what the other attorney and I can work out. What more can I do, Larry? Tell me. Would Nancy like to review my time sheets?'

He looked uncomfortable. 'The loss of revenue is a problem. We count it under JNR – justifiable nonrecoverable – but it's going to adversely affect our division's year-end totals.'

'Look, if Nancy Darden doesn't like the way I'm handling the case, give it to Bob Wilcox. It wouldn't hurt my feelings.'

One corner of Larry's mouth rose. 'It has been suggested – not by myself – that a male attorney might have more success dealing with Hispanics.'

Gail laughed. 'Fine. Take the case yourself. *Buena suerte.*'

Larry was silent for a few moments, then said, 'You say the other side is being stubborn as well?'

She nodded.

He pulled on his earlobe. 'I think what we have to do is put pressure on this Pedrosa fellow from another angle. He still wants to purchase Judge Strickland's property, doesn't he?'

'As far as I know. Why?'

'And there's no contract yet?'

'No. Ben's trying to decide how much he really wants to sell it for.' Gail paused. 'Wait a minute. If you're suggesting that we connect these two trans-actions . . .'

'As long as Ben is fully informed, it's worth considering.' He arched his eyebrows, waiting for a response.

It was also, Gail knew, clearly against the rules. 'I wouldn't be comfortable with that,' she said. 'And I'm sure the other attorney would have something to say about legal ethics.'

'There are ways to be subtle.' Larry's eyes seemed to glide along the fringed border of his oriental rug. 'One thing about Cubans – they're quick to understand subtleties. A very pragmatic people. Carlos Pedrosa isn't the only buyer out there, and he should know that.'

121

Gail finally said, 'Let me see what I can work out with the other attorney this afternoon before we start panicking.'

'Ethics can't be viewed narrowly,' Larry said. 'You have to remember that you are *right*. Your clients are difficult, granted, but they are in the right. That's the basis for legal ethics, knowing that what you do is *right*.'

She and Larry looked at each other for a few seconds. Finally he gave her what he might have intended as a professorial smile. She idly noticed that his bottom teeth overlapped, too crowded in his narrow jaw.

'You know, Gail, as attorneys we're all going to get into difficult situations. That's what we get paid for, isn't it? To be able to handle them. And we can't resort to abstractions to make the decisions for us. We have to rely on experience in the real world as well as on our inner belief. Do you follow?'

'I'll certainly do my best, Larry.'

'I have consummate faith in your abilities.' He pulled back his cuff. 'Well, time to go.' At the door he patted Gail's shoulder. 'Keep me posted.'

Her mind churning, Gail made her way along the corridor past other attorneys' offices, hearing through open doorways a few snatches of conversation, a message dictated, an unexpected peal of laughter. She squeezed her eyes shut tightly, then took a breath. The corridor seemed to go on forever, its end vanishing at a pinpoint.

She muttered to herself, 'God almighty, how did I get into this line of work?'

It occurred to her, as she took a shortcut through the library, zigzagging between shelves of the *Southern Reporter*, that she ought to toss the damn case in Jack Warner's lap. He was the senior partner in the litigation division. She should make him decide what to do with it. If, however, she could also avoid making Larry Black look like the flaming idiot he was. Larry wouldn't forgive her for that, and it was Larry, after all, who wrote monthly reviews of her performance.

At the top of the stairs, Gail caught her heel on the first step. She grabbed at the curving balustrade and righted herself, then took a long, slow breath. She felt the familiar tickle in her chest, heart thudding against her breastbone.

Even if she went to Jack Warner, he would expect her to handle the Darden case to its conclusion. That was his way – trial by ordeal. She was in a pit and he would be waiting to see whether she could climb out of it. The last thing she should do was ask him to throw her a rope. Partners could levitate themselves upward on will alone.

The word around the office was that of half a dozen associates being reviewed for partnership, only two would be chosen. A credible estimate, given the sad facts of life in the legal profession these days: too many attorneys scrabbling for business in a saturated market. It wasn't enough, she realized, to be good at her job. She would have to be more than good. She would have to be brilliant.

On the way into her own office, Gail found Miriam on the telephone.

'. . . *toda la noche*, and I slept not even an hour. *El niño me vuelve loca*, I'm telling you. *Pero* you can see where the tooth is coming in, *¿tú sabes?*, a little bump, *entonces* in a few days he'll be okay, my *mami* says. *Pobrecito, cómo llora*.'

Gail tapped on the glass partition and Miriam waved. '*Te llamo después*, okay? Bye.' When Miriam looked back at Gail, her smile faded.

'Don't we have things to do besides chat with our friends on the telephone?' Gail spun around and crossed the corridor to her office.

Miriam followed, dumping a stack of files on Gail's desk. Her brown eyes snapped with anger. '¿Qué te pasa? I don't like to be talked to like that. I do my work, don't I?'

After a moment, Gail sank back into her chair. 'Yes. I'm sorry. You do your work very well. Just try to remember there are other people around here to please besides me, okay?'

Miriam's chin was still raised, and she looked at Gail haughtily before she relented. 'Okay.'

Gail wanted to make amends. 'Is Berto sick?'

'No, just teething.' Miriam laughed, her bubbly humor back again. 'He was screaming so loud Danny had to sleep on the couch last night, the first time we've slept apart since we got married. He says he's going to buy Berto a set of false teeth.'

'I want a picture of that.' Gail smiled, pulling the files across the desk. 'Anybody call?'

Miriam held up four pink message slips. 'That Metro-Dade policeman, Frank Britton, wants you to call him back.'

'He'll have to wait.'

'And the Indian, Jimmy Panther. He didn't say what it was in regard to.' Gail only nodded. Miriam continued to flip through the messages. 'Ben Strickland says he has some papers for you to sign. And your husband can't pick up Karen from ballet this afternoon.'

Gail groaned softly. 'Just great.'

After Miriam went back across the hall, Gail angrily punched in the number for the marina and asked to speak to Dave. When he answered, she said, 'This is Gail. I got your message about Karen.'

'Yeah, I have to do an estimate up in Lauderdale.'

'You were supposed to pick her up. I can't possibly leave work so early.'

'What, have you got a trial or something?'

'You know very well I don't have a trial. I have a meeting. I have appointments. There is work I simply have to do today.'

'Ask Irene. Maybe Irene can help.'

'Irene is in no condition to go driving around Miami. She won't even leave the house to do her own grocery shopping.'

'Jesus. Look, I have to go. I'm with a customer.'

'Damn it, Dave.'

'I'm not the family chauffeur. You're her mother. You've got some responsibility in this, too.'

'I know that, I know.' Gail dug her fingers into her hair. 'Okay. Can you take her with you?'

'What?'

'Pick her up on the way and take her with you. She likes to ride in the truck. I'll come by the marina on my way home.'

After a long silence, Dave said, 'All right. Try to get here before seven. I'm playing tennis tonight.' He hung up.

Gail let the phone drop back into the cradle. She swiveled her chair around to face the window. What in God's name would she do if he left her?

As she continued to stare across her office, the cold possibility settled into her mind that he might do just that. She couldn't pretend they were riotously happy. Their marriage might die. And her first thought had not been how to save it, but what a separation would do to her schedule.

Gail shook her head as if to clear it. 'I can't think of this now.' She reached for the files, then remembered she had to call Ben.

* * *

Turner, Brown, Widdeman, Young & Strickland.

The brass letters spelling out Ben's last name shone more brightly than the others because they had been added more recently to the wood panel outside his sixth-floor office. The other names belonged to old buddies of his, men Ben used to go fishing with, or take up to Gainesville in his Winnebago for the University of Florida homecoming game.

Still flushed from her dash across Flagler Street, Gail opened the door to the waiting room, which was unoccupied except for a UPS delivery man talking through the little window to one of the secretaries. The room had dark green vinyl-covered chairs and a bookcase with an outdated set of *American Jurisprudence*. Framed prints of British barristers in wigs and billowing black robes were lined up over the long sofa. Gail had seen them advertised in the *Bar Journal*.

When the delivery man moved away from the window, Gail stepped forward before the secretary could slide the frosted glass back into place. 'I'm Gail Connor, here to see Judge Strickland.' Ben wasn't a judge anymore, but he liked the title.

The woman looked at her in a blank but friendly way, obviously having forgotten Gail had been here before. 'I'll tell him. Sit down.' She pulled the window shut with one finger. Her red dress wavered behind the bubbly glass, then disappeared.

Gail leaned on the counter and read the titles of the brochures displayed in plastic holders. *Should I have a will? What if I am arrested? How will title insurance protect my home?*

Ben had said if he'd known private practice was this good, he'd have left the bench years ago. Gail often wondered whom he was trying to convince. She knew he had enjoyed his position on the circuit court. Now he was just one more late-middle-aged attorney in a firm of them.

The inner door opened. 'Gail, come on in.' It was Ben. He wore no jacket and his tie was loosened. She followed his long strides past the secretarial area, then around a corner to his office.

When she had called he had told her it would be no trouble to send the corrected probate papers by courier for her signature. Gail had said she didn't mind getting out of the office for a few minutes. Besides, there was something she wanted to talk to him about.

They sat on opposite sides of his desk, she in a heavy oak chair that had once been in a turn-of-the-century jury box, Ben in his black leather armchair. He had brought his own furniture from the courthouse when he left – dark, masculine pieces scuffed from years of use.

Over the desk he had hung his favorite Florida landscape paintings, a square arrangement of four heavy gold frames that used to grace the waiting room outside his chambers. Sunset and endless sky over the saw grass prairie. Turkey gobblers in the Central Florida woods. A white heron rising out of a cypress swamp. And Ben's own property in Southwest Dade – rustic cabin, pines, and palmetto scrub.

He opened the file and slid some documents across the desk. They were the same forms she had read at Irene's, retyped with her own name. He gave her a pen.

'I spoke to Irene,' he said. 'She told me about the police searching Renee's apartment. Said she asked them to. I swear, that woman worries me.'

Without looking up, Gail signed the Petition for Administration, then the Oath of Personal Representative. 'I think she's beginning to realize how irrational it was. She didn't want me to mention it to you, because you'd think the same thing.' When Gail

127

came to the inventory – still to be filled out – she said, 'Oh, I forgot to tell you. They're keeping Renee's records for a few days.'

'What for?'

'Procedure, I don't know. Frank Britton – he's the sergeant in charge – said he'd send you a preliminary death certificate. Did he?'

'Nothing's come in,' Ben said, then added, 'Britton. That could be the guy who went out to see Irene a couple of nights ago.'

'What did he want?' Gail asked.

'She said they talked about Renee.'

'I wish he'd quit bothering her.'

Ben smiled. 'Oh, I think Irene likes the attention. She said Britton was a nice man. She fixed him some tea.'

'This is getting ridiculous. I wonder if you could find out what he thinks he's doing?'

'I could try. I know some people who could ask.'

'Ben.' Gail hesitated, then said, 'Do you think there's anything to it?'

'Oh, I wouldn't worry. Irene overreacted a little is all.'

'Be honest.'

His face grew serious, deep lines appearing in his forehead. 'I don't know, Gail. I've thought long and hard about it. Girl like Renee, she could have been into any number of things. Drugs, sickos of some kind. Kinky sex.' He glanced at her. 'Sorry if that shocks you.'

Gail shrugged a little, aware she found it strange to hear Ben talk about sex, kinky or not. 'No, it's all right,' she said. 'I wanted your opinion.'

'I wouldn't say this to Irene, you understand. She's pretty old-fashioned. She thought Renee was just a fun-loving girl who hadn't grown up yet.' Ben ran his thumb along the carved edge of his desk. 'I think there was more wrong with her. The night of the party. She was acting crazy. I don't know how else to say it.'

His eyes rested on Gail for a moment. He swiveled his chair toward the window. 'Lord, this is hard to – I took Renee out on the back porch – I mean, I pulled her by the arm and told her to straighten up, she was making a damn fool of herself. There was this—' he paused '—wild look about her. We were out there in the dark and she laughed and— She—'

Gail didn't move.

'She . . . put her hands on me. She said—' Ben shook his head and blinked. 'Doesn't matter what she said. Doesn't matter. She was not right in the head. I was thirty years older. And her cousin. Maybe she realized what she was doing and felt embarrassed, I don't know. I'm not going to remember her like that, though. I try to think of her the way she was, when she was a kid. But I figured you ought to know, honey. You asked me if I thought Frank Britton was barking up the wrong tree and I think he is. I think he's wrong as can be.'

Ben gripped the arms of the chair, slapping them for emphasis. 'Enough of that. Did you sign everything?'

Gail was still reeling. It took her a few seconds. 'No. There's one left.' She signed the last paper, then passed them all back.

Ben looked at Gail over the file as he dropped the papers back inside. 'You said you had something to talk to me about?'

For a moment, she could not think of what it was. 'Yes. Carlos Pedrosa.'

There was a clock on Ben's credenza, an antique bronze horse rearing on its hind legs, with a white dial in the pedestal it stood on. The clock said one forty-two.

'I'll have to make this fast,' Gail said. 'Remember I told you I have a case against the same Carlos Pedrosa you want to sell your property to?'

Ben reached for his cigarettes and lighter. 'I remember. You represent Doug Hartwell's girl.' He drew a cigarette out of the pack, then held it up between two fingers to see if she minded. Gail shook her head.

'Ben, this is between you and me, all right?'

'Sure. What's going on?'

'Carlos is stonewalling on discovery. He won't agree to a reasonable settlement – neither will my clients, to tell the truth.' She hesitated, then said, 'Larry Black suggested I use your property as bait.'

'What did you say?'

'I thought it was a bad idea. Now I'm not sure.'

Ben flipped his lighter open with one hand and hit the wheel with his thumb. He inhaled, then tossed the lighter back onto his desk. 'Who's the judge on this case?'

'Arlen Coakley.'

'I'll talk to him for you.'

'Ben—'

'Come on. Arlen and I go way back. We went to grade school together.'

'Absolutely not. I didn't come to you for that.'

Ben extended his arm to flick his ashes into a heavy pewter ashtray. 'You wouldn't accept help out of a pool of quicksand.'

She said, 'I only wanted to know if I was doing the right thing.'

He smiled with one corner of his mouth. 'Yes, honey. It's the right thing. I'm proud of you.'

Gail felt a rush of emotion so sharp it stung her eyes. She glanced at the bronze horse clock again and stood up. 'I have to go. Pedrosa's attorney is coming at two to talk about settlement.'

Ben looked at her. 'If you need help with Pedrosa, say so.' He got up and walked with her to the door. 'I'm of two minds with that sale anyway. I don't even like the guy. I wouldn't have talked to him if Renee hadn't introduced us. And what's the matter with his credit that he can't arrange a bank loan and pay me cash? Last weekend I was out there fixing up the cabin, and happened to drive by the construction site. Not a lot of activity going on. Makes me think I might have to foreclose to collect my money.'

Gail turned to him. 'Carlos Pedrosa is having problems?'

Ben laughed at the look on her face. 'I don't know. I'm just telling you what to say to him. Make him sweat a little.'

'How do you know he wants the property bad enough to sweat for it?'

Ben smiled, deep creases in his cheeks. He looked vital again, the years lifting off. He said, 'Carlos Pedrosa would make a lousy poker player.'

Running back across the street through slow, heavy traffic, the stench of exhaust in her nose, Gail remembered the ranch – scent of pine, clouds reflecting in blue pools of rainwater, wind sighing through the trees.

The painting in Ben's office looked like her memory, but she knew reality was something else. The artist hadn't shown the air conditioner hanging out the back window of the cabin, or the mosquitoes, or the weeds that choked the yard. And there were no people in the painting.

Every winter, before they lost interest, the Strickland descendants had converged on the ranch, clearing the underbrush and fixing whatever was broken, with beer and barbecue to follow. The last cookout Gail attended took place around Christmas before she was due to graduate from the university. Hardly anyone had shown up – a cousin and his wife and kids; Irene and Renee; herself and Dave, engaged to be married in the spring. Ben was there, of course, with his wife Shirley, who would die of cancer within the year, though no one knew it then. Their two sons had already moved north. Ben wore old jeans and cowboy boots. His hair was still dark brown, just beginning to go gray.

Renee told Gail she wouldn't have come at all, except that Irene wanted to show her off a little, now that Renee had made it through two semesters at Miami-Dade Community College. Renee laughed. *Big deal. Not like Miss Perfect with a three-point-eight at the U of fucking Florida.* She tugged the beer out of Dave's hand when no one else was watching and tilted it back, hanging onto his shoulder. She wiped her mouth. *Guess what? Ben's getting me a car. I'm not supposed to know.*

After lunch Irene brought out a chocolate cake with 'Congratulations' on it and Ben and Shirley gave Renee a set of car keys. Six months later, the car – a used Plymouth sedan Renee had hated at first sight – would spin out on I-75 and slam into a retaining wall at three in the morning. The highway patrol would say it was a miracle Renee walked away from it.

But on that afternoon at the ranch, Renee squealed and jumped up and down like a little girl. As the paper plates of cake were being passed around the long wooden table, Gail casually made her announcement. Rather than accept a position in management training at Southeast Bank, she would go to law school. Follow in Ben's footsteps and eventually make as much of a contribution to the community as he had made.

Ben nodded, evidently pleased. The cousins said how brave she was. Dave stared. Renee hardly spoke to her the rest of the afternoon.

For years Gail had remembered the last cookout at the ranch with a pleasantly fuzzy sense of nostalgia. Now the scene replayed itself more clearly. She had chosen her path that day, pushed along by the worst of motives.

Chapter Eight

As soon as she sat down at her desk, Gail buzzed Miriam. 'Has Anthony Quintana shown up yet?'

'Where did you come from?' Miriam asked.

'The back way. Is he here?'

'Yes, they called me from the lobby a couple minutes ago. I'll go get him.'

'No, wait.' Gail pulled the Darden file to the center of her desk. 'I want to make a phone call first.'

Gail hit the button for an outside line and dialed Charlene Marks's number. If kisses on the cheek and flirtatious repartee in the courthouse corridor had meant anything, Charlene knew Anthony Quintana well enough to give Gail some answers.

To her relief, Charlene was actually in her office.

'No, dear, I do not have a cot at the courthouse,' Charlene said with a deep chuckle. 'What's doing?'

'Anthony Quintana,' Gail said. 'I have a question.'

'Yes, he's single.'

Gail laughed. 'Not that question. I wonder if you could tell me what he does besides practice law. Is he connected to any businesses owned by Ernesto Pedrosa? That's his grandfather.'

When she had first taken on *Darden v. Pedrosa*, Gail had made a few inquiries to find out who the players were. Ernesto Pedrosa was eighty-two years old, a refugee from the Cuban revolution, and about as rich as anyone could reasonably get in Miami. Along with

135

his wife, Digna, and a few other Pedrosas who held minor shares, Ernesto owned not only Pedrosa Development but a Chevrolet dealership, a McDonald's on Calle Ocho, a strip shopping center in Hialeah, two office buildings, several hundred acres of land, and a good chunk of four banks, which he himself – a former banker in Havana – had founded. Carlos Pedrosa's name appeared on the list as manager of Pedrosa Development. Gail hadn't seen the name Anthony Luis Quintana Pedrosa anywhere. But if he had a stake in the company, she wanted to find out.

There was a long silence over the phone, then Charlene said, 'I know who Ernesto Pedrosa is, sure.'

'Well?' There was something Charlene wasn't saying. 'Come on, Charlene. What?'

'I can't get into it. I handled Tony's divorce.'

'Really,' Gail said. She knew Charlene couldn't ethically talk about a client's liabilities and assets. 'When was that?'

'Oh . . . about three years ago, I guess. Why do you want to know all this, anyway?'

'I have a case with him – Nancy Darden is suing Pedrosa Development, remember?'

Charlene took a moment, then said, 'Oh, yeah. Our esteemed Senator Hartwell's own little princess.' Gail heard a sigh over the line. She could imagine Charlene pacing back and forth with the phone clamped under her square jaw. 'Well, I can tell you that Anthony Quintana is not connected to any of Ernesto's operations, including the development company. His ex-wife didn't want to believe it, but there it is.'

Gail thought about that. 'Why? Anthony's his grandson.'

'They had some kind of falling out years ago. Ernesto is supposedly grooming his other grandson to take over. I forget his name.'

'Carlos Pedrosa?'

'Correct. Anyway, whatever Tony has, he made on his own, no thanks to *abuelito*. Ernesto's a real pissant.'

Gail remembered what Ben had told her: Ernesto Pedrosa had been heavily involved in anti-Castro activities. She asked, 'You don't know anything about Anthony Quintana's politics, do you?'

'Not really. I never asked.'

'One more thing. Somebody suggested to me that Carlos might not be doing so well.'

'Hard to believe, with Ernesto's money behind him. But you never know these days.' Charlene asked, 'What does Tony have to say about all this?'

'I'll ask him. Is he going to play straight with me?'

'I've never caught him in a lie, if that's what you mean.' There was a pause, then Charlene added, 'On the other hand, he won't necessarily tell you more than he has to.'

After Gail hung up she kept her hand on the phone for a second, thinking, then yanked open a desk drawer. She kept spare makeup and a mirror inside. For any other attorney she would not have touched up her mascara but decided to be on the safe side. Cuban men were an unknown quantity.

Gail was slowly turning pages in the Darden file when she heard movement at the door to her office. She looked up.

Miriam was behind Anthony Quintana, ushering him in. Catching Gail's eye, Miriam put both hands to her own cheeks and pretended to swoon. He did look particularly well turned out, Gail thought. Dark hair gleaming. Double-breasted suit the tan of *café con leche*. And his shiny black briefcase with the gold clasps. When he turned to nod at Miriam, her face snapped into its usual friendly smile.

137

Gail frowned at her.

'Shall I close the door?' Miriam asked sweetly.

'Please.' Gail rose from her chair and extended her hand across the desk. 'Anthony, I'm glad to see you again.' She had worn her high heels today, putting her at eye level. 'Won't you have a seat?'

He smiled apologetically, still standing. 'Could we talk downstairs? I noticed a coffee shop in the lobby. I had two hearings this morning and missed lunch completely. I'm famished.'

On her desk was the file, with lists of construction costs she had wanted to refer to, and the contract, and revisions to the contract. She wondered how it would look spread out on the lunch counter while she perched on one of the red-covered stools.

'Leave it here,' Anthony said. 'I have a memo pad if we want to make notes.' He dropped his briefcase into a chair.

'Well, I suppose we could do that.' She glanced at his briefcase. 'What is that made of?'

'This? Snakeskin. A client gave it to me.' Anthony ran his fingers over the surface, then picked it up and held it out to Gail. 'The last I saw of him before he jumped bail and went back to Panama. I would have preferred the rest of my fee.'

The skin was surprisingly slick. Gail drew her hand back. '*Tsk-tsk.* I've trained my clients *never* to jump bail,' she said.

He looked at her, amused. 'Another reason I should do more civil practice.'

She reached for the doorknob but he was already there, and held the door for her. 'Thanks,' she said. She was used to opening her own doors. Her nose quivered as she brushed past him. That cologne again.

There was no one else in the elevator. He touched the button for the lobby, then settled back against the

138

side wall, arms spread, hands resting on the brass railing, looking at her. His jacket was open far enough to show a bit of suspender at his belt line, the same brown-and-green swirly pattern as his pocket handkerchief.

Gail glanced at the floor indicator, where the numbers were counting down in digital blue. The finer points of her argument could wait until they had ordered coffee, but they might as well go over the status of the proceedings now. She had the advantage talking to a criminal attorney about a civil case.

She turned and opened her mouth to speak.

'How is your mother?' he asked.

'My mother?' She looked at him for a moment, then remembered Latins considered it polite to begin with inquiries about health or family before coming to the subject at hand.

'You're kind to ask about her,' Gail replied. 'I suppose she's as well as could be expected at this point.'

He nodded. 'And you?' His brown eyes were wide open, fixed on her, curious.

'We're both trying to adjust. Thank you.' Gail could not imagine that his concern amounted to anything more than good manners. But she should reciprocate.

'Your parents are in Miami?' she asked.

'My mother was. She died two years ago.' Then he added, 'My father is still in Cuba. A small town outside Camagüey City called Cascorro.' The *rrr* flowed off his tongue.

Gail wondered why Quintana senior had stayed in Cuba. And if Anthony had ever been back to see him. Other questions it was none of her business asking occurred to her. She asked an innocuous one. 'When did you arrive in Miami?'

'In sixty-five. I was – let's see – nearly thirteen. Speaking only Spanish, of course.' He laughed. 'But I

139

could also carry on a basic conversation in Russian.'

'Can you still?'

'*¡Alaba'o!* In my grandfather's house it was the first thing I forgot.'

The elevator opened and they walked into the tiled lobby. Through the glass doors leading out onto Flagler Street Gail could see a small patch of blue sky over the department store across the street.

She said, 'Here's the truth about the coffee shop in this building. They charge eight bucks for a sandwich and the waitresses are surly.'

'They couldn't ruin soup.'

'Yes, they could. Come on, there's a good place on Biscayne. It won't be crowded at this hour.' Besides, there would be a table between them. She could not imagine sitting elbow to elbow at a lunch counter.

Anthony followed her across the lobby. 'Is this what you do to weaken your opponents?'

'If you faint I'll carry you.'

She bumped into his arm as he reached to push open the door. 'Thank you,' she said, going through first. She blinked in the sunlight. They turned left, walking eastward toward the bay. Anthony put himself between Gail and the street. Such manners.

'I am curious about something,' Gail said. 'What ever happened to George Sanchez?'

'He still works for Ferrer and Quintana.'

'But not on this case.'

'George is primarily a title examiner and real estate attorney. I'm better at trial work.'

It had occurred to Gail, speaking to Charlene earlier, why Anthony might have taken *Darden v. Pedrosa* from George Sanchez. Estranged from his grandfather for too long, he could be using the case to get back in. If that were true, he would be more likely to settle than to risk a loss in court.

Gail said, 'I suppose it's convenient for your grandfather to have a family member handling the case.'

Anthony nodded. 'That too.' He stopped walking and touched her arm. 'Excuse me a minute.'

There was an umbrella cart under a clump of palm trees, a white box with two small wheels in front and bicycle tyres behind, pushed by a black man in a yellow tank top. A stenciled sign on the side said 'Jamaican Meat Pies'. Anthony Quintana was pulling out his wallet.

He turned to Gail. 'I know this man. He used to sell these in front of the Justice Building. Would you like one?'

The Jamaican – if he was Jamaican – grinned at her, a mouthful of white teeth under an orange Miami Hurricanes cap. 'What kind you want, pretty lady?'

'Not for me, thank you.'

'No?' Anthony shrugged. 'One only. Hot.' He held out his dollar and the Jamaican gave him a semicircular piece of pastry with fluted edges, wrapped in white paper. Anthony pulled a napkin out of a metal dispenser wired to the cart.

He started walking again – slower than necessary, she thought. He said, 'Have you talked to your clients?'

'Yes. Have you talked to yours?'

'Of course.' The meat pie was poised at his lips. He made a little sigh of pleasure. '*Riquísimo*. No one else makes them like this.' He bit into it, eyes half closing, leaning forward a little so nothing would drop on his suit. The pungent smell of ground beef and spices filled Gail's nose. He wiped the napkin across his mouth.

Gail fastened her eyes on the square, reddish tiles in the sidewalk.

'What do the Dardens want to do with this case?' he asked.

'They want a reasonable settlement,' she said. 'But let's wait until we sit down to talk about it.'

'Why?' He took another bite, folding back the paper. 'I can be as reasonable standing up as sitting down.'

She let herself look at him a moment longer, suddenly realizing what he was doing. Anthony Quintana was flirting with her. Not overtly, just enough to distract her attention.

'All right,' she said. 'We won't talk about who did what to whom. The question is, what's likely to happen in a trial? Neither of us is going to come out unscathed, obviously. But Pedrosa is not in the stronger position, not on the facts, and not with Judge Coakley. Your motion for recusal won't fly. He'll stay on this case like a pit bull.'

Anthony shook out his napkin and wiped his mouth again, then tossed the napkin into a trash basket. 'And if we have a jury?'

'Go for it.' She smiled at him. 'You told me you're a real whiz with juries. But here are two things to consider. One, you've still got Coakley on the bench. And two, I probably know my way around a civil courtroom better than you do.'

He stopped walking and the crowd parted, moving past them on the sidewalk. The sun cut across his face, casting shadows, making his skin glow as if polished. 'Then perhaps we should say to hell with settlement and go to trial, yes? What do you think?'

What she thought was that he would not have used that tone of voice with a male attorney. She leveled her gaze at him. 'Fine. Go to trial. If you're sure you really want to take that chance.'

'Would you cut me into little pieces?' Anthony gave her a slow smile. 'What would it be like, I wonder, to fight in court with you?'

Before she could think of a tart response, he shook

142

his head and began to walk. 'No, I don't have the time,' he said. 'Civil cases last too long and I lack the patience for them.' His hands accented his words as he spoke. 'In criminal law, at least, the issues are clearer and your cases are over quickly, most of them. Even the murder cases rarely take more than a year.'

'You told me you were going to give that up,' she said.

'Did I? No, I did not mean give it up entirely. I like my criminal practice.'

'Are you good at it?'

'Yes. I generally win the cases that should be won and arrange suitable pleas for the rest of them.'

'But your clients. Murderers, rapists, drug dealers—'

'They are not always guilty – not of what the state charges them with. Not even the murderer who pulls the trigger.'

'Why not? The victim is dead.'

'Gail, I am surprised.' He looked at her, enjoying this. 'What is the motive? Momentary rage or cold premeditation? If I persuade the jury it was the former, I save my client's neck. And besides, who can draw a clean line between guilt and innocence? Even in a criminal trial the result is often only a guess. In life, everyone is guilty of something.'

'That's rather cynical.'

'Not at all. Look at your clients, the bankers and businessmen – do you always believe the purity of their motives?'

She had to laugh a little at that. 'Mr Quintana, you are representing the businessman in this case, not I. He's the big developer who doesn't care if the construction is shoddy as long as he makes a profit. How innocent do you think Carlos Pedrosa is going to appear to Judge Coakley? Or to a jury of other home owners?'

143

Anthony slowed his steps, his face lighting up as if her argument were a Jamaican meat pie and he was going to finish it off. 'Well . . . Ms Connor . . . when I introduce into evidence each one of the seventy-three change orders requested – no, demanded – by your clients, then the jury may get a more accurate picture.'

They rounded the corner at Biscayne Boulevard. A gust of wind flattened Gail's skirt, then swirled it to her thighs. She pushed it back down, then noticed Anthony Quintana's eyes lifting from her legs.

She kept her skirt gathered in one hand. 'Then I suggest we go ahead with the depositions next week. I'm particularly eager to meet Carlos.'

'But you have met him, no?' Another gust of wind opened Anthony's jacket. His tie remained securely in place, pinned by a gold tie tack.

'No,' she said. 'I certainly would have remembered.'

'He came to the visitation for Renee.'

'Carlos Pedrosa?'

'Yes, just before I arrived.'

Gail frowned. 'I saw a man in the parking lot. You spoke to him. He was driving a silver Mercedes. About thirty, with a beard?'

'That was Carlos.'

'I thought he was a client of yours.'

Anthony laughed. 'You should tell him that.'

'Sorry,' Gail said.

'Does it surprise you he was there?'

'I suppose not, if he and Renee knew each other. You were there.' She walked for a while, remembering Carlos Pedrosa swinging his keys around his forefinger in the parking lot, grinning at her. She wondered how well he had known Renee.

'How did they meet, through your law firm's title company?' That was what Ben had told her, but she wanted to hear what Anthony had to say.

144

'Yes. My partner Raul Ferrer hired her. Raul runs the title company.' Gail's next question must have been apparent in her face. He added, 'Renee and Carlos were friends.'

She continued to look at him.

He shrugged. 'Forgive me, if I leave it at that. Carlos is my cousin.'

'Renee was my sister.'

'Even so.'

The wind had calmed beside the buildings on Biscayne, though the big multicolored flags at Bayside Marketplace three blocks north were still snapping westward from their double row of flagpoles.

Gail said, 'I've tried to imagine Renee sitting behind a desk with a calculator, going over figures for a real estate closing, and I just can't do it. It's so unlike her.'

'I never heard complaints about her work.'

'How long had she been there?'

'A year or so. Beginning part-time, then working to a full-time position. She did some of the closings for Carlos if the other closers were busy. Many of the buyers couldn't speak English.'

'Renee spoke *Spanish*?'

'Not fluently, but well enough. You didn't know this?'

Gail shook her head.

Anthony said, 'Do you remember the photograph I brought your mother?'

'Of course. What about it?'

'I once asked Renee who the other little girl was. She told me about you.'

'I'm afraid to ask.'

'"My beautiful, brilliant bitch of a sister. She can do anything."' Anthony smiled. 'Renee meant it as a compliment.'

Gail laughed. 'I doubt it, but thank you.'

145

'No, I think Renee meant everything she said. She was one of the most forthright people I have ever met.' He stopped walking, his brows lifting. 'Is this the place you wanted to bring me?'

Further along the sidewalk a Cuban restaurant faced the street. A ledge at the open window held a five-gallon insulated water cooler and a glass box of pastries. A man stood outside the window sipping thick black coffee from a tiny cup. Through the door Gail could see a few tables, most of them unoccupied.

'This place? Actually, I never noticed it before.' She looked back at him. 'But if you prefer—'

'Because I'm Cuban?' He shook his head. 'I had enough Cuban food as a kid. That's all I had until I was eighteen. I eat what my aunts cook when I go to their houses, but other than that, I never touch it.'

'How odd,' she said, following when he began to walk again. 'Isn't it?'

Anthony shrugged, palms moving outward and up.

Gail was still curious. 'You lived with your grandfather when you came to Miami?'

'Yes. And with my grandmother, my mother, a younger sister, two aunts, an uncle, and three or four cousins. Including Carlos.'

'What is Ernesto Pedrosa like? If you don't mind my asking.'

'Well, don't think he is uneducated because he has *arroz y frijoles negros* on his plate every day. He studied in New York and traveled around the world. He attended the ballet and the opera in Havana. My mother told me they had a French cook. This was before, of course.'

'Before the revolution?'

'Yes. Ever since he got here he won't eat anything but Cuban food at home.'

Anthony stopped at a fruit stand and flashed Gail a

146

smile. 'All this talk of food.' He said something in Spanish to the vendor too fast for her to understand any of it except the word *dos*. He pulled out his wallet.

The vendor – a buxom, red-haired Hispanic woman in tight pants – handed him two cups of chunked tropical fruit with plastic forks inside and rattled something back at him.

Gail asked, 'One of those isn't mine, is it?'

'Hold it for me, if you don't want it.' Anthony speared a piece of pineapple. She watched him chew. He was wearing yet a different ring, she noticed, a gold band with a brown striped cat's-eye. He had graceful hands. Gail imagined the women on the *Darden v. Pedrosa* jury watching Anthony Quintana instead of listening to her final argument.

But the case would be settled first. They were all reasonable people. Even Nancy Darden would be happy. Gail inhaled deeply, tilting her head back to let the sun pour over her face.

Anthony was concentrating on his fruit cup. Then he said, 'I'll tell you about my grandfather, since you seem to be curious. My grandfather's house in Coral Gables faces south. In his office he has a big desk – over which hangs a flag of Cuba with bullet holes in it.'

He poked through the fruit until he found a more or less square piece of mango. He held it up on the end of the fork. 'This desk is turned toward the southwest—' He rotated the mango. '—so that when Ernesto José Pedrosa Masvidal sits in his chair he is looking at Havana. So he says. *Veo mi Habana querida.*'

Anthony ate the mango, then laughed and gestured with his fork toward the other cup. 'I should have bought three of them.'

Gail looked down, swallowing a piece of cantaloupe. 'Oh, I'm sorry.'

'No, I bought it for you.'

'Well, then.' She took another piece, eyeing it carefully. 'What is this?'

'Mamey.'

She put it into her mouth and grimaced.

He grinned at her. 'You've never tasted mamey?'

'No. Bizarre.' She let it slide down her throat.

'You stay in your office too much.'

'How true.' Laughing a little, Gail brushed back the hair that had blown over her forehead. 'What a gorgeous day. I was outside earlier and didn't even notice.'

'We must have all our talks in the street, then.'

His eyes were so dark, and the eyelashes so thick, she could barely distinguish pupil from iris. What a fascinating face, she thought, wanting to decide objectively why she thought so. The angles. Or textures. Or because it was Hispanic and therefore different, although she could not tell in what way. Perhaps the contrast between dark and light. Rich brown hair, white shirt collar. Dark eyes, pale skin. More golden than pale, but lighter than Dave's, anyway, with a darker beard below the surface.

It took no more than a second or two for all this to flash through her mind, then Gail turned her attention back to the sidewalk ahead of them. She wished she could discreetly drop the half-full cup of fruit into a trash can. The sweet juice had run backwards off the fork and made her fingers sticky.

'I think we've gotten a little off the subject,' she said.

'Yes. You were threatening to go ahead with the depositions on Monday.'

'No, I was making a point. If we can't at least agree on a tentative settlement, we'll end up in trial, and neither of us really wants that.'

They walked around a cabbie loading a pile of luggage into the back of a taxi. A family of sunburned tourists –

British from the sound of them – stood to one side waiting.

Anthony speared the last piece of fruit in his cup. 'Well, tell me what you do want.'

She said, 'Pedrosa Development repays the Dardens what they have in it and they deed the property back.'

'We don't want the property back,' Anthony said. 'However, some adjustments might be made in the purchase price. For example, the pool could be included at no charge.'

She shook her head. 'This is an emotional thing for them, you have to realize that. Bill and Nancy are newlyweds, planning a family. They wanted a nice home and wound up with a construction nightmare.'

'I think you are talking to the judge, not to me.'

'Carlos can sell the house to someone else.'

Anthony's smile had gone. 'You're asking too much, Gail.'

'I'm willing to give up the loan interest. Maybe.'

'No. Take the property, Pedrosa will come down on the price. Get another contractor to do the work.'

'This isn't much different from what you were saying nearly two weeks ago.'

'Neither is what you are telling me.'

Gail stopped walking. 'Then go to trial.'

Anthony looked at her steadily for a few moments, then gestured toward the fruit cup she held. 'Are you finished with that?'

She glanced at it. 'Yes.'

He took both cups and dropped them into a trash can. 'I have something I want to show you.' He opened his jacket and reached into the breast pocket. 'A letter. The original is in my file.' He handed it to her, folded crisply into thirds.

There were four pages. It took Gail only a moment to recognize the loopy handwriting, and she turned to the last page to confirm it. A letter from Nancy Darden to Carlos Pedrosa, dated six months ago, when the conflict between them had blown out of control.

After beginning with a general expression of outrage, which was sprinkled liberally with exclamation points and capitalized words, Nancy Darden had suggested that Carlos Pedrosa was a lying thief who hired illegal aliens. That this was still America and they should all go back where they came from, including Carlos. That Cubans were known as the Jews of the Caribbean, which she guessed explained just about everything. That her father was a member of the United States Senate who was going to take care of this—

Silently cursing Nancy Darden, Gail folded the letter. Stupid, bigoted little bitch. She held the letter out to Anthony Quintana.

'Keep it,' he said. 'Perhaps Mrs Darden would like to reread it.' His easy manner was gone, something steely-edged moving into its place.

Gail put the letter into the pocket of her dress, speaking coldly, masking her uncertainty with indignation. 'What do you intend to do with this? It has no relation to the issues in the case. It isn't admissible as evidence, not in a civil trial.'

'I think you should discuss it with your clients before it becomes a problem for them.'

Of course, Gail thought. The letter could turn up in *El Herald*. The Cuban talk stations in South Florida, always hot to jump on politicians, would be sizzling. They had never liked Douglas Hartwell, even if he was a Republican. Oh, and the Jewish voters didn't like him either. And who else had Nancy insulted? Hartwell would be facing a contested re-election in the fall, and even a petty issue like this could make a difference.

Obviously Anthony Quintana had figured all this

150

out. And now he was still waiting for her response. He would, she decided, make an excellent poker player.

'What do you expect me to do, Mr Quintana?'

He spoke in a flat tone. 'As I said, I don't have the time or patience for civil jury trials. I want this settled.'

'On whose terms?'

'Make an offer.'

Gail felt vulnerable, dismayed by what she could now see only as her own carelessness. Nancy had told her she had written to Carlos Pedrosa but Gail had never asked for a copy of the letter. It was small comfort to know that most other attorneys wouldn't have asked either. There would be no excuses for losing this case.

She knew what Larry Black would do. If she took his advice, whom would she be trying to save, the Dardens or herself?

Everyone, Anthony had said, is guilty of something.

But Gail could only laugh, and she saw the surprise on his face. She looked across the wide boulevard, to the grassy, manmade hill on the other side.

'Since you appreciate forthrightness—' She turned back to him. 'I assume you do. You said as much, talking about my sister.' She waited, then went on. 'I don't like threats. Do what you want with that letter. I'm going to pretend I never saw it. I'm also going to pretend we don't have clients from hell and that maybe we can work this out. And if not—' Gail lifted her hands. 'If not, thanks for the fruit and I'll see you in court.'

Anthony looked at her for a moment longer. 'Clients from hell?' She said nothing. 'The house is more than halfway finished, Gail. You know the court will not cancel the contract.'

Her hands were wet with perspiration. She clasped them behind her back. 'Yes, I know. We'll pay the

151

contract price, but only labor and materials, no overhead, no profit.'

'And this is reasonable?' He gave her a look. 'What about the extras they ordered? The Jacuzzi. The oak floors. All of that.'

'All right. But only cost, no profit.'

'Agreed. Only cost.'

'We need to see your invoices.'

'Of course.'

'And the company pays loan interest.'

'Half. Both sides caused the delay.'

'Fine. Half.'

'And the Dardens can find another contractor to finish the house.' There was a vague smile. 'Perhaps an American company, where everyone speaks English.'

'Anything else?'

He made a dismissive gesture. 'Small details. Will your clients agree?'

'I'll let you know after I talk to them.'

'Yes. Call me.'

'Tell me something,' she said. 'What would you have done with that letter?'

He took a few seconds, then shrugged. 'Probably nothing.'

They stood looking at each other. Gail said, 'We never made it to the restaurant.'

'This was better. Don't you think?'

She returned his smile. 'Except for the mamey.'

With a hand briefly on her elbow Anthony turned Gail in the other direction, facing south again, and they began to walk.

She said, 'Assuming our clients agree to all this, how soon can I have copies of the invoices? I'll rely on you to make sure Carlos sends me everything.' When she didn't hear Anthony reply, she glanced at him.

His eyes were on her face. 'Come to my office next

week. I'll ask Carlos to bring the records and the three of us can go over them together.'

'All right. We have the depositions scheduled for Monday anyway. We may as well use the time.' She pushed her hair behind her ear.

He was still looking at her. 'Come early. We'll discuss details over lunch.'

'Yes,' she said. 'Good idea. We can draft the final settlement – assuming we really have one.'

'I think by then we will have.'

That afternoon, Gail listened to the soft purr of the telephone at the Dardens' apartment. Nancy was usually there by four o'clock. She taught kindergarten at a Montessori school.

'Hello?'

'Nancy? This is Gail Connor. I spoke to the other attorney today and we've worked out a tentative settlement.'

Gail explained that the case could drag on for months if litigated. That no one could tell what would happen in court. That the settlement was not perfect but acceptable. That Gail was confident it would be approved by Lawrence Black and even by Douglas Hartwell. And she explained – with just the right touch of regret, she thought – about the letter, its implications.

During this, there was dead silence on the line, followed by several interjected *uh-huh*'s and finally a series of impatient humming noises.

And then, as Gail expected, Nancy broke in.

'They're trying to twist everything I said in that letter. I'd like to know whatever happened to free speech in this country.'

Gail sighed audibly into the phone. 'I know what you mean, but we do the best we can.'

'Well, I don't like the way you handled this. I'm

153

sorry, but I don't. I think you should have spoken to us both first and gotten our approval. Bill might have told you to go ahead and talk to this other attorney, but you never checked with me. I didn't know what you were doing.'

'Nancy, let me remind you that we have litigated this case for nearly five months now, and it's time to lay it to rest.' Gail listened to a little tapping noise over the line. Nancy's long, French-manicured nails, perhaps.

'I think they should pay us all the interest on the loan. If you get that for us—'

Gail stood up, stretching out the phone cord. 'It's not a good idea to start nickel-and-diming Carlos Pedrosa. He's not keen on a settlement either.'

'Well, excuse me. Since when is over ten thousand dollars in interest a nickel and a dime?'

'Five thousand. That's half.'

'I'll get back to you,' Nancy said. 'After I discuss this with a few people. If you don't mind. I mean, if that is all right.'

'Certainly,' Gail said. 'But I advise you to do it quickly.'

Nancy made a little noise of exasperation and hung up.

Standing by her desk, Gail smoothed the creases out of the letter and put it into the *Darden v. Pedrosa* correspondence folder. Even if the letter had not backed Gail into a corner, it had done some good with Nancy Darden. The case hadn't been settled, but it would be, and by Monday, if her luck held.

She put the folder into a brown accordion file with the other Darden papers and dropped the file on the second shelf of her bookcase by the door. She wanted to review it all, but not tonight. On top of the bookcase were three other cases she would take home tonight.

Gail checked her watch. Four fifty-two. A client

would be coming in a few minutes. Then, if traffic were not too heavy, she could make it to the marina to pick up Karen by seven. Dave could do what he wanted.

At her window, Gail looked out at the buildings and trees to the north and thought of Monday.

She knew that Anthony Quintana did not intend for Carlos to have lunch with them. That the restaurant would be small and quiet. And that details about the case could be discussed over the telephone in advance, and that Anthony knew all this as well as she did. But she also knew that what is not stated between men and women is politely presumed not to exist.

Gail leaned forward until her head bumped against the glass and glanced down to the street, a sheer drop. The palm trees, foreshortened at this height, moved briskly in the wind. In the intersection she saw an umbrella cart and a black man pushing it. He could have been the Jamaican meat pie vendor, heading home. From overhead, the yellow and orange stripes looked like an exotic flower.

Chapter Nine

When Gail opened her eyes on Saturday, it was past eight-thirty. She jerked herself upright and grabbed the clock.

'Damn.' Someone had pushed in the alarm button. She got out of bed and dressed quickly in slacks and a cotton shirt.

Dave and Karen were in the kitchen, breakfast on the table. He glanced at her over the top of the sports section.

Gail said, 'You let me oversleep.'

'Hi, Mom,' Karen said. 'Daddy fixed me French toast.' Her mouth glistened with syrup.

'So I see.' She remembered this was what had awakened her, the smells of bacon and French toast and coffee drifting through the air conditioning vent. 'What's the occasion?'

'Since when can't I fix my own daughter breakfast?' Dave folded the paper into quarters and laid it on the neat stack already beside his empty plate.

'I didn't say you couldn't. It's just that you usually hand her a bowl and a box of cereal.'

There was only half a cup of coffee left in the pot. Gail poured it into a mug, then moved Karen's beach bag out of the chair opposite Dave and sat down. She stole a piece of French toast off Karen's plate and kissed her cheek.

'It's sunny outside. I'm afraid you'll fry like an egg.

Is there any sunscreen in your bag?' Karen was going to the beach with some girls from her Brownie troop.

'I don't know. Daddy packed it for me.'

Dave began to stack the dishes. 'Yes, Gail. Sunscreen and a change of clothes and two towels. I've got everything under control. Marilyn's coming by to pick her up in ten minutes.'

'I'm impressed,' Gail said. She poured a little milk into her coffee, then noticed Dave had on his Metzger Marine pullover. 'You're going to the marina this morning?'

'Yeah, I've got a few things to do.'

Dave dropped his silverware on his plate and lay his and Karen's juice glasses on top. The muscles in his arms were taut, the skin burned a ruddy tan. He had been outside with the men this week, he had told Gail, replacing the teak decking on a sailboat, stripped to the waist, sawdust on his hands instead of ink.

She said, 'I hope you plan to be here by the time Karen gets back.'

'I'm not sure.'

Gail looked at him. 'Remember I told you I'm going to work today? That's why I needed to get up early.'

He took the dishes to the sink. 'I might not be back until later. Why don't you pick her up at Marilyn's?'

'Because Marilyn isn't a baby-sitter.' Gail glanced at Karen, who was dredging her last bite of French toast through a puddle of syrup. 'All right. I'll be home by three. Marilyn wouldn't bring the girls back before that.'

The phone rang on the wall beside the refrigerator. Dave picked it up.

Gail wiped a spot of syrup off Karen's pink T-shirt. 'We could rent a video tonight. *The Little Mermaid*?'

'Mom.' Karen gave a little sigh. 'That is such a stupid movie.'

Dave held the phone out. 'Gail. For you.'

'Who is it?'

'Says his name's Jimmy Panther.'

Wincing a little, Gail got up. She had thought about calling him during the week but had never managed to do it.

'Good morning, Jimmy.'

'Hi, how are you?' His voice was deep and resonant even over the telephone. 'Your mother gave me the number. I was wondering if you found that clay deer mask at Renee's place.'

Her eyes automatically went toward the counter separating the kitchen from the family room. She had taken the mask out of the cardboard box to show Karen and had left it there all week.

'Yes, I did find it. I'm sorry I haven't gotten back to you.'

'I'd like to come pick it up. It would take me an hour or so to get there, though.'

'We're just going out. I could leave it on the porch. It's a safe neighborhood.'

'No, don't do that.' There was a silence, then Jimmy Panther spoke as if thinking aloud. 'I can't make it later today. Or Sunday. Maybe Sunday night.'

Gail said, 'This might be better: I could bring it to you tomorrow afternoon. Sell us a couple tickets on your airboat. My daughter has never ridden on one, and it's been years since I have.'

'I'd be glad to. Look for Everglades Adventure, about four miles past Krome Avenue on the Trail. However, you don't pay. This will be my favor. Your daughter's name is . . . Karen?'

'Yes. How did you know that?'

'Renee told me.'

When she hung up, Dave turned around from the sink. 'What did the Indian want, his deer mask back?'

Gail had told him about her conversation with Jimmy Panther.

'Yes, I'll take it out to him tomorrow. I didn't ask if you wanted to go along because I thought you'd be playing tennis.'

'Correct. I am.'

Just as well, she thought to herself.

She picked up the mask from the counter. Someone had dropped Oreo crumbs on it. She brushed them off, then sat back down at the table. The deer's long face was delicately formed, its round eyes slanting upward.

'It looks real old,' Karen said.

'It probably is.' Gail slid a forefinger around the crescent on its forehead. 'An old Indian woman made it, maybe when she was just a girl.'

Dave came to get Karen's plate. 'I wouldn't be surprised if he bought it at a souvenir shop. Turn it over, see if it says "Taiwan" on the bottom.'

Karen looked. 'It doesn't say that. Is Jimmy Panther his real name?'

'I don't know,' Gail said. 'I don't know much about him at all, except that he was Renee's friend.' Dave was rinsing off the dishes with the sprayer. Gail asked, 'Have you ever seen this mask before?'

'Not before you brought it home.' Dave spoke over his shoulder. 'She did tell me a story about him, though. She said they were walking downtown by the river, going across a parking lot, and Panther stops right in the middle of all that asphalt and kneels down and listens. He says he can hear his people weeping. Says that's where a bunch of them were murdered by the Spanish three hundred years ago.'

Gail said, 'You never told me this.'

'No. Renee said to keep it to myself. I guess it doesn't matter now.'

Their gaze held for a moment before he turned back

to the sink to load the dishwasher.

What else had Renee told Dave during all those Monday lunches? How much woe had he poured out to her? Or had they only laughed? Dave might have told Renee his favorite jokes before Gail heard them. They would have sat in the back of whatever restaurant they'd gone to, whispering, the waiter pretending not to notice only one of them wore a wedding ring. Dave would have paid the check in cash and put his sunglasses on as he left. Whether or not they had slept together was beside the point: there could be more intimacy in words than sex.

And knowing this, she had thought of Anthony Quintana more than once, not meaning to. He had called her on Friday. They agreed to meet on Monday to sign the stipulation of settlement in the Darden case. They could look at the draft over lunch, Anthony had said. And then he said he would take her to a Cuban restaurant. Cuban but as far from rice and beans as Paris from French fries. Had she ever been to Yuca in Coral Gables? No? But surely she knew it had been recommended by the *New York Times*? No? He explained how the name, which meant cassava, was also an acronym – young urban Cuban-American. Not that he himself was so young anymore, at forty-one, but the food – And here he sighed. Then said she really ought to know these things. She lived in Miami, after all.

Gail jumped a little when someone knocked loudly at the kitchen door. Karen whirled around in her chair. Her elbow grazed the mask, which slid toward the edge of the table. Gail barely caught it. 'Karen!'

'Polly's here!' Karen flew to the door.

Polly's mother Marilyn, wearing a long beach shirt and sandals, pushed her sunglasses up into her frosted hair.

'Hi, everybody.'

'Where's Polly?'

Gail said, 'Karen, go brush your teeth.'

'Mom, I have to leave!'

Marilyn came in. 'It's okay. I'll wait.' She had perfect nails and a tan Gail suspected she maintained at a salon. She spoke as if divulging a great secret. 'Guess who's going to be forty years old? Ryan. He's so gloomy. I want to give him a surprise party next Sunday afternoon. Can you come?'

'We'd love to.' Gail looked at Dave.

Dave crossed his arms, leaning on the counter. 'Well, if Gail says we're coming, I guess we are.'

Marilyn looked uncertainly from one of them to the other.

Gail said, 'We'll let you know. Our schedules are crazy these days.'

'Oh, I understand about that.' Marilyn made a quick smile.

No one spoke.

Then Karen came running back in. Dave swept up her beach bag and pulled her into a hug. 'Bye, princess. You be a good girl for Daddy.' He held her tightly, his eyes closed.

Karen squirmed. 'Daddy, I gotta go.'

He bent to kiss the top of her head. 'Love you.'

'Love you too. Bye, Dad. Bye, Mom.'

The kitchen door slammed behind her. Through the window Gail could see her running across the grass, climbing into Marilyn's new minivan, three or four other girls already inside, bouncing up and down.

Gail turned around. 'Why did you say that to Marilyn?'

Dave let a few seconds go by. 'Gail . . .'

She started across the kitchen. 'I have to go to work.'

'Wait. I need to talk to you.'

She turned around.

He flexed his fingers, then folded his arms. 'I've been thinking I might stay out at the marina for a while.'

'Why? What do you mean?'

'There's this cabin cruiser. The owner's flying back to New York for the summer and I told him never mind the dockage fee, maybe we could work something out.'

Gail only stared at him.

Dave said, 'You know how we've been lately. Not that it's anybody's fault. It just happens. Relationships have their up moments and their down moments. Maybe we need to clear out the cobwebs, see what we've got.'

She crossed the kitchen to stand in front of him, where he leaned against the counter. 'I don't understand.'

'Maybe we need a break from each other. It could do some good.' He exhaled, hands on his hips, as if he were trying to catch his breath. 'Come on. Don't make this hard, okay?'

'Dave, my God!' She laughed. 'What are we supposed to tell Karen, Daddy's gone to find himself?'

'I don't know. Tell her I'm working.'

'You tell her.'

There was no reply.

'Dave, this is ridiculous. I know we've got problems, but we won't solve them that way. Running off to the marina? I can't believe you'd do that.'

'What, is this a big surprise to you?'

'But you never *said* anything.' Gail pushed her hair back with both hands, then let them fall to her sides. 'All right. I know things aren't great. But we're both at fault. We never see each other. I come home, you're lacing up your tennis shoes. When do we talk?'

He laughed wearily. 'I can't deal with this anymore.'

'Have you even tried?' Gail waited, then said, 'We don't have to let this happen.'

'Gail—' Dave turned around and leaned on the counter, head dropping level with his extended arms. 'I feel like I'm going to die. I can't move. I can't breathe.'

'It's Renee, isn't it? You've been like this ever since the funeral.'

He lifted his head, smiling tightly. 'You mean I'm depressed or something? It'll all go away?'

'We could see someone,' she said.

'What, a marriage counselor?'

'Yes.'

'Do you really want to?'

Gail hesitated. 'I think it would help.'

'Do you really *want* to?' His blue eyes fixed on her.

'We should.'

After a few seconds, Dave picked up his coffee mug from the table, checking to see if he had any left. 'I'll tell you something I've figured out lately. Don't do things you don't want to do.'

Gail had thought – usually during one of their protracted silences – that she would be just as happy single. She had even – in an angrier moment – thought of his sixteen-foot open boat exploding in a ball of flame and sinking into the Atlantic. But reality was different.

She sat down sideways in a chair. 'Will you be here this weekend?'

'I don't know.' Dave ran water in his mug, then wedged it into a rack in the dishwasher. 'I'll probably take some stuff down there this morning. How about if I come over Sunday for dinner?'

'All right.'

'Or we could all go out if you'd rather.'

Gail swung her foot, legs crossed. 'How long have you planned to do this?'

164

He closed the dishwasher and seemed to concentrate on the buttons. 'I should have talked to you before about it. I know that. I'm sorry.'

'You made love to me last night. The first time in two weeks.'

He seemed unsure of how to respond. 'I care about you, Gail. I always will.'

'Knowing what you would say to me this morning.'

He took his truck keys out of his pocket. 'I'll give you a call tonight or tomorrow.'

'Fine. But let's not plan on Sunday dinner.'

He wasn't looking at her. 'Then Karen can go with me if you don't want to go.'

'Maybe you can explain all this to her.'

'I'm not worried about Karen,' he said. 'She's okay. She'll be okay no matter what happens. Don't you think she's smart enough to see what's going on already? If we force ourselves to stay together for her sake, we'll end up hurting her even worse.'

'What pop psychology book did you get that out of?'

'Look. Don't make me the bad guy. I'm not going to walk out on you. I'm going to keep on running the business and paying what I can on the household expenditures. I want to see Karen as much as possible. I expect us to work out a reasonable arrangement.'

After a few seconds, Gail said, 'You've been talking to an attorney. Who?'

'I don't think you need to know that.'

'Who?'

Dave considered, then said, 'Joseph Erwin.'

She laughed out loud. 'Joe Erwin? He's a divorce lawyer with screws for teeth. I hear he charges ten grand to take a case. What did you have to pay him for a consultation?'

Dave's voice was low, menacing. 'Don't make me fight with you, Gail.'

165

'That's what Joe Erwin does. Why else did you choose him? What did he advise you? Wait and see if you'd get any more money for the marina before you left? It was my money that started the marina, so don't think you're going to blithely walk off with it.'

He yelled, 'You love it, don't you? Controlling people. I know what you're doing. Punishing me for being friends with her.'

Gail yelled back. 'Friends? You met her for lunch for two years. You lent her money. You knew it was wrong because you hid it from me. You had a wife and a mistress, but you didn't have the guts to sleep with both of us.'

He leaned on the table, his face inches from hers. 'Gail. Fuck off. Go fuck yourself.'

Gail's chair fell over backward when she stood up. She was shaking. 'I don't care what you do. Leave. Go to hell. When I get back from downtown I don't want to see anything of yours here.'

'I'll move my things when I get ready to move my things.' He followed her out of the kitchen, walking beside her through the living room. 'Don't touch anything. And don't try to take the marina, Gail.' She could feel flecks of spittle on her cheek. 'Don't try it. I'm warning you.'

She whirled on him. 'Speak to your damn attorney on Monday. I'm not going to discuss this with you.'

Dimly, as if from a far-off place, she heard the doorbell chime – long, stately tones. 'I'm not here,' she said, going toward the bedroom.

He screamed after her. 'What am I, your fucking maid?'

She went into the bathroom and slammed the door, sponged off her face with cool water on a hand towel. She sank down onto the toilet lid, gasping, her forehead on her crossed arms. She heard the doorbell chime

166

again. After a few seconds, she raised up and saw herself in the mirror. Without makeup her eyes looked indistinct. Her permed hair was still flat from sleep, her skin blotchy.

There were three sharp raps on the bathroom door. 'Gail. You've got company.'

'For God's sake—'

'It's that cop.'

She opened the door. Dave held out a calling card between two fingers. It said, Frank Britton, Metro-Dade Homicide.

Dave was behind her when she walked into the living room. He kept going, through the dining room toward the kitchen.

Britton stood up from the end of the sofa. The garage door slammed and his head swiveled in that direction, then back to her.

'Good morning, Ms Connor,' Britton said. He was wearing the usual nondescript sports jacket and polite expression. At his feet was a cardboard box, and on top of that, a thick accordion file, its flap folded over and secured with a cord.

She nodded, not in the mood to return his smile. 'Sergeant. I'd offer you a cup of coffee, but I'm getting ready to go downtown.'

'Sorry for the inconvenience on a Saturday. I left a message at your office I'd be by.'

'You did? I missed it. It was one of those weeks.'

'I know how it is.' He motioned to the sofa as if she were the visitor and he the host.

She didn't move. 'I really am in a rush. What have you got, Renee's papers? If you could just leave them—'

'No, I can't do that. We need to go over a couple things. If not now, then I'm going to have to ask you to come out to headquarters. Sorry for the bother.'

167

He used a smile and a touch of regret, she noticed, to soften the rough edges. She didn't have to talk to him at all, but it would be easier to talk than argue.

She said, 'All right. I'll fix us both some coffee.'

The half cup she had poured herself earlier was cold and the pot was empty. She busied herself refilling it. Water, filter, coffee grounds, tablespoon. Neat measurements, channeling her thoughts. She observed her own hand holding the spoon. Not a tremor. The storm Dave had produced raged far beneath the surface. Britton's visit would keep it there for a while longer. After he left she would go to her office and bury herself in work for several more numbing hours. And then decide what to do. Probably call Charlene Marks. Ask if she'd mind doing a divorce for a friend. Gail took a sudden breath, her heart stopping, then starting again with a thump.

Britton had put the accordion file on the table. He remained standing, hands in his pockets, watching her.

Gail said, 'How do you take your coffee?'

'Black, thanks.'

She took another mug from the cabinet over the coffeemaker and placed it next to hers. Mismatched, she noticed idly. Hers with a Far Side cartoon, the other a souvenir of the Coconut Grove Boat Show.

He said, 'You and Renee had the same father, didn't you?' When she looked at him, he explained, 'You're a lot taller.'

'Five-nine. Not that tall. Our father was over six feet,' Gail said. 'Renee took after our mother. Sergeant, do you want to sit down?'

Glancing toward the table, Gail noticed the overturned chair and started to cross the kitchen to pick it up. 'Sorry.' She wondered how much shouting he had heard before he pushed the doorbell.

'No, I've got it.' He smiled and turned the chair

upright. As he sat, he reached for the deer mask still on the table. 'Looks like the same one you got out of Renee's apartment.'

'It is. I'm delivering it tomorrow.'

'So did you get back over there? Everything cleaned out?'

Gail shook her head. 'My mother is supposed to go with a friend of hers and a helper this morning.' She poured the mugs full of coffee, then added milk to the one with the cartoon on it. Britton scooted his file further along the table when Gail sat down. They faced each other across a corner.

'You're not going along?' he asked.

'No.' Gail had not insisted when Irene had said she could take care of it herself.

Britton sipped his coffee. 'Mrs Connor apparently wants to donate the clothes. And sell the condo. The market is pretty good in the Grove right now.'

'You seem to know a lot about what my mother wants to do, Sergeant.'

'We've talked a few times. She reminds me of an aunt of mine, back when I was a kid in Ocala. That's where I'm from. Florida horse country. You ever been up there?'

Gail made a polite smile. 'Not recently.'

'Well, it's changed. Fast food and traffic.'

She waited for him to get to the point.

Britton sipped from his mug. 'I talked to your mother on Tuesday, I believe, and she mentioned the money Renee left you. What was it, a couple hundred thousand? I didn't think Renee had that kind of money.'

'She didn't. It was in a trust.' And Britton must have known this, if he had talked to Irene.

Britton leaned back in his chair, puzzled. 'I was wondering how come you didn't mention it.'

'Excuse me?'

169

'At Renee's apartment. When we were talking about Renee's estate.'

After a moment she said, 'I suppose I forgot.'

'You forgot.'

Gail gave him a long, steady look. 'Yes. My sister had just killed herself. You can understand that her trust wasn't the first thing on my mind.' Let him make of that what he wanted, she thought.

Britton put down his coffee and unwrapped the cord from around the accordion file, then lifted the flap. 'I brought you something. I twisted the ME's arm and got a preliminary death certificate.' He handed her a single sheet of paper, a form with typing in the blanks, a raised seal at the top.

Gail glanced at it long enough to read a few of the lines. *Renee Michelle Connor. Age 29. Cause of death: Exsanguination. Due to or a consequence of . . . Pending investigation.*

She turned it over on the table. Britton's eyes were on her, concerned. She smiled. 'It looks so cold.'

'Yes, ma'am. You do need the certificate to open the estate, though.'

She nodded. 'Thanks for bringing it. And you really don't have to call me ma'am. I'm younger than you are. It makes me feel strange.'

Britton chuckled and settled back in his chair again. It creaked a little under his stocky form. 'Okay, let me get your thoughts on something. Your cousin Ben Strickland's handling the estate, right? Last week he called the captain about us closing the investigation. Why would he do that?'

'He wouldn't.' Gail sat silently for a moment, then recalled her conversation with Ben. 'No, this is a misunderstanding. If he called it was only to find out what was going on.'

Britton frowned, thinking. 'That wasn't exactly how

I heard it. Didn't you ask him to call?'

Gail said, 'Yes. I wanted him to find out how long this is going to take. All those nice chats you're having with my mother aren't doing her any good. She needs to put this behind her. So do I, frankly.'

'I sympathize. But I've got a young woman dead and a lot of different opinions as to whether or not she could have taken her own life. In the last couple days I've talked to several of her friends and co-workers. Most of them said no.'

'Then they didn't know her very well. Renee showed whatever side of herself she wanted to show.'

'And what was the real side?'

'Afraid. Lonely. Unable to cope when things got difficult for her. I think she finally just gave up.'

Britton sat silently for a while. 'Why was she like that?'

'I have no idea,' Gail said. 'A product of her lifestyle, most likely.'

'We ran her name through the computer,' Britton said, 'and came up with half a dozen arrests. And two as a juvenile, but those files were sealed when she turned eighteen. There was a drunk and disorderly, a trespassing, a misdemeanor marijuana possession, and two driving under the influence. And a case last summer for trafficking in cocaine. Did you know about that?'

Gail drew a sharp breath. 'No. My God. What was she doing?'

'Basically coming back from the Bahamas on a fishing boat with the wrong kind of people. They didn't find much, half a kilo, but the guys had priors. They skipped after the bond hearing. Renee's case was dropped before it got to arraignment.'

'Well. Now you understand what I mean about her lifestyle.'

Britton took off his glasses, held them up to the

light, then worked a paper napkin on the lenses. 'No, I don't think she was into drugs. She was showing up at work every day, on time. And helping to plan a baby shower for a girl at her office. Like I mentioned the last time we talked, there are several things about this case that bother me. No hesitation marks on her wrists. Tossing the razor blade after she cut herself. And she went out on that boardwalk after dark? No flashlight? No bug spray?' He put his glasses back on. 'It makes you wonder.'

Britton opened the file again. The jumble of papers Gail had seen before in Renee's desk had been rearranged into neatly stacked folders.

He said, 'That box out there in the living room, you can have all that. I don't have any use for it. Old photos, notes from classes she took, papers regarding her condo, and so forth. What's in here are things I want to keep awhile. If I thought you needed it for the estate, I made copies and they're in the box too.'

'Copies? Such efficiency,' Gail said. 'When do we get everything back?'

'It shouldn't be too long.' Britton pulled a folder out of the file and opened it on the table. There were envelopes inside. A dozen of them, mostly white, a couple red, a pink, a dark green, a blue. The size that greeting cards come in. Britton lifted the torn flap of one envelope and withdrew a card, passed it to Gail.

On an empty white background there was a tiny cartoon figure holding out a flower. *Just to let you know* . . . She flipped it open. . . . *that I'm thinking of you.* Underneath in black marker was scrawled the initial D. And under that a note: *I hope the $$$ comes in handy. Don't worry about returning it.*

Gail closed the card.

Britton said, 'They're all from somebody named "D".' He opened more of them and showed her.

172

Merry Christmas to my favorite elf. Happy Birthday . . .
When you're feeling blue . . . Hope your day is a happy one
. . . Cards that might have been purchased at any
drugstore on the spur of the moment. Dave's taste
hadn't been brilliant. Their banality embarrassed her
more than their number.

Gail tossed the last one back on the stack. 'They
weren't having an affair, if that's what you're thinking.'

'You're sure.'

'Yes.' When he continued to look at her from behind
his gold-rimmed glasses, Gail said, 'Dave and I have
already discussed this. And you'll understand if I tell
you that the conversation is private.'

Britton spread his hands as if concurring, then closed
the folder and put it to one side. 'I'm going to keep
these for a while.'

'Fine.'

She checked the clock on the microwave. 'I'm
expected at my office at ten,' she said.

'Okay, but let me ask you about one more thing.'
Britton rubbed the back of his neck. 'Renee died early
Sunday morning, as near as we can tell.'

Gail couldn't hold back a little smile. 'I was at work
by eight and my husband had a tennis match.'

. There was a momentary silence, Britton looking at
her. 'You know, all that stuff you hear on TV – the
person died between eleven and eleven-fifteen, whatever
– that's wishful thinking. We've got a bigger time span
on your sister, with her lying in a foot of water for over
twenty-four hours.'

His eyes went over Gail's face, as if noting its pallor.
'But I didn't want to ask you about that just now. I'm
curious about your mother's birthday party. Mrs Connor
told me about it, but I'd like to get another perspective.
Who all was there?'

Gail tapped lightly on the handle of her mug with a

fingernail, making a faint clinking noise. 'Her friends were there. Most of the family, except the ones out of town. Neighbors.'

'Your daughter wasn't there.'

'No, she was spending the night with a friend of hers down the street. It wasn't really a party for children.'

'Do you suppose you could give me a list of who was there?'

'This minute?'

'No, you can think about it, let me know. Mrs Connor gave me some names, but I'd like to make sure I have everybody.' Britton leaned an elbow on the table. 'Did Renee come with anyone?'

'No, by herself.'

'How was she at the party? Happy? Depressed?'

'It's hard to say. She had a lot to drink.'

Southern Comfort, Gail remembered. In a rocks glass. Renee dunking a cherry up and down by its stem, asking Irene's eighty-year-old neighbor if he could make a knot in it with his tongue. The old man laughing, red-faced, finally wheezing.

There was no need to tell Britton what Renee had done to Ben on the back porch. Let Ben tell him, if he wanted to.

'When did she leave?'

Gail looked up. 'I don't remember exactly. Nine, nine-thirty. I left shortly afterward.'

'Mrs Connor said your husband drove Renee home.' Britton seemed to want an explanation.

'Yes,' she said. 'She was too intoxicated to drive herself.'

'He drove her car?'

'Yes.' Renee had been laughing, her arm around Dave's neck as he half-carried her to her car. Beams of white swept across the shrubbery in Irene's yard, red taillights disappearing up the street.

174

'And you got home – How?'

'In our car.'

'Did you go by Renee's to pick him up?'

'No, I went straight home.'

'Why was that?'

Because they had argued. Because she had told him to find his own way home, hitchhike, walk for all she cared. 'Because he said he'd take a taxi.'

'About what time did he get home?'

'I'm not exactly sure.'

'Can you give me an estimate what time it was? Ten? Eleven?'

'Who remembers things like that? I may have been asleep. I don't know.' She glanced at the clock again. 'I'm sorry, but I really do have to get ready for work.'

Britton stood up. 'There are a couple other areas I need to cover. How about if you come on out to headquarters Monday? I'll give you a tour of the facility.'

'Monday is difficult.'

He seemed surprised, his eyes widening a bit. 'I know you're a busy lady, but don't you want us to find out what happened to your sister as soon as possible?'

'Don't play games with me, Sergeant. Of course I'll talk to you, but I cannot bend my entire schedule around to do it. If you call my office I'll see when I have some time available.'

Britton looked at her for another second, then put the folder back in the file and closed the flap.

'I expect cooperation, Ms Connor. This is not a game. Your sister was murdered.'

Chapter Ten

From the living room window Gail watched Frank
Britton back his sedan out of the driveway. Plain
hubcaps, blue light on the dash antenna on the roof.
She could see the neighbor across the street staring as
he picked up his recycling bins at the curb. *Honey, there
was a cop over at the Metzgers'. What do you think is going
on?*

Gail let the curtain fall back into place.

Until now she had managed to think of Frank Britton
as a minor annoyance – Irene's grief incarnated into a
functionary of the Metro-Dade Homicide Bureau. He
would go away once the right paperwork had been
filled out. Gail could not imagine he was serious about
murder. Until now.

Renee had known some dangerous people. Not just
decadent – dangerous. She might have gone willingly
with one of them to that park in the Everglades, to do
God only knew what.

But apparently Britton was pursuing other theories.
He had shown Gail the cards from Dave. The
implication was clear: a secret affair, a moment of rage.
Dave could lose his temper. Britton knew it, if he had
been listening at the front door.

Impossible, Gail thought. Dave wasn't capable of
murder.

She let herself sink into a chair.

Perhaps Britton was thinking of a conspiracy, she

and Dave planning it together, concocting alibis. Money was motive enough, two hundred thousand dollars, which she had forgotten to mention when Britton asked about the estate. Or did he think she had killed Renee by herself? Gail laughed at the thought. Britton wasn't that stupid.

Maybe he wanted to make lieutenant. He could shake the tree and see what fell out. Former deb of old Miami family slashed by crazed drug lord. Or by frustrated lover or jealous sister, take your pick. With no hard evidence, Britton was playing with theories. Stacking and shuffling, trying to find patterns.

And two and two are five. The simplest answer was, Renee had killed herself.

When the medical examiner had pulled back the sheet, Gail had held her breath. She had looked at a face they said was Renee's, but the colors were all wrong. Gray and rubbery. Pieces missing. But not as bad as she had feared. Gail stared until she heard someone ask if that was her sister. And she had nodded. Since then she had the feeling that the torn and bloated body in the morgue was real and that the Renee of her memory was disappearing, fading in and out like a distant radio signal.

Gail stood up from her chair. The living room was silent, utterly still, only a thin wedge of light angling across the ivory-colored carpet. Ivory carpet, white walls, track lighting, blue sofas. She had let a decorator do it, not having the time herself. She still didn't like it.

She went back through the dining room to the kitchen and called Bob Wilcox at the office. *Sorry, I can't come in today, Karen is ill. No, nothing serious, but I simply can't leave. Don't worry, you'll do fine at trial.*

As she hung up it occurred to her that Bob had found her excuse flimsy. *He* would have made arrangements. He wouldn't have blown off an entire day because his kid had a cold. 'To hell with it,' Gail muttered to herself, surprised at how little she cared what he thought.

Her legs shaking, she sat down at the table and rested her cheek on one hand.

The deer mask was still there. She turned her head to look at it. Slender face. Empty, rounded eyes, staring back at her.

The clouds had rolled in before noon, and by two o'clock Marilyn's minivan had appeared in the driveway. It was pouring, a spring deluge. Gail had packed Karen up into the car, along with the box containing the deer mask. It was now tucked securely under her arm.

Holding a black umbrella in the other hand, Gail guided Karen up a flight of steps on Flagler Street to the plaza of the cultural center. The wide, red-tiled plaza connected library, art gallery, and historical museum. From beyond the encompassing wall she could see the courthouse, its pointed top shrouded in low-hanging clouds.

The sky was the color of dirty gray cotton, more mist than rain. Karen ran out from under the umbrella, her image reflecting in the wet tiles. She skipped, spun, then came down flat-footed in a shallow puddle, laughing.

'Karen!'

Just outside the museum Gail shifted the box so she could fold her umbrella. Karen pulled open the door. The dark-tinted glass wall and doors were fogged with condensation, the air inside chilly.

Karen saw Irene first. She was sitting at the information booth, the only person in the lobby. 'Hi, Gramma.'

Irene wore her Miccosukee jacket, standard for museum volunteers. Its sleeves were too long and Irene had rolled them up on her thin wrists. She leaned over the polished wood partition far enough to reach Karen. 'Well, look who's here. Hello, bunny.' She patted her head. 'My, your hair is damp. Do you want a sweater?'

'No way.'

Gail put the grocery bag next to a stack of brochures. 'I didn't know you were back at the museum.'

'And here I thought you had come all this way to see me,' Irene scolded.

'Of course we're glad to see you.' Gail kissed her cheek. 'Did you finish at Renee's?'

Irene gave a quick shake of her head. 'I couldn't go, just couldn't do it. I woke up this morning and just lay there staring at the ceiling. I called Dr Price and he said I should do something, anything. So here I am. My legs ache like the dickens, but there's only an hour until we close, so I suppose I can make it.'

'You're glad to be back, though.'

'Oh, well. I suppose I should be. People have been very kind.'

Karen was spinning around on one toe, the rubber sole of her sneaker screeching on the tile floor.

'Karen, stop that.'

She did. 'Can I go in the gift shop and look around?'

'No. Wait here,' Gail said, then spoke to Irene. 'When I called they said Edith Newell was working today.'

Irene nodded. 'She's doing a tour upstairs. Some children from St Hugh.'

'Mom. Can I go upstairs?'

'No.'

'Oh, Gail, for heaven's sake. Let her go. You're too strict. She'll be no trouble at all. And she certainly won't get lost.'

'Can I, Mom?'

Gail finally nodded. 'Okay. But don't touch anything.'

'I know, I know.' Karen skipped across the lobby, then disappeared up the carpeted stairs.

Irene looked after her, then said, 'Why don't you all come over for dinner? I haven't felt much like eating lately but if I had someone to cook for . . . Unless you and Dave already have plans.'

Gail couldn't think of anything to say except, 'Dave does have plans, but I'll bring Karen.'

'Well, don't come if you have things to do. I know how busy you are.'

'Irene, please.'

'You sounded like you didn't really want to, that's all.'

'No, it's fine. I want to.' Gail propped her umbrella against the booth and put the box on the counter. 'Tell me what you think about this.' She pulled the mask out of its nest of bubble wrap. 'It's a deer mask. I found it when I was at Renee's apartment with Sergeant Britton.'

Irene picked up the mask, turned it around. 'What an odd thing this is.'

'Did she ever show it to you?'

'No, never. It's Native American, I can tell that much.' Irene looked up. 'Is this why you wanted to see Edith?'

Edith Newell, the museum's director of education, had made a personal crusade of Florida history. She knew Indian artifacts better than most Indians did.

Gail said, 'Jimmy Panther says he lent the mask to Renee, but it might belong to the museum. Edith would know.'

Irene frowned. 'Jimmy wouldn't steal from the museum.'

'Renee was working here as a volunteer and they were friends.'

'Gail, honestly! You think the worst of Renee, you always did.' Irene put the mask back into the box.

181

'I'm only trying to find out where it came from.' She stopped speaking when an older couple crossed the lobby from upstairs, then passed the desk on their way outside. 'I don't think the worst of Renee. I don't even know who she was.'

Irene looked at her strangely. Gail leaned over the partition to put the box on the desk.

'I'm going upstairs to find Karen,' she said.

The stairs, covered in dark tweedy carpet and decorated with a polished brass handrail, went up to a landing, then up again, turning around a ten-foot-high Fresnel lens from an old lighthouse that had once stood on a reef near the Matecumbe Keys. The museum was so quiet today that Gail could hear the electric motor turning the pedestal under the heavy glass. A light had been placed inside for effect, and white beams swept in a slow circle.

Halfway up she remembered Renee climbing these same stairs.

It had been a year ago, perhaps less, a party to woo museum donors – live music on the plaza, hors d'oeuvres and champagne in the lobby. This stairwell was dark that night, except for the light sweeping around. Gail had noticed Renee unclipping the velvet rope that closed off the second floor. Renee climbing these stairs in a striped Miccosukee jacket and a miniskirt, flouncy black taffeta. A man following a few steps behind, tilting his head to see up her skirt. Renee laughing at him over her shoulder. The stairs turned and their bodies moved out of sight. Renee's size-five feet in their high ankle-strap sandals, toenails painted red. His light gray trouser legs behind her, catching up.

Gail reached the top of the stairs. 'Karen?' She could hear children's voices somewhere to her left.

A ramp led past glass walls, a diorama of the wetlands:

saw grass, stuffed birds, and reptiles. An alligator with slitted eyes that seemed to follow her. Gail felt a sudden chill. Renee had lain in the shallow water of the Everglades.

At this hour the museum was nearly deserted. Gail could still hear the children ahead, but saw no one. She made her way past the archaeological dig, Tequesta Indians, Spanish conquest, a cannon hauled up from a shipwreck.

She heard running and laughter. Karen had probably joined the children from St Hugh's – Edith Newell's junior assistant tour guide.

Gail hadn't told her yet about Dave.

Driving through the rain on the way here, with Karen chattering away about something or other, Gail had thought of asking him to come back. She would go to him, take both his hands, and tell him . . . Tell him what? That she couldn't exist without him?

From ahead came the thumping of children's shoes on a wooden ramp, voices getting fainter.

Gail passed quickly through the early settlers' exhibit – the facade of a frame house, glass cases full of tools and dishes and clothing, as if someone had spilled an attic trunk. The path was darker here, the exhibits lit by spotlight.

Ahead of her she saw a photograph, a grainy, life-size enlargement of a dozen people standing outside the first dry goods store on Flagler Street, before it was even named Flagler, back when it was still paved with limestone rock. A horse and wagon waited at one side. Most men wore collarless white shirts, another a straw hat, others had beards or mustaches. The women's blouses were buttoned to their chins. All stared straight into the camera, nobody moving, the sun cutting harsh shadows on their faces.

In the front row stood Benjamin and Addie

183

Strickland, her great-grandparents. A squinting young man and a dour girl of twenty who looked as though she had just bitten into a lime.

Gail turned her head, glancing to her left. A wooden streetcar, painted dark red, its iron wheels jacked up so they barely touched the floor. There was a chain across the open door.

She whirled back toward the photograph and laughed out loud.

'Yes. So that's what she meant.'

Gail had seen Renee later at the benefit on the plaza – she remembered it now. The moon floated over the buildings downtown. A band from the islands played steel drums. Renee – a plastic glass of champagne in each hand – was picking her way through the crowd, her hips moving to the music. Gail thought she was probably stoned.

Are both of those glasses for you? Gail asked.

No, one's for him. Her hair swinging, Renee turned toward the man sitting at a small table. Dark eyes, closely trimmed beard, open collar.

Renee said, *Is he not delicioso?*

If you like chest hair. Is that the same man you took upstairs half an hour ago?

Maybe. Renee's lips curved into a smile. *I've always wanted to do it right in front of Benjamin Strickland.*

She had left Gail standing there glaring at the flouncy miniskirt twitching its way across the plaza. The man had stood up, pulled out a chair. On his face had clearly been written a post-coital, indolent sexuality.

Now, remembering this, Gail frowned. He was familiar somehow. That lazy smile, the short black beard, dark eyes. She had seen him before. Or since. The eyes, of course. So like Anthony Quintana's. It was his cousin.

'Carlos,' she whispered. 'Carlos Pedrosa.' He had

looked directly at her outside the funeral home, swinging his car keys around his forefinger.

And Renee had brought him *up here*?

As if drawn, Gail walked toward the streetcar, then unfastened the chain and climbed up the steps. The museum lights shone dimly through the open windows, on the two rows of wooden seats and the levers where the conductor had stood. A dented metal sign said, 'Colored to the Rear.'

Gail went further in, the streetcar creaking softly. She swung around a pole and dropped into a seat. From ten yards away, across the aisle and through the windows on the other side, Benjamin Strickland and his tight-lipped wife Addie looked back at her.

Renee had sat here, Gail imagined, in this first seat, the only one with any leg room. Carlos Pedrosa had glanced around, then climbed the stairs behind her.

Gail heard a door slam somewhere and jumped. If anyone walked by she might duck down rather than explain. They wouldn't notice her in the darkness. She felt a rush of excitement, of pleasant fright.

He would have sat beside Renee on this scratched wooden seat, put his arm across the back of it. Or around Renee, more likely. Looking at him on the plaza, Gail had thought he was not the sort of man to waste time.

They might have heard music coming faintly from below. Faraway voices. Then the rustle of black taffeta. The soft rasp of a zipper. Shifting on the narrow seat, someone nearly falling off. Stifled laughter. Legs and mouths opening. A moan. The wood in the old streetcar creaking.

Over his shoulder Renee would have seen the photograph.

Gail looked at it now through the window. Great-grandfather Strickland, the sun glaring off his face, his shirt, the white limestone rock on Flagler Street.

She stood up and reached for the metal handrail. The narrow streetcar was too dark, the museum so quiet she could hear her own breath. She swung herself down, then fastened the chain back across the entrance. She had been upstairs too long.

Gail found Edith Newell at her desk in the basement of the museum. Open books and historical magazines lay every which way on her desk. The deer mask was propped up on a stack of them.

Edith Newell had always reminded Gail of a wading bird – elbows stuck out at an angle, head bobbing on its long neck, her voice thin and piping. Over seventy and never married, she still lived in a white frame house off Brickell Avenue in a stand of orchid trees, a glitzy condo on one side of her, a twenty-five-story bank building on the other. To the despair of developers, Edith had sworn to leave her property to the county for a park.

Gail knocked on the open door of the tiny office. 'Miss Newell?'

Edith laid down a rectangular magnifying glass and motioned to Gail. 'Hello, darling. Come in. I must say, this is extraordinary, what you've brought.'

Gail sat down. 'I thought it might belong to the museum.'

'Oh, my, no. If it were a part of our collection, I would most assuredly know about it. I know everything we've got and this was never here. Your mother explained you found it at your sister's residence?'

'Yes. You know Jimmy Panther, don't you?'

'Indeed.'

'He says he lent it to my sister. That his grandmother made the mask.'

'His grandmother?' Edith drew the word out. 'This

186

isn't Miccosukee. The Miccosukees didn't do masks.'

'Could it be Seminole?'

Edith Newell's eyes, magnified behind thick glasses, fixed on Gail. She smiled patiently. 'No, dear. The Seminoles and Miccosukees are like brothers, both from the Creek Nation in Georgia and Alabama. Their ancestors migrated into Florida in the eighteenth century. Most of them signed the Fort Dade peace treaty in 1837 during the Seminole War. The Miccosukees are the ones who didn't want to. They went into the Everglades to hide and the Army finally gave up looking for them. This mask certainly predates that period.'

'Oh,' said Gail.

'Now as to what tribe made this mask—' Edith knitted her fingers together. She had big hands, knuckles the size of walnuts, having wielded pickaxes and machetes in her time. 'Tequesta,' she announced. 'If it isn't a forgery – and I don't think it is – this is a Tequesta mask, but of a unique type.'

She flopped a book around so Gail could see it. One page was taken up with color photographs of half a dozen wooden masks. Gail recognized a catlike face, a bird, others that made no sense to her. Most of them were cracked, the wood dark and crumbling at the edges.

Edith said, 'These are prehistoric masks from the Key Marco site on the southwest coast. They're all carved of cypress. Notice the style. The crescent on the forehead? The big ears? Similar to the mask you brought me. However—' Edith lightly touched it, a caress. 'This is of another material entirely – fired clay.'

Gail looked at the deer mask as if she might see something different this time. 'Tequesta? Didn't they die out?'

'Good. I see you aren't completely ignorant. The

187

Tequestas were never numerous or vital. They were extinct by the middle of the seventeen hundreds.'

'So the mask could be fairly old?'

'Old? My dear, the ones in that picture date back two to three thousand years.' Edith Newell's thin voice rose higher. 'The Tequesta hunted and fished. They built chickees – you know, those palmetto frond huts – but next to nothing remains. Everything rots so quickly in this climate. We've found projectile points they traded from Indians further north. Beads. Fragments of clay pots, but none intact. Cups or knives made of conch shells. But only a few masks. Very few. Most of them have fallen to dust. So when you bring me *this*—'

Laughing a little, Edith bounced on the seat of her chair. 'What a find. The historians will go mad over it.'

Gail stared at her for a moment. She had never seen Edith behave this way. Her wispy gray hair seemed to stand on end.

She said, 'Miss Newell, Jimmy Panther once told my sister his people were murdered by the Spanish. Could he have meant the Tequestas? If they're extinct—'

'Oh, yes. I've heard that story. He claims to be the last descendant of the Tequestas. Rubbish.' Edith settled back in her chair. She smiled. 'I'll tell you about Jimmy Panther. His grandfather was white. Did you know that?'

'No.'

'Oh, yes. By the name of Gibb. He ran a rum boat to Cuba for Al Capone during Prohibition. If it were up to me,' Edith said, 'I'd make Jimmy prove ownership before we hand the mask back to him.'

'How could we? It certainly isn't ours.'

'You found it in your sister's house.'

'In an old box with a shipping label to the gift shop where he keeps his airboat. And Renee never had an interest in Indian artifacts.'

'Well, what would Jimmy do if we let him have it?' Edith asked crossly. 'Sell it to a collector, probably, and we'd never see it again.'

'Is it valuable?'

Edith considered. 'Since there's a ban on the importation of pre-Columbian art from Latin America, that runs the price up a bit. A cypress mask in good condition would go for four or five thousand dollars, if you could buy one at all. This mask could easily be triple that.'

'I had no idea it was worth so much.'

'Money,' Edith snapped. 'As if that were the only thing that mattered. I could weep. No, I don't speak of you, dear. Your roots go down deeply here. All those people pouring in. Thousands of them. They don't care about tradition. Bulldoze it all. They don't give a hoot as long as they can live in brand-new air-conditioned houses and drive their cars on brand-new roads until every last blade of grass is paved over and every drop of water is sucked out of the ground.'

She tilted her head to look at Gail straight through her glasses. 'You won't give the mask back to Jimmy Panther, will you?'

'He expects me to bring it to him tomorrow afternoon.'

'Oh, no.'

'I could put him off for a while,' Gail said, 'but he has more right to it than we do.'

Edith held up a forefinger. 'Here's what. Let me send it off to an archaeologist friend of mine at the University of Florida. I'll make sure it isn't broken, don't worry about that. He knows every important primitive artifact ever found in this state. If this mask is genuine, he'll know who it belongs to.'

'What if he's never seen it?'

'Then I'll ask your mother to talk to Jimmy. He likes

189

Irene. Maybe she can persuade him to sell it to the museum for a reasonable price. God knows we don't have much money to spare. The county would rather spend millions of dollars for a Grand Prix racecar track.'

'Miss Newell, if I let you keep the mask for a while, you must promise me something.'

She looked warily at Gail. 'And that is?'

'Don't tell anyone about this. Renee was involved somehow. Let me find out what it means.'

'Done.' Edith mimed locking her lips and tossing the key. 'I won't say a word.'

'And make your friend promise too.'

'Yes, dear.'

Gail turned the mask around, shadows from the reading lamp playing over the crescent on the deer's forehead and the painted lines around its eyes. Fifteen thousand dollars' worth of clay? It had nearly smashed to bits on her kitchen floor this morning. Renee had kept it cushioned in a heavy box and hidden on the top shelf of her closet. She must have known its value.

Gail would have to explain to Jimmy Panther why she wasn't going to bring it back tomorrow. Maybe she could strike a deal: the Tequesta mask if he told her the truth about what Renee was doing with it. Or better, how Renee had become friends with the part-white Miccosukee grandson of a Prohibition rumrunner.

Irene crossed the kitchen to get the ice cream out of the freezer. 'No. Dave's going to come back, you'll see. He can't throw away eleven years just like that.'

'Yes, he can,' Gail said. She reached into the cabinet for two bowls – one for Irene, one for Karen, who was still stretched out on the living room carpet in front of the television with the orange striped cat. Applause and laughter from a game show drifted down the hall.

190

'Then let him be by himself a while,' Irene said. 'Men like their freedom, especially at that age. But they come home if you handle it right. He's a responsible man. Talk to him.'

'I'm not sure I want to talk to him,' Gail said.

'Don't you *care* what happens? Your marriage is falling apart and you stand there calm as can be.'

'Mother, please. Let's not get into a debate. I just thought you should know.' The big gray cat – Muffin – twined around Gail's ankle and she gently shoved it aside.

'That's the price you pay.' Irene dug into the ice cream with a scoop. 'A woman can't let her husband think she wears the pants in a marriage, I don't care what the feminists say.' She let the scoop of fudge ripple fall into a bowl.

'I am what I am,' Gail said wearily.

'What you are,' Irene replied, 'is a mother with a daughter to think about. You might have to raise her alone. I did it with two daughters, and it's no bed of roses, let me tell you.'

The cat leaped to the counter, sniffing at the carton. Irene pushed him away with her elbow. 'Naughty kitty. Down.'

Gail said, 'Don't give Karen too much. It's nearly dark. We should go before it starts to rain again.'

Irene appeared not to have heard. 'I could have remarried. I was asked three different times.'

'Why didn't you, then?'

After a moment, she said, 'I didn't love any of them. Romantic notion, wasn't it? I didn't need to worry about money. I had Ben to help out with discipline from time to time, so I didn't feel the need to find a substitute father for you girls. Probably a mistake, I can see that now. You girls needed a man's influence in the home. Renee did, anyway. I didn't know what to do with Renee except let her have her way. She was like me when I was young, and I couldn't bear to say no to her. You were the one I leaned on.'

'Did you?' Gail held out two spoons from the silverware drawer.

Irene didn't take them. She put her hands over her face. 'I've failed you, too.'

'Mother, I'm fine. For heaven's sake.'

'All right. All right, I've stopped.' She fanned her eyes. 'Yes, you're fine. You're strong. You don't need people so much, not your husband, not even your mother. I used to worry about that but I guess it can be a virtue if you want to survive in this world.'

She dropped a curl of ice cream on a saucer, which she set on the floor. 'Muff, Muff, good kitty kitty.'

Eyes closed, Muffin licked at the ice cream, tail twitching. Irene's fingers moved lightly through the fur behind his ears. 'Yum yum yum.'

Gail watched for a while, then said, 'I don't think you're weak at all. You're just . . . subtle. Like Renee. She had a talent for getting what she wanted with the least amount of effort.'

Irene stood up, giving Gail a sideways look. She went to put back the ice cream. 'You'll need help with Karen, I suppose.'

'I hadn't thought that far ahead.'

'Apparently not,' Irene said.

'You know how you hate to drive. You hardly leave the house.'

'One has to make sacrifices.'

Gail smiled. Irene finally had something concrete to worry about. 'Mother, you haven't been so cheerful in weeks.'

'Cheerful? What are you talking about? I'm positively horrified at what's happened to you.' She picked up the bowls. 'Wait till reality sets in. Wait till you go to

192

bed alone every night as I did, you'll see.'

Irene sat on the floor next to Karen, easing herself down carefully, spreading paper napkins across their laps. She hugged Karen as if she had just pulled her from the rubble of an earthquake, then the two of them ate their ice cream, facing the television.

Unnoticed, Gail went outside, the grass in the backyard soaking her sneakers. She stood on the concrete edge of the seawall. The bay lapped softly against it, almost a dead calm. To the south a line of clouds stretched across the darkening sky.

It had been easy to think Renee had cut her own wrists. There was a kind of justice in that – if not divine justice, then at least a balance. You couldn't live as Renee had lived and get away with it. Suicide made sense. Murder didn't fit the equation. It was accidental, like lightning or a falling tree limb.

Gail had never wanted Renee to *die* – that was a hideous extreme – she had only wished, occasionally, that Renee would get what she deserved. That her sports car would rust; that she would put on fifty pounds; that men would stop wanting her; that she would finally *realize*.

It had been easy to assume that out there on the end of the nature walk, under the moon, with a razor blade poised over her wrist, Renee had finally realized that she had gotten it all wrong.

Arms outstretched for balance, Gail walked along the seawall, wondering how she could have been so damnably presumptuous. She didn't know Renee. She had made up details to suit herself, as a means of proving her own virtue. She who had never made a wrong step in her life. Successful job, happy home, loving husband. As if any of that were true. There was more truth in Renee's laughter. In twelve-dollar filet mignons, making love in a museum, and a clay deer mask.

If only the truth were easy to find. Gail had no idea where it lay, only that she had never bothered to look for it.

Gail felt a raindrop on her shoulder, then another. She stopped walking. The line of rain extended across the water like a tattered gray curtain.

Chapter Eleven

When Anthony Quintana's secretary showed Gail into his office at 1:30 p.m., she registered an immediate impression of black leather furniture, stucco walls, and thick gray carpet. Anthony and another man – Carlos – turned around from a glass wall. Past them Gail saw an atrium, green with lush tropical plants and flowers. A small fountain cascaded silently down ferny, rough-hewn rocks.

Anthony crossed the office. 'Gail, come in.' He led her to an arrangement of sleek leather chairs facing the windows. 'This is my cousin, Carlos Pedrosa. Carlos, Gail Connor.'

'How do you do,' she said.

'How are you?'

The fingers that briefly closed over hers made Gail doubt that Carlos Pedrosa had ever swung a hammer in his life. His shirt – open at the neck – pulled a little over his stomach. He wore a fashionably wrinkled nubby tan suit. He smiled at her, white teeth in a short beard. He had the look of someone hardened to the rigors of partying all night. Gail could see why Renee had been attracted.

As she sat down, she put her briefcase on the floor beside the slab of polished marble that served as a table. There was a folder on it labeled 'Pedrosa, Darden vs.' Anthony took the chair to her left, facing Carlos. The three of them made some small talk.

Earlier this morning she had spoken to Anthony's secretary by phone. *Please tell Mr Quintana that I will not be able to meet him at noon. An emergency has come up, so awfully sorry.* Gail had decided a cowardly tuna sandwich was better than the exotic menu at Yuca.

Now Anthony was opening the folder on the low table, one forefinger turning back the cover. He wore his gold and diamond ring today and a suit the color of bittersweet chocolate. Inside the folder were several documents computer-printed onto crisp bond paper. He drew them out, looked over at Gail. His eyes matched his suit.

Gail reached into her briefcase for her notes.

Anthony said, 'This is the stipulation of settlement to be filed with the court. You received a copy of this by fax, no?'

'I did.' She uncrossed her legs and leaned forward, scanning the first page, then the second. She pointed. 'This provision should read "not including materialmen and other potential lienors."'

Anthony moved closer to find it, clicking his gold pen. His sleeve brushed her arm. 'Where? Yes, I see.' He added the words in flowing blue ink. She placed a check mark by the provision in her notes.

A high-pitched beeping noise came from the vicinity of Carlos's belt. He pushed his jacket aside and turned it off, then resumed staring through the window. He looked bored.

She went back to the documents, skimming a voluntary dismissal and a release of claim. The last pages consisted of closing documents, samples of papers which would transfer title to the Dardens. They had been prepared by Vista Title Company. It hardly seemed possible that Renee had done this sort of work, preparing closing documents. Or that she had lasted a year at Vista without getting herself fired.

'My clients would like to close at the end of the month,' she said.

'We can do it next week,' Carlos said. 'Sooner the better.' Gail noticed that Carlos spoke without an accent; if he had not been born here, he had certainly come as a small child.

'According to the stipulation for settlement,' she said slowly, 'we have up to thirty days.'

'Tony, what is this?' Switching to Spanish, he asked a question too fast for Gail to understand it.

Anthony replied in English, 'Because we need court approval first and that takes time.'

Gail slid the documents to her left. 'Everything else appears to be in order,' she said.

'Good.' Anthony lifted the phone on the small table between their chairs and pressed a button, telling his secretary to come in for a moment.

It had slowly been dawning on Gail, as her body sank further into Anthony Quintana's soft leather furniture, that last week's saunter down Flagler Street had been no accident. Meat pies and fruit cups and mild flirtation. Settlement for dessert. From the moment he had shaken her hand at the door, Anthony's manner had been businesslike, nothing more. The Darden case was just another done deal. Case closed. She felt slightly foolish. And vindicated for canceling lunch today.

Carlos's beeper went off again. He fumbled for the small black box at his waist. 'Guys, guys, give me a break.' He laughed a little. 'You never get a minute's peace.' The box went silent.

He settled back again, arms spread, jacket open. One foot was propped on his knee, bouncing up and down. He wore pale blue, laced shoes with thin soles, a dark smudge on the back of the heel from driving.

Gail said, 'My clients will want an owners' title policy,' she said, 'as provided by the contract.'

'We're not going by the contract anymore.'

'Let them have it,' Anthony said.

'*¡Coño!*' Carlos muttered the epithet almost too softly for Gail to hear it. His foot stopped bouncing. 'We usually give the buyers a bottle of champagne, too. What kind do they want, Dom Perignon?'

Gail said, 'That would be marvelous. Thank you.'

When the secretary came in, Anthony showed her where the changes were to be made.

After she left, Carlos coughed into his fist, then sat quietly for a while, looking at Gail. There was a chunky gold watch bracelet on his wrist.

'You look like Renee. No, you do. I mean, not exactly like Renee, but I can tell you're sisters. It's the mouth and chin.' He made a vague gesture around his own chin. 'Doesn't she look like Renee? What do you think, Tony?'

Anthony's expression was unreadable.

Carlos spoke solemnly. 'She was . . . Renee was really something. It shocked me totally, what happened, you know?'

Gail murmured an appropriate response, then found herself unable to look away from this man. Renee had slept with him. Had engaged in . . . whatever they had done in her bedroom. Pornographic videos and groans of ecstasy. Or laughter, more likely, knowing Renee.

Tapping the pages of her notes together, then folding them, she glanced at Anthony. Then dropped the notes into her briefcase. 'Mr Pedrosa—'

'Carlos.' He took a portable phone out of his bag, a thin black one that unfolded like a wallet. She had never seen a telephone so small.

She smiled. 'Carlos. On another matter. Judge Strickland instructed me to tell you that he is willing to sell at thirteen hundred per acre, five percent down, mortgage at eight percent for twenty years, to balloon after five. I can draw up the option if the basic terms are acceptable.'

She heard Anthony say, 'What property are you referring to?'

As he stood up, Carlos made a dismissive gesture with his hand. 'It has nothing to do with this case. The company's signing an option on some acreage.' He held up the phone. 'Excuse me a minute.' He spoke over his shoulder to Gail as he punched in the numbers. 'I'll get in touch with Ben later in the week.'

Gail glanced at Anthony. She had not thought the purchase would be complete news to him. 'Ben Strickland is my mother's cousin.'

'Yes,' he said, as if he already knew that much. Gail supposed Renee might have told him. He was watching Carlos, who stood by the atrium wall, one hand in his pocket, the phone at his ear.

Carlos bounced a little on his toes. '*Oye, Bernardo. Es Carlos. ¿Qué pasa?*'

Gail hadn't noticed it until now, the uneasiness between them. And now she remembered the odd scene outside the funeral home. Anthony hadn't shaken Carlos's hand. Neither, in fact, had come within five feet of the other. Curious, she wanted to poke at this anomaly to see what would happen. Both men had known Renee. Renee had introduced Carlos to Ben.

She said to Anthony, 'Pedrosa Development wants an option on three hundred acres.'

When Carlos finished his phone call, Anthony said, 'Why do you want to buy a tract that size?'

'To build on, why else? It's what we do. We build houses.'

A flicker of something cold went through Anthony's eyes. He kept them on Carlos. 'What's the total price?'

'Depends on how many acres I get. Don't worry about it.' He hadn't moved from the glass wall, and his features were shadowy against the light outside. 'Tell the judge okay, but I'll call him.'

'You can call me,' Gail said. 'I'm handling it.'

'That's fine. Give me one of your cards.' He came across the room.

When she reached across the table to hand her business card to Carlos, she kept her eyes on his face. 'You should know the judge isn't happy about having to hold such a large mortgage. He's concerned that the company is having difficulty raising cash for a proper down payment.'

Carlos flipped the card between his fingers. 'This is not a discussion I want to get into right at this time.'

Gail gave him an innocent look. 'Oh, I'm sorry. I assumed that Mr Quintana was your corporate attorney.'

'No,' Carlos glanced at Anthony, who sat looking at him from under half-lowered eyes. 'Raul Ferrer is. Tony just handled this one thing, the Darden case, that's it. Plus Tony does my DUIs.' He laughed. 'Just kidding, I only had one.'

Anthony said, 'Has Ernesto approved this purchase?'

Carlos raised his hand, pointing as if he couldn't decide what to say. Finally he broke into fast, idiomatic Spanish. He was smiling but Gail didn't think he meant it.

Anthony said quietly, 'English, please.'

'Sorry,' Carlos said, looking at Gail. 'Sometimes I forget.' He slid the phone back into his leather bag.

'Would you prefer to discuss this in private?' she said.

'No, that isn't necessary.' Anthony glanced up. 'Have a seat, Carlos. We are making our guest uncomfortable.'

Carlos sat, looking toward the door, waiting for the secretary to come through it.

'Gail, you should be aware,' Anthony said, 'that contracts for the purchase of real estate can only be signed by Ernesto Pedrosa, as president of Pedrosa Development.'

Carlos's head snapped back around. 'Tony—' He muttered something, then said to Gail, 'I'll get Raul Ferrer to write up the option and Ernesto can sign it.'

'Ben wants me to prepare the papers,' she said.

'That's not how it's usually done.'

'It's the way he wants to do it.'

Carlos said, 'Okay, fine. Call me when it's ready.' He took a business card from a holder in his coat pocket. 'My beeper number's on there too. You can reach me anytime at the beeper.'

'It would be better,' Anthony said, 'if Ms Connor took the papers to Ernesto herself. He may have questions.'

'*Este no tiene nada que ver contigo, Tony.*' Nothing to do with you.

'*Es mi asunto mientras que él sea mi abuelo. Yo no voy a—*' It is my business . . . my grandfather. Gail lost the rest in a blur of syllables.

'*¡Por favor!*' she said, breaking into a heated reply from Carlos.

Both men looked at her.

'Yes. I believe I would prefer to speak directly with Ernesto Pedrosa.'

After Carlos left, promising to have his equipment off the Darden property within twenty-four hours, Anthony closed the door to his office.

'Thank you for staying,' he said.

Gail nodded, doubting that Anthony wanted to clear up a few minor details on the Darden case, as he had said. She watched him drop the file on his desk. An oddly shaped desk – a slender black triangle with rounded corners, resting on curves of glass. Light came from somewhere underneath, creating the impression that the desk, the ultramodern red lamp, and all the neatly stacked files and papers might float upward toward the ceiling.

Anthony followed her when she wandered across the office toward the atrium. She had thought that this might be a common area for the building, but had seen no one walking by. She could see now that it was enclosed, private to Anthony Quintana's office, with panels above to admit light. Ficus vine grew thickly on the wall ten feet past the window.

'Send your decorator over to see me,' she said. 'If I had an office like this, I'd live in it.'

He reached up to click open a latch. With a push, one of the glass panels rolled smoothly on wheels in a track. Gail could hear the burble of the fountain now, a musical splash of water on sunlit rocks.

'Sometimes I have slept here,' he said, 'when preparing a case.' He nodded toward the long black sofa near the office door. 'I live on Key Biscayne, so this is easier.'

Gail pulled her eyes away from the sofa. 'What did you want to talk to me about?'

Anthony leaned a shoulder casually against the glass. 'When did you learn my cousin wanted to buy the property from Judge Strickland?'

'A couple weeks ago.'

He continued to look at her.

She said, 'I assumed you knew.'

'Carlos does not tell me everything he does.'

'Apparently.'

'Are you able to discuss this with me?'

'I doubt Carlos would approve,' Gail said.

'You are not his attorney.'

'And you are?'

Anthony smiled. 'Very proper of you.'

'Prudent,' Gail said, then added, 'Actually, there's

not much to tell. Carlos wants to buy a piece of my cousin Judge Strickland's property just west of Krome Avenue. Ben has about two thousand acres, total. He used to go hunting out there. Not anymore. What's accessible by land he keeps fenced and there are some very touchy dogs roaming around, possibly feeding on the occasional trespasser. Frankly, I can't imagine lawns and sprinklers and neat little three-bedroom houses, but Carlos told Ben that's what he plans to do with it.'

Anthony shook his head a little. 'How can he? Isn't that a wetlands area?'

'Ben doesn't care about your cousin's business sense, only his bank account. And that's what bothers him. Carlos wants to put about two dollars down.' She crossed to the chair Anthony had sat in before and sat sideways on the edge of it, facing him.

He said, 'How long have these negotiations been going on?'

'As far as I know, Carlos contacted Ben a few weeks prior to Renee's death. She introduced them, as a matter of fact.' Gail asked, 'Are you opposed to the purchase?'

'I'm not certain.'

She watched him for a minute, then said, 'I probably would agree with Carlos that this isn't your business, but frankly, I don't want to see Ben lose money if a contract for sale is eventually signed. You're in a better position to check it out than I am.'

Anthony appeared to be listening to the fountain in the corner of his atrium. Finally he turned back to Gail. 'Could you have the proposed offer drawn up this week?'

'Yes, I should think so. It won't have Ben's signature on it, you understand.'

'One of my aunts is having a party at my grandfather's

house next Friday evening. Carlos will be there. And I will. You could deliver the contract.' He spoke casually, but Gail sensed her answer was important to him. After a second, he added, 'It's a family gathering, so if you wish, bring your husband.'

'I can't imagine Mr Pedrosa would want to be disturbed during a family occasion.'

'He'll be glad for the diversion. And don't be concerned about coming to his house. He suffered a mild stroke last year and rarely goes out. Most of his business is conducted at home.' Anthony raised his brows. 'Would that be convenient for you? He lives here in Coral Gables.'

Gail could see the point to this. For reasons of his own, Anthony did not want Carlos getting to the old man alone. He wanted to be there, and having Gail bring the papers was one way to insure it.

She said, 'I'd have to call Carlos and let him know.'

Anthony nodded his assent.

Gail put her briefcase on the table and clicked it open, sitting down to put her copies of the signed and dated Darden papers inside. 'Thank heaven this case is over. If I have any problems setting a closing date, may I call you?'

'Of course,' Anthony said, not returning her smile. When Gail reached for her purse, he said, 'Wait. There is something else.'

He sat down in the chair opposite, looking at her intently.

After a second or two, Gail said, 'What?'

'A homicide detective from Metro-Dade spoke with me this morning.'

'Really. The intrepid Sergeant Britton, no doubt.' She let her purse strap slide off her shoulder. 'What did he ask you?'

'Routine things. What I knew of Renee, what she

was like, who her friends or enemies were. I see you are aware of this.'

Gail laughed softly. 'Too aware.'

'May I ask you what evidence he has? Do you know?'

'He says the razor blade wasn't found close enough to her body and there were no hesitation marks.' Gail paused. 'That means—'

He nodded. 'I know what hesitation marks are. What else?'

She relaxed a little into the chair, remembering she was talking to a man who was fluent in the language of criminal procedure. 'Nothing. No hard evidence. Just the supposition that she wasn't the sort of person who would do this to herself.'

'Does he have a theory who did?'

She shook her head. 'If he does, he hasn't told me.' Anthony didn't need to know about the cards Dave had sent Renee, which Britton had found so fascinating. Or the inheritance. Or even Renee's trip back from the Bahamas with a drug smuggler. None of which meant murder. She said, 'How well did you know my sister?'

The dark brown eyes fixed on her face, unblinking, then he shrugged a little. 'We were friends.'

'Not as close as Carlos.'

There might have been a smile. 'No. They knew each other better. Are you asking my opinion on the likelihood of suicide? I told Frank Britton that I didn't know.'

'What would you tell me?'

'Ah.' Anthony considered for a moment. 'I would say to you that I agree with him.' He watched her reaction. 'Renee had . . . How can I put this? She was curious about everything. She would talk to complete strangers and they would answer willingly. She had few inhibitions and no pretensions. I think she found life too interesting to leave it. No, I do not believe she killed herself. The next question is obvious. As to that, I truly do not know.'

'But she was so unhappy. She—'

Leaning forward, Gail rested her arms on her knees. 'This is confusing. Everyone has an opinion of Renee and none of them match. I thought I knew her.'

Anthony was still looking at Gail, the light from the open windows cutting across his face. 'I remember the photograph of the two of you on the swing.'

'Yes. My mother has it in her bedroom now.'

He said, 'When I lived in Cuba I had a best friend, Juanito. I left when I was a boy and didn't see him for over twenty-five years. He finally came to the US and he walked into my office, right through that door. I knew him immediately. He is bald now, and fat, but I knew him.'

Gail smiled. 'A nice story.'

His hand lifted from his lap, fell back. 'Only that. It may not apply.'

He walked with her to the door. 'Sixteen forty-two Malagueña,' he said. 'That's my grandfather's address. I can give you directions.'

'You don't have to. I know the street.' Of the dozens of Spanish-named streets in Coral Gables – Alhambra, Granada, Cordova – this one had a reputation for being hard to find and harder to afford. 'Very fancy,' she said. 'I think the city fathers let me drive down it once on my way to have our Rolls-Royce serviced.'

For the first time, he laughed, his mood changing. 'You will find that my grandfather is a simple man.'

'A simple man with a bullet-riddled flag over his desk. Will we be in his study? I have to see whether you were making that up, about his desk facing Havana.'

'No, it's true. Ask him.'

'I might do that. See you about seven-thirty. I have some family arrangements to make, but I should be

206

there by then.' She shifted her briefcase and held out her hand.

His grip was strong, the fingers warm around hers. Not the sort of hand to swing a hammer or a tennis racquet, she thought. More the type to twist the cork out of a champagne bottle.

She pulled away, waiting for him to open the door. He didn't. 'I'm sorry your clients took you away from lunch today,' he said. 'I had looked forward to it.'

'Yes, so had I.' Gail smiled. 'Oh, well. What can you do? These emergencies happen.'

The subtle lifting of his brows, before he turned the doorknob, said he didn't believe her for an instant.

Charlene Marks's office was on the seventh floor of Dadeland Towers, on the southern urban fringe of Miami. This afternoon she and Gail had taken the elevator down to O'Herlihy's Pub on the first floor of the building. They found a booth in the back. O'Herlihy's had fifty kinds of four-dollar imported beer and bartenders in striped aprons who could spin cocktail shakers like batons. At four-thirty it was just beginning to fill up with the happy-hour crowd of suits.

Charlene was tapping two Tylenols out of a purse-size box of them. 'Look, it's not that bad. You'll get past this, I swear.'

Gail downed them with the rest of her zinfandel. 'I didn't think he'd be so greedy.'

'I wouldn't blame Dave. It's Joe Erwin, the scum-sucking bastard. He always starts off asking for the moon. Don't worry. There's no way I'm going to let him screw you on this.'

Gail knew that. Charlene was tough.

They said she carried a .22 on her thigh, that she had shot a client with it when he complained about her fees. 'Ridiculous,' she would say, but in a way that left

207

you wondering. But it was absolutely true, Gail had been assured, that when Charlene Marks was a prosecutor, she would wear a low-cut dress to final arguments, and lean over the jury box with a necklace that spelled out G-U-I-L-T-Y in tiny gold letters. Rumor had it that she and the current governor had been lovers.

Shortly before Gail arrived for her appointment, Charlene had talked to Dave's attorney. Erwin had made Dave out to be nearly penniless, and referred to Gail as an heiress. He demanded the business and half the house. As for Karen, he expected shared custody, the father to have said daughter on alternate weekends, holidays, and birthdays, plus a month in the summer.

Gail wasn't too worried about Joe Erwin. By some of the men Charlene Marks had smilingly sliced to ribbons, she had been called pushy, a bitch, and a dyke. She had never been called a loser.

Now Charlene was filling her legal pad with notes. She turned to a new page. 'At least we don't have to ask for your maiden name back. Smart of you to keep it. I've been married four times. If I'd taken their names I'd be known as Charlene Marks Steinfeld Brown Lidsky DeMarco.'

Charlene's smile vanished when Gail leaned her head against the back of the booth. Charlene tapped the empty wineglass with her pen. 'I think you need a refill.'

'God, no, I'd be on my ass. I have six files to look at tonight.'

'Don't you get it yet? The partners over there work you schmucks like slaves. Especially the women. Shit yes, weed 'em out.'

'Well, Charlene. Some of us schmucks plan to have our own slaves someday.'

'If you don't drop dead first.' She tilted back her

208

glass, then looked for a long moment at Gail. 'What's the problem with you and Dave? Really. You haven't told me squat.'

Gail thought for a while. 'Nothing I can isolate. You just go along, the way people do, assuming everything is all right. Then one day it isn't. Except you don't even realize it. Maybe Renee dying made Dave suddenly feel mortal, I don't know.'

Charlene pulled the olive off her cocktail spear with her front teeth. 'I know he's only been gone two days, but are you okay?'

'Fine. I should be miserable, but I'm not. Maybe I knew all along this was going to happen, but didn't want to admit it.' She laughed. 'My ego has been bruised more than anything.'

'Don't feel weird. Half the women in America would throw their husbands out if they could. I should know.'

Gail checked her watch. 'I have to leave. Karen will be home soon.'

Charlene snatched up the check before Gail could reach it. 'No, no. When you get this princely inheritance Erwin was talking about you can treat me to a drink.' She left a twenty on the table.

They went single file past the bar with its noisy crowd of mostly men. One or two of them recognized Charlene and she waved and smiled, avoiding conversations.

She spoke into Gail's ear. 'Men have their uses, marriage not necessarily among them. You want my advice? Go have an affair. Buy a box of condoms and a couple bottles of wine and rent a hotel room on South Beach.'

Gail laughed.

'I mean it. It clears out your mind wonderfully.'

As Gail flipped through the mail, she watched Karen

209

getting herself a snack. Open and close the cookie jar, two Oreos neatly placed on a napkin. Pour a glass of milk, wipe up a little spill.

How self-sufficient she was. Gail had so seldom been at home at five o'clock to notice.

The red light on the answering machine was blinking. She pushed a button. The tape clicked, then spun out a message. 'This is Blockbuster Video. You've got a couple tapes still out . . .'

Gail let the machine spin. Last Sunday Dave hadn't come to pick up Karen for dinner after all, explaining he needed to get settled. Gail knew what he was doing: lying low until Karen had settled.

Karen had taken it well enough, Gail thought. 'Are you and Daddy getting a divorce?' She knew the word. Several of her friends' parents were divorced, remarried, or living in all sorts of combinations.

The next message was from Dave.

'Call me at the marina. It's important.'

Gail waited until Karen had taken her cookies into the family room and turned on the television.

'It's Gail,' she said when Dave answered. 'I just got home. I had an appointment with my attorney this afternoon.'

There was a momentary silence. 'Gail, I'm sorry about all this.'

'Joe Erwin doesn't seem to think so.'

She heard him exhale softly. 'We'll work it out. Look, I called for something else. The cop was by to see me today. Britton. He came on Saturday, then again this morning. I finally told him to get lost. Listen, what did you say to him about me taking Renee home the night of Irene's party?'

Gail pulled a stool over and sat down. 'Just that you drove her car and then came home later in a taxi.'

'What time did you say I got home?'

'I couldn't remember.'

'All right.' There was a silence on the line. Then Dave said, 'I told him it was after midnight. I could be wrong about that.'

'I have no idea. I was barely awake.'

'That was the second time. The first time, I walked around the Grove for a while, then came home about ten-thirty. Your car was gone. So I went out again. To be honest, I didn't feel much like being home, the mood you were in.'

'Wait a minute. I'm not sure I understand this.'

'I came home twice, Gail. The first time was around ten-thirty but you weren't there. Where'd you go?'

Gail stood up, stretching the phone cord to make sure Karen was still in front of the television. 'Renee's. I just drove by to see if she was up. I wanted to talk to her, but I chickened out. I sat in the driveway for a few minutes, then came home.'

'Jesus. Why didn't you tell me this before?'

'I didn't think of it. And nothing happened. I didn't even get out of the car.'

'Do you know how that *looks*? Don't mention it to Britton, I'm telling you.' There was a silence over the phone. Then Dave said, 'If anybody asks, I came home about eleven. We went to bed.'

Gail heard the noise of cartoons on the television, Karen's laughter.

'Gail, are you still there?'

'Yes.'

'It'll be okay. Listen, is Karen around?'

Gail called her to the phone.

While Karen talked to her father – she seemed a little formal with him – Gail stood at the open door of the refrigerator staring vacantly at the contents.

Close to eleven, Renee had been home. Her car was in her parking spot. A kitchen light was on. Who was

211

with her then? What were they doing? If Gail had stayed there a few minutes more—

She turned around when she heard the click of the telephone. Karen had hung it up.

'Did you have a nice talk with your dad?'

'Okay.'

'How about McDonald's tonight?'

Karen shrugged.

Gail crossed the kitchen for her car keys. 'Come on. We'll go out.' She bent to kiss the top of Karen's head. 'You don't have any homework, do you?'

'Well . . .' Karen smiled.

'So do I. We'll do it later.'

Gail left her stack of files on the counter.

Chapter Twelve

Number 1642 spread out over two lots at the end of Malagueña Avenue, a narrow street of overhanging trees and long driveways. As she passed Ernesto Pedrosa's open ironwork gates, Gail saw a sprawling two-story stucco house, a red tile roof, a heavy door under a vine-covered portico. Cars jammed the driveway and parked along the sidewalks in both directions. She had to drive a block and a half before finding an empty plot of grass not in someone's manicured yard.

At the front door Gail pushed the buzzer, waited awhile. Salsa music was coming from somewhere. Crickets chirped in the tangle of bushes under the front windows. She heard laughter, voices speaking Spanish. The tap of heels on tile. Then the door swung open.

The pretty, dark-haired woman standing there smiled. '*Buenas*,' she said slowly, quizzically, taking in Gail's business suit and briefcase. The music was louder now.

'*Soy Gail Connor*. Umm. *¿Señor Anthony Quintana está aquí?*'

The woman smiled as if she should have known. '*Ah, si, entre. Perdóneme. Señora Connor.*' She drew Gail inside, closed the door. More Spanish.

'*¿Usted habla inglés?*'

The woman laughed gaily. 'Sure. Sorry about that. I'm Anthony's cousin Elena. He said you were coming. We'll find him. *Mami, ahora vengo.*' She told the older woman sitting on the sofa with three others that she would be back. 'Come on, I saw him a minute ago.'

She led Gail through the large room with its heavy furniture and high ceilings, then down a hallway, people coming and going. A little girl with a pacifier on a ribbon watched Gail hurry along beside Elena.

'Do you live here?' Gail asked.

Elena glanced at her. 'Me? No, I used to. I got married ages ago.'

The music switched smoothly from instrumental to vocal. It had to be a live band, Gail realized. They passed a huge kitchen, racks of pots overhead, women clattering dishes, the sweet aroma of roast pork and garlic. Finally the hall opened out to a screened patio that might have held a hundred people – laughing, talking, filling plates at a table heaped with food. And dancing. The other end of the patio had been turned into a dance floor.

The band was on a small platform. Four men in tuxes – keyboard, guitar, conga drums, a horn – backed a singer whose hips and feet moved as if on ball bearings. He wore a wide-shouldered white suit and lime green shirt. His black hair was tied into a little ponytail.

'Ms Connor?'

Gail wasn't aware she had stopped walking. Elena pointed. 'Anthony's over that way.'

They made their way through the crowd, the peplum on Elena's yellow silk dress bouncing as she clicked along in her high heels. Nearly all the women here wore clingy, ruffled things that emphasized their bodies. Elena stopped to greet someone. '*Gisela, ¿qué tal?*' They pressed their right cheeks together, a kiss in the air. Gail's eyes went back to the band.

Renee had dated a Hispanic boy in junior high. They had danced the *merengue* in Irene's kitchen, radio turned way up. A Wilfrido Vargas tune. Gail remembered that too. Renee and the boy, both of them small and graceful. Shoulders level, backs straight. His hand on Renee's waist, her fingers on his shoulder. Turning back and around, then a spin, carried by the steady rhythm. He tried to show Gail, six inches taller. She turned the wrong way and stepped on his foot. Laughing, Renee held out her hands. *Feel it, you goose. Don't think. Just move with it.*

On Ernesto Pedrosa's patio the singer in the white suit pulled the microphone closer to his mouth, words pouring out like liquid. *Morena, que no me trates así. Ay, mami, ¿porqué me duelas a mí?*

Elena took Gail's elbow again. 'He's here. I saw him a minute ago. Yes, over there.'

Gail had expected – had almost hoped – to find him dancing. But he was standing in a group of other men along the side of the patio with a drink in his hand, his jacket off and his collar open. He saw her and smiled. His eyes moved quickly over the people behind her, then back to her face. Ignoring her extended hand, he lightly kissed her cheek.

She knew, with a sudden, giddy rush of pleasure, that he had been looking for Dave and that he was glad she had come alone. He took her arm and pulled her out of the way of a teenage couple dancing by.

'This is a marvelous party,' she said, laughing a little. 'What's the occasion?'

He leaned closer so she could hear him. 'My aunt's seventieth birthday.'

'Do you always celebrate like this?'

'No, her son-in-law's parents just arrived from Havana, so it's for them, too. And also for one of the *municipios en el exilio.*'

Gail had heard of these groups of exiles from towns in Cuba. They were combination social clubs and planning committees, having picnics while deciding

215

such things as who would run for mayor and what public bus system to have when they finally went home again.

Anthony introduced her to the other men. One she recognized as a Miami City Commissioner. She supposed her briefcase and the announcement that she was a lawyer with Hartwell Black and Robineau put her firmly in the category of business associate, not female friend.

Finally he took her arm. 'I would suggest you have something to eat, but my grandfather said to bring you in as soon as you arrived. I think he wants to go to sleep.'

'Are you sure this is convenient?'

'Yes, don't worry. He's expecting you.' Anthony glanced around, then noticed Elena. 'Elenita, see if you can find Carlos and tell him Ms Connor is here, will you?'

'Sure.' She smiled at Gail.

Gail couldn't hold back a delighted laugh as Anthony escorted her through the crowd with a hand lightly on her waist. 'Do you know, I've never been to a Cuban party before?'

'No?'

'I've missed a lot.'

'You see.' He wagged a finger at her. 'Too much time in that office of yours.'

Anthony picked up his jacket from the back of a chair in the hall. 'Perhaps you can stay after the meeting.' He straightened his cuffs. 'You might like to hear the band, taste some of the cooking.' He smiled. 'It wasn't catered from Yuca, but I admit – it's pretty good.'

In Ernesto Pedrosa's study at the opposite end of the house, the music seemed to come from far away. Gail walked slowly across the room, whose dark corners were illuminated only by a silk-shaded floor lamp. Anthony flipped a switch and two other lamps came on at either end of a sofa upholstered in brown leather, cracked from age. She smelled expensive cigars and musty books.

Directly in front of her was the desk, not as big as she had expected. Its right end came out further into the room than the left.

'Haven't you ever wanted to . . .' Gail made a pushing motion with her hand.

'I did once, for fun, and he chased me through the house with his belt.' Anthony turned on the brass desk lamp.

'Did he catch you?'

'Unfortunately, yes.'

Her eyes lifted to the flag, a red triangle and white star on the left, three blue and two white stripes across. The lower right edge of the flag was tattered and stained. There were, indeed, several holes in it.

She glanced at Anthony. He shrugged.

On another wall a washed-out blue banner bore the numbers 2506 in faded yellow. A black and white photograph hung beside it, a formation of men in Army fatigues, the same banner flying behind them.

'What is this?'

'*Brigada 2506* invaded Cuba at the Bay of Pigs in 1961,' Anthony said. 'They meet here from time to time. Those who are left.'

Gail walked past a bookcase crammed with papers and heavy books, then to an illuminated glass case. Inside, a faded red ribbon had been draped across an open book of poetry. *Versos Sencillos*. The pages were yellowed, the stanzas written in Spanish. Beside the book was a photograph of a man with a high forehead and small mustache. He wore a black coat and wing collar.

217

'José Martí,' she announced.

'Very good.'

'There. I know something about Cuban culture.' She studied the paintings on the wall. Old Havana. Varadero Beach. Hills and oxcarts and palm trees. She glanced at Anthony. 'And you grew up in this house.'

'Yes. The Pedrosa Museum of Cuban History.'

He took her briefcase and put it beside one of the chairs facing the desk. When he turned back around his eyes went toward the door. He made an almost imperceptible bow.

'Señor, buenas noches.'

Ernesto Pedrosa came in, leaning a little on his cane. He wore a long-sleeved white linen shirt with four pockets – a *guayabera* intricately pleated and stitched.

Gail could see now where Anthony had gotten his height. Pedrosa was even taller, a slender man with a gray mustache. Now he was looking at her through his heavy, black-framed glasses.

Anthony said, *'Abuelo,* may I present *la señora* Gail Connor. My grandfather, Ernesto Pedrosa Masvidal.'

She held out her hand. His was cool and dry, a big hand that enveloped hers completely.

'Mucho gusto en conocerle, señor.' Gail had learned that from Miriam before leaving the office today. She must have pronounced it right, because Pedrosa glanced at Anthony with the pleased surprise of an aging relative for a child who has done something particularly clever.

'Que bien ella habla el español.'

Gail shook her head. 'No, I don't speak it well enough to hold a conversation.'

'It doesn't matter.' The old man chuckled. Behind the thick glasses were a pair of light blue eyes. 'Welcome. *Bienvenida a mi casa, doctora.'*

'Doctora?'

Anthony explained. *'Doctora* is a term of respect for

your profession as a lawyer.'

Pedrosa still held her hand. He brought it briefly to his lips. '*Sin amor de mujer no hay razón para vivir.*' He smiled, then turned toward his desk, walking with a limp around the end further out into the room. 'Translate, *nieto*. These are words for a younger man.'

Anthony smiled as if the two of them were sharing a private joke. 'Without the love of a woman there is no reason to live.'

Gail said softly, 'What a charming man.' But this old charmer, she recalled, had helped launch armed raids on Cuba and bomb a Little Havana radio station.

Anthony touched her elbow. 'Come sit down.'

Pedrosa hooked his cane on the edge of his desk and eased himself into his chair. Beside the lamp was a tray of crystal liqueur glasses and a bottle. 'Anthony, *por favor*. My hands are stiff tonight. May I offer you a glass of cognac, *Señora* Connor?'

'Yes, thank you.'

Anthony loosened the cork, which squeaked a little as he turned it.

'That's enough,' his grandfather said, and pulled it out the rest of the way. It was a short, heavy bottle with an ornate gold label. Gran Duque de Alba. Pedrosa filled three glasses, then hesitated.

'Where is Carlito?'

'He is coming.'

Pedrosa filled a fourth.

Anthony gave Gail a glass, took one for himself, then sat down to her left.

Pedrosa tapped the cork back into the bottle with the heel of one hand. 'I hope you will forgive me, *señora*, if I desert you after we talk. The day has been very long.' He sighed, smiling at her. 'Do you know that we had a stable of horses when I was a young man. Yes. I fell off so many times I surprise myself still to be alive. You don't think of breaking your neck when you are young.'

The door opened. Pedrosa looked across his office. '*Entra.*'

Carlos went around the desk to his grandfather. '*Abuelito, ¿cómo estás?* You're looking good tonight.' He put his arm around Pedrosa's shoulders and kissed him on the cheek.

Pedrosa gestured toward the remaining glass of cognac. Carlos took it then nodded at Gail.

'Hi, glad to see you again.' He pulled a chair closer to the desk, completing the semicircle facing the old man, Gail in the middle.

Pedrosa raised his glass. '*Salud, dinero, y amor.*' He smiled at Gail. 'Health, wealth, and love.'

The cognac was sweet, rich, sublimely smooth.

Pedrosa said, 'Do you have children, *señora*?'

'I have a daughter, nine years old.'

He professed amazement. 'Nine! You are so young.'

Gail made a noncommital smile. She would allow this old man his opinions. 'You are very gracious, *Señor* Pedrosa. And your family as well. I met Elena . . . your granddaughter?'

'One of several.' He cleared his throat, sipped his cognac. 'I have two daughters living, four granddaughters. Eleven great-grandchildren. And two grandsons, whom you see here.' He motioned to them, then said, 'I had a son. He died at Playa Girón. You call it the Bay of Pigs.'

Carlos leaned on the arm of his chair, closer to Gail. 'That was my father. Tomás Pedrosa Betancourt. I never knew him.'

Gail remembered what Anthony had told her: His own father was still in Cuba. She glanced at him. He sat casually, legs crossed, holding his glass of cognac on his knee.

Carlos said, 'We never got his body back. Someday, *si Diós quiere*, I'll put flowers on the place where he died.'

Pedrosa raised his glass. '*Si Diós quiere.*' He turned to Gail. 'My sympathy for your sister, *señora*.'

'Thank you,' Gail said, surprised. 'Did you know her?'

'I met her once,' the old man said, and did not elaborate. He said, 'Carlos has told me that Judge Benjamin Strickland is your relative.'

'My mother's cousin.'

Pedrosa nodded. 'I have not met him, but I have heard of him. And of your family, of course. The Stricklands, an old family in Miami. Now we may do business together.'

Gail took this as her cue to begin. 'I hope that we can. Carlos wants Pedrosa Development to have an option on three hundred acres of Judge Strickland's property in southwest Dade County. If you wish, we can discuss the specific terms.'

'No, I am familiar with them. But my other grandson disagrees with the purchase on any terms. Perhaps he will explain this.' The old man turned his gaze to Anthony.

'I do disagree,' Anthony said. 'Never until now have you purchased land without a clear idea of what is to be done with it. There are no subdivision plans even sketched out, no discussion with the architects—'

Carlos interrupted. 'Where did you get this information?'

'From your office,' Anthony said, then went on. 'The price per acre is reasonable, but three hundred acres is a lot of money. The company is presently holding more land than cash.' He smiled slightly at Carlos. 'According to your own financial statements.'

'You know as well as I do what they prove.'

Gail could see Pedrosa's eyes move to her, then away. She took a sip from her glass. Carlos had just admitted shading financial statements.

The leather in the old man's chair creaked. 'Anthony is my blood, Carlos, as you are. I will listen to what he has to say.' He held up his hand. 'And we will not discuss the company.'

After a moment Anthony said, 'This property isn't technically wetlands – I asked about that, too – but close enough to require an environmental study. They may not allow us to build anything on it.'

Carlos stared. '*Us?*' He looked back at his grandfather. 'Tony never wanted any part of the business. Now it's *us.*'

'Wait.' Pedrosa said to Gail, 'What is your opinion, *señora*? Is the judge selling swampland?' He smiled, but Gail knew he could not have found it amusing.

'Part of the property is low-lying, true. It could be filled if you get the permits, but you might not. We've discussed this with Carlos. Developers used to be able to get whatever they wanted, but not anymore, at least not easily. The contract would have no warranty as to zoning.'

Pedrosa took another swallow of cognac.

. Carlos said quickly, 'People are moving in that direction. If we can get the land cheaply, I say do it. This isn't a contract to purchase, it's an *option*. We're not required to buy anything. We're going to do a survey. An option gives us a chance to decide if we want to go through with the deal.'

Gail heard Anthony's breath come through his teeth.

'Yes, Carlos. We all know what an option is. We also know it is foolish to gamble any amount on these odds. Consider what to do with the land before the contract is signed. Why rush into this?'

'I am not a gambler,' Pedrosa said. His big hand tapped a slow rhythm on his desk.

Above the beard, Carlos's cheeks were hot. 'The real estate market is coming back and we have to be ready.' He sat stiffly on the front of his chair. '*Abuelito*, I've worked for you for eight years. I proved myself. Ever since you had your stroke, if you notice, other people have been showing up a lot. Excuse me, but that's the way I see it.'

Anthony spoke softly. 'Carlos. *Después*.' Later.

Gail wanted to slip out of the room. No, she admitted to herself, she wanted to hear what these men would say if she weren't here. Except that it would be in Spanish. Only politeness had kept the conversation in English so far. She focused on the flag behind the tilted desk.

Pedrosa wiggled the cork out of the bottle. '*Señora?*' When she declined, he refilled his own glass.

Finally he said, 'I am not opposed to any of my family taking part in my business, if that is what they want to do. There is a place.'

Gail sensed the tension in Anthony's body. She said, '*Señor* Pedrosa, if you need more time to decide about the purchase, I can speak to my cousin.'

He appeared to be considering that.

Carlos stood up, took the bottle of cognac and twisted the cork out. 'Tony's a good lawyer. If he wants to give that up, start in the business . . . Okay with me. But I wouldn't put him somewhere really visible. People know he's got ties to Cuba. Some of them might not like that.'

'Ties? My father and sister are in Cuba. Everyone knows it.'

Carlos watched the cognac gurgling into his glass. 'I heard you were just down there last month. What did you do? Did Marta take you to Havana for another talk

223

with the Ministry of Trade? She wants you to invest down there, right?'

Gail had never seen Anthony's eyes so dark. '*No voy a discutirlo contigo.*' Not going to talk to you about it. '*Es mi asunto*—'

Pedrosa's angry, astonished voice broke in. '*¿Fuiste otra vez? ¿A santo de que?*' You went again? For what?

Gail's eyes flew to Anthony's face.

'*¡Son mi familia, mi sangre!*' My family, my blood. '*No permito que ellos sufran*—' I won't let them suffer . . . Gail lost the rest of it.

The old man's fist came down on the desk so hard the brass lamp bounced. '*¡Malagradecido! ¡Te salvé de eses asesinos y así me pagas!*' I saved you from those murderers and you repay me like this.

Anthony sat as if carved from stone. Carlos sipped his cognac.

Then Pedrosa smiled tensely at Gail as if suddenly remembering she was there. There were spots of red high on his cheeks. 'Señora. I hope you will pardon us. If you have the contract . . .' He gestured toward the door. 'Carlos. Tell Digna to come in.' To Gail he said, 'Digna is my wife. She is secretary of Pedrosa Development Corporation.'

Gail nodded and reached into her briefcase. For an instant her eyes met Anthony's. She laid the two-page option and an extra copy on the desk.

'*Dame la pluma.*' Pedrosa looked up at Anthony and pointed to the pen in the holder at the edge of the desk, out of his reach. '*Dámela.*'

For a long moment, Anthony did not move. Finally he leaned over far enough to remove the pen from its holder and give it to his grandfather. Not looking at him, Pedrosa tilted the papers toward the desk lamp, turning the page for the signature line.

The door opened and Carlos came through it,

followed by a plump woman in a dark blue dress. She must have been in her late seventies, but moved as briskly as a girl. Gold filigree earrings swung from her earlobes.

She smiled and nodded at Gail.

Anthony, who had stood respectfully when she entered, sat down again.

Pedrosa opened a drawer and withdrew a chrome-colored seal. '*Digna, firma el contrato y ponle el cuño.*' She put on her glasses, signed, then squeezed the corporate seal over her signature, making a little *uumph* of effort.

Pedrosa said, '*Gracias, mi vida,*' when she kissed his forehead. She left as quickly as she had arrived. The door quietly closed behind her.

Gail glanced at Carlos. He was finishing off the last of his cognac, putting the empty glass back on the tray.

Ernesto lifted a heavy, leatherbound checkbook out of his top drawer. '*Doctora*, do you require a certified check?'

'It's not necessary from you, *Señor* Pedrosa.'

When he finished and tore it out of the book, she reached for it reluctantly. Ten thousand dollars, written in a shaky hand, from his personal account.

He said, 'You and the judge will take care of the details with Carlos.'

'Yes.' She folded the check and dropped it into her briefcase along with the signed option.

Pedrosa gripped the arms of his chair. 'Now you must excuse me. I am tired. I am going upstairs.' He picked up his cane, placing it carefully. Carlos rushed around the desk but Pedrosa waved him away. '*Déjame. Estoy vivo.*' I am still alive.

From the middle of his study, he bowed slightly to Gail. 'It was a pleasure, *señora*. My house is yours. You must come back for dinner anytime. My wife is an excellent cook.'

'Good night, *Señor* Pedrosa.'

Anthony had risen from his chair. Pedrosa glanced at him then moved stiffly toward the door, which Carlos opened.

'*Buenas noches, abuelito*,' Carlos said, watching him pass. 'Do you need help getting up the stairs?'

'No.'

When he was gone, Carlos smiled at Gail. 'Okay. Looks like we're in business. Hey, Tony, don't be like that. Come on, man.' He held out his hand. 'Come on. It's business. No hard feelings.'

Anthony only glared at him until Carlos shrugged.

'Suit yourself.' He said to Gail, 'So did you get something to eat? A drink?'

Gail shook her head. 'Thank you, but I should be getting home.' Karen was waiting for her at Irene's.

'Well.' Carlos bounced on his toes. 'I guess you'll let me know when Ben signs the papers.'

'Yes, I will.' Gail put her purse over her shoulder. Anthony held the door. 'I'm leaving too. I'll go out with you.'

Carlos said, 'No hard feelings, Tony. I mean it.' He had his hands in his pockets this time.

Anthony gave him a blazing look and stalked out of his grandfather's study without a backward glance.

They were beyond the iron gate before he finally stopped walking. The light from the row of lamps along the wall shone dimly through the leaves.

'You shouldn't have been drawn into our family bickering,' he said. 'I didn't expect it would turn out this way tonight.'

'I feel disloyal somehow,' Gail said.

'To whom?'

'Perhaps to you. I was on the wrong side.'

He shook his head. 'No. Your loyalty is to Ben Strickland, only that.'

'This may sound odd,' she said, 'but I think you and your grandfather are very similar.'

Anthony looked at her steadily.

'Not in your politics, obviously, but there is that stubborn, aristocratic manner. Carlos doesn't have it. He probably wishes he did.'

The music seemed to come from far away now, echoing across the golf course and back again. A car came by, pulling into another driveway.

Gail said, 'Well. I should go.'

'Where are you parked?'

She laughed and pointed over his shoulder. 'About a mile that way.'

He finally smiled. 'I'll drive you.' His gray Cadillac was beside the wall.

When he pulled alongside her car, he turned off the engine, leaving the parking lights on. She thought he might be coming around to open her door – unnecessary, but a pleasant courtesy. He turned slightly in his seat to face her. In the semi-darkness she heard the fabric of his jacket sliding against the leather seat.

Anthony said, 'You probably wanted to have something to eat. Let me take you somewhere else. We can talk.'

She hesitated, a bit too long. 'Thank you, but I have some cases to review tonight.'

'It's still early.'

'I'm married.' When he made no response, she looked through the windshield, laughing a little. 'Sorry. That presumed a lot, didn't it?'

A few seconds passed. He said, 'When I asked you to lunch the other day I told myself it was to discuss the Darden case. There may have been other reasons.'

She turned her head to look at him fully.

'I won't act on them.' The amber dash lights shone dimly on his face. His eyes were lost in shadow.

She smiled. 'Very gallant, *Señor* Quintana.'

His slight shrug was noncommital. 'We've just settled a lawsuit. A cup of coffee to celebrate wouldn't be out of order. As colleagues?'

'As friends,' she said after a moment. 'Perfectly in order.'

Then she thought of Renee dancing the *merengue* in the kitchen, laughing, holding out her hands. *Feel it. Don't think.*

Gail took out her car keys. 'I'll follow you.'

Chapter Thirteen

They sat in the restaurant at the Hyatt Regency Hotel on Alhambra Avenue, only a few other customers left in the room. Their table was reflected in the windows looking out over the terrace with its splashing fountain and the palm trees wrapped in tiny strings of lights.

The waiter had long since cleared the plates. They had ordered only dessert – one chocolate mousse, one raspberry tart. On the table now: glasses of sauterne, their second. *Her* second, anyway. Maybe her third, she couldn't remember. Excellent sauterne. Anthony had ordered a whole bottle of it.

Gail propped her chin in her hands, classical guitar music drifting from the cocktail lounge across the hall.

They had talked about where she went to law school. Where he went to law school – Columbia, on scholarship. *God, you must be smart.* They had talked about the new Japanese movie in town – *Who has time to see a movie?* Talked about the hassles of a big law firm.

Anthony was leaning back in his chair, relaxed. Looking at her across the table. Gail smiled at him, cheeks warm, feeling the wine. But not showing it, surely not.

They had talked about Montreal, which they had both visited. He liked to snow ski, had learned when he lived up north. They had talked about their kids. His son and daughter lived in New Jersey with his ex-wife.

Talked about taking them to Disney World last Christmas.

She watched the lines appear on either side of his mouth when he smiled. A shadow of beard on his upper lip and chin. Such a straight nose.

He hadn't asked about her husband. Hadn't asked if she would like to do this again sometime.

Only listened. Listened more than he talked, she realized after a while. Unusual for a man to do.

His top three shirt buttons were undone. She wanted to press her fingertips into the hollow at the base of his throat, then along his collarbone. She could see his pulse. Slow. Steady.

No knees bumping hers under the table. He was keeping his distance. Leaning back in his chair. Looking at her. His dark eyes touching her. Only that.

She blinked. 'I'm sorry. What—'

'I asked where you went to high school.'

'Ransom-Everglades,' she said.

He considered. 'Exclusive school, isn't it?'

'Oh, you don't *know*.' She giggled, caught herself. 'The sons and daughters of Miami's white Republican elite. Lah-de-dah. The girls went to teas and had coming out parties.'

'You were a debutante?'

'At the Riviera Country Club. A couple dozen perfect little debs on their fathers' arms. Except my father died when I was thirteen, so Ben escorted me.'

'Judge Strickland.'

'Yes. I wore a frothy pink dress. Not me at all.' She lifted her wineglass. 'I'm not pink and frothy, am I? Do you think?'

'Not at all.'

'It was awful. Imagine. You're eighteen, wearing this tight, scratchy dress and white gloves and a stiff smile and everyone is wondering if you'd be good

230

enough to marry their pimply-faced little Rodney.'

Anthony smiled.

'Well, you know what I mean.' Gail laughed. 'Someone actually phoned about Karen going to cotillion and I said absolutely not.'

'What is that?'

'A dance class. Learning how to behave oneself at society events, to be more accurate. They start early, don't they? Pre-teen.'

'I'm trying to visualize Renee as a debutante.'

'Renee? She laughed at the whole idea, particularly after they kicked her out of Ransom-Everglades in the ninth grade. She was right, of course, not going to those stupid deb parties.'

Anthony picked up the bottle of sauterne. 'I hear some admiration there, no?'

'Probably. But I'd never have said so. Not then.' She watched the wine swirl into her glass, pale gold. 'That was back when my mother wanted to preserve the impression that the Stricklands were still somebody in Miami. But most of them had already jumped ship.'

'Where to?'

'Broward County or even further up the state. Ben's sons went to New York. My cousin Nancy said she was tired of checking her driveway for muggers every time she got back from the grocery store. Linda said she wanted to live in the USA again. Absolutely no sense of adventure, any of them.'

Gail put down her glass. 'All right, your turn.'

'My turn?'

'Would you mind if I asked you something about your family?'

He turned one hand palm up. 'Ask.'

'Why did your father stay in Cuba?'

'Ah. I thought you would get to him sooner or later. Luis Quintana Rodriguez. He's an unrepentant revolutionary. Sixty-four years old now. He was blinded and lost one arm in a skirmish with some exiles in 1963.'

Gail drew in her breath. 'And you let me go on and on about teas and coming-out parties.'

'It was interesting.'

'Sure. My exotic American childhood. You were just down to see him?'

'A few weeks ago. I've been back several times since I left.'

'Obviously your grandfather doesn't approve.'

'Unlike what happened tonight, it rarely comes up. And my father doesn't ask me about my life here. I guess if you lose your sight you don't want to think it was for nothing.'

'But he let you come to the United States.'

'He didn't *let* me.'

Gail waited. 'You escaped in a rubber raft?'

Anthony shook his head.

'Hijacked an airplane?'

He smiled. 'All right, this is what happened. No mysteries. My mother – Caridad Pedrosa – was the youngest daughter of a rich Havana banker. My father was a nobody from a farm in Camagüey province, his mother a *mulata*, descended from slaves. They met in Havana, where he had come to work his way through the university. Somehow Caridad eluded her chaperones. Ernesto found out and locked her in her room, but it was too late. She was already pregnant. Ernesto had to let them marry. My sister Marta was born six months later.

'Then Luis, my father, became involved with the socialists. The Batista government threw him in jail. They beat him. They might have killed him if he hadn't been related to Ernesto Pedrosa Masvidal. He didn't see my face until I was two years old. When he got out

232

Ernesto gave him a job in the bank, which he hated. One day he told my mother he was going back to Camagüey. She could keep her soft life in Havana or follow him.'

'What did she do?'

'She followed him, of course. Luis was her husband, the father of her children. And he was a passionate man, very idealistic. I remember the trip, hours and hours in the back of an open truck. My mother had three children by then, and expecting another. We lived on his parents' farm. Soon after, my father joined the rebels in the Sierra Maestra – the mountains.'

'She must have loved him desperately.'

'Yes. But when you have four children, feeding them *yuca con mojo* instead of steak, and there are chickens and pigs running under the house and . . . Well, when your husband has another woman from time to time, romance and passion don't last too long.

'The summer after Batista fell, my grandfather got word to Caridad that the family was leaving Cuba. A car would come for her and the children while my father was away. But it came early. Marta and I were not there and she had to leave without us. I was seven, my sister ten. I have never cried so hard, but then my father told me the revolution needed men, not babies. I didn't cry again.

'He was injured two years later. I remember going to the military hospital. My father's face was wrapped in bandages. Fidel Castro himself had pinned a medal on his chest, which my father could see only with his fingers. He was thirty-four years old.

'By then my life in Havana was only a dream to me. In Camagüey I ran barefoot and fished with my best friend Juanito and went to school. One day my aunt told me they had arranged for me and Marta to visit our mother. My father was back in the hospital and

233

knew nothing of this. Marta didn't want to go. She was fifteen, old enough to decide. I got on a DC-6 and half an hour later – Miami. Naturally they never had any intention of letting me go back. Ernesto must have spent a fortune on bribes.'

Anthony smiled across the table. 'And that is how I came to America.'

'You were practically kidnapped.'

'I felt this for a long time, yes. I was homesick, speaking no English, getting into fights with the American boys on the street. I drove my mother to tears. But finally, you know, you learn the new language and you go to McDonald's and ride a new bicycle and pretty soon – if you are thirteen years old – you let go.'

'Will you go back someday?'

'To live?' Anthony turned his wineglass by its stem. 'Never. Marta took me to see our grandfather's house in Havana. It's been cut into apartments. I don't think it's been painted in thirty years. A sad country. Everything is too much in the past. What I have is here.'

They sat silently for a while. 'I am sorry about your father,' Gail said.

'You lost yours completely.'

Guitar music drifted faintly through the open doors. Gail glanced out the window and saw Anthony's reflection in three-quarter profile. There was more to him, she was certain, than he had told her. How had he reconciled the competing passions of Luis and Ernesto? There was more than could be learned over one bottle of wine. She doubted there would be another. There were no more cases to settle.

'A personal question for you,' he said.

She turned.

'What happened between you and Renee?' When

Gail didn't immediately respond, he asked, 'Is that too personal?'

She shook her head. 'No, it isn't that. I could give you an easy answer and say it was sibling rivalry. I could say we never got along. But you remember that photo of Renee and me on the swing. How she was laughing? She was one of those adorable kids who find everything funny. And I adored her too. I couldn't help it. Even when I was mean to her, I couldn't be for long.'

Gail lifted her fingertips to her cheeks. For a few seconds the restaurant dimmed, as if fragments of a dream had intruded on her waking mind.

'What is it?' Anthony asked.

'Just . . . Renee.' Gail smiled shakily. 'How odd. I saw her so clearly just then. A flash, nothing more. Usually all I see is . . . When I went to identify her body. That's what I see, so I try not to think of her at all.'

Anthony said nothing, waiting for her to go on.

She took a slow breath. 'As to what happened between us . . . I've thought about this a lot. Sometime after our father died, we both changed. I became withdrawn and distant. I stayed in my room reading or sometimes only staring at the ceiling. She became angry. She lied, but in ways our mother wouldn't notice. And – How can I say this? Sexually advanced. What she said, how she acted. She started sneaking out of the house, meeting older boys. You don't need a PhD in psychology to figure that one out.'

Gail paused. 'Anyway, our mother was lenient with her, trying to make her happy again. I was only aware of the injustice of it all. Me getting straight A's and no pats on the head because I didn't need them. Renee getting what she wanted. Poor little Gail, right?'

'Are you bitter?'

'No. Well, I used to be. Not now. When she killed herself I thought it was some kind of proof that she was wrong and I was right. Now I don't think it's that simple. I'm not bitter. I'm mystified. And so regretful. I could have changed things between us.'

'Do you blame yourself for what happened?'

'In a strange way, I do feel guilty. Not for her death, of course, but . . . You know. If only. If only.'

She tilted her glass, watched the light bounce off the wine. 'If I weren't so buzzed I wouldn't bore you with all this.'

'No, I asked you.'

Gail looked up. 'Why? It's a dull topic, compared to what you just told me.'

Anthony put his forearms on the table, hands loosely clasped. How utterly foreign he seemed to her in that moment, for reasons which had nothing to do with his Hispanic features or the lingering accent. She simply did not know what he was thinking and didn't know what words to use to find out.

'Gail.' Anthony took the wineglass from her and pushed it aside. 'Listen to me.' His voice was quiet. 'I have a friend in the State Attorney's Office, a prosecutor. I asked him about Renee's murder.'

Her eyes fixed on his face, waiting.

'I wanted to know, specifically, if they have enough evidence for an arrest, and if so, of whom. He said the police are still investigating, but there is a primary suspect. You.'

She felt one moment of giddy incredulity before she grasped what he was saying. 'Me? They suspect me? Why?'

'I don't know. He wouldn't get into specifics.'

The waiter appeared, a young blond man in a red vest. 'Will there be anything else for you folks?'

'No, thank you.' Anthony barely glanced up at him.

The waiter left. 'You don't have to discuss it with me. There may be reasons you prefer not to.'

She started to laugh, but gasped instead. 'What are you telling me? I should hire a criminal attorney?'

'At some point you should consider it, yes. For now, I am offering my advice as a friend.'

'This is impossible.'

He spread his hands. 'But not something to be taken lightly.'

'I suppose Britton thinks I did it for the money. I inherited two hundred thousand dollars from Renee.' Anthony's brown eyes held no expression. 'That's a lot of money, I know. It was a trust our grandfather left us. It's complicated.'

'Never mind. You can explain it later. Did the police ask you where you were when Renee died?'

'You really think she was murdered. Don't you?'

'Yes. What did you tell the police about an alibi?'

'Who could have done this? I don't even know who she was involved with. Last year she was arrested with some men bringing cocaine from the Bahamas.'

'Gail.'

She laughed a little, running her fingers through her hair. 'All right. Where was I when she died? There was a party at my mother's. Dave took Renee home. Britton might think I was jealous, because he found greeting cards that Dave sent Renee. Birthday, Valentine's. Sometimes for no reason at all.'

'Slow down.'

She closed her eyes for a moment, started again. 'I might as well tell you. Dave and I are separated. It has nothing to do with Renee. Or maybe it does, but not the way Britton thinks.'

'Were they having an affair?'

'They had lunch together occasionally. Regularly. For almost two years. He says he never slept with her.'

'Do you believe him?'

She nodded. 'You'd have to know Dave to understand.'

He looked at her for a moment, then said, 'When did you find out about this . . . arrangement?'

'He told me just after she died. After.' Gail pressed her knuckles into her breastbone, waiting for her heart to settle. 'What am I going to say to Karen? What about my job?'

'An investigation doesn't mean you will be arrested,' Anthony said. 'You don't have to say anything to her yet. Are there criminal attorneys at your law firm? You may want to consult with one of them.'

'There's one. He does white-collar crime. I don't know anyone else. I'd appreciate your help.'

'Then listen to what I tell you. First, don't talk to any policemen, I don't care what they say. If you're dumb enough to talk to them, they will hang you with your words. I know Frank Britton from other cases. He's not the country boy he appears to be. Do you understand?'

She nodded.

'Next, don't discuss the facts of this case with anyone. Innocent words can be misconstrued and your closest friends could be subpoenaed to testify against you. Yes?'

'Yes.'

'And tell your husband and the rest of your family not to talk to the police unless a lawyer is present.'

'How is that going to make me look?'

'Don't think about that. If you are contacted by the police for any reason, you tell them, "I would like to talk to you, but I was instructed by an attorney not to say anything. Otherwise, I would be glad to help." And if this occurs, call me immediately. Will you do that? Gail?'

238

'Yes.' She took another deep breath, then said, 'Am I supposed to mention your name?'

He hesitated. 'If you wish, but I cannot become officially involved unless I am retained.'

'Oh, God. How much—'

'No.' Anthony took her hand and enclosed it in both of his. 'I'll monitor the situation for now. Don't worry.'

'I've never been—' She laughed shakily. 'I've had two speeding tickets in my life. That's it.'

He smiled and let her hand go. She felt cool air where his had been. He said, 'This is what I want you to do. Tomorrow morning you will call me and I'll give you a list – a long one – of things for you to write down. What happened and when, that sort of thing. What Britton asked you or Dave and what you told him. That way, if something happens, we will be prepared. But we'll talk about that tomorrow. Now, it's late.'

Gail glanced at her watch. 'Almost eleven.'

'Where's your daughter?'

'With my mother.'

'Are you all right to drive?' He reached inside his jacket.

She nodded. 'Tell me something. Don't criminal attorneys ever ask clients if they're guilty?'

He pulled a business card and a pen out of his wallet, looking at her. 'Not if they already know the answer.' He wrote on the back of the card. 'That's my home number. Anytime after eight.'

She put the card in her purse, then spoke over her shoulder when he came around for her chair. 'You asked me about Renee so you could decide if I did it.'

'Forgive me. I prefer innocent clients when I'm lucky enough to find them.'

Gail stood up, still a little out of breath. 'Once you told me everyone is guilty of something.'

'Did I? And what could you be guilty of?'

'Not this.'

Chapter Fourteen

Five or six years ago, the last time Gail had driven out to Ben's property, she had turned off Krome Avenue after the U-Pick strawberry field. The field was gone now, plowed under, a realtor's sign erected on two posts. For Sale – Residential Zoning. She turned and headed west, gravel pinging the underside of her car for a mile or so.

Ben had left the gate open for her. A barbed-wire fence extended on either side of it, running between the trees and a weed-choked drainage ditch. Gail rolled her window down and followed the dirt road that ran straight back into the property. Her tires splashed through a pothole and bumped over fallen branches. She came finally to a clearing where a tin-roofed shed and a faded concrete-block house faced each other across a plot of rocky ground. A dented aluminum fishing skiff leaned against the shed wall. Gail pulled in beside Ben's white Lincoln, turned off her engine, and got out.

Then she heard the barking. A black mutt sped around the corner of the shed, teeth bared. Ben followed close behind.

'Hey! Shut up that racket. Quiet!' As Gail came out from behind her door, the dog trotted back over to Ben. He patted its head. 'Go sit down. Go on.'

She caught her breath. 'Are his friends around?'

'They saw a rabbit and took off into the woods.' Ben

laughed. 'I won't let them eat you.' He took off his work gloves and stuffed them into the back pocket of his jeans.

She picked up the plain white envelope on the passenger seat and held it out to him. 'A present from Ernesto Pedrosa,' she said. 'His offer, signed and sealed.'

'You came a long way to bring me this.'

'I don't mind. The check's inside. A personal check, but you shouldn't have any trouble with it.' She closed her door, then noticed the pile of junk beside the shed – a battered lawn mower, old tools, a torn mattress, scraps of lumber.

'You work fast.' She had telephoned Ben's house at nine o'clock, catching him on his way out. 'I can't believe you're doing all this yourself.'

'Somebody's coming this afternoon with a truck.' Ben wiped his forehead with a handkerchief. Sweat glistened on his neck and patterned the front and underarms of his blue work shirt. He grinned at her. 'I can still get around, little girl. Come on, I've got some sodas in the cooler. Want one?'

'Not for me, thanks. I just had lunch.'

She followed him across the yard. Under her sandals the ground was unyielding, a thin layer of dirt over white limestone. Ben folded the envelope and stuck it in his shirt pocket.

'I thought Karen might come along,' he said.

'Dave's going to take her to a movie this afternoon.'

Ben picked up a piece of two-by-four and sent it sailing end over end into a tangle of Brazilian pepper. 'I don't know why I keep this place. Nobody comes out here anymore. I ought to sell the whole tract.'

Gail shaded her eyes. 'Where's the section Carlos wants? He said he'll need access to do a survey.'

'That way, toward those trees. They better bring a machete and some bug spray. Tell him to let me know when and I'll put the dogs in the shed.'

As they walked across the yard Gail studied the cabin – what they had once called the cabin, a single-story block house built in the forties. It seemed to be in the final stages of decrepitude – broken panes in the windows, mildew creeping upward from the ground. The roof, which overhung a concrete porch, bore a thick layer of pine needles. It probably leaked.

The dog trotted along beside them, tongue lolling out. At the end of the porch Ben lifted the lid on his cooler. 'Nothing for you? Sure?'

She shook her head, then noticed the shotgun propped beside the screen door. 'What's that for? Trespassers?'

'Just the legless kind. Last time I was out here I saw a rattlesnake in the yard.' He popped the tab on his soda, tilted it back, then stood looking at her a minute. 'Irene told me about you and Dave.'

Gail nodded.

'I hate that, honey. He's a good man. Maybe the business has him down. I could talk to him.' He put his hand on her shoulder.

'No,' she said.

He turned away and stepped onto the porch. 'Well, don't say I didn't offer.' There was a sheet-metal dog feeder as far under the roof and away from the weather as possible. Two big bags of dog chow lay beside it. Ben set his soda on the windowsill and pulled one of the bags upright. The black mutt tapped across the porch, tail wagging.

Gail knew she had to be the next to speak. 'I appreciate your concern, though. I do.'

He slit the bag open with his pocketknife and lifted the bag to the feeder. 'How's Karen taking it?'

'I'm not sure. She hasn't said much.'

'You ought to think about what you're doing, is my

243

opinion. Kids shouldn't grow up in a broken home.'

'Ben—' Gail didn't want to start a discussion that would end up nowhere. 'Ben, I came about something else. The police think I killed Renee.'

He stood there holding the bag upside down, looking at Gail, long after the last chunks had rattled into the feeder. She stuck her hands into the back pockets of her slacks.

'Jesus H. Christ,' he finally said.

She laughed softly. 'Can you believe? Because of the money, I suppose. Dave wasn't home to say I was with him. And everyone knows how Renee and I disagreed. It all fits, in some nightmarish way.'

'Where did you hear this?'

'From Anthony Quintana. He and I were on that case together – Doug Hartwell's daughter. I mentioned that at Irene's, didn't I? He has a friend at the State Attorney's Office and he asked what was going on.'

'Are they crazy? It was suicide.'

'Not according to the police,' she said.

'God almighty. They're saying *you* did it? This is the grossest example of police incompetence I have ever heard of.' He jumped down off the porch. 'I'm going to have somebody's butt for this.'

'Ben, there's nothing we can do. If we make a stink they'll think I'm trying to hide something. They haven't arrested me yet. They might not. But do me a favor. Don't say anything more about it than you have to.'

'That homicide detective – What's his name? Britton. He asked me some questions a couple weeks ago. Came back another time. I figured it was routine. You know, because your mother wanted them to look into this.' Ben groaned softly. 'Oh, lord. Irene. Did you tell Irene?'

'Not yet,' Gail said, 'but I will. I spoke to Anthony Quintana this morning and he said I should discuss it with the family in advance, so no one is taken by surprise.'

Ben looked at her steadily. 'You're certainly calm.'

'Focused is a better word. And on two or three hours' sleep last night. The call to arms, I suppose.' She rocked back and forth on her toes, her hands still in her pockets. 'I want to ask you something.'

'Sure, what?'

'It's — It would be hard to talk about this with Mother.'

Ben waited.

Last night her thoughts could have marched across the bedroom ceiling in illuminated letters, they were that clear. Gail began slowly, recapturing them.

'What surprises me most is that Frank Britton believes I could have done it. Forget motive or opportunity. He thinks I had the capacity. Why? Does he see something in me that I've missed? I've never been one to doubt myself before. But now — Look. My marriage has fallen apart. I hardly know my own daughter.'

'Gail, honey—' Ben scratched the side of his face. 'I know you've had your troubles lately—'

'That isn't it. I don't think that's it.' She sat down on the edge of the porch. The boards were cracked and dry, the nail heads coming up. She picked at a splinter. 'What does he see? That I hated her? I didn't. Truly, I didn't. Okay, I resented her sometimes, but — It was more my fault than hers. I didn't want to hear what she had to say. I didn't care. To learn that about yourself — That there's a willful lack of understanding. That you made things worse.'

Ben sat down beside her. He rubbed the heel of his hand down his thigh as if easing a cramp. Gail noticed the lines his tendons made under the skin, the curly white hair on his forearm. 'What are you doing, blaming yourself for the way she was?'

'No. Although I probably contributed to it. The point is, I didn't know her. Who is this person that Frank Britton says I – Who was she?'

The dog came over from the feeder and stretched out beside them. Ben scratched its muzzle. After a second or two he said, 'Well, I wouldn't worry about it now. You turned out all right, honey. Renee didn't.'

Gail stared idly at his knee, the faded denim. A line of tagalong thistles stuck to the laces on his work boot. She knew he would never understand. He couldn't. There was simply a gap between them. No connection.

'Aw, come on.' Ben's arm went around her shoulders. He shook her a little. She tensed, feeling awkward and embarrassed. Then she turned her head into his neck and let out a long, slow breath. The scent of soap and sweat was in his shirt.

Gail closed her eyes. 'When I was a kid, I was so jealous of her. My pretty sister. The one who always got what she wanted. What I wanted.'

His voice vibrated in his chest. 'What did you want?'

'Affection, isn't that what every kid wants?' She laughed softly. 'It sounds so stupid now. So childish. I wanted to be noticed. I thought nobody liked me as much. Which was probably true, given my attitude. I'd lie on my bed in the dark listening to the rest of you having a good time. Wishing someone would make me come out. I could have opened the door, couldn't I?'

He shifted a little as if he were about to move away. He didn't. It occurred to Gail that he was being polite; that she was being maudlin. Then she felt him lightly kiss the top of her head.

He said, 'Honey, I'm sorry you felt that I – that Irene and I – didn't show you as much affection as we did Renee. I never intended to butt in and take your dad's place, but I got the feeling you resented me because you thought that's what I was trying to do. So

246

I sort of left you alone. Renee was easy to get along with. Well, she knew how to get on Irene's good side, that's for sure. Mine, too. I never knew we made you feel like this. Didn't seem like you wanted anybody.'

He patted her cheek, bent down a little to look into her eyes. He smiled, deep lines in his face. How old he looked now, she thought. And as a child she had thought he was so handsome.

Suddenly Gail stood up, his arms sliding away. The knowledge had hit her with an impact that left her dizzy, why she had never told him how she felt, fifteen or twenty years ago. Not because she hadn't wanted to be closer to him, but because she had, too much.

'Gail?' She felt his hand on her back.

She had wanted him. Not knowing, at that age, what it was. She had lain in bed under her pillows, aching, listening to the rumble of his voice. Hearing Renee's laughter. Her silvery, piping songs at the piano. And in the dark behind her eyelids Gail had played elaborate, bloody scenes of her sister's death.

When she turned around Ben was still looking at her, probably trying to figure out what the hell was going on.

'You want to sit back down? Are you okay?'

'No. Yes, I'm fine.'

'Maybe you need to get a good night's sleep,' he said.

'I guess so.' She rolled a rock under her sandal, glanced toward her car. 'Well. I need to get home. Make sure Karen's ready. Dave's going to pick her up. I think they're going to a movie.'

'You said already.'

When she looked back, Ben was still watching her. 'We're going to take care of this, Gail, this thing with the police. First thing, I'm calling Ray Hammell. Best criminal lawyer in Miami.'

She pushed her hair off her forehead, raking her fingers through several times. 'No. I can't – Let's talk about this later. I want to go on home.'

'I'm not going to let you hire some Cubano who thinks he can score a big fee off you.'

'We didn't even talk about money!' She held up her hands, aware how sharp her voice had been. She started over. 'This is my problem. I'm not asking you to get involved.'

Ben petted the dog, his hand moving quickly over its glossy fur. 'Quintana represented Renee once, did he tell you that?'

Gail numbly shook her head.

'No, I guess he forgot to mention it,' Ben said. 'Your sister got herself into trouble last year. Again. She hired this Quintana fellow. I didn't even know she had been arrested until the bond hearing. She called me, crying. Ben, Ben, what am I going to do? I've fucked up my life. You've got to—'

'This was for trafficking in cocaine.'

He stopped, puzzled that she knew.

'Frank Britton told me,' Gail said.

Ben nodded. 'Big trouble this time for Little Sister. Fifteen years, minimum mandatory sentence. No possibility of parole. I wanted to get her the best, not some guy she met at the office. I suggested to Quintana that he withdraw. He didn't want to.'

'You told me at Irene's you had never heard of him.'

'I didn't want to get into it with you. Having to explain all this. Anyway, the case was dismissed, so he had no client. I guess you could say the case withdrew from him.'

Gail stood silently, then said, 'Drug cases don't just vanish from the system. Britton told me that's what happened. Did you have anything to do with it?'

His mouth was a thin line.

'Ben?'

'I'm going to tell you this, but I don't ever want to hear it mentioned again. I talked to the judge in her division. He spoke to the prosecutor. Renee had no idea what was on the boat. They understood that. We take care of our own, or try to, when we can. But the administrative judge didn't see it that way. He found out and wanted my resignation.'

Stunned, Gail couldn't decide if what he had done was noble or reprehensible. He had saved Renee, but at the cost of his career.

Ben sat back down and patted the dog's neck. 'I have no regrets, except that it didn't do any good. Renee fell back into her old ways soon enough.' He glanced at her. 'I'll tell you one more thing, though maybe I shouldn't. She was expecting a child when she killed herself. I think that's why she did it.'

'I know,' Gail said. 'I read the ME's report.'

'I called him up. Wanted to know what happened to her. Figured she was full of drugs or something, but no. Another surprise. I didn't tell Irene.'

'I did.'

He tossed a stray twig into the yard. 'You shouldn't have.'

'I think it was Carlos Pedrosa's. I'm pretty sure they were involved.'

'That son of a bitch.' Ben looked at her sharply. 'Now you see how dumb it is, having Quintana for your lawyer? A blood relative of the man sleeping with your sister?'

'Carlos and Anthony aren't exactly on the best of terms.'

'Oh, come on. Say Carlos caught her with somebody else and killed her. Latinos are hot-blooded like that. And say Quintana knows he did it. You think he's going to turn him in? Family? Not likely, not if he has you on the hook. Maybe he's using you to find out what kind of a case they have.'

'That is so farfetched.'

'Okay, let's see how smart you are. Did you go to him or did he approach you?' He must have read the answer in her eyes. 'Case closed.'

She sat down heavily on the porch. 'Nothing makes sense to me today.'

'Only today?' Laughing, Ben let his gaze drift across the weedy yard to the trees beyond. 'I feel like that all the time. All the damn time. It's not us, honey. It's this place.'

He looked back at Gail. 'You know, last week I took a drive up the state a bit. Said to myself maybe I could find a few acres. Arcadia, Zolfo Springs. It's so quiet up there. Green and quiet. You can still leave your doors unlocked. People go to church on Sundays. If we were smart, we'd all get the hell out. Damn county's full of crazies. Irene's afraid to drive around at night. I keep expecting to hear about you getting mugged or raped. Now look what's happened. Even the police are crazy. We haven't changed, everything else has gone nuts. This isn't Miami anymore. It's moving right out from under us. Twenty percent black, over half Spanish, more of them pouring in. We're a minority. A minority in our own country.'

'Ben, stop it. Don't be like that.'

'I'm so goddamn sick of having to mince my words. People get pissed off if you speak the bald truth. Why in hell bother anymore?'

Suddenly he pulled the dog off the porch by its collar. 'Get down. Go on, Barney. Scram.' He patted Gail's arm. 'You stand over there by your car.'

'Why?'

'Just do it.' He motioned her away, then stepped up on the porch, grabbed his shotgun, and lightly jumped back to the ground. 'And stick your fingers in your ears.'

By the time he braced the shotgun on his hip, aiming at the cabin, Gail was behind her car. He fired. The middle section on the wooden screen door shattered. He pumped the gun, the red plastic shell spinning out to one side. The next blast hit a window. Glass exploded into the house.

Her mouth open, Gail let her hands fall from her ears. The echo was still reverberating. The dog was howling behind her, circling.

Ben looked over his shoulder. 'Gail, come here. I can rack one more into the chamber. I'll let you do the other window. Pretend it's Frank Britton. But watch out for my dog feeder.'

He pumped the shotgun. Another shell flew out.

She screamed at him. 'Ben, what the hell are you doing?'

After a moment he crossed the yard and lay the gun on the porch. He stood with his back to her, looking at the ragged hole in his screen door.

Chapter Fifteen

Miriam waved the file in Gail's direction as she came in. 'The foreclosure case for one-thirty.'

Gail looked up from her desk. 'Thanks. Just throw it in my briefcase. That is the Yancey file, correct?' In her state of mind, Gail was double-checking everything.

Miriam held it up. 'And all the documents are inside. With copies.'

'Good girl.'

While Miriam unloaded more files on the desk, Gail noticed the chicken salad sandwich still sitting in its deli paper on her appointment book. She had eaten a quarter of it and that had tasted like cardboard. Nerves, she supposed. Breakfast had been no better. Wrapping up the sandwich, she aimed it at her trash can and returned to the notes she had been reviewing.

There were twenty-three pages of neat, handwritten notes on paper from a yellow legal pad, accumulated over the past three days for Anthony Quintana. He had told her on Saturday what he needed to know. She had not written in one continuous stream, but had divided her thoughts into sections and subsections on separate pages. Her background – educational, personal, and so on. Dave. Karen. Family history and financial matters. Conversations with Frank Britton. The night of Irene's party. Details about Renee – as far as she knew them.

Gail had not numbered the pages, aware as she came to the end of each section, laying them out on her desk or kitchen table, that they might be shuffled or rearranged. She had tried to write only facts and dates and times, but it wasn't easy. If she wrote about Britton's showing her the cards Dave had sent to Renee, she would have to explain why Dave had sent them. That would require her to admit the failures of their marriage. Gail could not write that she and Renee had argued the night of Irene's party without revealing her own resentments. As the stacks of pages grew, she saw herself more clearly, with faults she hadn't known were there. Gritting her teeth, she had kept writing.

She had set an appointment with Anthony Quintana for five o'clock this afternoon, which now she couldn't keep. Larry Black had just dragooned her into covering a deposition in Fort Lauderdale. Perhaps she would put the notes for Anthony in an envelope and drop them off at Ferrer & Quintana on her way home tonight. But first, she had a question of her own: Why hadn't he told her he had represented Renee?

'Miriam?' Gail adjusted her straw to reach the last of her iced tea. 'When you finish, would you see if you can get Anthony Quintana on the phone? And make sure I'm not disturbed while we're talking.'

'I'm almost done.' Miriam opened a file and unfolded the metal clasp, poking the prongs through the holes in a letter. 'You know, if I ever can go back to school,' she said, 'I would love to be an attorney.'

'You would, huh?' Gail turned another page.

'Yes. It is so exciting.'

'Well, you've got the brains, Miriam, but – Let me see your teeth.'

Miriam laughed. 'Why?'

'You can't get into law school unless they're filed into points.'

A light flashed on Gail's telephone, an outside call coming through the switchboard. Miriam reached for it before Gail could turn in her chair. 'Ms Connor's office . . . One moment, please, I'll see if she's available.' She pressed the hold button. 'It's Jimmy Panther.'

Gail held out her hand. She had put him off too long. Miriam left with three files and a microcassette full of instructions.

'Jimmy, this is Gail Connor. I know you must be calling about the deer mask.'

'Right. It's been . . . what, over three weeks since you found it? If you're too tied up to bring it out here, I could come to your house.' The voice was polite, as usual, but this time it held an undercurrent of annoyance.

Gail said, 'At the moment, I don't have it. Saturday before last I took the mask to the Historical Museum and let Edith Newell look at it. You know Edith, I believe.'

'Yeah.'

'She thought it might be genuine Tequesta. I let her send the mask to a friend of hers at the University of Florida, an archaeologist. He's going to give an opinion.'

'You sent it to Gainesville? This is my property you're talking about.'

Gail rolled a pencil on her desk, its edges clicking. No reason to tell him everything. 'Let me explain. I found it in Renee's condo. As the executor of her estate I have a duty. This isn't meant to be personal, Mr Panther, but for all I know the mask could be a valuable artifact from a museum. How can I be sure who it belongs to?'

Behind the silence over the phone, Gail heard people talking. A cash register. A door opened, closed. He was probably calling from the gift shop on the Trail.

Then Jimmy Panther said, 'If that mask is Tequesta, I'm as surprised as you are. My grandmother – her name was Annie Osceola – told me she made it. She kept it in a heavy wood box under her bed, wouldn't let anybody touch it. She said when the time came she would tell me the legend of the mask.' He paused. 'Not many people know this,' he said, 'but Annie Osceola was a descendant of the Tequestas.'

'Is that so?' Gail said. 'I thought they died out.'

'They did – except for a few who went to Cuba.'

'Cuba?'

He didn't elaborate. 'Where is the mask now? Still in Gainesville?'

'I could find out.'

'If it's broken,' he said, 'I would be very upset. Very.'

After some grumbling, Jimmy Panther agreed that Gail could call him back later in the week. Gail hung up and pressed the intercom.

'*Sí, señora*,' Miriam said, her voice sliding up and down the scale.

'Miriam, do me a favor. Call Edith Newell over at the Historical Museum and see if she's heard from her friend in Gainesville. She'll know what you mean.'

Gail went back to the notes on her desk, flipping through till she found the page about Jimmy Panther and the mask. So now the Tequestas had migrated to Cuba. Well, well. When Jimmy's white grandfather was running rum for Al Capone to and from Havana, he may have met Annie Osceola. Fascinating. Maybe she had been a dancer at the Tropicana. Maybe Anthony Quintana was a distant cousin of Jimmy Panther's. Gail started to write.

When her telephone buzzed she automatically picked it up.

'Mr Quintana on line one,' Miriam said. 'And the lady at the museum says she got it this morning. Whatever it is, she has it.'

'Thanks.' Gail glanced up to make sure her door

was closed before pressing the button. 'Anthony, this is Gail. I'm glad you're in.'

'Has something happened?'

Gail slowed down, realizing she must have sounded out of breath. 'No, Sergeant Britton hasn't jumped out of the bushes yet. Do you have a minute?'

'Of course.'

With thumb and forefinger she ruffled the bottom edges of the twenty-three pages of notes. 'Over the weekend I talked to my cousin Ben Strickland. Your name came up, naturally. He told me you were Renee's attorney on a drug case last year.'

'Ah. This is true. And you would like to know why I didn't tell you. At the time – last Friday night – I believed you had enough to think about. I would have brought it up eventually.' When Gail did not reply, he said, 'I knew Renee through the title company. She was my client for only a week, then the case was nolle prossed.' He paused. 'Judge Strickland must have told you the State Attorney's Office dropped it.'

'Yes, he told me.' Gail wondered if Anthony knew what part Ben had played in this. She asked something else. 'Do you know if Renee was guilty?' Before she finished the question she could visualize him smiling at it.

He said, 'Guilty of what? Of trafficking in cocaine? No, I don't think so. Of knowing it was on the boat? Yes. She said she knew. That's not a crime. I would tell you more about it now, but I'm on my way out. We'll talk this afternoon.'

'I can't make it,' Gail said. 'I'm getting sent to cover a deposition. If you have a mail slot I can leave my notes at your office. There's no rush, is there?'

She heard a door open, heard his secretary ask a question. Anthony told her to wait a minute. Then he said to Gail, 'I've heard nothing new about the

257

investigation. Call me later at home, would you do that? We should discuss what is likely to happen next.'

After hanging up, Gail returned to her notes, putting her personal history into reverse chronological order. Less personal that way.

Miriam knocked and opened the door far enough to lean inside. 'Gail? While you were on the phone, you got a couple of calls. One, Carlos Pedrosa was asking about the option again, whether you got it back from Judge Strickland. I told him no, not yet.'

Gail nodded, paper-clipping pages together. 'Who else?'

'Frank Britton of Metro-Dade.'

She looked up.

'He said you could come by headquarters and collect your sister's papers. I have the address if you need it, out west of the Palmetto Expressway.'

'Did he say anything else?'

'No. Just that. And to call if you have any questions.' Miriam closed the door again.

Gail drew in a deep breath. Surely this couldn't be a ploy to get her there, to snap the handcuffs on. If he wanted her, he knew where to find her. Another thought occurred: if he was giving the papers back, he might be giving up the investigation. Ben needed the papers for the estate, but she couldn't possibly go pick them up herself. But if she didn't, what would Britton think? Then again, Anthony had told her not to care what Britton thought.

She spun in her chair, reached for the phone, dialed.

Anthony had already left.

At one-twenty Gail walked quietly into the courtroom on the tenth floor of the Dade County Courthouse. The session had started at one o'clock, Judge Henry Cooper's afternoon list of all matters short of a trial.

Her case was set for one-thirty.

She took a seat along the aisle toward the back. Other attorneys sat here and there in the six rows of wooden benches. The long seats faced front, like pews in a chapel, separated from court personnel by a low partition. A jury box was tucked into a corner to the left of the judge's elevated desk.

Henry Cooper was new to the court, a mid-thirties black man with a luxuriant mustache. He wore his judicial robe even in the halls, either to compensate for his youth or to hide his running shoes. They still flashed beneath the flowing robe as he walked.

In the breaks between cases, the attorneys whispered to each other. There would be no attorney on the other side of Gail's foreclosure case. The defendants – Simon and Rita Yancey – had never filed an answer to the complaint or obtained counsel, and it was too late now. Absent compelling reasons, no decent attorney would take a case after default was entered. Like going to a doctor to cure rigor mortis. Some attorneys would do it, of course, delaying the case by any means, filing bankruptcy or all manner of spurious motions. They would advise their clients: Live in the house a few extra months for free. Cheaper than rent.

Sometimes the defendants would show up on their own. Gail scanned the people in the room, not seeing anyone who looked like a husband and wife. Then, across the aisle, on the second bench, she noticed a man in a suit that pulled across the shoulders. He was twisting his neck as if his collar were too tight. Light brown hair, a bald spot. She would bet money this was Simon Yancey.

He was holding a large manila envelope on his lap, which probably contained all the documents connected to the house. Deed and mortgage, warranties for the appliances, insurance, title policy. Maybe even photos.

The Yanceys lived in Miami Springs, near the airport. Aside from their credit history, Gail knew nothing about the Yanceys except what she had gleaned from a copy of a letter in her file, the original sent to the judge last week. Single-space typing, cramped margins, an indignant tone.

'Dear Judge Henry Cooper, This to officially protest what is being done to me and my family. They are trying to put us out of our home. We got behind but since then we have sent the payments but they keep sending them back to us . . .'

The clerk called the next case. An attorney Gail had met at a bar meeting maneuvered past her. They smiled politely at each other as Gail shifted her knees to one side. She watched the man push open the low swinging door, announce his presence to the court. She wondered if he would have smiled at her if she were out on bail on a murder charge.

Before she left the ranch on Saturday, Ben had told her not to worry about making bail. He would lend her the money, if it came to that. And then he had apologized for blasting out his screen door, making her swear not to tell Irene.

That night Gail had told Irene about Frank Britton. Irene had burst into tears, raged at the police, and finally blamed herself for causing all this trouble. She had never done what Gail had feared – hesitate. Not for an instant, before flinging her arms around Gail's neck.

It made no sense to burden Karen with this, on the heels of her father moving out. Irene had come over a few times when Gail was late getting home. She had fixed dinner. They had talked. They had even talked about Renee. Gail could see how the three of them – herself, her mother, and her daughter – had become closer. Terrible that it had to happen this way.

Gail noticed the balding man in the ill-fitting coat shift in his seat. He was looking around the courtroom, studying the faces of the female attorneys. Besides Gail, there were two others, one arguing a case and the other in whispered conversation with someone in the back. He spotted Gail.

Large eyes, whites showing beneath the iris. Heavy jaw, a thin mouth. Younger than she had expected, probably under thirty. He looked at her blankly for a few seconds, then turned back toward the front. Apparently Mrs Yancey couldn't get off work.

These were the kind of people Renee had dealt with at Vista Title Company. Normal people, buying houses. It wasn't likely, but maybe Renee had done their closing. Renee would have known more than their credit report. If Renee had been sitting here beside Gail she might have whispered, *Simon was a baggage handler for Pan Am, until it went under. Now he works as an air-conditioning mechanic, off and on. Rita is the cafeteria manager at Springs High School. They have a Harley and ride with the motorcycle club on weekends.*

Renee's miniskirt would have crept up her thigh. Legs crossed, swinging her foot. The warmth of her shoulder against Gail's arm. And her perfume – Shalimar.

She would have laughed softly, pulling Gail closer. *Simon's not wearing his earring today. A diamond Rita gave him when they were in high school. They have two boys, really cute. Tommy has a learning disability, but he's smart if you really listen to him. Joey's an angel, he climbed right up in my lap at the closing.* Gail remembered what Jimmy Panther had said in her office. Renee was good with the kids at the Historical Museum.

If Renee were wearing Gail's tailored skirt and jacket, if she had her name on Gail's bar card, she would have told the man at Atlantic Financial Services to let the poor guy catch up on his mortgage, for God's sake. *Don't be such a putz.*

Renee might have had a storefront office near the tomato fields in Homestead – speaking Spanish would help. She would have brought a bottle of Irish whiskey to Father Eamon Donnelly. She would have defended illegal immigrants against the INS, would have gone to their parties, would have danced the *merengue* or the *cumbia* on Saturday night, and slept with one or two of them, maybe even at the same time. Would have piled them – men, women and children – into her red sports car with the top down and gone cruising to Key Largo, radio blaring.

Renee would have known the details of a stranger's life; Gail didn't even know the details of Renee's.

Father Donnelly had held his fraying prayer book in his hands. *In the end, we are all forgiven.*

Gail gradually became aware that the court clerk had called the case twice. 'Is someone here from Atlantic Financial?'

She picked up her briefcase, walked down the aisle, and pushed through the swinging door. Simon Yancey was already in front. The clerk handed the file to the judge and sat back down. The clerk was a middle-aged woman with a sweater thrown over her shoulders.

Gail opened her own file on the counsel table to her left. 'Your honor, I'm Gail Connor of Hartwell Black and Robineau, for the plaintiff. This is a motion for final judgment of foreclosure in *Atlantic Financial Services v. Yancey.*'

The judge looked up from the file. 'Mr Yancey?'

'Yes, sir.' Yancey set his folder on the other table, pulled out some papers. 'I realize that we're behind on the mortgage, your honor. We owe about three thousand dollars, but we can bring it up to date.'

'Let the plaintiff's attorney speak first, all right?

262

Then you can have your turn. That's how we do it.'
Judge Cooper went back to reviewing the file.

'Okay.' Yancey held the papers in one hand and
cracked the knuckles of the other with his thumb.

Gail gave the affidavits to the clerk, who passed
them up to the judge. A neat stack of documents. She
explained each one. When she was finished, the judge
nodded toward Yancey.

He took a couple steps forward. 'I called this lady
three or four times and she never called me back. She
had her secretary talk to me. Her secretary said if I
didn't pay the money they were going to put me out. I
told her I can bring the payments up to date. I got laid
off last summer but my wife and me are both working
now.'

Yancey glanced down at his papers, gave one to
Gail, another to the clerk, who handed it to the judge.
'I've taken the liberty of making up a payment schedule.
It shows if we pay an extra two seventy-six fifty a
month we'll be back on track by the end of the year.'

The judge looked at Gail. 'What can you do for
these folks?'

Gail had already discussed the case with someone at
Atlantic, the sound of a keyboard tapping as they talked.
He had pulled up the account on a computer screen
and told Gail that the company didn't want to fool
around with the Yanceys anymore.

Feeling rotten, she didn't look at Yancey. 'My client
is not willing to allow reinstatement, judge. The
defendants have been consistently delinquent and this
is the second time a foreclosure action has been filed
against them. A default has already been entered.'

'Yeah, but I'm working now. We can pay it.'

'Mr Yancey—' Judge Cooper seemed sorry he had
to say this. 'After default the plaintiff has a right to
proceed with foreclosure if it so chooses.'

263

'But I called her.' The judge was shaking his head. 'I've got a wife and two kids at home. Is that fair? Where are we going to live? I thought America was supposed to be a free country. What kind of freedom is it—'

'Did you receive a copy of the summons and complaint, sir?'

'What kind of freedom is it when a man is put out of his own home?'

'Sir—' The judge waited until Yancey was quiet. He tapped a page in the file. 'Sir, you were served with a copy of the complaint and there is no timely response from you in the file. It says right here on the summons that if you fail to respond in twenty days, judgment may be entered against you.'

Yancey's voice was shaking with tension. 'I know what this lady wants. She wants to stick me with a thousand dollars in attorney's fees. For what? And five hundred bucks in costs. She ought to be investigated.'

The court clerk sympathetically rolled her eyes at Gail. Another nut. What can you do?

Judge Cooper reached for his pen. 'I understand how you feel, Mr Yancey; but the plain fact of the matter is, you have to pay attention to legal documents. You ignore them at your peril. Now you have twenty days to redeem the property, or it will be sold at public auction. I'm sorry, but that's the law.' Judge Cooper lifted papers until he found the order of foreclosure.

Yancey turned around, breathing sharply. He kicked the chair at the end of the counsel table nearer him. It spun, tipped, and thudded to the floor. Yancey's eyes narrowed into slits. He headed toward Gail, his voice trembling.

'Bitch. You better watch yourself, you cunt.'

264

Gail stumbled backward. The judge leaped out of his chair, poised as if he might vault over his desk. He yelled, 'Bailiff!'

Yancey grabbed his papers off the table, pushed past the swinging door and up the aisle. The door clattered on its hinges. Two attorneys by the courtroom entrance moved out of his way.

After a few seconds, Judge Cooper sat back down, smoothing his mustache. 'I wouldn't worry about it, Ms Connor. People get upset. They calm down.'

Gail dropped her hand from her heart. 'Any other line of work wouldn't be half as exciting.'

There was nervous laughter among the other attorneys in the courtroom.

The bailiff appeared at the door. 'Judge? Everything okay?' The court clerk put the overturned chair back beside the table.

Judge Cooper picked up his pen. 'Please make sure Ms Connor isn't disturbed on her way out of the courtroom.' He finished signing the order.

Gail found Edith Newell in the reading room of the museum, yellowed newspaper clippings spread out around her at one of the long tables. Edith looked up, her gray eyes huge behind her glasses.

'Hello, dear. My, you look exhausted. Sit down here, just move that stuff over a bit. I'm finding out oodles of things about Dan Hardie. Our Prohibition sheriff, don't you know?' She smiled. 'Well, never mind that. You came for another reason, didn't you?'

Except for the two of them, the reading room was deserted, the air chilly and dry, suited to old books and crumbling papers. Gail shivered. 'Is the professor sure it's genuine?'

'Oh my, yes. No doubt at all. Tequesta, about twenty-five hundred years old.' Edith laughed. 'He begged me for it. Begged me. But he was a good boy, sent it right back, not a scratch.'

'And no idea where it came from?'

'No, I'm sorry to say.' Edith pushed her sweater sleeve up her arm. Its cuff was loose, the fuzz turned to little balls. 'You didn't get any information out of Jimmy Panther?'

'He says his grandmother kept it in a wooden box under her bed. A family heirloom, was the impression I got.'

Edith hooted. 'For two thousand years?'

'Her name was Annie Osceola,' Gail said. 'Does that sound familiar?'

'Well, not precisely, but Osceola is a common name among both the Seminoles and Miccosukees.'

'He also said the Tequestas migrated to Cuba.'

'Yes.'

'*Yes?*'

'Some of them. They went with the Spanish. About 1720. We could look it up, you want to?'

Gail studied the rows of shelves. 'I wish I had the afternoon free. Edith, do you think one of the volunteers would like to earn a little extra money?'

'Oh, don't ask them.' Edith began to stack the newspaper clippings. 'I'll do it for free, if you promise to give the museum a shot at that clay deer mask.'

'It isn't mine, Miss Newell.'

'Maybe not. But if we prove it isn't his, either—' She dropped the clippings into a box and closed the lid. 'There's something fishy going on, don't think there isn't. What do you want me to find out?'

Gail squeezed Edith's hand, then took a legal pad out of her briefcase. 'Anything on Jimmy Panther. Check the public records. Birth certificate, school records, military, employment . . .' Gail's pen flew over the paper. 'And general information on the Miccosukees

266

and Tequestas would be helpful.' She looked at Edith. 'Did you ever see him with Renee, when she worked here?'

'Oh, yes.' Edith thought for a minute. 'They were quite friendly.' She caught Gail's expression. 'Not like that, dear. You know. *Friends*. The way men and women used to be friends, before sex got so prevalent. Although I can't imagine what they saw in each other.' She smiled. 'Nothing against Renee, of course. She was a charming girl, in her way.'

Gail sat quietly for a moment. 'When did Renee begin working at the museum?'

'Well, Renee was hired about a year and a half ago, I believe. Part-time.' Edith lowered her voice, although there was still no one else in the room. 'It doesn't matter if I tell you this now. Your mother made a contribution to cover her wages. Renee was having problems finding a job, apparently. At first she was utterly unreliable. I had to speak to her. I said, Renee, this will not do. She began to come around.' Edith was silent for a moment, her eyes on the ceiling. 'Starting early last year – February, March – Renee worked part-time here at the museum and part-time for some kind of insurance company.'

'Vista Title Insurance,' Gail said.

'Yes. By last fall, I believe, she was working full-time for them, although she would still come see us now and then.'

'When was Jimmy Panther hired?'

'He was never an employee. Jimmy only came in to use the reading room. He would do a lecture whenever he wanted to. He became quite a hit. Upped our contributions considerably. One has to give him credit for that.'

'So they met about eighteen months ago?'

'More like a year ago, perhaps less.' Edith nodded

toward the next table. 'It was right over there. Renee and I were indexing catalogs and in he walked, with his beads and long black hair over his shoulders. He looked straight at Renee. Oh, the expression on her face. She whispered, 'Edith, look at that Indian coming in the door.' Well, he walked right over and I introduced them. I'd met him at a Miccosukee festival, so I knew who he was.'

Through the glass door Gail could see the lobby and the stairs leading to the second floor. 'You said he came to the museum to use the reading room. Do you know what for? I mean, if he wanted to sit and read he could use the library across the plaza.'

Edith gave a wide smile. She had teeth too perfect to be anything but purchased. 'Aren't you clever. Let me think.' She turned around in her chair. 'Jimmy would use the card catalog, then he'd go to the shelves and get whatever it was. Then he'd sit down at the last table. He had a zippered briefcase, I remember that now, with a notebook in it.'

'Was he reading about Indian artifacts? Tequesta history?'

Tiny lines appeared around Edith's mouth as she pursed her lips. 'I don't know. He sat with his back to the wall and wouldn't say a word about it. If he went to the men's room he'd reshelve the books and take all his papers with him.' She lightly touched Gail's wrist. 'And sometimes Renee would sit with him, but that was more recently.'

'More recently when?'

'A few months ago? After the first of the year?'

The last table was bare, three chairs on either side, neatly aligned. Gail got up, looked at the chair where Jimmy Panther had probably sat. 'He never checked anything out?'

'Oh, no. We don't allow that.'

'But they do at the library,' Gail said.

'Indeed,' Edith said. 'And the records are on computer. I have a friend over there. Shall we ask her to look him up?'

Gail nodded. 'Let's say running back at least a year.'

'Maybe some of the staff at the museum know what he was working on.'

'Try not to be obvious.'

'Oooh, isn't this fun?' Edith unfolded her long legs from under the table and picked up Gail's legal pad, tearing off the list of things to do. She hesitated. 'What are we looking for?'

Gail shrugged, smiling a little. 'I suppose we'll know when we find it.'

Chapter Sixteen

It was nearly six o'clock when Gail pulled into the parking lot at Metro-Dade Police Headquarters. The ultramodern building, curves and glass and bright color, sat on several acres of landscaped lawns. Keys in her hand, and caught between dread and curiosity, she stared through the windshield of her car. If Frank Britton had any evidence to arrest her, he would have done it already.

In the lobby she told the duty officer – a woman in a tan uniform – why she had come: to pick up papers belonging to Renee Connor. The woman looked over her shoulder at another officer writing on a clipboard. A row of black-and-white TV monitors flickered behind him. She asked, 'Britton. That's Homicide, right?' He nodded.

Gail said, 'When I called, he told me he might be working late. If not, he said I could pick them up from anyone.'

'Okay, let's see.' The woman dialed a number on the phone. 'You can sit down if you want to.'

She didn't, only wandered from the reception counter to the middle of the lobby. Glass walls on either side, a profusion of philodendrons hanging from second-floor planters. Along the wall, trophies from the last Pig Bowl. A memorial to policemen killed in the line of duty T-shirts for sale. Say No to Drugs. The place was as upbeat as a high school guidance office.

Gail rubbed the taut muscles in the back of her neck. Her head ached deep behind her eye sockets. Irene had said she would pick Karen up from dance class and make dinner, not to worry. Gail would go home – assuming they didn't drag her off in leg irons – as soon as she pushed her notes through the slot at Ferrer & Quintana.

'Ms Connor!' Britton had come through a side door, tie loosened, ID badge clipped to his shirt pocket. He smiled at her, shook her hand. 'Nice to see you.' He lightly rapped on the counter. 'Betty, give me a second floor badge.'

Gail said, 'You want me to go upstairs with you?' She could see a long, carpeted hallway through the glass.

'Sure, I'll give you the twenty-five-cent tour.'

'Thanks, but I have to get home. My daughter's waiting for me.'

'Some other time, then. Come on up and get the papers.' He handed Gail the plastic-coated badge. She clipped it to her lapel. 'You ever bring your little girl to an open house?' They went down the hall, around a partition of glass bricks, then to the elevator. 'Kids like the weapons collection. We've got everything from an anti-tank gun to a pistol made to look like a ballpoint pen, all seized right here in Dade County.'

As Britton described the technological wonders of the toxicology lab, Gail wondered if Anthony Quintana had heard correctly from his friend at the State Attorney's Office. A suspect didn't mean a prosecutable case. Or maybe Ben had worked some magic with the State Attorney since Saturday.

Britton finally led her through a door marked Homicide Bureau, then past gray upholstered dividers. She heard laughter over one of them, someone telling a joke. A man walked past wearing a black T-shirt. On the front: *Metro-Dade Homicide*. On the back, a skull and the words: *When your day ends, ours begins*.

Britton stopped to speak to a young woman behind a desk. 'Hey, hon. Where'd the Connor file go?'

She barely glanced up from the computer screen. 'Still in room two, unless somebody moved it.'

When Britton closed the door, background noises disappeared. Gail looked around. It was a small room, perhaps eight by eight. Off-white walls. Light gray table, molded chairs on tubular chrome legs. A fat accordion file lay on its side on the table.

Britton unwound the cord that held it shut. 'Have a seat for a minute. I want to make sure it's all here.' He sat in one of the chairs. After a few seconds, Gail took the other.

She said, 'What's this, an interrogation room?'

'It's where we bring anybody when we need a quiet place to talk. I ought to put in a couch and a TV.' He walked his fingers through the folders inside the file. 'I haven't spoken to your mother in a while. Next time you see her, give her my regards.'

Gail put her purse on the table and crossed her arms.

Britton said, 'Are you okay? You look a little tense.'

'I'm fine.'

'I could get you some coffee. A cup of tea?'

She gave him a smile. 'No, thanks.'

He went back to the file. 'How long have you been a lawyer?'

'Seven years.'

'I went to law school, lasted a whole semester.' He smiled at her, pulled a folder out, pushed the accordion file to one side. 'I'm sorry all this happened to you, Ms Connor. I spoke to your husband at the marina not long ago. I gather you two have split up.'

Gail nodded. 'It's an amicable separation.'

'Well, that's good.' Britton lay his hands flat on the folder. 'I'm going to show you a letter. We didn't find this among your sister's papers. We got it from Barnett Bank last week. But before I talk about that, let me tell you what I think happened to Renee.

'We found her at Ibis Park about ten-thirty in the morning, Monday, March 8. She had been floating in a foot of water off the end of the nature walk since about midnight Saturday night, give or take. Her wrists had been cut. She bled out before she hit the water. We didn't find any traces of fabric in her lungs or nose to indicate suffocation. We also didn't find any bruises on her neck to show she'd been choked unconscious, but light bruises could have disappeared, given the length of time she was in the water and the damage done by the animals out there. They go after soft tissue. A test of the vitreous humor – the fluid in her eyeball – showed an alcohol content of point one-six. Alcohol in vitreous humor doesn't dissipate after death. Before she died, Renee was drunk enough to have passed out, given her size. If that's what happened, she wouldn't have felt a thing.

'We went back and found marks on the nature walk that match scuff marks on her Reeboks. She was a little woman, five-one, a hundred and five pounds. It wouldn't have been hard to put her in the car unconscious, drive her to the park, then get her to the end of the nature walk. We didn't find any fingerprints on the door handles, steering wheel, gearshift, or rearview mirror. None, not even hers. Somebody wiped off the prints, locked her purse in her car, walked to the main road, hitchhiked back to town.

'We found the razor blade about eight feet away in the water. We found a pack of the same kind of razor blades in her kitchen drawer, two missing. Whoever did this had been in her house. And that person knew she had attempted suicide with a razor blade once before.'

The room seemed to shift, grow smaller. Britton continued to speak, that soft cracker drawl, his blue eyes showing a kind of regret behind the glasses.

'Ms Connor, what I've found – and I've been in homicide about as long as you've been a lawyer, if that means anything – I've found that most people don't mean this to happen. They get mad, they lose their temper, then they're afraid to admit it. But it's a human weakness. We all have a dark side, I really believe that. Push anybody too far and it comes out.'

His eyes were fixed on her – gentle, concerned. 'Dave and Renee were pretty close. He gave her money. He sent her cards. And she was pregnant. Could have been his baby. If they weren't having an affair, it sure looked that way, didn't it? And your mother was giving her money, too. Mrs Connor told me about that, said you didn't like it.'

Gail pulled herself to her feet as if her body were weighted, catching her heel on the leg of the chair, stumbling. 'I would like to have my sister's papers, Sergeant. And then I would like to leave.'

He remained seated. 'You're not a bad person, Gail. You had a little too much on your mind. Money problems, marriage problems. You thought about Renee's trust fund. Dave's business was in trouble, the money would help.'

'I didn't even know about that until after she was dead! I didn't kill her. How could you think that?' Gail grabbed her purse off the table and turned the doorknob. The door was locked. She whirled around. 'Let me out.'

Britton stood up. 'Gail, I wish to hell I could stick this on somebody else, but I can't. We thought of Dave because he took her home, but he went to a bar

275

afterwards. We found his charge card records. Everybody who could possibly have had a reason to kill Renee can explain where they were. Can you?'

'Open this door.'

He picked up the file, came around the table. 'Renee's neighbor saw your car in her driveway about eleven. You went by to see if your husband was with her. I can understand that.'

'I didn't go in!'

'We found your fingerprints on the kitchen counter over the drawer we took the razor blades out of.'

'You never took my fingerprints.'

'They're on file with your bar application, Gail.'

'This is bullshit! The only time I was in her apartment was to get a dress for her to wear in her casket. I told you that!'

'Yes, but you also told me you went straight upstairs. And a couple other odd things. Your mother was going to handle the estate, but you talked her into letting you take over. When she wanted us to investigate Renee's death, you asked Ben Strickland, the former judge, to get us to leave it alone.'

'That's a lie.'

Britton waited, then said, 'Gail? It's better if we get this straightened out now. You've got a daughter. A good job. What if we have to come pick you up at work, all those people around, do you want that to happen?'

Gail spoke through a wave of dizziness. 'I'm not going to talk to you.'

'Why not?' he asked softly. 'There's nothing wrong with the truth, is there? Don't make it worse on yourself.'

'My attorney told me not to talk to the police.'

He shifted the file in his arms, frowning a little. 'An attorney already? That's kind of a surprise.'

'His name is Anthony Quintana.'

Britton nodded. 'I know him. You've got yourself mighty high-powered counsel for someone who says she didn't do anything.'

'Open this door or I will sue you for false imprisonment.'

He looked at her for a long moment, then held out the file. 'You want to take this with you? I'm keeping the cards from Dave. Plus her financial records and a few other things, but we've made you copies.'

Gail hugged the heavy file to her chest.

Britton turned the knob with one hand, pressing a button underneath with the other. Then he glanced back at the table. 'I almost forgot. There's a letter you ought to have.' He went back to pull it out of the folder, then held it so she could see it.

'This is a copy of the letter Barnett Bank sent you on your thirtieth birthday. Says here they enclosed a check for $200,000 and a copy of the trust papers.' Britton folded the letter into thirds, lifted the flap on the file she held, slid the letter inside. He said quietly, 'Gail, you said you didn't know about the money. You've known for over three years. But I'd rather believe this happened because you argued with her and got mad. Tell me that's how it was.'

Britton was standing closer now and she could feel the warmth in his hand when he laid it on her shoulder. 'Gail, tell me this wasn't premeditated. I wouldn't want to see you up for first-degree murder. Come on, talk to me. Help me out.'

Gail was shaking so violently the flap on the file wobbled up and down. 'My attorney's name is Anthony Quintana. If you wish to discuss the case, call him. Now open this door.'

Half a mile down the street, Gail found a telephone outside an Exxon station. She dropped the quarter to the pavement twice before she got it into the slot. She pressed the buttons. Her fingers were colder than the metal.

'*Esta es la oficina de Ferrer y Quintana. Deje su mensaje al sonido*—' She hung up, found another quarter, turned the card over.

It rang six times before he answered.

'Anthony? This is Gail.' She waited until a diesel truck roared away from the pumps. She cleared her throat. 'Would it be convenient for me to bring my notes by your house instead of your office? I need to talk to you as soon as possible.'

He sounded far away. 'Is there a problem?'

She watched the traffic on the road. 'Yes. You could say that.'

Chapter Seventeen

Anthony Quintana's townhouse on Key Biscayne was one in a U-shaped arrangement of them, half-hidden behind banyan trees, the driveway stopping at a seawall. Gail drove slowly, looking for the right number, squinting into the sun. The Miami skyline stretched out on the other side of the bay.

She parked in front of his garage, then got out, juggling a large manila envelope and the heavy accordion file with Renee's papers in it. Now she wished she had accepted his offer to come pick her up, to hell with being stoic. Her hands ached from clenching the steering wheel. She took a deep breath and locked her car.

The front door was set back in a tiled entranceway, an ironwork security door barring access. It was cracked open. She slipped through. Involuntarily looking around to see if she had been followed, Gail hurried to the front door and pressed the buzzer. Bahama shutters covered the windows.

After a few seconds, Anthony opened the door and pulled her inside. 'What have you done, Gail?'

If her arms had been empty, she might have thrown them around his neck in relief. She laughed instead. 'Don't tell me that you told me so. I know you told me, and I talked to him anyway. Just tell me I haven't screwed up too badly.'

He led her through the small foyer.

'Britton was good,' she said. 'I should be so good cross-examining opposing witnesses. He made me want to confess everything I ever did, including the time I stole a tube of Maybelline lipstick from the drugstore when I was eight years old.' She handed him the mailing envelope. 'Here. The notes you asked for.'

He frowned, looked inside, pulled them out. 'Ah. Yes.'

'And Renee's papers are in this file. I'll need them back.'

Gail set the accordion file and her purse on a long table behind the sofa. A dark green leather sofa, pouffy pillows. Her eyes traveled around the room: thick rugs on a polished tile floor; shelves crammed with books. French doors led to a terrace. Beyond the terrace, a narrow inlet, its surface bright with sunlight, boats on the other side.

Gail glanced back at Anthony. 'I thought you'd live in a penthouse with black lacquered furniture and a wet bar.'

He was watching her. 'What did you tell Britton?'

'Nothing directly.'

'What indirectly, then?'

'I confirmed that I went to Renee's house the night she died.'

'*Diós mio*,' he muttered. 'Even I did not know that. What were you doing at Renee's house?'

'Nothing. I was going to go in and apologize for yelling at her. I sat in my car for a while, then left.' Gail studied Anthony's tightly set expression. 'There's something else. My fingerprints.'

'What about them?'

'First I told Britton I'd never gone anywhere in her apartment but upstairs for a dress, then later I remembered I'd been in the kitchen, too. They found my fingerprints. She kept razor blades in one of the

280

drawers, and – God, this sounds so awful. Now he thinks I was lying.'

Still holding Gail's notes, Anthony folded his arms across his chest. 'What else did you say?'

'That I didn't know about the money in the trust until after Renee died. But he had a letter from the bank, showing they had mailed me a copy of the papers.'

'The two hundred thousand dollars you told me about?'

'Yes. Maybe the bank did send me a copy, but I swear to you I didn't notice the survivorship provision. At the time I was more interested in the check.' Gail pushed her curls off her forehead. Her hands were shaking. 'What do you think, counselor? Have I shot myself in the foot?'

Anthony held up the envelope. 'What you will do is write down everything you remember about your conversation with Frank Britton, while I read this.'

She nodded. 'I'll need some paper. Anthony, do you have any aspirin? My head feels like someone is clomping around inside in golf shoes.'

'Have you eaten?'

'No.'

'I was about to make dinner when you called. There's enough for both of us. Come.' He walked through a small dining area toward his kitchen, separated by a wide counter. Gail followed, aware that this was the first time she had seen him out of a suit. He wore a loosely fitting silk shirt the color of plums and pale linen slacks, smooth across the hips, pleated in front. She inhaled a subtle, woodsy fragrance. Scented soap, perhaps. His hair looked freshly washed, darker than its usual brown, comb marks still in it.

He sat her down on a high chair at the end of the counter. She sank gratefully into the soft upholstery. He tapped two capsules out of a plastic bottle into his hand, his gold bracelet glittering against the hair on his forearm. No rings. His fingers opened over her outstretched palm.

She said, 'Britton left a message at my office, come pick up your sister's papers. Sounded innocent enough. I said, well, if he asks me anything, just smile and mention your name. Easy right? But you don't know what it's like. He's so friendly. You start to think he's your pal. And then – Snap!'

'I told you so.'

'Thanks a lot.' Anthony filled a glass with bottled water from the refrigerator. She said, 'Britton never read me my rights. Whatever I said can't be used against me, can it?'

'You weren't under arrest. If you are not in custody they can use anything you say.'

'Can they lie to me?'

He set the glass on the counter next to her. 'Was he wearing a Boy Scout uniform?'

'*Damn* it.' Gail tossed the capsules into her mouth. She followed them with a deep gulp of water. 'You should have seen him. Sitting there so smugly.' She gave her voice an accent. 'You did it, Miz Connor, I know you did it! Now, did you *plan* to do it in advance or did Renee make you mad? Because if you only lost your temper, then maybe we can keep you out of the electric chair—' Gail leaned her head on her palms. 'Oh, God.'

She felt Anthony's hand close around her forearm, then pat it lightly. '*No te preocupes*. You'll be all right.' He poured her a glass of red wine.

She laughed. 'Do I look that strung out?'

He unwrapped a plate of cheese and handed her a knife and a box of crackers. He leaned on the counter opposite her. He may have showered, but he hadn't shaved, and stubble darkened his jaw and upper lip.

282

'I will tell you about a case Frank Britton was investigating. Three or four years ago a cruise ship executive was found dead in his hot tub. Four bullets in his chest. The wife said burglars had come in and stolen their jewelry, attacked her, and killed her husband. She had the bruises on her face to prove it. Britton believed her. A good woman, two kids, a member of a church. But Britton's lieutenant brought her in a second time. She confessed. Her husband had beaten her once too often and she shot him.'

'Good for her.' Gail laid a slice of cheddar across a cracker, gave it to Anthony, and made another for herself. 'So now Britton is leaning on me.'

'Tomorrow morning I'll call him and find out what he intends to do. He and I are on good terms.' Anthony chewed the cracker. 'But we'll talk about Britton after dinner.'

'He paid you a compliment today,' she said. 'He wondered why, if I were innocent, I had to hire such high-powered legal talent.'

Anthony smiled, lifting the lid on a copper pot. Steam rose and an aroma of something rich and meaty filled the kitchen.

Her nose quivered. 'I'm going to swoon. What is that?'

'Beef stroganoff,' he said, stirring with a fork. 'I can't take the credit. It's from a deli.'

'Who cares? My refrigerator's full of cold pizza and leftovers from my mother's house.'

He put the lid back on the skillet, turned off the heat, then emptied a bag of fresh pasta noodles into a pot of boiling water. 'Five minutes, then we eat. Do you like salad?'

'I'll eat whatever you put on the plate.' Gail dabbed at her lips with a napkin, the taste of sharp cheese still singing on her tongue. 'May I use your phone?'

He nodded toward the end of the counter. Gail stopped halfway. An unzipped black leather pouch lay next to his car keys. With her forefinger she lifted the open edge far enough to see inside. Dark gray metal, cross-hatched wooden grip. 'Your trusty forty-four?'

'No, a pistol. Nine-millimeter, semiautomatic. I keep it in my glove compartment. Or on the seat in certain parts of town.'

'I may be one of the last unarmed motorists in Miami,' she said, picking up the phone.

Anthony put the gun in a drawer.

She grinned at him. 'Afraid I'll use it when you tell me what your legal fees are?'

She dialed the number at her house, then watched Anthony set out plates and napkins while she told Irene she would be late. Pottery plates, green linen napkins. More wine. Irene told her not to worry, dinner was on the stove for Karen. Gail asked to speak to Karen, reminded her to do her homework. *Love you, sweetie. Mind Grandma.*

When she hung up Anthony was looking at her.

Gail eased the frown she knew was on her forehead. 'I haven't yet decided what to tell my daughter.'

'The truth.' Anthony nodded toward the patio. 'Open the doors. It's cool enough this evening, we'll eat outside.'

Taking her wine with her, Gail crossed the room to unlock the French doors. A ceiling fan hung under a blue striped awning that ran the width of the townhouse, privacy walls on either end, baskets of white and pink impatiens at the roofline. Sisal mats lay on the tile floor. A screen door opened onto steps, then a grassy lawn, then a concrete dock. The sun had nearly set, light slanting into the little harbor, the colors vivid, saturated with orange.

She walked to the railing and studied the stern of a

sailboat moored on the other side of the inlet. *Snookums* – Providence, RI. A barechested man on board was throwing a line to a woman on the dock. In the waning breeze the rigging made soft bell-like dings against the aluminum mast. Gail took a deep swallow of wine, its warmth finally thawing the chill of Britton's gray interrogation room.

When she came back inside, standing for a moment in the doorway, Anthony said, 'Look around if you wish. Master bedroom upstairs, my study down the hall. Not a large house, but room enough for my children when they visit.'

Gail had already noticed their eight-by-ten color photos on the bookcase. Luis and Angela, both of them with Anthony's dark hair and eyes. A smiling boy about twelve, a teenage girl in a white off-the-shoulder gown. Gail picked up her picture. The girl looked more like a woman.

She heard Anthony's voice from the kitchen. 'That's her *quinceañera* portrait, taken in December when I flew her down for the party.'

Gail knew that daughters of traditional Cuban families celebrated their fifteenth birthday as a special coming-of-age event. Rich or poor, every girl would have a party.

'You gave her a *quince?*'

'Is that surprising?'

'Well—' Gail put it back. 'I thought you were more . . . modern.'

'*Y menos cubano.*' Less Cuban.

She heard him laugh. She took off her jacket and laid it over the arm of the sofa, noticing the magazines on the square coffee table. *Time. The New Republic. Miami Mensual.* A novel – Gabriel García Márquez, *El Amor en Los Tiempos del Cólera*, a bookmark stuck in the middle. A stack of office files. Also on the table were several fat little birds carved from dark wood. She picked one up, put it down. She lifted the lid of a cigar box. The smell of tobacco mingled with the leather from the couch, distinctly masculine. She read the label. 'Naughty boy. Havana cigars. Does your grandfather know?'

Anthony smiled through the cloud of steam rising from the noodles. 'A present from a client. He smuggled them in on his boat from the Caymans.'

She glanced toward the inlet. 'What did he do, tie up to your dock?'

'Yes, to tell the truth, he did.'

She closed the lid of the cigar box, aware that everything in this room intrigued her. Each piece of furniture or item of decoration had a texture or smell to it. She wanted to touch each one, feel its weight, close her eyes and sniff.

His snakeskin briefcase lay across the seat of a soft upholstered armchair. She sat on the matching ottoman, pulled it onto her lap. 'You don't know what kind of snake this is?'

'The client or the briefcase?'

She looked around at him. 'Oh, one of those? I've had a few myself, the ones you'd like to send slithering back to the jungle.'

Anthony filled two glasses with ice. 'In this case, he did just that.'

She remembered. 'The bail jumper. What was he charged with, anyway?'

He poured water into both glasses before answering. 'You know the name Nelson Restrepo? A friend of Manuel Noriega. And the CIA. If Nelson is still alive, I would be surprised to hear it. He was one of ten defendants in a massive drug case a few years ago involving the Medellín cartel.'

'Isn't that when they had the federal building roped

286

off? I bet I saw you on the six o'clock news with this guy.'

'Probably. He was the one with his coat pulled up around his head. He was found not guilty. The feds screwed up what little evidence they had against him.' Anthony pulled a tray off the top of the refrigerator. 'I keep the briefcase as a reminder of why I don't do big drug cases anymore.'

She put it back on the chair. 'Well. I'm glad you've turned to murder. So to speak.'

When the food was ready she helped him carry it all outside. 'What's the procedure with criminal attorneys?' she asked, rolling out place mats on the table. 'Am I supposed to sign a contract? How much do you charge an hour, anyway?'

Anthony put down the plates. 'I don't charge on an hourly basis for this type of case. It's usually a flat fee.'

'Well, what's usual in Miami?'

'Generally for a first-degree murder defense the minimum is one hundred thousand dollars. Plus costs.'

'Oh.'

'If I decide to represent you.'

'Well. Why shouldn't you?' She laughed. 'I'll just write you a check. And another one to the bail bondsman.'

He pulled a chain on the ceiling fan. Its white blades began to turn. 'No. Don't expect bail. There is no automatic right to bail in first-degree murder. I – or whoever represents you – would have to convince the judge that you should be released. And I will be honest with you. It rarely happens. Twice that I have heard of.'

He held her chair and Gail sat down – calmly, because there was nothing else to do. 'I'd be in jail until the trial was over.'

'Yes.' Anthony sat opposite, his eyes not leaving her

face, as if weighing how well she was taking this. 'Eat your dinner.'

She picked up her fork. 'How long would I be in jail? I mean, if there's a trial?'

'Six months to a year.' He passed her a basket of rolls. 'Let me tell you the procedure. If the police decide that there is probable cause to arrest—'

'What do they do, send uniformed officers to take me away?'

'Shh. Listen, I'll tell you. Britton might seek a grand jury indictment first, but if he believes he has probable cause, he can arrest you without one. Then the indictment would follow. In either case, I would say to him, Frank, allow me the courtesy of surrendering Gail Connor to you. She is not going to flee. Her family is here; she has strong ties to the community. Let me bring her in. And I think he would allow it.'

Gail nodded. Her stomach felt queasy, but she forced herself to eat. 'And then what?'

'You appear before a magistrate within twenty-four hours. He would say, Counselor, this is a nonbondable offense, file the appropriate pleadings before the judge assigned to the case. I would do so, but it is highly unlikely, as I have told you, that bail would be granted.'

'Unlikely. But possible?' She noticed Anthony had not touched his food.

'Remotely possible.'

'And if it happened, how much is bail? Assuming.'

'Probably a million dollars.'

She put down her fork and looked past the railing on the porch to the sailboat across the inlet. The sun had set now, the colors fading to gray. 'How ironic. Renee died and left me all that money and I have to use it to prove I didn't kill her.' Gail glanced back at Anthony. 'Of course I can't collect if I'm not found innocent, can I? And that's really all I've got. My family would help. I

288

think I could manage your fee.'

'And costs. Say twenty for that. I would want to put an investigator on the case immediately.'

She nodded.

'You should talk to other attorneys.'

'Shop around for the best quote, you mean?' Gail went back to her salad. 'No. If Frank Britton thinks you're hot stuff, I trust his opinion.'

She felt Anthony's eyes on her and looked up. In the fading light, the purple silk seemed more a shadow than a garment.

He said, 'You understand that I must treat you like any other client.'

'Of course,' she said lightly. 'I am quite able to separate friendship from business. I have to do that in my own practice.'

He nodded. 'You mentioned that you and your husband separated. Have you filed for divorce?'

'No, not yet. We decided to work out a settlement first.' With her left thumb Gail involuntarily touched the place where her wedding ring had been. Her hand felt naked. 'Should we put everything off for now?'

'It would be best. Will he help if I ask him to testify?'

'I think he will.'

'Where is he living?'

'On a boat at our marina. He hasn't asked to come back.'

'You could ask him.'

Gail shook her head, took a bite of bread.

'Pride?'

She reached for her wine. 'I don't think so. Does it matter?'

'Forgive me for the personal questions,' he said. 'Your relationship with your husband may be important.'

'Well. Hmm. Why haven't I asked Dave to come back?'

'Perhaps because of his friendship with Renee.'

Gail shook her head, considering the lights coming on in the houses across the inlet. 'That doesn't bother me anymore.'

'Are you still in love with him?'

She smiled. 'Should I say so on the witness stand?'

'Gail. There is one thing you must do. Unequivocally.' Anthony's words were clipped, the Spanish accent coming through. 'When I ask you a question – here, now, or whenever we discuss this case – you must answer it.'

Her back straightened. 'Look. You don't have to pull that Latino male act with me, all right?'

He said nothing, but she saw his lips firm into a tighter line. Finally she looked away. 'I'm sorry. That was uncalled for.'

After a moment, Anthony returned to his dinner. 'The prosecution will be looking for motive. Love – obsessive love. Jealousy.'

'I was never . . . obsessed with Dave.' She pushed her hair behind her ear. 'All right, you want to know the truth? Dave's a responsible guy at heart, very conscious of what ought to be done. I probably haven't asked him to come back because I'm afraid he would.'

Anthony finished the thought for her. 'And you don't find duty sufficient reason to stay in a marriage.'

'I suppose you think that's heartless of me.'

He paused, then said, 'My wife – my former wife – took Luis and Angie to my grandfather's house, weeping. What a horrible man she was married to. She expected this man – me – to bring her back, as I had done before. This time I said fine, you want to leave, leave.' Anthony made a wry smile. 'Another of my sins. And then I allowed her version of the truth to stand, being too proud – too foolish – to contradict it. My family – the Pedrosas – made their judgment about me.

It took a long time for them to see me again as I am.'

He turned his chair slightly and pushed his plate aside. 'I told you that because it has stuck with me as a lesson on the importance of image. If your case goes to trial, the jury will get one version of the truth from the prosecutor, another from me. Juries want a murder trial to resemble a TV show. An image they can grasp. The good woman caught in a nightmare, unjustly accused.'

Anthony's fingers played with his knife, setting it upright, sliding down the handle, turning it again. 'Of course we will fight every piece of physical evidence the state produces, but the jury will be looking at *you*. Gail Connor, condensed into a few days. For me to do that – to do my job of establishing your innocence – I must have the reality, not the image. By the time we walk into the courtroom, I will know everything about you.'

For a long moment Gail stared at him, his features less distinct now in the twilight. He was not asking for her consent. He would take what he needed from her. She pressed her hands together in her lap to keep them still. Astonished at its impact, she had felt a clearly sexual stirring. He wanted to open her in a way that was more than physical. Already she was deciding what she would tell him, what she could hold back. Not everything was relevant. There were things . . . a swirl of self-involvement and jealousy and incestuous adolescent passion – none of it the image of the woman he would want to create in a courtroom.

After a while, Gail moistened her lips. She smiled. 'Fine. Ask away.'

He glanced at her plate. 'If you are finished, we can go inside. I want to read what you wrote, and then we'll talk.'

While he made coffee Gail used his guest bathroom, then came out to see him already reading, her pages spread across the kitchen counter as coffee drizzled into the pot.

He looked around at her. 'You've written a lot about this Indian, Jimmy Panther.'

'I can't tell you how it ties in.'

Anthony turned a page. 'But I agree with you. It is odd, about the mask. After you speak again with your friend Edith Newell, I would like to know what she has to say.'

Gail smiled. 'I'll mail you more pages to read.'

She kicked off her pumps and sat on the end of the sofa, her feet curled under her, sinking into dark green leather, one of Anthony's legal pads on her lap. He had instructed her to put down everything she could remember about her meeting with Britton and also – unless she had already included it in her notes – reasons why Dave might not have been truthful about having a purely chaste relationship with Renee.

A few minutes later Anthony set one cup and saucer on the coffee table near her and another opposite, where he eased himself into a lounge chair, feet on the ottoman. He reached over to turn on a floor lamp beside the chair. His eyes caught Gail's.

'You have a question?' he asked.

'Why do you think Dave lied?'

'Why assume he was telling the truth?'

Gail smiled, shaking her head. 'I know Dave better than that. We've been married for nearly twelve years.'

'You didn't know he was seeing Renee. Sending her cards. That's quite something to keep from a wife for – how long? Two years?'

'Wait a minute. What are you saying?'

'First I will give you a theory, which I have developed through observation. Premeditated murder is an intimate act with a simple motive based on passion. Hatred or love or greed, all passions. When a woman is the

292

victim, I assume sex is involved. I start from these premises. If the conclusion is different—' Anthony shrugged. 'Well, I am willing to be surprised. Now let us imagine that Dave wanted Renee too much, then killed her in a rage when she refused him.'

She laughed. 'You couldn't tell a jury that. It isn't true.'

Anthony flipped through the pages of her notes. 'You wrote that he has a hot temper, which he expresses now only on the tennis court. What do you mean by "now"?' When she didn't answer, he looked back at her. 'Has he ever struck you? Gail?'

She said, 'That was years ago. I told him I would leave. He never did it again.'

There was a silence. Anthony said quietly, 'How badly were you hurt?'

She shook her head. 'Not much. He didn't mean to.'

'Did you have to see a doctor?'

'Yes.'

After a moment, Anthony gestured toward the legal pad. 'Write it down. Everything. And the doctor you saw. I may look at your medical records.'

'It doesn't matter. Britton says Dave has an alibi. They have his charge card receipts at the bar he went to.'

'Did Dave tell you where he went?'

'No.' Gail paused. 'I wonder how the police found his receipts. He usually pays cash.'

'Then Britton was lying.'

'Bastard.'

'If you were guilty, you might have caved in at that point. It is possible, however, that Britton found someone – a bartender – who thinks he saw Dave that same night and not another. Britton has to eliminate other possible suspects. What we must show is that the times don't correspond. That Dave could have established an alibi, then gone back to Renee's house.' Anthony turned more pages. 'And if not for passion, for money. You say the marina was in trouble. That was the business he started. All he had.'

'But when I told him about the money he was completely surprised.'

'It appeared so to you. If the trust papers were in your house, he may have seen them. When Renee reached thirty the money would go to your mother. Before that, to you. Indirectly to him.'

Gail looked down at the legal pad, remembering what Dave had said. He had planned to buy a new high-lift truck. Add more boat storage space to the marina. She unclipped her pen from the top sheet. 'I hate thinking this way.'

'I would hate to see you in prison.'

She wrote for a while, remembering that Dave had not decided to leave her until after she had told him no, she would not put more money into the business. Over the rim of her coffee cup she noticed Anthony gather up her notes and tap them together on his thighs, making a neat stack, which he fastened with a paper clip.

She set the cup back in the saucer. 'I have another question.'

He looked at her.

'Was Renee having an affair with your cousin? You wouldn't give me an answer before, when I hinted at it that day on Flagler Street. And here's another question. Would you protect Carlos? I told Ben Strickland you were my attorney. He suggested you might throw me to the wolves to save Carlos.'

Anthony leaned over to put the notes on the table, then crossed his legs at the ankle. 'Is that what you think?'

'I told Ben no. That you don't like Carlos very much.'

His expression didn't contradict her. He said, 'Ben Strickland is wrong about throwing you to the wolves. Completely. As for your first question – Yes. They were having an affair.'

'For how long?'

'About a year. They met when she went to work for Vista Title. The construction company used Vista to handle some of its closings, as you know.' Anthony picked up his coffee. 'I asked Carlos the same thing you're getting to. He says he was with another woman the night Renee died. Apparently it was enough of an alibi to satisfy the police. They talked to her.'

'She could be lying.'

'Perhaps.'

Gail stood up and stretched her arms over her head. 'Such a nice guy, Carlos. Having an affair with my sister and in bed with somebody else. If he was.'

'I doubt he killed her. It isn't his style. Petty violence, perhaps. But this – It indicates a degree of control and calculation I doubt Carlos possesses.'

'Now who's assuming things? Murder – an act of intimacy and passion with a simple motive. You said it.' Gail sat on the edge of the coffee table, her knee brushing the ottoman. She noticed that Anthony's cream-colored socks matched his shoes.

She said, 'Your grandfather mentioned he had met Renee. Once. Not a favorable impression, I gather. And if what I saw the other night was any guide, Carlos would do back flips through flaming hoops to please Ernesto Pedrosa. After all, Carlos has to protect his status as heir apparent to the Pedrosa empire, right? You might be a threat if you'd stop going down to Cuba to see your father. Of if you'd kiss Ernesto's butt as much as Carlos does.'

Anthony was smiling a little, elbow on the arm of his chair, head supported on extended fingers.

'Let us assume, ladies and gentlemen of the jury, that Renee was in love with Carlos. That she wanted to marry him. The father of her child—'

'Are you sure of that?'

Gail spread her hands. 'An assumption.'

'All right. Continue.'

She got up and began to walk back and forth in her stocking feet. 'Carlos has been putting Renee off for months. She was fun to have around, but not the sort of girl you bring home to granddad. One Saturday night last March, after a disastrous party at her mother's, her brother-in-law brings her home, drunk. He leaves. Carlos is waiting for her upstairs in bed. Or maybe she calls Carlos and says come over. Now. She refuses to have another abortion; this is her last chance for a baby. She threatens to go to Ernesto, to go public, to chain herself to one of Carlos's bulldozers. Renee knows how to get what she wants from men. It looks bad for Carlos, then she passes out. He's been her lover long enough to know what those scars on her wrists mean. He throws her in her car, drives to the edge of the Everglades, carries her to the end of a nature walk. It's dark, but there's a moon, bright enough for him to take her wrist, to guide the razor blade—'

Her words came to a sudden halt. Gail drew in a shaky breath. 'This, ladies and gentlemen, is what happened. You have seen Mr Quintana destroy the credibility of Carlos Pedrosa's alibi witness. You have heard Carlos Pedrosa admit on the stand that Renee Connor was obsessed with him. That his grandfather would have disowned him if he had married her. These facts, I submit to you, create a reasonable doubt that Gail Connor, the victim's . . . loving sister—'

Gail made a little face, hiding the tremor in her lips. 'Well. I guess that's why I do commercial law.'

'Not bad,' Anthony said. 'If Hartwell Black lets you go, come see me about a job.'

She let her gaze drop to the carpet, then walked across the room and through the French doors. In the darkness she could see easily past the screen. The inlet was shiny black, the sailboat quiet at anchor on the other side. Small shaded lamps in the low concrete wall of the dock cast pools of light. Music came from a fishing boat further up.

She heard Anthony's footsteps. 'Gail?'

After a minute, she said, 'You know, if I could only figure out who she was . . . I'm going to be on trial for her murder and I can't help you – or myself – because I don't know why this happened. Isn't that what the police look for first? The reason?'

He stood beside her. 'I should have sent you home after dinner. We can talk later. There's no hurry.'

Gail lightly pressed her fingertips on the screen, unwilling to go just yet. 'You told me about your friend Juanito, remember? How you saw him after all those years and he hadn't really changed? Well, I don't know about Renee. I don't recognize her at all. Carlos probably treated her like a whore. But to Dave she was the opposite. Unsullied as a virgin. Edith Newell thinks she was immature. My mother thinks she was misunderstood. Ben says she was mentally ill, some kind of pervert. And you . . .' Gail glanced at Anthony. 'You liked her. For her honesty. What did you mean?'

He took a few seconds to answer. 'Just that . . . if you asked her what she thought, she would tell you.'

'Yes.' Gail smiled. 'And sometimes even if you didn't ask. How come she got all the courage? She said things out loud I was embarrassed to think of, even if they were true. When we were children she would run along the seawall behind our house, doing cartwheels, scaring our mother to death. She liked being on the edge. Almost as if she wanted to fall off. She went to extremes – a bitch one minute, weeping the next, then laughing at herself. Maybe she was mentally ill, a little. Or giving a spontaneous reaction to what she saw around her, I don't know.'

Gail turned around to face him, leaning on her hands, the metal railing of the terrace behind her. 'Listen, I didn't come out here because of what you said about Hartwell Black letting me go. I'm not that nervous. Sure, this scares the hell out of me, but I know I'm innocent. And I've got some high-powered legal talent, right? What can happen?'

Anthony said, 'It seems Renee did not get all the courage.' Behind him, the light from the living room fell across the terrace floor in a long rectangle. The ceiling fan spun slowly, its blades barely visible.

She said, 'When I was talking to you before, describing what happened to her, how she died, it was as if I were there. I could see her, but not whoever was standing over her. He was only this dark shape.'

Gail pulled her hands out from underneath her hips, turning up her palms. 'She had such small hands. They were slender and pale, like a little girl. I could put my thumb and forefinger around her wrists. When she was in the hospital, and the bandages were on, she laughed and held out her hands. She said, "Look what I've done, Sis. I sure as hell trimmed my nails too close this time."'

Gail smiled, then stood quietly for a moment. 'Renee looked utterly exhausted. Almost as if she wished she hadn't come back, but she was lying there making jokes about it. Her eyes had circles under them, but still they were like two spots of blue light in her face. So blue. It made me want to buy contacts.'

'Yours are blue.'

'Compared to yours, maybe. But not like hers. Mine have more gray. No, no. Renee had the looks, although she would deny it. She never liked that little gap between her front teeth, did you ever notice that? And that one dimple. She used to sit around with her finger poked into her other cheek to make a pair, but of course it didn't work. And the earrings. Four holes in each ear. Our mother cried over it. No, I'm not kidding, she did.'

Gail lifted her hair away from one ear. 'Look. She did mine, too.'

Anthony leaned closer. 'Four holes? Where?'

'Two in each ear. I only use one, and the other hardly shows. I was nineteen. She said it wouldn't hurt. She lied.' Gail laughed, then let her hair fall back into place, her smile fading. Suddenly aware of the floor tilting under her, she grabbed the railing, holding on, the metal cold under her hands.

Anthony said something. A question.

She heard her own voice at a distance. 'I'll never find her now. Someone did this and it's too late. Whatever she was, she didn't deserve this. Not this. And I was moaning about saving my own skin. Whoever did it should burn in hell. I don't care why he did it. I hope he dies.' Gail's breath was coming quickly now, burning her chest. 'I would use a razor on him myself and watch him bleed to death. He did that to her. My sister.'

The water in the inlet ticked softly against the dock, lights wobbling on its surface under a black sky. The Everglades must have been this dark.

She sank, spinning in slow motion. A sudden slide of warm silk on her cheek. The terrace floor rushing toward her, then the porch railing above, falling away.

White fan blades, circling. Something under her shoulders, then warmth around her head.

Her eyes opened to complete darkness. She rolled her face away from Anthony's chest. She lay across his thighs, his arms circling her, his back against the railing.

She blinked, tried to smile. 'Did I break anything?'

'No. I caught you. You fainted.' He loosened his arms.

'Please. Not yet.' She turned her face into his shirt again, felt him pull up one knee to brace her back. They sat like that for a while. She could hear his heart under her ear. A steady, rapid thud.

She turned further and felt silk against her mouth. 'I wonder what Renee would do now.'

His breath stopped. Gail slid her hand up his shirt to his open collar, along his scratchy jaw, into his hair, thick and soft between her fingers.

The Spanish words he whispered Gail didn't understand. Then his breath was on her temple. 'Gail. I'll be your lover or your attorney. But not at the same time.'

'So proper.' She let her head fall back, his arm under her neck. With one finger, she outlined his lips, touching the peak at the centre, the lines on either side. 'I wanted to do this the first time you smiled at me. In the courthouse. Remember? It seems so long ago.'

His eyes closed. He sucked her finger into his mouth, bit down, stroked with his tongue.

Gail pushed herself up on one arm, her hand dropping from his mouth to the buttons on his silk shirt, one then another.

'*Jesucristo*.'

She buried her face in his chest, breathing in, hair tickling her nose. She moved down, her lips on his skin, her fingers undoing his belt.

'*Por Diós, ¿qué me estás haciendo?*' What are you doing to me? His hands clenched in her hair. '*No pares, mi cielo. No pares.*' Don't stop.

Chapter Eighteen

'Daddy!' Karen ran down the dock toward the big sailboat moored at its end, her sneakers thumping on the wooden planks. Gail followed more slowly, careful not to get her heels caught in the crevices. Dark green water lapped at the pilings and sparkled in the early-morning sun.

Dave was loosening the tiedowns on the sail cover, getting ready to cast off. The sails would not go up until he had the boat in the windier passage of upper Biscayne Bay. The mast bobbed slightly as a sportfisher passed by, low wake fanning out, engine rumbling.

Gail carried Karen's yellow zipper bag – sunscreen, hat, change of clothes. Dave had arranged this trip last week. He and Wayne, his engine man, had to deliver a forty-eight-foot sloop-rigged Swan to Key Largo; someone at the marina there would drive them back up to Miami. *Let Karen come along*, Dave had said. *She can miss one day of school.* Normally Gail would have given him a flat no, but she knew Karen missed her father.

Now Karen was running back and forth alongside the boat, her ponytails bouncing like the ears of a puppy. Swinging around the mast, Dave came to the edge of the cabin top. He wore old tennis shorts. His arms and legs were brown, the hair on them bleached pale blond. Last night Gail had lain awake trying to imagine Dave at the end of that nature walk, standing over Renee's body. She couldn't see it. And today, with the sun bathing everything in clear white light, the idea seemed positively obscene.

He smiled broadly at them. 'Hi. You girls are early.'

'Can I get on, Daddy?'

'Come aboard.' He turned back toward the cockpit and called to the other man standing there. 'Wayne, give her a hand.'

Wayne stuck the wrench he'd been holding into the pocket of his blue work pants and swung Karen off the dock as lightly as a rag doll. He was a black man somewhere past sixty. He had told Karen once, straight-faced, that he had been born in the engine room of a Merchant Marine freighter and suckled on diesel fuel instead of mother's milk.

Karen went below, exploring. Gail leaned down a little to look through the portholes in the hull, hoping Karen would look out. Lately she had held her more than usual, and missed her almost viscerally when she was out of sight.

When Dave jumped down from the cabin top, Gail gave him Karen's bag. 'I'm going to work late tonight,' she said. 'Can you take Karen by Irene's?'

'Sure, no problem.'

'Dave, I need to speak to you.'

He stood there for a moment with the bag in his hands, then hung it over a spoke on the ship's wheel. He said to Wayne, 'You want to go ahead and check out that oil line?'

'Take your time.' Wayne smiled at Gail. 'Nice to see you again.'

'You too.'

They walked back along the dock toward the marina. By this hour, nearly eight o'clock, most of the sport fishermen had already headed out. A few people were going into the ship's store, a flat-roofed building connected to a machine shop that smelled of oil and acrid welding torches. From halfway down the dock Gail could see the weeds behind the building, the sagging chain-link fence.

Lifting his cap by its bill, Dave smoothed his hair, put the cap back on again. He said, 'Somebody made me an offer on the marina. Not a great offer, but enough to pay off our bills, plus about half the second mortgage on the house. I'll sign the house and everything in it over to you. And you can have whatever you think is fair for child support.' Dave glanced at Gail. 'My attorney says I'm crazy, but it's what I want to do.'

A pelican, beak tucked on its belly, watched them from a piling. The sound of hammering came from inside the shop.

Feeling unaccountably adrift, Gail studied the weathered wooden planks as they passed under her feet. 'Dave, I'm sorry about the marina.'

'Don't be.'

'Would you still work here?'

'I could, that's part of the deal. But you know what I'd rather do? Take some time off, do some sailing. There are a couple of boats around here the owners want to get rid of. I could pick one up cheap. Maybe catch some of the tennis tournaments on the islands.'

'Maybe you should listen to your attorney,' she said.

Dave laughed. 'He's eating me alive on fees. You know how attorneys are.' The pelican flapped away from its perch as they approached it. 'What does a man need to be happy, anyway? Not so much . . . stuff. Possessions are a trap.'

They looked at each other. He must have read something in her face. He said, 'You don't need me, Gail. You never did.' Their eyes held long enough for them to recognize the truth in that.

At the end of the pier the sloop whined, coughed, and settled down to a steady purr. They turned to look at it, Gail squinting into the sun. Wayne was at the helm station panel by the wheel. He waved.

Dave made a thumbs-up. 'Sounds good,' he yelled. 'Let her run.'

When he turned back, Gail said, 'I want to tell you what's going on with Renee's murder investigation.' Anthony had told her not to discuss the case with anyone. But Anthony didn't know Dave; she did.

They wandered across the parking lot, then past the shop, the clang of metal occasionally coming from inside.

She told him about her meeting with Frank Britton.

'They think I did it. That I took her to that county park and faked her suicide because I thought she was sleeping with you. Or to get the money in her trust fund. Either reason, I suppose, would be enough. They're probably going to arrest me. And if they do, there's no way I'd get out on bond. I'd be in custody for as long as a year, until the jury comes back with its verdict.' She smiled. 'I assume it would be not guilty. Anyway, you'd have to take Karen till then, you and Irene.'

'Oh, God. I don't believe this.' Dave had stopped walking. His face was ashen under the tan. 'Oh, Gail.'

'We need to put the divorce on hold. Is that all right for now?'

'Jesus.' He leaned against her, fumbling for her hand. 'Whatever you want. I don't believe this.'

She said, 'I have an attorney. He's going to talk to Britton today and see what's going on.'

They moved out of the path of a pickup truck hauling a skiff on a trailer. Dave said, 'Listen, I told the police I went to a bar after I dropped Renee off. I could have made a mistake with the time. If you need me to cover for you I will.'

'You mean, offer me an alibi?'

306

'Sure. Screw Britton.'

'I don't know. The jury might see through it. For now, just answer me some questions, okay?' Dave nodded. 'When did you get to Renee's house that night?'

'Nearly ten, I'm pretty sure.'

'Did she seem eager for you to go? As if someone might have been upstairs?'

'Not that I remember. She didn't rush me off.'

Gail thought about that. 'If no one else was there, then the person who did it came by unexpectedly. Or she might have called him after you left. Was she sober enough to use a telephone?'

'Yeah, I'd say so. She didn't talk much in the car on the way, sort of lay there with the seat back and her eyes closed. She made it into the house on her own.'

'How long did you stay?'

'Ten minutes?' Dave's eyes seemed to focus on the mangroves on the other side of the channel. 'I wanted to stick around and make sure she was all right, but she told me to go on home. She said, 'Go on home and make up with Gail, she's pissed off at me enough as it is.'

'Did she talk about anybody she was having problems with?' Gail watched Karen climb the ladder from below, run across the cabin to the prow, and lean out over the water, her ponytails dangling.

He said, 'That trouble Renee got into last summer. Maybe she was still involved. I got the impression, before she died, that she had something going on she didn't want me to know about. Maybe it was drug dealers that did it.'

Gail had told Dave about Renee's arrest but couldn't remember how much. She had learned from Anthony only last Friday that Renee had known what was on board the boat. Gail hadn't talked to Dave since then.

She asked, 'Did Renee tell you about this?'

'Yeah. She did.'

'And?'

He took off his cap again, straightened it on his head. 'Okay. This is what happened. Last summer she asked me to help out a friend of hers. He needed some work done pronto on a sportfisher and he'd pay cash. I said fine. A couple days later two guys pull up in a forty-four-foot Striker, running pretty ragged. Wayne and I were supposed to overhaul the engines, two Detroit diesels. So we pull it into the shop. And there's a quick-release port in the hull.'

Gail frowned. 'What's that?'

'It's a smuggler's trick. We see them in boats we get in here from time to time. They put drugs in it, and if the police board, you can push a lever and it lets the stuff go down. You lose a few kilos of coke but you save your ass.'

'You knew they were drug smugglers and you did this?'

'No, not really certain. Not—' His hands fell to his sides.

'What were their names?'

'I only heard one. José. José García.'

'Like John Doe.'

'I didn't ask for ID, Gail.'

'What did they look like?'

'Both Spanish. José was muscular, mid-thirties. A mustache. The other guy was skinny, a little younger. I asked where they were from, didn't get any answers. José wanted the work done within two days. I said no way, not for twelve cylinders, unless you go two thousand per cylinder. He gave me five thousand down, said I'd get the rest later. I'd have told him to take a hike if Renee hadn't said they were okay. Wayne and I busted our asses but we did it. Damn good job, too.'

'Did Renee come along with him?'

'No. We were supposed to have lunch the next week, but she didn't show up. Come to find out, she was in jail at the time. One night after closing José shows up with his friend. They said they were out on bond. They had to drop the drugs but the police found cocaine in one of their duffel bags. They were pissed that someone set them up and thought of me because I hadn't gotten paid. They slammed me up against the wall in my office. Wayne heard what was going on and came in with the gun we keep behind the counter. I thought they were going to kill me. Hell, I don't know who set them up. Could have been nobody. A fluke. The Marine Patrol cruises by, the guy tries to avoid them. Bingo. José, his friend, and Renee were nailed coming around Bill Baggs State Park about two in the afternoon.

'Renee called and said she was sorry for getting me into it. She went along with them to Freeport because she thought it would be exciting. Jesus. Exciting. She said it was stupid, what she did, and she was tired of doing stupid things. She promised to pay me what they owed. I told her never mind, it was my own fault. Her case was dropped, so I guess it didn't turn out too bad. I hear José and his buddy skipped the country.'

'Did Renee tell you why her case was dropped?'

'No. She just said it was.'

'Ben talked to the right people.'

'Yeah? I guess it pays to be a judge.'

'Who was the friend she was doing this for? One of those two men?'

'She wouldn't say, but I can guess. Carlos Pedrosa.'

'What?'

'She was dating him, if you want to call it that.'

Gail nodded at this confirmation. 'Yes. But that doesn't mean he got her involved in drug smuggling.'

The engines on the sloop quieted. Wayne appeared on deck, coming up out of the companionway. He made an okay sign with his fingers.

'Be there in a second,' Dave yelled. He looked back at Gail. 'Carlos Pedrosa wasn't exactly a member of the Jaycees, you know what I'm saying? They used to get together and do cocaine, before she got off it. Plus I got the feeling he was hurting for money. A big score like that would help. I'd like to know where he was the night she died.'

'With another woman,' Gail said. 'So I heard. Not that Carlos was entirely without sentiment. He came to the funeral. You were on your way out and nearly hit his car. A silver Mercedes coupe.'

'I don't . . . Oh, yeah. Vaguely. Sorry I missed.'

'And I'm sorry it took you this long to tell me what happened last summer.'

'Come on, Gail. How was I going to do that?' He reached out and took her hand. 'Look, I meant it, what I said before about an alibi.'

'Thanks.'

He held on to her. 'You want me to move back in? I will, if it would help.'

'Thank you, but it's not necessary.' She laughed a little. 'Unless I'm in the Women's Detention Center, then somebody has to water the yard.'

He put his arms around her and she closed her eyes and hugged him back, feeling the familiar weight and scent of his body.

Then she kissed him lightly on the mouth and let him go. She studied her car keys. 'Have a good time today. Make sure Karen wears her life vest.'

As Gail drove out of the parking lot she could see Dave in her rearview mirror, looking after her.

It took her until nearly nine-thirty to locate Carlos

Pedrosa. His gold-trimmed Mercedes was parked in front of a house under construction, on a turnaround at the end of a bare new street in a subdivision way out on Coral Way called Versailles. Carlos's attempt at international flavor, she supposed.

Gail had passed herself off as a realtor to the girl behind the desk at Pedrosa Development Company – a suite in a corporate plaza on West Kendall Drive, its walls decorated with artists' drawings of houses in Pedrosa subdivisions.

Versailles had a naked look to it. Spindly trees. Concrete foundations poured, not much going up. The models were done, three of them, painted in pastel, flags flapping outside, signs in Spanish and English. Gail hadn't spotted any customers. The subdivision was on a dead-end road, saw grass on the other side of the wall encircling the property. Across the street, another tract was up for sale. Getting out of her car, she could hear the pop-pop-pop of a nail gun. Three men were laying shingles. They stopped what they were doing and looked at her.

Gail picked her way carefully across the rocky front yard. Two pitted two-by-twelve planks lay as a ramp to the door. The interior smelled of joint compound and dust. She walked through to the back, past two workers hanging drywall. Carlos was on the patio with a roll of blueprints in his hand. The man he was talking to – big arms, a leather tool belt – saw her first. Then Carlos turned around. He had his dark glasses on. His shirt was open at the collar.

'Gail Connor, how you doing? You came all the way out here?'

'How's business?'

'Business is great. Everything is great.' He smiled at her, teeth white against his short black beard. 'So, did you bring me the option from the judge?'

'No, I wanted to talk to you about something else.'

'No option? Man, I left . . . must have been six messages at your office.'

'I haven't seen Ben in the last few days.'

Carlos spoke to the carpenter. '*Momento*, okay?' He stepped over an aluminum wall stud. 'See, Gail, the thing is, I have to figure out what I'm going to do with that property. And I can't do that until I get the survey. And I can't survey it until I get the option. You want to see if he'll get going on this?'

They stood in the shade at the edge of the patio. Gail said, 'Actually, I came about something else entirely. I'll get to the point. The police think my sister was murdered.'

'I'm not surprised. They asked me some questions.' Carlos looked at her through his sunglasses. 'This is a terrible thing that happened.'

'The police aren't having much luck, so I've decided to see what I can find out. I didn't know her friends. We weren't close the last few years. Did she ever mention that?'

'She might have.'

'I understand you were with another woman the night Renee died.'

After a hesitation, Carlos said, 'Yeah. Which I am not going to get into because I don't want the young lady bothered.'

'Of course.' Gail wished she were as good at this as Frank Britton. Lawsuits were easier: in a courtroom she usually knew the answers to the questions. 'I've heard rumors my sister may have been involved in cocaine trafficking. The police drop hints, but they won't tell me anything.'

Carlos's mouth dropped open. 'Renee?'

'You knew she had been arrested, didn't you?'

He was tapping the blueprints against his leg. 'Wow.

So maybe one of these people—' Carlos glanced away when a sheet of plywood landed with a bang across two sawhorses. The carpenter pulled a tape measure off his tool belt, running out the end of it. He marked a line. Carlos looked back at Gail. 'So when was this?'

'Last summer, but the case against her was dismissed. She never told you?'

'No. But if the case was dismissed, then I doubt she was majorly involved. Rest your mind on that, Gail.'

'You never knew her to take drugs?'

'Well, she might have smoked grass now and then.'

'With you?'

Gail could see her reflection in Carlos's sunglasses, two tiny, dark faces. He said, 'Now and then. It's no big deal.'

'When did you meet her?'

'I don't know. When did she start working at the title company? Whenever that was.'

The scream of a power saw shattered the silence. His face turned toward the carpenter, who was lopping a few inches off the plywood. Gail wished she could hold the saw at Carlos's throat, her finger on the button.

When the saw whined to a stop, she said, 'Was it your child she was pregnant with?'

The sunglasses swung back in her direction. 'Renee was pregnant?'

'Stop pretending you don't know anything,' she said sharply, and knew the moment the words were out of her mouth how desperate they sounded.

His eyes were fixed on her. In the bright sun she could see dimly beyond the gray lenses. Dark eyes under thick, straight brows. Like Anthony's, she thought suddenly. But this face was more blatantly sensual. Fuller, redder lips. The kind of face Renee might have seen over her as she lay tied to her bed with that black silk cord the police found in the nightstand.

He finally said, 'And don't you pretend you didn't come all the way out here to see if I killed her. The answer is no. Renee and me had something special going and it tore me up when she died. You find out who did this to her, I'll personally take care of him for you.' Carlos held up the blueprints. 'If that's all, I got work to do.'

Gail found a pay phone inside a Denny's restaurant up the street.

'Hartwell Black and Robineau.'

'Gwen, this is Gail Connor. Let me have Miriam, please.'

She dropped the phone to her shoulder, not wanting to hear the on-hold music. Carlos Pedrosa hadn't been as stupid as she had thought. But he had been more frightening. Yes, that would have appealed to Renee as well. Sexuality and danger. Living on the edge. Going on a drug-smuggling trip because she thought it would be exciting.

Sex with Carlos, virginal romance with Dave. Fragments of a life.

'Gail!' It was Miriam on the line, sounding agitated. 'Where were you? I didn't know how to get in touch with you. I called your house.'

'What happened?' Gail had the phone back at her ear.

'You missed that big meeting at nine o'clock with Jack Warner and Larry Black and the rest of the litigation department. I told them you had a personal emergency, but I don't think they believed me.'

Gail closed her eyes. 'Oh, no. Oh, shit.'

'Are you all right?'

'Miriam, you want to know the truth? I forgot.' She struck the wall with the flat of her hand. 'Damn. Look, tell Larry—' She laughed. 'Tell him it slipped my mind.'

'Are you serious?'

'Weep into his wing tips. Say I'm in an agony of remorse.'

'I'll rephrase it, okay?'

Gail leaned against the edge of the phone booth and watched the waitress pouring coffee at the counter. 'Any other dire emergencies I should know about?'

'Carlos Pedrosa called about the option.'

'I know. I just spoke to him.'

'And Jimmy Panther called about the mask. He left a number and said for you to call him as soon as you can.'

Gail wrote it on her notepad.

Miriam said, 'Is that the Indian mask you took over to the museum?'

'Yes. I'll explain it one of these days. As soon as I can figure it out myself.'

'And Anthony Quintana called twice. He said it's important. Here's the number—'

'No, I've got it.' He would want to tell her the result of his phone call with Frank Britton.

Miriam asked, 'When are you coming in?'

'What have I got on the schedule?' Miriam told her. Gail said, 'Nothing we can't move around. Reset everything for after two. I should be back by then.'

Gail's next quarter went for a call to Anthony's office, which she dialed without looking at his card. He was with a client, hold on.

'No, don't disturb him. I'll try back in half an hour.' She checked her watch. 'Before eleven, anyway.' She hung up, then stood there staring blankly at the pay phone, seeing only Anthony's face over her last night on his living room floor. They hadn't made it to the bedroom. She had a rug burn on her butt. Beard burn on her face and tenderer places. He was saying things

315

she probably couldn't have found in a Spanish dictionary. A foreign tongue.

'Miss, are you using the phone?'

Gail jumped. An elderly woman was behind her, waiting. 'Sorry. No, I'm finished.'

She had a cup of coffee and wished it had been decaf. She checked her watch again and wondered what Britton had told Anthony. Her heart was beginning to jump.

At the telephone again she pulled open the phone book and looked up Vista Title Company. She didn't want to hear what Frank Britton had said. Not yet.

Delores Perrera lived with her husband, Julio, and her mother in an apartment building behind Westland Shopping Center in Hialeah. She would still have been working as a post-closer at Vista Title, she explained to Gail, except that she had a weak uterus and the doctor was afraid she'd miscarry for the third time. It had been her mother who had opened the door when Gail knocked, Loly staying on the sofa, her stomach a gentle mound under a long white T-shirt. She wore tight black knit pants and red pumps with little heels.

It had taken Gail a few minutes to realize where she had seen her before – at Renee's funeral. The woman she had uncharitably pointed out to Dave as a pregnant exotic dancer, coming in with a pimp. Not a pimp after all. Her husband, Julio, now downstairs changing the water pump on his Trans Am in the parking lot.

Loly struggled up when her mother brought in two *tacitas de café*. Gail had protested coffee, but the mother had smilingly ignored her. The silver-colored tray held little china cups and a plate of *pasteles*. She retired to the kitchen, which Gail could see through an open archway. A spotlessly clean room, like the rest of the apartment.

316

'My mom the hostess,' Loly said. 'You don't have to drink it.' She bit into a pastry. 'I'm going to name my baby Renee if it's a girl. What do you think?'

Gail smiled. 'She'd have liked that.' Loly was the woman whose baby shower Renee had been planning the week before she died.

Loly settled back against a pillow. 'Like I said on the phone, I'll tell you what I can about her.'

'You may have heard. The police think she was murdered.'

Loly nodded. 'When they came around the office asking questions, before I quit, I thought something was going on. I call up over there a lot – you know, my friends and all – and we talk about it.'

'Let me ask you this. What was Renee's relationship with Carlos Pedrosa?'

'He was her lover, I guess you'd say. He took her places. Bought her stuff. She said they went to Jamaica for a week. But they weren't engaged or anything.' Loly glanced toward the kitchen. Her mother was washing dishes. 'Are you telling me you think Carlos did it?'

'I don't know. But a stranger didn't kill her,' Gail said. 'A stranger wouldn't have bothered to fake a suicide. Carlos was supposedly with another woman at the time, but I have my doubts.' Gail sipped her espresso, pinching the cup by its tiny handle. Vile black stuff, intensely sweet.

'Oh, my Go-o-o-d.' The last word stretched out. Loly had the tip of her forefinger in her mouth, thinking. When she noticed Gail looking at her she said, 'Betty Diaz. I heard she was talking around the office about Carlos. How they were going out and stuff. I said, *What?* Betty Diaz?'

'Oh. It's true, then.'

'No, you don't get it. This girl is so—' she circled

317

her hand in the air, looking for the right word. 'Not ugly, but – I mean, Carlos and Betty Diaz? And then Teresa – she's the receptionist over there – she goes, Oh, Betty was saying how she had to talk to the police and all, acting like she's so big.'

'Do you think she would lie for him?'

Loly shrugged. 'She might, if she thought he really liked her. God. She'd be stupid to think that.'

Gail put her cup down carefully. 'How well did you know him?'

'Carlos? He didn't come in a lot. We'd say hi to each other, that's about it. Mostly I know him from what Renee said.' Loly adjusted the pillow under her back. 'Okay, you want to know about Carlos? I wasn't going to say this but right now I don't care. He was embezzling money from his company. Renee knew about it.'

'Pedrosa Development?' Gail stared at Loly.

'I found out because I had to issue some checks at the title company and the money wasn't in the file from the builder. We assign every closing its own file—' When Gail nodded, Loly went on. 'Renee said don't worry about it, take it out of another file for now. See, what Carlos was doing was taking money from one file to pay another. He couldn't catch up. The houses weren't selling fast enough to cover the shortages. But listen, Renee didn't do any of that, okay? It was Carlos. And George Sanchez. He's the Vista title examiner. The two of them were in on it.'

'George Sanchez, the attorney who works for Ferrer and Quintana.'

'Yes. Renee just figured it out, I guess. She was very smart. But she didn't want to get Carlos in trouble. She said he was trying to pay it all back.'

Before his grandfather got wind of it, Gail imagined. Or before Anthony found out. Either one just as fatal for Carlos. Now she had the real reason Carlos had

318

dragged his heels settling the Darden case. He hadn't had the cash to give their down payment back; he had to make sure they took the house. For an instant Gail wondered if Anthony was aware of this. No. If he had known, Carlos would be out on his ass. Anthony would have seen to that. Ferrer and Quintana owned the title company. Carlos and George Sanchez had been – might still be – screwing around with the company trust accounts as well as stealing from Ernesto Pedrosa.

'Renee could have made trouble for Carlos,' Gail said.

'I don't think she would have told anybody,' Loly said. 'That would be turning in a friend.'

'How trusting of him.' The second sip of coffee wasn't as jarring. Gail got through half the cup. 'Did Renee tell you she was pregnant?'

'Yes. She wouldn't say whose it was, but probably Carlos. I mean, who else? She didn't sleep around.'

'Do you know if she was pressuring him to marry her?'

'Not that I know of. She never talked about marriage like it was something she would do. I don't think—' Loly's eyes went to the floor, then back to Gail. 'Renee knew she couldn't have got married and had it turn out good. You know?'

Gail shook her head.

Loly shifted on the pillow again. 'Well, she was real nice and fun to be with and all, but – How can I put this? She was like . . . broken. I knew she tried to kill herself before because I saw the scars and asked her about it. She told me stuff. Doing drugs, getting down under ninety pounds one time. And she used to date these men that were really – you know, like would beat her up and stuff. And she'd laugh about it, like it was funny. I didn't think it was funny.'

Loly reached over and laid her hand on Gail's arm.

'No, come on. It's okay. I talked to her, you know? I go, *chica*, you can't keep doing this stuff. I thought she was getting better. She *was*. When I heard she committed suicide, I said, *what*? It didn't make sense to me. She wanted that baby. Yeah, that's what she said. She wanted it. Maybe she got pregnant on purpose, who knows? Everybody needs somebody.'

'Because she couldn't have Carlos.'

'No. She didn't *want* Carlos.' Loly balanced her cup and saucer on her stomach. 'I asked her. I go, Renee, you must be really in love with this guy. She says, No, you only want what you can't have.' The cup moved up and down with Loly's breathing. 'I think she was in love, but not with him. She wouldn't tell me who, but I have my opinion. Carlos's cousin. You might know him, since you're a lawyer, too. Anthony Quintana? He's a partner in the law firm next door.'

Gail leaned over to put down the tiny cup and saucer, avoiding Loly's eyes. 'Yes. I do know him.'

'I heard they had something going at one time. He's a real good-looking guy, you know? Whenever he'd come in the office, which wasn't too often, I'd see how she'd get. Once I caught her crying in the bathroom after he left. She told me to mind my own business. Yeah. That guy must have messed her up. And he wouldn't even look at her.'

A cabinet door closed in the kitchen. Through the window Gail could hear the rush of cars on the expressway. She took a breath and looked around for her purse.

'Well, I ought to go.'

'Stay for lunch. It's no trouble.' When Gail finally said she absolutely had to be downtown in half an hour, Loly walked her to the door, then kissed her on the cheek.

'Come back and see the baby in three months,' she

said, then drew back and studied Gail's face. 'You know what? When I first saw you, when my mom let you in, I thought you were Renee. Crazy, right?'

The key to Renee's condo in Coconut Grove was still on Gail's key ring. She had let a realtor in last week to see it. Women from Irene's church had already cleaned out everything but the furniture, upstairs and down, and a truck was supposed to come tomorrow for that, taking it all to a shelter for the homeless. The closets and dressers were empty, only a few hangers left, or a drawer half open. Gail herself had been through the place two weeks ago, throwing everything remotely provocative into a white plastic garbage bag – videotapes and magazines; a lingerie bag full of soiled underwear; the collection in the nightstand. She had tossed the bag into the Dumpster at the end of the parking lot.

Now Gail sat on the edge of the bed in Renee's bedroom. She faced the hall, her jacket off and sweat tickling down her back. She had opened the window and raised the miniblinds. It hadn't done any good. The electricity was off.

Without the sheets and pillows, without the Georgia O'Keeffe print of the open orchid or the clothes on the floor or the knick-knacks on the dresser, it was only a room. Gail closed her eyes. There was still the faint scent of Shalimar. Or maybe she was imagining it.

She wondered if the sound of a fist on flesh had ever echoed in this room. If Renee had brought them here, those men who would hurt her. Probably not. They must have belonged to those darker years when she had tried to kill herself; when she was hardly ever sober or civil; when she had finally spent weeks in a psychiatric hospital.

What horrified Gail, thinking of Renee drawn to pain and death, was that in one small, dark corner of herself, she understood. She had anesthetized herself with work as Renee had done it with drugs and alcohol. Dave hadn't known how to reach her. He had long since given up trying. Five years ago, worn raw by days of arguments, she had slapped him; he had struck back, breaking her nose, blood all over their bedroom. Then he had dropped to his knees and sobbed.

But in one bright, clear instant before it happened, his fist coming toward her face slowly, silently, she had felt a lightness, a letting go. Stop struggling, stop fighting. Stop everything.

Gail turned her head far enough to see the satiny blue fabric of the mattress, tufted and stitched. She slid her hand along the edge.

Possibly – no, almost certainly – Anthony had been on this bed with Renee. Gail didn't regret last night, only that he had not told her. She smiled. An uncommon breach of manners for this man.

Whom had he kissed last night, that deep, drugging kiss that stopped them dead in the living room, sinking to the rug, not even getting so far as the couch?

And in that instant before he entered her, before the barrier of flesh was breached, her fingers loosened from his shoulders as though she were dropping from the edge of a cliff. He could have done anything to her then. *No pares.* Don't stop.

Gail hadn't known who she was in that moment, couldn't have said her own name if he had asked her.

Her eyes opened. The room was intensely hot and still and her dress was soaked with sweat. She got up, pulled down the window, locked it, then picked up her jacket and purse from the bed.

She called Anthony from outside the post office on Grand Avenue. 'It's me,' she said. 'Checking in before I go downtown. What did you find out from Britton?'

322

'Where are you, Gail?'

'Coconut Grove.'

'Good. Not far. I want you to come to my office, right away. Can you do that?'

There was something else. Gail tensed. 'Why?'

'Frank Britton wants me to bring you in.'

Chapter Nineteen

Anthony was waiting for her when she arrived at Ferrer & Quintana. He closed the door to his office and told his secretary they were not to be disturbed for any reason.

Standing beside his desk, Gail managed a small laugh. 'I was afraid there would be a SWAT team outside waiting for me.'

He smiled gently and gestured toward one of the client chairs. 'Sit down. I have some good news. The State Attorney has agreed to bail.'

Gail sank into the chair, her legs going weak beneath her. 'You did that? Oh, Anthony. How?'

'It wasn't easy. Listen carefully. We don't have much time. I told Frank Britton I would have you at his office by two o'clock and it is nearly that now. I expected you to call long before you did.'

She wanted to reach for him, but the formality of his manner confined her hands to her lap.

He sat in the chair next to her, adjusting the knee of his gray suit. He wore a silver and black tie, a spotless white shirt. 'I called Britton at seven-thirty this morning. He said he had intended to call me anyway, because you gave him my name. He will allow me to take you to his office. You will be arrested, paperwork will be filled out, and then you will be taken to the Dade County Jail. There is more paperwork, the bail bondsman will appear and – if all goes well – you will be released.'

Still trembling, Gail nodded.

Anthony said, 'After I spoke with Frank Britton, I called your house but there was no answer.'

'I was – I took Karen to the marina early this morning. She's with Dave now in Key Largo. He plans to take her to my mother's.'

'Good. I telephoned your cousin, Ben Strickland, and suggested ways in which we might obtain your release. First, he assured me that he and your mother would take care of the bond, whatever it was. Then we discussed how to approach the State Attorney. It had to be done by persons who know you but who are not friends of the State Attorney. If the *Miami Herald* could suppose for a minute that favors were granted, you would have no chance at bail. None.

'Judge Strickland and I made a list. Jack Warner and Larry Black from your office, the president of the Florida Association of Women Lawyers, the priest at your church, a few others. No politicians. By noon all of them had spoken on your behalf. They said that you are not going to flee Dade County, that you have long-standing ties to the community, that you have never been charged with a crime . . .'

Gail listened while Anthony quickly related the discussions with the prosecutors, who had finally agreed to a bond of $1,250,000. Ben had made arrangements with the bonding company.

'So much. Dear God.'

He seemed still incredulous that it had happened. 'I did not dare expect this, Gail. It is, as I have told you, very rare.'

'Then I chose a good attorney.'

Leaning forward, he took her hands. His felt so warm she knew hers must be frozen.

He said, 'I'll go with you to Metro-Dade headquarters, and through the procedures there, but after that you will have another attorney. No, you must listen. Ben Strickland recommended Ray Hammell. I agree. He's an excellent lawyer. One of Hammell's associates will meet you at the jail. Do you understand?'

She closed her lips on what she had started to say, then nodded. She studied the dark edge of his coat sleeve on a white cuff, a platinum ring, the fingers curled tightly around her hand.

He said, 'I can't represent you.'

'Because of what we did?'

'Yes.'

She smiled a little, looking away. 'You shouldn't have let that happen.'

'I know. But if I were in trouble myself, I would trust Ray Hammell. I trust him with you.'

'Not that.' Gail looked back at him. 'You should have told me about Renee.'

'Renee?'

'You were her lover.' When he didn't reply, she said, 'Am I wrong?'

He finally shook his head. 'How did you know this?'

'It doesn't matter.'

'It was over a year ago,' he said.

'No explanations.'

'Gail—' His eyes followed her as she rose to her feet.

She said, 'It's five till two. We don't want Frank Britton to come looking for me.'

The next hours ran together, one into the other. Frank Britton received them in the lobby of the Metro-Dade Police Department building. He and Anthony shook hands, exchanged pleasantries. And then Britton led them up the same way he had taken Gail the day before. He sat her down in his office, asked if she would like a cup of coffee, had someone bring it. Anthony gave Britton a document signed by Raymond

327

F. Hammell, Esq., that said she would make no statements. Britton had a search warrant and asked for her house and car keys. He promised to return them. Paperwork was filled out, copies given. Then Frank Britton said it was time to take Gail down to be photographed and fingerprinted. A uniformed officer walked with her, and she looked back over her shoulder at Anthony standing at the other end of the hall.

She rode to the Dade County Jail in a green and white Metro-Dade patrol car, handcuffed. A female officer sat in back with her, not saying much. There were scuff marks on the Plexiglas behind the front seat, and the handles had been taken off the doors. The car smelled like dirty underwear. Traffic was beginning to stream out from the city.

Inside the jail, the corridors echoed, fluorescent lights glared overhead. A guard – a black woman in a gray uniform – guided her by the elbow. She took off the handcuffs and put Gail in a plastic molded chair in a small room to wait with several other women, most of them poorly dressed and sullen. They stared at her. After nearly two hours the guard came to get her, but didn't put the handcuffs on again. She took her to the lobby where a young man in a dark blue suit was waiting. He handed her her purse. He said his name, that he was from Ray Hammell's office, and that he was here to take her home.

In Renee's old bedroom at Irene's house, Karen lay under the quilt with all three cats stretched out around her, one across her chest, the others curled up by her hips. Gail scratched between the orange cat's ears and it began to purr.

'Well, if the kids at school tease you, what are you going to say?'

Karen sighed. She looked tired, Gail thought.

'I am going to say . . . the police have made a big mistake and my mom didn't do anything wrong and she will prove it.'

'Good girl.'

'And if they don't shut up I'll punch them.'

'Not good.'

They both smiled. Then Karen said, 'Do I have to go to school tomorrow?'

Gail straightened the lace trim on Karen's pajama top. 'No. Not if you really don't want to. See how you feel about it in the morning.'

'Are we going to live with Gramma now?'

'For a while. Is that okay?'

Karen pulled the sleeping cat up to her chin and stroked its back. 'I wish we could go home. Daddy too.'

'Oh, sweetie. I'm sorry things are so hard right now.'

Gail could think of nothing else to say. She kissed Karen, holding her for a while, feeling the warmth of her small body. She smelled of soap and freshly laundered cotton. Gail finally pulled away, turning out the lamp on the nightstand. Dim light came from the hall.

'Mommy.'

'What, baby?'

'Are you scared?'

'Not so much anymore. It'll be okay.'

Karen said, 'You can sleep in here with me if you want to, so you don't get nightmares.'

Gail tucked the quilt around her. 'Well, maybe I will. Thank you.'

She heard Ben's voice at the door. 'Are you girls turning in?' He came in quietly. 'Good night, Little Bit.'

Karen held up her arms. 'Good night, Ben.'

He leaned down and kissed her. 'Don't let the bedbugs bite.'

'Your beard is itchy.'

He lightly pinched her cheek. 'And you're my little flower, aren't you?'

Gail smelled the bourbon on his breath. 'Ben, please. It's nearly ten-thirty.'

She left the door open a crack so the cats could stick a paw through and get out. They walked toward the living room, Gail in her robe and pajamas.

Ben put his arm around her shoulders, pulled her closer. 'My God. Seeing you and Karen in there – It's like Renee was back again, alive. Sweet Jesus, what's happened to us all?'

She maneuvered out from under his arm. When he looked at her, she said, 'Sorry. I'm tired.'

'You going to work the rest of the week?'

'Of course. This is no time for an unpaid vacation.' Dave had made a trip to the house and brought back her clothes and makeup. He planned to stay there through the weekend, in case she needed anything.

Ben said, 'All right, Friday I'll come by and take you over to Ray Hammell's office.' She had an appointment at four.

'You don't have to. He'll probably make you stay outside.'

'No arguments. You're not going to go alone.' Ben spotted his glass on a coaster on the coffee table and went to retrieve it.

Irene, wearing her glasses, was still curled up on the far corner of the sofa with the phone at her ear, her address book open on her lap. She was calling everyone in the family, in-state or out. Earlier she had phoned both the headmistress of Biscayne Academy and Karen's third-grade teacher to prepare them for the eleven o'clock news.

Gail followed Ben into the kitchen, where he set his glass in the sink. She poured herself a mug of milk.

Ben scowled. 'If we'd had Ray Hammell on this from the beginning there might not have been an arrest. I'm talking from the minute Britton got that bug up his ass. Hammell can smell a lousy case before it gets to the State Attorney's Office and the cops know it. That Cubano attorney of yours waited till Britton was about to come get you before he did anything about it.'

'He got me out, Ben.'

'Bull. I got you out. He called wanting to know what the hell to do. I was the one who got you out. What's he doing, taking the credit? And who's going to pay a hundred and twenty-five grand in bondsman's fees?'

Gail put her milk in the microwave and pushed the buttons. She hated it when Ben started raving. She told him what she had already told him several times tonight. 'I appreciate what you did for me, Ben. You know I'll pay you back.'

'That's not the point. How many murder cases has he done? He's a damn drug attorney, don't you know that? He defended some of the biggest cocaine cowboys in South Florida. Where do you think he got his money? All those guys are hand in glove. Wouldn't surprise me a damn bit if he knew what Renee was into even before she did, he came in so fast after she was arrested.'

She stared at the numbers counting down on the microwave. 'He had nothing to do with what happened to Renee. It was Carlos.'

'What do you mean?' Ben crossed to the cabinet where Irene kept his Wild Turkey.

'I think Carlos was involved in that drug operation she got caught in. I can't prove it, but that's what I think.'

Gail explained what Dave had told her – the boat,

the botched drug run. That Carlos used to supply Renee with cocaine.

She said, 'He needed money because he was embezzling from Ernesto Pedrosa's construction company. He tried kiting checks on closings at Vista Title. Renee found out about it. Maybe they both planned the drug run to the Bahamas, I don't know. But if it had succeeded, he'd be home free. As it turned out, she was the one who got stung.'

Ben eyeballed an ounce of bourbon into his glass. 'The guy's a damn menace. And he thought he was going to buy my property. I'm glad I told Quintana to forget it.'

'When?'

'Today during one of our many phone calls. I told him to tell his cousin Carlos the deal is off. I tore up the check and mailed it back.' Ben tipped back his glass, then said, 'With what you tell me now, I think Ray Hammell better put an investigator on Carlos Pedrosa.'

'So do I.'

Irene appeared at the kitchen door. 'Well, I've called everyone I can possibly think of,' she said. 'And tomorrow I'll stop your newspaper for the next two weeks. You'll be here that long, won't you? And Dave's going to see about the lawn man.' She tossed her notepad on the table. 'Anybody want some tea?'

Gail said, 'I'm about to go to bed and Ben was just leaving.'

'She's rushing me off, Irene. Gail's little way of telling me I've had too much to drink.'

Irene reached up to pat his cheek. 'Go on home then. I'll take care of things here.'

He took her hand. 'Irene, come up to Arcadia with me. Both of you, soon as this damn trial is over. I'm buying some property up there, did I tell you? We'll build a house, what do you say?'

'Ben, hush.'

'I can't take Miami anymore. It's going to kill us. Look what it did to Renee. What it's doing to Gail.' He gave Irene his glass. 'Put a little ice in there, will you, honey?'

She poured the bourbon into the sink, then filled a cup with coffee and set it on the table. 'Drink that.' Ben sat down and lit a cigarette, his lighter snapping open and shut. He moaned softly and put his forehead in his palm.

Irene said, 'Gail, go to bed. You look positively exhausted.'

Gail held up her mug. 'I was a little hungry.'

'Then I'll fix you a cheese omelet. Sit. It'll just take a minute.' Irene went to the refrigerator. 'By the way. Jimmy Panther phoned yesterday and asked me to talk to you about that mask. I said I'd call him today. I hope he'll forgive me if I don't because I am not putting that phone to my ear one more time tonight.'

'Jimmy Panther called you?'

'He's sweet on me, I think.' She laughed.

Gail watched Irene crack eggs into a bowl. Precise taps. Breaking the shells open with one hand, then dropping them neatly, nested in their other halves, into the garbage disposer. Gail wanted to let go, to weep on her mother's shoulder, to feel those small, precise hands stroking her hair.

Gail said, 'I want to see what Edith Newell has to say. He and Renee were working on something together. I don't know what, but she's going to help me find out.'

'Renee never said anything to me.'

'Well, it's just too weird to be ignored. He found her body, didn't he? How did he know where to look?'

333

Irene turned around from the stove. 'Gail, you can't be serious.'

'In my position, I take everything seriously.'

Ben spoke up. 'My guess is he was going to make a few more of those masks and try to pass them off as real.'

Irene gave him a look over her shoulder. 'He would never do that. It isn't like him. Jimmy Panther has no regard for material gain. He says the Indians live the way all people are meant to live.' The whisk clicked on the sides of the bowl. 'He's a true shaman, as far as I'm concerned. You listen to him talk sometime. It's a religious experience.'

Ben extended his cigarette in the direction of the ashtray. The ashes fell on the table. 'Jimmy Panther, AKA James Gibb, was once arrested for auto theft. Does he tell that to the visitors at the Historical Society when he's asking for donations?'

'Everybody has mistakes in his past.' The eggs sizzled when she poured them into the pan.

'Irene, you are a gullible, silly woman.'

'That's not very nice of you, Ben.'

He held up his cup. 'How about some more coffee?'

She slammed her spatula down on the stove. 'You come over here and expect to be waited on. I'm busy with Gail's omelet. I think you ought to call a cab and go home.'

Ben stared at her for a second, then pushed himself up. 'Irene . . . my dear . . . you are correct. I ought to go home. But I can drive myself four damn miles.' He crushed out his cigarette. 'Ladies. Good night.'

Gail felt an odd rush of pity for him, aware of her abruptness earlier. She smiled at him as he passed. 'Good night, Ben. Thank you.'

He stopped and crooked both arms around her neck, pulled her out of her chair. His chest pressed tightly against her breasts, bare under her pajamas and cotton robe. She stiffened but didn't draw away.

He lightly kissed her lips. 'Don't you worry, darlin'. Everything's going to be all right.'

Gail came out of Irene's walk-in closet with an extra pillow. Irene was back on the phone. Her cousin Marian, who lived in Charleston, had just heard from Boyce in Atlanta who had spoken to Patsy in Tampa.

One finger on the light switch, Gail stopped, looking down at Irene's dresser, at the bifold frame Anthony had brought to the funeral. She picked it up, saw the two girls in the backyard swing. The other frame showed Renee standing in the stern of a boat, big smile, and behind her a harbor in some Caribbean town or other. How pretty she was. Of course Anthony would have been attracted.

Renee was wearing white shorts and a hot pink tank top. The wind lifted the brim of her straw hat. Her hair was dark blonde, not platinum. She must have stopped bleaching it at some point and Gail hadn't noticed. She studied the small hand holding down the hat. The nails were bare and clean.

'Look at you,' Gail said softly. 'That's why I couldn't get a fix on you. Nobody else could either. Everybody with different opinions, telling me different things. You were changing. Becoming yourself, probably. Who would that have been, I wonder?' Gail brushed her thumb over the tiny face in the photograph. 'I think I would have liked you, Sis.'

She started to put the photo back, then let the pillow slide to the floor and held the photo closer to the lamp. Two thin lines of light ran over Renee's collarbone, meeting at a pendant that hung between her breasts – a gold heart outlined in tiny diamonds. A present from Irene on Renee's twelfth birthday.

Gail opened the first drawer of Irene's jewelry case, then another. From the third she lifted a small plastic zipper bag with a tag on it from the medical examiner's office. Connor, Renee. It held the earrings she had worn – gold loops, four pairs in various sizes. A pearl ring for the little finger of her left hand. Bangle bracelets. But no necklace.

Gail sat down on her mother's bed and dialed her home number. Dave answered on the sixth ring.

'I was beginning to think you were back at the marina,' she said.

'I didn't want to pick it up. I just watched Channel Seven news.' He exhaled. 'Jesus. Are you guys okay over there?'

'More or less. Mom's handling everything. She's wonderful.' Gail's eyes were stinging. 'Karen's not sure if she wants to go to school tomorrow.'

'Tell her to stay with Irene. She can miss the rest of the week. You probably should, too.'

Feet still on the carpet, Gail let herself drop slowly backwards on the bed until she stared straight up at the ceiling, tightly gripping the phone.

'What's the matter, Gail?'

Her voice was thick, her throat too tight. 'I'm tired, I guess.'

He laughed, not unkindly. 'It's been a shitty day, who wouldn't be?'

'Oh, Dave.' She closed her eyes, silence on the phone. 'What happened to us? I thought we were okay. I did. Not perfect, but we had a balance. Balance ought to be worth something.'

'Gail—'

'You should have told me. You should. I never saw it coming.'

'Maybe I didn't either.'

She wiped the tears off her temples. 'You said I

never let you near me. I was cold. Is that what you really thought?'

'I don't know. I was probably mad at you at the time.'

She laughed. 'People usually tell the truth when they're pissed off. Haven't you ever noticed? Well, the truth is, Dave – and I'm not even pissed off at the moment – the truth is, I have had a few rather odd revelations recently. I feel like I'm dangling over a dark pit. And it's not under me, it's inside.'

'Gail. Honey. You ought to go to bed.'

'Yes, I'm talking too much again.'

'Come on. I didn't mean it like that.'

'You're a very nice man, Dave. Irene said so and I agree with her.' Gail sat up and reached for a Kleenex in the box on the nightstand. 'I'm sorry I didn't make you happy.'

There was a long silence. Then he said, 'You want to come back here tonight?'

'Do you want me to? No. It's late.' She blew her nose. 'I really did have a reason to call you. Seriously. A question.'

'Okay.'

Gail reached around behind her for the photo in the bifold frame. 'Was Renee wearing her necklace the night of the party?'

'What?'

'You know. That diamond heart she always wore. Did she have it on?'

'Why?'

'Dave, please.'

There was a silence. 'Yes. She did.'

'You're sure?'

'The chain got caught in my watch strap when I was helping her out of the car. Yeah, she had it on. Why do you want to know?'

'Because the coroner didn't find it on her body.'

'Well, I didn't take it.'

'Dave. I know that.'

It took him a few seconds. 'Jesus. Somebody still has her necklace. Whoever did this has her necklace.'

Gail said, 'Let me ask you something else. Do you remember the name of that boat you worked on?'

'What boat?'

'The boat you worked on for what's-his-name. José Garcia.'

'Come on, that was last summer.'

'Don't you have any paperwork? The registration number? Anything?'

'Maybe. I'd have to look through my records. What are you thinking?'

'I don't know yet.' Gail stood up, tucking the Kleenex into her pocket. 'But I'm not going to sit around waiting to see what's going to happen to me.'

She glanced at the photo again, the two girls in the swing. Renee laughing. Gail leaning back, arms extended, holding on.

Chapter Twenty

'Gail, we're going to take you off the front lines for the time being. Believe me, it's better all round.'

Jack Warner – late fifties, fastidiously groomed to hide it – was head of Hartwell Black's commercial litigation department. Called into his office, Gail had guessed this was what he was going to tell her.

Her picture had appeared in the paper Thursday morning, a file photo from a charity event she had gone to five years ago. Perfect hair, sparkly earrings, the director of the Florida Philharmonic standing next to her in a tux. Socialite Miami lawyer charged with murder, released on bond. She had laughed at 'socialite'. Then nervously waited for the explosion from the State Attorney's Office, a demand that her bail be rescinded. Nothing so far.

The firm had made a statement to the press. *Regrettable incident. Confident of Ms Connor's innocence. An excellent attorney.* They had referred all questions to Ray Hammell.

Gail let her hands rise, then fall back into her lap. 'Jack, I'm just grateful you're not booting me out the door.'

He smiled, shook his head. 'We wouldn't do that. But you see the problem. Clients get nervous. Having their attorney accused of a serious crime, even wrongly, they're going to start biting their nails. And you're not going to be as effective.'

Unlike Larry Black, who occupied the other chair facing Warner's desk, Jack Warner could be brutally direct. She didn't mind. For the last two days the other attorneys had treated her as though she had been diagnosed with a fatal disease. Most of them had come by her office to tell her how awful this was, but nobody stayed for long. And nobody – not even Jack Warner – had asked if she was guilty. At least, not so she could hear it.

He gestured toward Larry Black. 'Larry can help you decide who to farm your cases out to, until this blows over. Can you do that by Monday, Larry?'

Larry nodded. Gail knew his moods well enough to know that his composed expression was phony: he hated this. He looked at her, his embarrassment showing for a second. 'We'll still need you on those files. Pleadings have to be prepared. Motions, briefs. The rest of the time—' He tried for a smile. 'We've got more than enough to keep you busy, helping out in the other departments. No reduction in salary, of course.'

'I appreciate that, Larry.'

Her career at Hartwell Black and Robineau – as anything but an associate attorney – was over. It bothered her less than she had thought it would. Other things weighed more heavily on her mind.

Jack Warner stood up. 'Gail, if you need anything, you come see me. Time off, whatever. We're going to be as supportive as we can possibly be.'

With a hand on her shoulder, he walked her to the door.

By twelve-thirty, with Bob Wilcox covering her morning calendar, Gail had dictated memos on most of her files – two major litigation cases, fourteen middling lawsuits, and thirty-seven other matters in various stages of completion. Now they were stacked all over her office, each pile with a microcassette on top. Miriam had brought them sandwiches from the deli around the corner. She had said she would stay as late as Gail needed her, no problem. Then she had burst into sobs.

Gail stood in front of her desk with her microcassette recorder, flipping through pages.

'In *Merkin v. Bayside*, answers to interrogatories are due May 11, but I told client May 4. Push him on this, otherwise he'll forget to do them at all.'

Her words flowed smoothly onto the tape. She reached for her coffee and realized that her heart was steady as a metronome and had been for days, ever since she had realized exactly how much trouble she was in. Battlefield courage, she supposed.

Half an hour later she flipped the last file shut and stacked it on four others. Rotated her shoulders. Put down the recorder and picked up the telephone.

She dialed Anthony Quintana's office, not knowing if he would be there. He was. The moment he spoke she felt short of breath. The intensity of this reaction surprised her.

'Gail,' he said. 'Are you all right?'

She closed her eyes, leaned on the edge of her desk. 'I called to say thank you. I'm sorry it took me two days to do it.'

'I understand. Where are you, at your office?'

'Oh, yes. They've decided to keep me out of sight of paying customers for a while, though.'

'That's too bad. A trial lawyer without a court-room.'

'For now.' She walked the phone cord around her desk, sat in her chair, and crossed her legs. 'I told Ray Hammell's assistant – I can't remember his name – that I'd left Renee's papers at your house.'

'Do you want me to bring them to you? Better still, come pick them up. This weekend, perhaps. I'd like to talk to you.'

She drew in a slow breath, aware suddenly of what had glided just beneath the level of her consciousness, more intense in dreams – physical sensations so acute she had been brought awake, orgasmic, blinking into the darkness, her pulse racing.

She said, 'It would be more convenient if you took them to Mr Hammell's office.'

He paused only a moment. 'If you prefer. He'll have them on Monday.'

'Anthony, you need to know this. The day before yesterday I spoke to someone who worked with Renee at the title company. Dolores Perrera, do you know her? They call her Loly. She's expecting a baby.'

'Ah. Yes, I remember her.'

'She told me something Renee had found out about Carlos. Whether or not it's true, I can't say. Carlos was embezzling from Pedrosa Construction. George Sanchez was helping him cover it up with money from Vista Title. Do you know anything about this?'

There was a silence over the line. Then quietly, 'No.'

'As I said, it's only an allegation, but I have to tell Ray Hammell about it. I'm sorry. Carlos is your family.'

'Of course you must tell him. Do you have any more details of this? How Carlos did it? How much he took?'

'I don't know,' Gail said. 'Loly said that Renee wasn't involved, other than knowing about it.'

'Perhaps I should talk to her myself. Or to George Sanchez.' The voice was quiet, the undertone deadly.

'Be nice. Remember you're getting it third-hand.'

After a few seconds, Anthony said, 'Is this how you learned about me and Renee? From Loly Perrera?'

342

'Yes. Not because I asked her directly. It came up in conversation.'

'And based on that conversation, you find it more convenient if I take Renee's papers directly to Ray Hammell's office.'

'Anthony—' She laughed softly, forehead leaning into her fingers. 'Let's not get into a discussion about it.'

She listened to the silence. Then he said, 'You're right. This isn't the time.'

After she hung up she sat for a few minutes, not moving. She felt as though her emotions were liquid, trembling at the rim.

An affair with Anthony. Oh, yes. If she could pretend he had never slept with Renee, then devastated her by shutting her out. Anthony had ended it, Gail was sure of that. Renee had loved him even after the affair was dead. Gail turned that bit of knowledge over in her mind – Renee had loved. And Gail loved her for that. She wanted to put her arm around her shoulders, huff indignantly, and tell her what other sisters would have said. *Well, forget that guy. He's not the only one. You're better off without him. Stop crying, you hear me?*

On the second floor of the Historical Museum there was an exhibit of Tequesta Indians. Stiff, dark-skinned mannequins, coarse black hair. The man sitting by a plastic orange fire, carving. The barebreasted woman holding a tray of food. The child watching his father. Behind them the museum staff had built a chickee, hung a dugout canoe, and painted sawgrass on the wall.

Gail leaned against the railing while Edith Newell talked, from time to time consulting a tiny spiral notepad.

'He's forty-four years old. He lives in a trailer west

343

of Miami, not out on the reservation. In fact, he never lived on the reservation, as far as I know.'

'Did he change his name legally to Panther?'

'No, that's his mother's name. I seem to recall he told me his mother was from the panther clan. Both his parents are deceased. Jimmy went to public school, not the reservation school, under the name Gibb. He dropped out of high school and went nights. He claims to have attended college, but if he did, it wasn't in Florida. He was in the US Army from 1968 to 1971 as James Gibb, honorably discharged. Never married or divorced in Dade County.'

Edith waited until some visitors had walked slowly past the exhibit, speaking French. Her cheeks were flushed with excitement, Gail noticed. Edith had delivered her report in the hushed tones of a B-movie spy. 'Jimmy is three-quarters Miccosukee but he was raised in town. Now he's gone back to his roots, you might say.'

Gail said, 'I heard he was charged with auto theft.'

Edith took her thumb out of the notepad, found her place, tilted her head to look through her trifocals. 'I was just getting to that. Yes. Magistrates' Court, February 1968. It doesn't say he was convicted, though. But there were others. What do you call it? A rap sheet?' Edith let Gail see the list. Drunk and disorderly. Trespassing – four of those. Possession of controlled substances. Driving under the influence. Resisting arrest.'

Edith pulled back her notes. 'Jimmy was a very bad boy.'

'Nothing recent?'

'No, this is all in the sixties.'

Gail was still amazed. 'How did you find all this?'

'It wasn't hard. My nephew's a lieutenant with the Miami Police Department.' Edith slipped her arm through Gail's. 'My dear, you know I would walk over hot coals for you. If necessary, I would have made the Clerk of the Circuit Court himself look up the records – his wife's my bridge partner. But do tell me. What does this mean for your case?'

'I don't know, Edith. Didn't you ever – maybe when you were digging in an archaeological site – come across something completely out of place and you just couldn't go on until you figured out why it was there?'

'Oh, certainly. Like a gold pocket watch in a Tequesta burial mound. I found that once and never did figure it out.' Edith opened her notepad again. 'But to go on.' She glanced around. Her reedy voice sank to a low monotone.

'Books he checked out of the main library during the past year and a half. A lot of adventure novels – men like that sort of thing, don't they? A Chinese cookbook, several books on religion and mythology, three on treasure hunting, two on archaeology in the Americas, three on state and local history' – she flipped to the next page – 'eight about Native Americans and of that, six on Florida Indians. Then there were two on Cuban history and four on Spanish explorers.' Edith looked up, smiling. 'That was the summary. I have the itemized computer printout in my office for you.'

'You're incredible,' Gail said. 'Do you have any idea what he was doing in the reading room?'

'Yes. An educated guess, mind you, since he was very secretive about it. Tequesta Indians. One of our staff members saw him looking at color slides on artifacts. Somebody else remembers he was looking at early Spanish maps of South Florida. I checked with the county archaeologist—'

'We have an archaeologist?'

'Oh, yes, dear. Very nice young man. He told me that Jimmy Panther was one of the volunteers at the

345

digs. Now, I didn't know this, because I haven't been to any in years. My hip replacement, you know. They did the Ferguson Mill site on the Miami River and then after that several of the burial mounds in western Broward County. Burial mounds, in fact, are where we generally find artifacts of any value.'

Edith put her head closer to Gail's. 'You know what I think, don't you?'

'That he stole the mask from an archaeological site.'

'Exactly.' Edith pulled Gail further along the railing around the exhibit, to a glass case. It contained three wooden masks carved into the shapes of animal heads, the wood nearly black from age. 'The Tequesta and other prehistoric tribes used these in their hunting ceremonies and often buried them with their owners. A burial mound can contain dozens of skeletons. Hundreds, if the site was used extensively. It takes months to unearth them properly. Months of painstaking, exacting work, otherwise you destroy more than you find.'

Edith nodded down at the case. 'Now, these masks here, even as old as they are, aren't nearly so valuable as that mask you brought me. You can't possibly let Jimmy Panther have it back now. If it's taken from the ground and it's prehistoric, it belongs to the State of Florida.'

Gail turned around from the exhibit, let her eyes wander. Across from where they stood, life-size cutout photographs of archaeologists sifting dirt from a site downtown, before a fifty-four-story bank building had been erected on the spot. The Miami skyline made up the background. Edith Newell, several years younger, in her baggy trousers and straw hat, carried a pick.

And Jimmy Panther had told Renee, walking across a parking lot downtown, that he could hear his ancestors weeping. The Tequesta who had been murdered by the Spanish.

'Do you think there's anything to his claim that he's descended from the Tequestas?' she asked, looking back at Edith.

Edith snorted. 'And I'm descended from the Babylonians.'

'None of what you've told me ties in to Renee, as far as I can see.' Gail put her hands on her hips, walked back and forth. 'Last time I was here you told me how they met. You said he came into the reading room and looked straight at Renee.'

'Yes.'

'Did you have the impression that it wasn't a chance meeting? That he knew she was there?'

'Hmm. Possibly. What does this mean?'

'I wish I knew. Did she ever go to the sites with him?'

'I asked. Bob never saw her there, and he would have recognized her. He knew Renee.'

Gail turned back around, staring at the Tequesta woman as if she could deliver some answers on that carved wooden tray she carried.

'There was a man in here once, with Jimmy Panther.' Edith came up beside Gail, her big, square hands curving over the exhibit rail. 'I've seen Jimmy talk to lots of people, so it probably doesn't mean anything.'

'Up here?' Gail asked.

'No, dear, down in the reading room. It wasn't that long ago. I didn't recognize him, and I know most everybody that comes in.' Her eyes turned upward as she tried to remember.

'Would he have signed the guest book?'

'Maybe. Maybe not, if he was with a member of the Historical Society. Jimmy was a member.'

'What did he look like?'

'Hispanic. Although he could have been Arabian or Italian, I don't want to generalize.'

'In Miami?'

'Well, Hispanic, then.' She nibbled at her lower lip, the lipstick already reduced to a dark pink line.

'Tall, short? How old? Bald? Glasses?'

'I'm trying to see him again, be quiet. He was sitting, so I don't know how tall he was. A nice-looking man, not old. Dark hair and eyes. I remember because he looked at me. And a beard, I think. Or a mustache.'

Gail touched her arm. 'Edith. Think hard. A beard?'

She closed her eyes, opened them. 'Yes. A beard.' Then she said, 'Renee was sitting with them. It was a month or two before she died.'

The initial meeting with Ray Hammell was to have taken an hour, sandwiched between another client and a hearing in federal court. After an hour and a half Hammell sent his associate to the federal courthouse.

Gail had come with Ben, who knew Hammell. Ben had brought a draft on his investment account. $90,000, representing a $75,000 down payment and $15,000 toward costs.

She hadn't wanted him there, and he probably suspected as much, but she had said nothing. He had earned his seat beside her on Hammell's sofa.

Gail had seen Ray Hammell on television last year, successfully defending a cop against charges that he beat a teenager into a coma. Hammell could have passed for a minister, with his blue suit, round face, and air of polite indignation: How in God's name could my client have been accused of such a thing?

He had let her see the indictment handed down by the grand jury this morning. She felt queasy reading it, the words shifting and melting on the page.

State of Florida v. Gail Ann Connor . . . that Gail Ann

Connor did, unlawfully and feloniously, from a premeditated design to effect the death of a human being, kill and murder Renee Michelle Connor, a human being, by cutting her wrists with a razor blade or other sharp instrument, thus causing loss of blood leading to her death, in violation of Florida Statutes 782.04(01) and 775.087, to the evil example of all others in like cases offending and against the peace and dignity of the State of Florida.

Hammell had spoken to the prosecutor assigned to the case. 'They aren't seeking the death penalty.'

A tremor ran through her. She hadn't considered that. Hadn't imagined – She cleared her throat. 'Then what do they want? Do you know?'

'Worst-case scenario. If the jury convicts and we lose all appeals, then you're probably looking at a sentence of twenty-five years, parole in ten. Worst-case.'

Gail gave the indictment back to him, told him no, she didn't want a copy of it.

He explained the procedure: The state would set an arraignment within twenty-one days of her arrest. He would enter a plea of not guilty on her behalf. Motions would be heard, discovery demanded, evidence produced, depositions taken. The prosecutor would offer a plea, which Hammell would consider. Or not, depending. The trial would most likely take place around the end of the year.

As to its outcome . . . Hammell had smiled slightly. He never made guarantees or predictions. He would wait and see what kind of case they had.

Now Ray Hammell stood at his window overlooking Brickell Avenue, the light making a penumbra of his gray hair. A young black woman named Alisha – his law clerk – sat at the corner of his desk taking notes. Her pen was poised, waiting.

Gail summarized what she knew about Carlos

349

Pedrosa. His affair with Renee. Dave's suspicions that he had been behind the botched drug run to the Bahamas. She heard Ben say, 'Oh, lord,' when she told Hammell about the boat Dave had worked on.

'*La Sirena*. It means mermaid in Spanish.' Then she unfolded a sheet of paper. 'This is the boat model and registration number. It might have some connection to Carlos.'

Alisha said she would check it out.

Gail told Ray Hammell what she had learned from Loly Perrera.

Hammell said, 'All right. We're going to put our investigator on Betty Diaz before we contact her personally. Let's see what's going on there. If Carlos has dropped her, if he's upset her in some way since this happened, maybe we can use that.'

Alisha wrote it down.

He added, 'I'm going to talk to George Sanchez at some point. If he was working with Carlos Pedrosa on this embezzlement, we'll need to know more about that. I want to find out how much Renee knew. Maybe George can give us an idea.'

Gail said, 'Today I told Anthony Quintana what was going on with Pedrosa Development. Should I have?'

'Well—' Hammell crossed the office and sat down on the arm of a chair facing the sofa. His foot swung back and forth. 'You shouldn't talk to anybody, all right? General principle. But I wouldn't worry about Anthony. He and I have already discussed your case at length. I'd like to speak to him again before he mentions this to George Sanchez, though. I think he could tell us how best to approach George.' He looked over his shoulder. 'Alisha, put a call in to Mr Quintana, please. Right now?' She nodded, picked up the phone.

Gail said, 'Are you aware that he and Carlos are cousins?'

'Oh, yes.' Hammell's nod revealed he knew more than this. Anthony must have told him everything.

Ben leaned forward, elbows on knees, his brow creased. 'What about a motion to dismiss? We might get this case dropped before it goes to trial.'

Hammell took a long, contemplative breath. 'Mmmnn. No, I doubt the judge would grant a motion to dismiss unless we come up with something really solid. I think we can expect a trial. But I'm encouraged with what I've heard today. The state's case won't be a lock and we'll have room to attack it.'

Ben went on, 'Carlos Pedrosa had a reason to want Renee dead. He probably lied to the police about his alibi. Seems to me we can use him to establish a reasonable doubt that Gail was involved.'

'If in fact the evidence points in his direction, and if he can't explain it all away.'

'We don't have to prove he's guilty,' Ben said. 'Just create a reasonable doubt that Gail did it.'

'Sounds simple,' Hammell said, 'but you have to tread cautiously when throwing accusations of murder at a potentially innocent man.'

'Mr Hammell?' Alisha was hanging up the phone. 'Mr Quintana's in court. I left a message for him to call you before he does anything else.'

'Thanks.' Then Hammell leaned over, gave Gail a firm pat on her knee. 'How're we holding up, young lady?'

She smiled.

'You ready to come back Tuesday and talk to me for two or three more hours?'

'I might sleep all weekend, then I'll be ready.'

'Good. Get your rest.' He stood up. 'I want to hear some more about that Tequesta Indian mask. Bring it with you, let's see what it looks like. We might have another angle here, you think?' He turned toward his

351

desk. 'Alisha, have some photos taken of Carlos Pedrosa. Discreetly. Then I want you to show them to – What's the lady's name, Edith Newell? Yes. At the museum.'

Ben got up from the sofa. 'Ray, I want to thank you for everything. I brought you a check, damn near cleaned house on this one. You still want it?'

'Afraid so. Alisha has the contract in her office, you can go take a look at it.' Ray Hammell held out his hand. 'Gail, don't worry too much right now, that's the best advice I can give you. It always looks confusing at first. We'll sort it out.'

Fifteen minutes later, Gail and Ben got into the glass elevator. Her head throbbing, she watched Miami rise toward them from twenty-two stories below.

Ben leaned with both hands on the chrome handrail.

'I don't suppose you want me to come with you next Tuesday.'

'No.'

'Gail—' He laughed soundlessly, his gaze going back to the trees getting closer. 'I don't begrudge you my time or my money. Neither does Irene. What I do object to is, you seem to think it's your due.'

'Oh, Ben—' Letting out her breath, she turned to face him directly. 'No lectures right now. Okay?'

'You asked me what was wrong with you, I guess that's it. You take. You assume. You want people to do for you, no questions. You accused Renee of being like that, and with good reason. But you're not so different. And if that's the problem with you and Dave, I don't blame him for wanting out.'

The elevator bumped gently to the ground and the doors slid open. On the walkway outside Ben looked back at her, his expression fierce.

'You coming?'

She pushed away from the handrail, hardly trusting herself to speak. 'I'm going to walk back to my office. I need the exercise.' She got a few yards past him, then turned around. 'Maybe we are alike, I don't know anymore. But she had more guts than I did. She tried to see things as they really were. Even herself.'

Chapter Twenty-One

The following Wednesday, abandoning a stack of files on her desk, Gail drove out to Everglades Adventures and Gifts with the Tequesta mask in her trunk. Past Krome Avenue, heading west, the road eventually narrowed to two lanes, a canal and saw grass prairie on the right, a strip of woods on the left. Gail turned into the parking lot, nosing up to the fence that extended from the gift shop. On the fence in flaking paint an Indian poled a dugout canoe toward an alligator with open jaws. *See Our Zoo of Rare Animals and Reptiles. Alligator Wrestling. Airboat Rides $8.00.*

Gail left the box in her trunk. Ray Hammell hadn't known what to make of the clay deer mask. It would have found its way back to Edith if Gail hadn't thought of something else to do with it today.

Inside the gift shop she maneuvered past a group of tourists poking through the souvenir T-shirts, then cut around a rack of postcards. She passed an open table of handmade dolls, then stopped and went back to it. The tiny dolls wore patchwork skirts, smiles embroidered onto brown heads made of palmetto fiber. She picked one up. Karen didn't much like dolls, but she would like to have a present to unwrap when she came home. Dave had taken her to his parents' house in Delray Beach for spring break. School would start again on Monday. Already Gail wanted her home again.

From time to time, as now, the thought of separation from Karen would come into her mind, chilling her like cold, gray rain. She hadn't asked Ray Hammell what might happen, afraid to hear his answer. She had imagined holding Karen on her lap in a room with a dozen other mothers, molded plastic chairs and stained carpet. Or seeing her through glass or wire.

Gail took a doll with a turquoise skirt to the cash register.

A woman about fifty, with skin like unironed cotton, looked up from putting price stickers on beaded earrings. 'That's ten-sixty, with tax,' she said.

'I'm looking for Jimmy Panther.' Gail gave her the exact change.

'You the lady that called? He's about finished out back. Go on. You don't have to pay.'

The doll in her purse, Gail went through the door that said 'Everglades Zoo. $4.00.'

On about a quarter acre of land, palmetto-frond chickees shaded cages of snakes and birds, raccoons, wild pigs, two black bears, and several tawny Florida panthers stretched out asleep. Gail read a reassuring sign that said the big cats were recuperating from accidents, or they were so old they couldn't live in the wild anymore. She wondered if it were true.

A dozen or more people gathered along a low chain-link fence in the back, watching what was going on beyond it.

Jimmy Panther, wearing blue pants and a faded red T-shirt, sat astride an alligator over ten feet long. Two others lay unmoving in the shade of a chickee behind him. A fourth floated in the shallow moat that separated the tourists from the gators. Gail leaned against the trunk of a palmetto palm, waiting. She had seen an alligator show before.

Hands clamped around its mouth, Jimmy held the

creature's head up. The scales on its neck were pale and shiny. The clawed feet dug into the sand. The muscles in Jimmy's arms stood out.

'This is what we call bulldogging. You've got a gator pinned. You want to tie him up, but you need both hands to do it. So you hold his mouth shut like this.' Jimmy stuck the alligator's snout under his chin and pressed it to his chest. He extended his arms. The crowd murmured and a camera flashed.

Jimmy grabbed a handful of loose skin under the alligator's jaw, the other hand curling over its nose. He shifted his weight and pulled the long jaws apart. Pointed teeth. More flashes from the camera. He let go and the mouth closed with an audible snap.

In one motion he stood up and stepped back. The alligator crawled to the edge of the moat and slid into the water, tail moving side to side, eyes just above the surface.

'So now you know what to do if you find an alligator in your backyard.' The crowd gave the expected chuckle and began to drift away. He dusted the sand off his knees. 'Thank you for coming to Everglades Adventures. Be sure to stop in the gift shop to purchase tickets for the airboat. Billy Osceola will be your guide.'

He noticed Gail then, and nodded at her. His hair was untied today, flowing over his shoulders and halfway down his back. He walked along the fence. 'You missed most of the show.'

'So this is what you do for a living.'

He picked up a metal bucket by the gate, then opened the latch. 'This and other things.' He went around to dig some bills and coins out of a can marked 'tips' wired to one of the fence posts.

Gail followed him across the yard, unsure of how to start this conversation. It would have been easier in her office, behind her desk. She said, 'I've lived in Miami all my life and I seemed to have missed the Miccosukees.'

He glanced at her. 'We're on display seven days a week at the Indian Village, go about fifteen miles down the road to the reservation.'

There was a spigot on the gift shop wall and he turned it on, holding the bucket under it. The water swirled pink for an instant and what looked like a piece of chicken skin spun in the vortex. Jimmy turned off the spigot and sloshed the water into the gravel alongside the building. An Asian couple with a small child stood nearby watching the bear pad back and forth in its cage.

Jimmy set the bucket upside down to drain and wiped his hands on a towel. He jerked his head to flip his hair over his shoulder. 'Where's the deer mask?'

'In my car.'

His expression said he had expected as much. 'What do you want to talk about?'

'Could we go somewhere else?'

He hung the towel on a nail, then led her to an opening in the wood fence. They came out behind the gift shop. The bare white ground sloped to a splintery platform with a railing around it made of two-by-fours, overlooking a weedy slough. The airboats would come past this spot, she supposed. She could see where the water hyacinths had been pushed aside, the channel disappearing into the saw grass. A dented Pepsi can floated in the weeds. Vine-tangled trees arched overhead.

Jimmy turned around an aluminum porch chair. 'Sit down.'

There was only one chair. 'No thanks.' She heard the insects chirring in the saw grass. She had half expected Jimmy Panther to refuse to talk to her, to call the police, to pull out his knife and demand his mask.

But he was only looking at her through slightly narrowed black eyes. 'What do you want to know?' He walked to where she stood at the railing.

'I want to know about Renee.'

'You're her sister.'

'We didn't see much of each other the last few years. I suppose you knew that.' Gail could see no change in his expression. 'You must have heard I've been charged with her murder.'

He said, 'Did you do it?'

'No.' She let out her breath. 'Look, I need your help. I thought – I hoped – you'd talk to me. If my attorney knew I was here he would probably fire me as a client.'

Gail turned her head toward the channel. The bright water threw dancing glimmers into the trees. 'I've never been a defendant before. I've defended other people – not in criminal cases, but they've been in danger of losing their last dime. I've seen them waiting, bewildered, probably hoping to God I didn't screw up. I always thought I'd hate to be in that position, waiting for somebody else to decide what's going to happen to me. I won't do it with my own case. So here I am. Pissing you off. Using whatever I can – including something that belongs to you – to find out about my sister.'

'The police talked to me already,' Jimmy said. 'They wanted to know if I saw anybody around when I found her. If I knew who might have wanted her dead, when was the last time I saw her. Where I was that night. I was home. I've got a trailer not too far from here.'

On the other side of the building an engine started up, an unmuffled roar. The sound grew, moved. Then Gail saw the airboat turn into the channel, a man wearing blue ear protectors in the high seat, three tourists down below, holding on. The propeller spun in its cage, picked up speed, the rudders straightening out. Gail put her hands over her ears, felt the wind tug at her skirt. Kicking up a froth of mist, the airboat vanished into the saw grass. The noise faded.

Jimmy Panther was still waiting. Gail asked, 'When you found Renee, was she wearing her gold necklace? She used to wear a necklace with a heart pendant, outlined in little diamonds.'

'I wouldn't know. I only got close enough to tell it was her, then I came on back here and called the police. Why'd you ask about the necklace?'

'We can't find it.'

His brows rose a fraction.

'You can also tell me who you are.' Gail bent to set her purse down on the deck and noticed how tense her muscles had become. 'Tell me how you can be part Tequesta when they've been gone for over two hundred years.'

'You want a history lesson?' He looked at her for a minute, then said, 'Okay. About 1700, when the Yamassee invaded from the north, they killed a lot of the Tequesta and sold others as slaves to the British. By 1750, most of the Tequesta had died out, but there were a few who intermarried with the Yamassee. Some of those remembered who they were and passed it along. My grandmother told me stories that her grandmother told her, and her people before that. The Yamassee later became part of the Seminoles. And the Miccosukees are part of the same group. Sure, the blood is diluted, down to a few drops, maybe, but the memory is still there, in the legend. Is that what you wanted?'

Gail said, 'What about your grandfather? Edith said he was white.'

'Hiram Gibb, came from Massachusetts. He sailed a trading boat from Miami to Key West and married a Seminole woman, Millie Cypress.'

360

'I heard he was a rumrunner for Al Capone.'

Jimmy Panther finally smiled, his slightly crooked teeth barely showing. 'He made a living that way, later on. He knew the backcountry, how to get a boat in and out of the mangrove channels. What else did Edith Newell tell you about me?'

'That you got into trouble with the police when you were younger. Auto theft, among other things.'

'That's a long time ago. You want to know about it?'

'Sure.'

There was the smile again. 'I hung around a bad element. Rich white boys at Miami High. My father owned a gas station and we lived in town. I didn't want to have anything to do with the Indian school. I liked acid rock and blonde girls and muscle cars. You know what muscle cars are? GTOs, 427 Ford Fairlanes, Roadrunners? These boys, they came out to Krome Avenue to do midnights, they called it. Straight highways, no cops, no traffic back then. Sometimes they'd blow the engines, break a fly rod. There was a big demand for parts. They started reporting their own cars stolen. They'd take out the parts, dump the car in a canal, and get paid for it. I helped, I'm not denying that. I was a couple years older, knew how to work on cars, so I fixed them. Then the insurance company noticed that all these guys were friends. You know who one of them was? Paul Robineau. Right, he's in your law firm.

'What I heard later was, the investigator went to Paul's father. He and a few other families paid the losses to keep their sons out of trouble, but they needed somebody to point the finger at. They gave me a choice – jail or the military. Paul went to Harvard that fall. I got to Vietnam just in time for the Tet Offensive.'

Jimmy glanced around when something splashed in the water. A blue heron had flapped down on the opposite shore, settling its wings against its body. Ripples moved slowly outward into the hyacinth and saw grass, sending flecks of sunlight into the trees.

'They made me a sniper.' Jimmy Panther's black eyes were still on the slough. 'Marines. The VC Hunting Club. When we went out, we called it going into Indian country. I did that for a while. Too long. Then I stayed stoned so I wouldn't be tempted to shoot at the wrong people. They put me on supply, then sent me to a base in Texas. Nothing but sand and rocks. After my discharge I lived in about ten states, doing this and that. I worked at Caesar's Palace in Las Vegas, in an Indian act. Buckskins and a feather headdress. I decided I might as well come on home.'

He flicked a leaf off the railing. 'As long as the Dade County Commission isn't totally bought off, and the city doesn't suck up what's left of the water, I guess I'll have this view to look at for a while. We used to live by hunting and fishing. The game's about gone and the fish are full of mercury. So we run airboats and make souvenirs for the tourists. To tell the truth, it's not too bad. But the white people have this thing about us lately. They feel guilty. I got invited to speak at a Christopher Columbus seminar. *The Herald* ran my picture a couple times. I've had old ladies tell me they're going to leave money in their wills to the tribe. This one guy, had to be about your age, said he was ashamed he was born white.' Jimmy Panther laughed. 'Fine with me, as long as it lasts.'

Gail studied his profile past the rim of black hair – curved nose, rounded jaw. She had never seen an Indian male's face so close. If he had to shave more than once a week it was only because his grandfather was white. Renee must have been fascinated.

'How did you become friends with my sister?'

He turned slightly. The light shifted on his hair, a

362

blue-black shimmer that caught the silver in it. 'I met her at the museum, got to know her.'

'Before you saw her, did you know she worked there?'

'Irene might have mentioned it. Yeah. I think she told me her daughter was a volunteer.'

He lies so well, Gail thought. 'Tell me about her. What was Renee like then?'

'A hard question. How do we know what's in another person's head?' He leaned his elbows on the railing and seemed to study the purple hyacinths floating in the slough. 'The first time we talked, we got into a conversation about legends and myths and religion, which I know something about because I studied it.'

'In college?'

'Out west. And I've studied on my own, as well. We had some pretty good discussions. She liked to talk about spirit, about separating your spirit from the world, the pure from the evil. I told her you can't. They're inseparable, like light and shadow. You have to accept both of them.'

'She was arrested for trafficking in cocaine. Did she tell you that?'

'Yes. I told her she took risks because she was afraid of death, and she wanted to see if she could touch it and survive.'

'Did she say anything about who she was involved with?' He didn't answer and Gail began to wonder if she had only thought the question in her head. She added, 'Did she say whose boat it was?'

'A friend of hers. She didn't say who. She said he didn't know she'd gone and he was mad as hell when he found out. I don't know whose it was.'

'Could it have been Carlos Pedrosa?'

Another silence. He seemed to be trying to figure out how much to say.

'You knew he was her lover,' Gail said.

Jimmy nodded.

'And her source for cocaine, before she got off it?' His expression did not contradict her. 'What did Renee tell you about him?'

'Not a lot. Cuban builder.' Jimmy walked further into the shade, then sat in the lawn chair, extending his legs in front of him. He wore slip-on blue canvas shoes, still sandy from the alligator pit. 'She was going to have his baby.'

'I heard.' Gail turned her head to watch the heron wading in the shallows. 'Did she want to marry him?'

'No. They weren't seeing each other so much before she died. Her decision.'

'How did he feel about that?'

'Not too good, from what she told me. He wanted her to get rid of the baby, they could go on the way they had. She wasn't sure. I told her to keep it. I said it was a way of starting over with her own daughter, a new life.'

'Why do you say it was a daughter?'

He raised one shoulder in a shrug. 'Because it was.'

'What else do you know about Carlos Pedrosa?' she asked.

'Less than you know, probably.'

'Do you think he's capable of murder?'

Jimmy Panther tented his fingers, tapped them against his chin. 'If he was pushed.'

Gail took a chance. 'Edith saw you with Carlos and Renee in the reading room at the Historical Museum about six weeks before Renee died.'

Jimmy Panther said, 'More from Edith Newell.'

'What were you doing?'

He continued to look at her without expression, then said, 'He was interested in Florida history. Renee brought him to talk to me.'

364

'What about?'

'Various things. The Spanish period, mostly.'

His answers were getting shorter, Gail noticed. 'You spent a lot of time in the reading room. What were you studying?'

'History. Indians. I'm planning a cultural museum out here. It pays to know something about my own culture.'

'Which? Miccosukee or Tequesta?'

He let his clasped hands down on his lap. 'Seems like we're back to the mask.'

'Why did Renee have it in her closet?' Gail asked.

'I told you. She was showing it to shops in the Grove.'

Gail laughed, and surprise flickered across his face, then vanished. She said, 'Oh, come on. You knew how valuable it was. I'm surprised you ever let it out of your sight. You said your grandmother made it. No. Not true. Not even true that your grandmother kept it under her bed. I think you found it in a burial mound, perhaps courtesy of our unwitting county archaeologist.'

Jimmy Panther's impassive stare was his only reply.

'It's not easy to sell pre-Columbian artifacts you take out of the ground,' Gail said. 'It's highly illegal. They belong to the state. You need someone with connections. Someone you can trust. Like Renee. The girl with a reputation. Renee knew all kinds of people, including Carlos Pedrosa. You lent Renee the mask so she could show it to him. So far, so good?'

Jimmy didn't answer. The air was heavy, no wind coming through the trees. She could hear a jet high overhead.

'But Carlos wouldn't have been interested if there were just one artifact. How many masks are there? Or pots. Or whatever. There had to be enough to make it worth his while. Then, before a buyer could be found,

Carlos and Renee argued. She wanted out. She knew things that could ruin him. He killed her. And the mask was still in her closet.'

Gail lifted her hands, let them fall. 'Maybe he killed her. Maybe they even fought over the Tequesta mask. I think he had his motives, but I can't prove anything.'

'Good for you if he did.'

'Yes,' Gail said. 'Good if he did.'

'You've got some interesting theories,' he said.

She pushed away from the railing, stood looking down at him in the chair. 'Jimmy, I'm not trying to get you in trouble with the state archaeologists. I'll make Edith Newell swear the mask never existed. You can have it and no one will know. Look, my attorney is going to contact you about all this, but I want to hear it for myself. I want you to tell me about Carlos Pedrosa.'

After a few seconds he asked, 'What do you mean about Renee knowing things to ruin Carlos?'

'He was embezzling from his grandfather. She helped him hide it.'

'Yeah. She said he was in trouble and she wanted to help him out.' Jimmy Panther looked up at Gail, his eyes going into slits in the sunlight. 'She let people use her. Carlos for one. Before she died, though, she was doing some heavy thinking. She was angry. You could look at her and see it. You could stand next to her and feel the heat pouring off. She was mad at somebody, that's for sure. I knew something would happen, but I didn't know what.'

Gail moved out of the way when he rose to his feet. He wasn't a tall man, but broad, the faded T-shirt snug across his chest.

He said, 'Okay. Carlos was going to find a buyer. I got the mask where I told you, from my family. Where they found it, I don't know. It hasn't got anything to do with Renee dying that I can see. I never heard her and Carlos disagree about it.'

'What are you going to do if I give it back to you? Let him sell it?'

'No. That deal is off. It was never meant to be. There was disharmony with Carlos Pedrosa. Maybe that's one reason Renee died, you never know. I feel bad about that.'

Gail said, 'Would you consider donating the mask to the museum?'

Jimmy smiled again, shook his head, the light glinting off his hair. 'Tell Edith Newell it belongs to us. The people out here, where it came from. We won't let it go again.'

In the parking lot, the cardboard box on a mildewed picnic table under the trees, Gail opened the flaps. She turned back the bubble wrap and cotton batting that Edith had put inside. The Tequesta mask was nested in the center. She pulled it out carefully, blowing away some dust on its forehead. In places the dark red surface still gleamed, remnants of a rich patina.

Jimmy traced the crescent on the deer's forehead. 'That means it's a peaceful creature,' he said. 'The ones that eat flesh, like the bobcat or panther, they have lightning over their eyes.' He made a jagged motion with one finger.

Gail gave the deer's face one last look – flaring ears, gently rounded eyes – then tucked it back into the box and handed it to Jimmy Panther.

Chapter Twenty-Two

Miriam came into Gail's office with some phone messages and went out again. Gail flipped through them.

Edith Newell from museum, has more info. Do you want to renew your Film Festival membership early for next year? Call Anthony Quintana.

Gail returned to her book, Volume 403 of *The Southern Reporter*. She was drafting a cross-reply brief for an appeal. Insurance underwriter bitching about a three-million dollar judgment. Subsidiary company wanting a share. Gail wished she could throw it all out her window and watch the pages spin and flutter to the street. If her window weren't caulked and screwed shut.

She tossed her pen onto a stack of research notes and looked at the messages again.

Call Anthony Quintana.

He had called twice yesterday and she hadn't called back. The memories of him and Renee were too close to the surface. He had lied to her about that. A lie by omission. She turned the piece of paper facedown, feeling as though she had just run up a flight of stairs. Whatever he wanted, he could wait.

She checked her watch. Eleven-thirty. Ray Hammell should be back from court.

He wasn't, and his associate was with a client. She asked to speak to his law clerk.

When Alisha came on, Gail said, 'I meant to call yesterday afternoon and got busy. You guys don't have to bother showing photos of Carlos Pedrosa to Edith Newell. He was the man at the museum. Jimmy Panther says so.'

'What'd you do, go talk to this Indian on your own?'

'Tell Ray I couldn't help myself. Jimmy also confirms Carlos was the father of Renee's baby. Carlos wanted her to have an abortion, and apparently they argued about it.'

'Ooh. Ray's gonna like that.'

'I thought so. Jimmy will talk to him. But I don't think the Tequesta mask had anything to do with Renee's death. How about Betty Diaz? Any news on her?'

'We're looking,' Alisha said. 'We had someone keep an eye on her over the weekend. Carlos was nowhere to be seen. There's nothing going on between those two, far as we can tell. I think Ray's going to give it another week or so, then drop a subpoena on her.'

'Maybe she's a good liar.'

Alisha laughed. 'You never heard Ray get hold of somebody. I'll give you the deposition transcript, you remind me.'

'What about that boat, *La Sirena*? I want to hear some more good news,' Gail said. 'Tell me it belonged to Carlos.'

'It didn't. I just got the phone call on that an hour ago. Hang on, let me find my notes.' There was the clunk of a phone hitting a desk. A while later, pages turning. Alisha said, 'The boat was seized and forfeited to the state . . . Okay, here it is. The owner was Nelson Restrepo, a Colombian with an office in Panama, doing business – if you can call it that – in South Florida. They would've brought him in, but he'd already left the country. Jumped bail on a bank fraud charge.'

Gail leaned way back in her chair. 'Oh. My my.'

'My my *what*?'

'Is this the same Nelson Restrepo who was on trial for cocaine trafficking a few years ago? It's not exactly a common name.'

There was a pause. 'Gee, I don't know. I wasn't down here then. Why?'

'Something else for you to mention to Ray Hammell. Restrepo was a client of Anthony Quintana.'

'Is that so?'

'This is getting complicated. Tell Ray—' Gail's laugh trailed off.

'Tell him what?' Alisha prodded.

'I don't know what to think of this.'

'You're on trial for murder, you don't have to think. Let Ray figure it out.'

Gail said, 'The boat was seized just south of Bill Baggs State Park. That's on Key Biscayne. Anthony lives there. He has a dock in his backyard.'

'Uh-huh.'

'And they – Anthony and my sister had an affair last year. Did he mention that to Ray?'

'Nope. Or if he did, Ray didn't tell me about it. They've had some fairly long discussions about your case, but I don't think this little item came up.'

Gail traced through her eyebrow with a forefinger, smoothed it down again, wondering if Anthony had told Ray Hammell why he had withdrawn from the case. Ray, *no puedo*. I can't do it, man, because your client had her face in my lap and her hand on my zipper.

'Gail, you still there?'

'Yes. I'll talk to Ray about this later. Tomorrow. We have an appointment at four o'clock.'

Gail picked up Anthony's message again, then held it over the trash can. She had learned not to believe in coincidences. She didn't know what was going on exactly, but something was. Son of a bitch. He had been lying about more than Renee.

She scanned the message about the Film Festival. No point in buying tickets for a week of foreign films. The warden wouldn't let her out to see them. She crumpled the slip of paper.

She frowned at the message from Edith Newell. More info? She got her purse out of her desk drawer. Might as well walk down to the museum, maybe grab a sandwich on the plaza. Besides, she had some info for Edith. The Tequesta mask wasn't coming back.

Edith Newell pushed her glasses up and squeezed the bridge of her nose. She gave a long sigh and took her hand away. Her glasses dropped back into place.

She said, 'I suppose you had to. I apologize for snapping at you, dear. God knows I might have done the same thing, in your position.' She rolled back from her desk, the wheels on her chair squeaking. 'Never mind. I said I'd help you and I will. Come on.' She glanced at her watch – a man's Timex with a stretchy gold band. 'I've got a few minutes before I'm due at the Conservancy.'

They made their way along the corridors in the basement, then up the stairs to the lobby, Edith favoring her bad leg, grumping at Gail's suggestion that they use the elevator.

Edith explained about requests for copies. Up until the first of the year, when a new operations manager had put a coin-operated copy machine into the reading room, anybody who wanted copies had to fill out a form and give it to a staff member.

'Then they'd have to wait for the person to go downstairs and make copies in the office,' Edith said. 'A quarter a page.'

Gail held the door to the reading room and followed Edith inside. Several high school students sat at the long tables with open boxes of old photographs. The noise level dropped when they saw Edith.

Edith spoke close to Gail's ear. 'I found a whole drawer full of receipts in our bookkeeper's office, going back since we opened. Imagine keeping such trash. Well, what's a museum for, I ask you. Anyway, the name of the person wanting the copies would usually be on the receipts, and sometimes what was being copied. Sometimes not.'

They walked along the rows of bookshelves and filing cabinets to the rear of the reading room, where two microfiche machines sat under gray plastic dustcovers.

Gail said, 'You found Jimmy Panther's name.'

'Indeed. The first notation was two and a half years ago.' Edith led Gail to a metal cabinet with wide, shallow drawers. 'I looked for what he wanted copies of. There must have been more that no one thought to jot down, but here's what I found, all noted within the last year. I stuck them in here.'

She gestured for Gail to move out of the way, then opened the top drawer, which slid smoothly out on rollers. Inside were maps and four plastic zipper bags. Edith laid the bags on top of the cabinet. Two contained yellowed pamphlets, one a faded paperbound report of some kind, and the last a single sheet, its edges crumbling. All the bags had numbers on them. Filing codes.

'These two here—' Edith slid the pamphlets closer '—are requests to the US Congress dated 1833 and 1836 for additional money for a survey of the great swamp. That was before it was called the Everglades. There's a tiny reference in both of them to locating Spanish gold supposedly removed by the Tequesta

Indians from the ship *Santo Espiritu* in 1732.'

Edith held out the bagged sheet of paper. 'This is from an 1872 surveyor's report,' she said. 'Josiah Tinsley describing ancient Indian encampments on hardwood hammocks – islands – in the east Everglades.' She whisked the sheet away and replaced it with the report, bound in faded blue paper. 'And this. An 1878 US Army Corps of Engineers geological survey, same area. Water levels. Ground elevation. This is before they started cutting in all those drainage ditches and canals. It's mostly dry land now.'

Edith rolled out the drawer again. 'Look. Maps.' She closed it, opened the next. 'This cabinet is full of maps, top to bottom. Road maps, survey, Army maps—' Bracing herself, she came up slowly from slamming the bottom drawer shut. 'Accessible to anybody. And yes, several people saw him back here looking through these drawers.'

'Lost Spanish treasure buried in the Everglades?' Gail gave Edith a sideways glance. 'And Jimmy Panther was trying to find it.'

'Oh, who knows what he was really doing?' Edith stacked the plastic bags and handed them to Gail. 'Here. If you want to, run downstairs and make copies. Tell Rosa I said no charge. I'd do it myself but I haven't got time.'

Gail followed her back through the reading room. Edith's voice dropped to a whisper again.

'You asked me a while ago about the Tequestas going to Cuba? I looked it up yesterday. The Spanish government in Havana sent a ship to rescue them from attack by another tribe in 1711. Two hundred and seventy went to Cuba, most of them died, and some returned home. Then they came under attack again and in 1732 the Spanish sent two more ships. The *Santo Espiritu* was one of them.'

Gail pushed open the glass door. Laughter was echoing in the lobby. Two rows of schoolchildren lined up at the stairs.

Edith headed for the main entrance. 'The legend is – and I hadn't thought of this for years, until I saw those papers – the Tequesta came on board for food. They got into the rum, sailors and Indians alike, and by morning the Indians were gone. So was the captain's strongbox. Coins, bars. Who knows what was supposed to be in there?' She made a snort of laughter. 'The Spanish crown jewels.'

Outside, she stopped walking, squinting in the sunlight that poured into the plaza. Gail could feel the heat radiating off the red clay tiles. People sat at the umbrella tables eating lunch and talking. The wind snapped the flags outside the library.

Edith clipped round sunglasses over her regular frames and put them back on. 'Apparently it wasn't enough to worry over, because after a cursory search the Spanish turned their ships around and went back to Havana. But stories of buried treasure are so compelling, aren't they? The gold – assuming the Tequestas even took it – never turned up, so people naturally assume they buried it. Every so often we get reports of destruction of Indian mounds. Idiots. They think there's something in them besides old bones and broken artifacts.'

'Maybe Jimmy Panther thought so, too.'

Edith started walking backward, eager to be on her way. 'No, dear, don't you believe it. He's not stupid. The only thing he found was the Tequesta mask, and I'd give half my remaining teeth to know where from.'

Gail held up the plastic bags with the papers inside. 'Then what's all this for? And those books he checked out of the library on lost treasure?'

The only reply was a dismissive wave. Then Edith

375

hurried across the plaza, a gangly, wispy-haired woman in clunky sandals and men's khaki trousers.

Gail pushed off from the edge of Irene's pool, arms extended, angling deeper. Dark, silent water. She drifted, eyes closed, feeling her body rising slowly, breaking the surface, cool air on her skin. She rolled face up. After burning off the day with twenty laps, she was coasting, catching her breath. Through the screen on the back porch, the sky was a deep, luminous blue, rosy purple toward the west. Crickets set up a steady chirr in the hibiscus.

She heard Irene drag a chair closer to the edge of the pool. She wore plaid shorts and a sleeveless top, her red hair fluffed out from her head.

'Come in with me,' Gail said.

'With my baggy knees?' Irene sat down, backlit from the kitchen, the gray cat curling up by her feet.

'Mother, you're silly. You and Renee and I went skinny-dipping in this pool a few years ago.'

'Did we?' Irene laughed. 'Yes. I think we were tipsy on margaritas. Remember how we giggled? I loved watching you girls. My daughters. Two sleek creatures risen from the sea. So lovely.'

Gail crossed her arms on the edge of the pool, her toes grazing the bottom. 'Before all this happened, I never thought about the good times we had.'

'There were some.' Irene's smile was unsteady. She put her cigarette to her lips, then exhaled a blue cloud. 'I just got off the phone with my dear cousin. The traitor's putting his tackle box and two of his old pals in his Winnebago, and they're all leaving for Arcadia Saturday at dawn. Goodbye to civilization for a whole ten days.'

'So it's you and me for Easter dinner. Dave won't be back with Karen until Sunday night.'

'I don't feel like cooking,' Irene said. 'Why don't we go out somewhere fancy and spend some money?'

'Okay, but you'll have to let me pay for it.' Gail waded to the curved steps in the corner, leaning forward against the water.

Irene got up to bring her a towel. 'Ben says he's going to find five acres and a house next week. He's serious. I told him I'd visit, but that's it. You need me to help with Karen and I couldn't possibly leave Miami.'

Water streamed off Gail's body. She took the towel and dried her face and arms.

Irene said, 'Anthony Quintana called when I was talking to Ben.'

Gail bent to do her legs. 'What did he have to say?'

'Nothing. I told him I was on the phone, could he hold on, but he said no, you have his number at home, please call.'

Gail made a noncommittal shrug.

'What's the matter? He seems like a nice man.'

'Frank Britton seemed like a nice man.' She wrapped the towel around herself and went inside.

She was dressed and sitting at the desk in the den with a stack of books, copies, and notes before she decided she might as well see what he wanted.

. She dialed his number and he answered on the second ring.

'This is Gail,' she said.

'Ah. I was about to think you were avoiding me.'

She hesitated, then said, 'What did you want to talk to me about?'

A glass clinked in his kitchen. Water ran briefly. Anthony said, 'I wouldn't have called you at home, but something came up late this afternoon. Ray Hammell asked me about a certain boat owned by Nelson Restrepo. He didn't say how he knew Restrepo was once a client of mine, but I assume you told him. Yes?'

'Yes,' Gail said. 'You should have told him yourself.'

'What have you created in your mind? Have you turned me into a drug dealer as well as a seducer of your sister?'

Gail studied the pigeonholes in the desk, wooden squares and slots with a 1989 'TV Guide', rusty paper clips, curling photos, old letters, cards. 'I'm sure Ray can fill me in on what happened with the boat. We have an appointment tomorrow.'

'No. I'm going to tell you myself. Leave now, you can be here in twenty minutes.'

She laughed, surprised. 'I'm not going over there. Ray Hammell would smack my hand with a ruler if he found out, and he'd be right.'

'Then you name a place,' Anthony said. 'I'll meet you.'

'I'd love to, but I have an appellate brief due by Monday, and I'm already on thin ice.'

He exhaled. 'Gail. Listen to me. It isn't Nelson Restrepo I want to talk about – although you ought to know the truth. It's Renee. You want to know about her, I'll tell you. You won't hear it from Ray Hammell.'

They agreed to meet under the flags at Bayside, a few miles down Biscayne Boulevard from Irene's house in Belle Mar. Gail came around the corner from the parking garage and spotted him. Pacing slowly toward the row of green metal benches bordering the walkway, then back again, people going by him in both directions. No tie. Jacket pushed back, hands in his pockets, narrow hips.

Gail watched him as she came closer. The curve of his throat as he glanced toward the black sky. How he moved. Looking toward the street, turning back. His gaze falling to the herringboned bricks, then toward the marina. Leaning down to peer at tropical fish in the window of a store, then drifting back toward the street. Finally seeing her. Not moving now. Waiting.

When she reached him, Anthony said, 'Would you like to have a drink?' He tilted his head toward the Argentinian restaurant. 'Tapas isn't crowded.'

'No,' she said. 'Let's walk.'

On a Thursday just past eight-thirty the crowds were still fairly thick, all the boutiques and stores and pushcarts doing a good business. Cruise ship passengers. Kids on spring break.

Gail was wearing slacks and a light sweater, sleeves pushed up, the thin strap of her purse across her chest, in case someone tried to grab it. They went past the intersection of two wide corridors, shops in both directions. The walkway opened onto a wide area of fountains, tables, chairs. The daiquiri stand was decorated with huge cartoons of fruit. A crowd had gathered around a mime juggling stuffed parrots.

Anthony said, 'This is ridiculous, meeting here.'

'It's convenient,' she said.

'It's safe.'

She gave him a noncommittal look, then stepped back to let a woman with a stroller pass. 'Should I tell Ray Hammell we talked?'

'It's up to you. If he does not approve, tell him it wasn't your idea.'

They walked toward the water. A striped-shirted gondolier was poling a middle-aged black couple past the docks. An anniversary, perhaps. The woman wore a corsage.

'Anthony.' When he looked at her she said, 'Did you tell Ray about you and Renee?'

'Of course. I told him it was why I had to withdraw as your attorney. Not entirely true, but he was satisfied with the explanation.'

Gail kept her eyes on Anthony for a moment,

wondering if he were lying. Wondering what difference it could make to her either way. They went up a few steps then along a sidewalk, marina on their left, jazz coming from speakers overhead.

He said, 'I suggested you come to my house because it would be private, not because I wanted anything else.'

'Really?'

He shrugged.

She said, 'Look, we ought to get something cleared up right now. Things got a little out of hand over there last week.'

'Out of hand?'

She slowed down. A group of teenage girls had stopped just ahead. 'I'm not blaming you.' When the girls veered into a swimsuit store Gail began to walk again. She said, 'It was dangerous and foolish. For both of us. I want you to know how I feel about it.'

Anthony inclined his head, a reluctant assent.

They came to the end of the shops. A combo at the open-air Brazilian nightclub was playing samba music. Waiters rushed around with trays full of drinks – pineapples and coconuts and tall, fruity-colored glasses.

She turned to Anthony. 'So tell me about Nelson Restrepo.'

Someone bumped him from behind and his mouth tightened. 'Not here,' he said.

They went down the sloping sidewalk, the music fading a bit. Ahead of them was the black water of Biscayne Bay, the lights of the Port of Miami, dark shapes of islands beyond.

He turned right, kept walking, going past Bayside into the park, buildings ahead of them, streetlamps along the seawall. The wind was blowing off the bay, chilly for this late in April. Gail could hear the water slapping against the huge rocks dumped as tide breaks. There weren't so many people here. Anthony kept between her and the park. She wondered if he had his pistol with him. She pulled the sleeves of her sweater to her wrists, crossed her arms.

Anthony said, 'Nelson Restrepo owned the *Sirena*. After the acquittal in his drug case, we went fishing in the Keys to celebrate. We took one other trip together, Bimini. About a year later, Nelson was arrested on conspiracy to commit bank fraud. He put up the bail and went back to Panama. He called and said he would send a check for my attorneys fees – he never did – but meanwhile I could use his boat. My partner Raul and I took it out a few times. Then I met Renee. She and I went with another couple to Nassau.'

'There was a quick-release port in the hull.'

'Yes. Nelson had bought the boat used, not knowing it was there. He thought it was funny. Ironic.' Anthony glanced at Gail. 'That's the boat in the photograph I gave your mother.'

Renee in the straw hat. Renee in the pink top, no bra. Gail said, 'You took the picture?'

'Yes. That was the last time I saw the boat. Renee knew about the release port, by the way. I showed her. When she was arrested, she didn't tell me it was on board the *Sirena*. I assume now that Carlos was looking for a boat such as that one, or that he knew people who were, and that she suggested it to him. As to how he acquired it, or who else was involved, we'll never know, unless Carlos tells us. I explained all this to Ray this afternoon.'

Anthony stopped walking, watching Gail intently, as if her thoughts might write themselves on her face. Gail hardly knew what they were. They whirled, changed shape and meaning. The explanations seemed obvious, then too easy.

His hands moved outward, palms up. 'What else do you want to know about it?'

'When did you learn the *Sirena* had been seized?'

'This afternoon. Ray told me.'

'Nelson Restrepo never called to ask about his boat?'

'No. It was never in my care. And as I told you, Nelson may be dead. He had enemies.' Anthony waited, then said, 'I am telling you the truth. I want you to believe that.'

'Is Ray going to question Carlos?'

'Yes. I doubt he will be truthful.'

Gail saw Carlos's sunglasses, the beard, his white teeth showing in a smile. The wind flipped the edge of Anthony's jacket. He was still watching her.

'What's Ray Hammell's opinion of Carlos?' she said.

'That he makes a better defendant than you do.'

'Well. Do you think he killed my sister?'

Anthony took several seconds. 'I don't know. Your jury might buy it. Particularly if his alibi is shot down.'

'Have you talked to him?'

'I haven't been able to reach him.'

'Does he know you suspect him of embezzlement?'

'No. Ray Hammell told me to hold off on any confrontation. But I told Raul about it and we're looking through the books. And we're checking the real estate closings George Sanchez handled.'

Gail doubted George Sanchez would have a job much longer. Carlos either. Excommunication by his grandfather was the lesser of his worries. He could face a murder indictment. So much the better for Anthony.

She walked to the edge of the seawall, the wind blowing her hair back. She felt a prickling sensation in her spine, Anthony standing behind her. What did she know about him? That his father was a blind ex-revolutionary; that his rich grandfather had once been a terrorist; that Anthony wanted it all, but in his own

382

way. They were alone, she and this man who had made love to her sister. Who might have done more than that.

Overhead the clouds raced westward, pale gray shapes illuminated from beneath by the lights of the city.

'What about Renee?' she said, not looking at him.

'Renee. Yes.' He moved to stand beside her, his face in shadow. 'I want to tell you how we met, what happened to us, and why.'

Gail said, 'I thought you might tell me . . . about *her*. That's what I expected.'

Anthony stood motionless, squinting slightly into the wind. His slight Spanish accent made him seem more remote to her.

'We met at a bar in Coconut Grove. Typical, no? I was alone, she started a conversation, and . . . what you might expect to happen, happened. The details don't matter. After my divorce that had become common for me, meeting women in that way. I must have been trying to make up for fourteen years of unrewarded fidelity. Renee was what I wanted then. She was younger, attractive, uninhibited. She made me laugh and I needed that too. We were together – intensely – for several weeks before I realized what I should have seen at once. She couldn't . . . achieve sexual satisfaction. She said it didn't bother her.'

The collar on his shift lifted, then settled. 'It bothered me. I might have ignored this if not for the rest. There was a part of her completely sealed off. I pushed her to tell me and she became hysterical. I never asked again. She often acted like a child. I am not referring to childish behavior. I mean literally a child. She called me Daddy when we made love. She talked like a little girl. When I told her to stop, she wouldn't, not until I lost my temper. Once she threw something at me. A

383

glass. In my own house. When I told her to get out, she cried. And then wanted me to punish her.'

When Gail turned away Anthony grasped her arm. 'You think I could do that? No. Nor could I end it. Not then. I knew she had once tried to kill herself. We endured another week or two. I was exhausted from the strain of it, not sleeping, making mistakes in my work. Then she said she loved me. Whatever it took, whatever I wanted, she would do it. But I knew it was over. I worried for days how to tell her, afraid of what she might do. But finally I did tell her. And she laughed and said it was good while it lasted. I will admit to you, I was relieved. She had only a part-time job at the historical museum, so I arranged a position at Vista Title. That's where she met Carlos. Soon she forgot about me.'

'Did she?' Gail was shivering, her jaw tight, her arms across her chest. It wasn't the wind.

Anthony's eyes were searching her. 'Renee became better. Happier with herself. You should know that about her, too. We spoke a few times afterward, and that was my impression.'

Gail could barely get the words out. 'Why did you tell me these things?'

He took some time to answer. 'Because you have the wrong idea of what I am. I would never have told you this if you had not found out about Renee and me. Never. I knew she would come between us. She's in your mind too much. When you were with me last week you told me what she was like. You described her. On the terrace, as you fainted, you said you saw her.'

'I said that?'

'Yes. You called her name.'

Gail turned her back on the wind and held her hair with one hand.

384

Anthony was closer now. She could feel the heat of his body. 'When you came to – when I was holding you – Renee was still there. You did what you thought Renee might have done. You said that, too. But it wasn't Renee I made love to. It was you. Do you think that I touch you and think of Renee? Gail, you're nothing like her. Believe me, I would know.'

She laughed. 'Oh, God. Stop. What did you expect would happen? Two adults, unattached. I come running to you to save me from Frank Britton. My hero. Plus you're tall, dark, and macho. Add a couple hours of intense conversation. *¡Salsa!*'

He leaned around her. 'And that's what you think? An impulse? I have wanted you since the day we walked on Flagler Street. The moment you told me to go screw myself with that letter from Nancy Darden to Carlos, or words to that effect.'

She looked back toward Bayside. 'Anthony. You're a dangerous man. I don't need this. I really don't.'

'And what did you call me? Latino macho—?'

She knew he saw her smile. 'More or less.' She could feel the heat pulsing through her body. Stupid, stupid, she thought.

He said, 'For you – tell me if I'm wrong – it wasn't an impulse either.'

'I don't know you,' she said. 'I don't know what I want with you.'

'No?'

'No,' she said.

'We should find out,' he said.

'Oh, you think so.'

'Yes. We should.'

'Tell me something.' She turned her head. 'Do you always make love in Spanish?'

A smile started at the corners of his mouth, moved to his eyes. She could have fallen into them. He said,

385

'Come home with me. I'll show you.'

She nodded, feeling the desire. She could hardly breathe. He kissed her and she turned to him, slipped her arms under his coat. Warm, solid. The delicious scent of him. Whatever he had done, she didn't care.

His tongue went into her mouth, along her teeth, going deeper. She pushed her hips against him. He was ready. She wished she had a skirt on. Wished no one else was there, she would pull it up herself. She slid her hand between them, heard him groan.

He tightened his fingers in her hair and tilted back her head. His mouth went to her ear. She shuddered, sagged against him. In clear English he told her what he would do to her.

It was somewhere near dawn. A pale gray light was coming through the curtains. She had awakened to the sound of ringing. A telephone.

Anthony was speaking softly, not to wake her, propped up on one elbow. Gail closed her eyes, burrowed deeper into the blankets, felt the warmth of his bare hip and thigh.

Gradually she became aware that the tone of his voice was wrong. She pulled the blanket away from her face, blinked.

'Who else did you call? . . . No, I'll do it, as soon as—' He ran his fingers into his hair. 'Okay. Thank you.' He quietly replaced the phone but didn't lie down again.

She sat up and touched his back. 'Anthony?'

He turned his head to look at her. 'Carlos is dead.'

Chapter Twenty-Three

The rain had slackened to a light mist by the time Anthony turned his Cadillac onto the Loop Road. The Loop ran south off the Tamiami Trail, making a meandering U shape before cutting back north.

Gail sat in the passenger seat. It was just past eight in the morning. She had told him he might as well take her along, because she would follow in her own car if he didn't.

Anthony turned the windshield wipers to intermittent. He hadn't said much during the trip from Key Biscayne. His hands were tight on the wheel, his body hunched forward a little. He kept the speed up, trees and tangled bushes blurring past, tires rattling over the potholes. He had told her what he knew. Late yesterday afternoon a cane fisherman had noticed the back end of a car about four feet under the water in a weedy pond. The fisherman flagged down a state trooper when he got back on the Trail. It was raining hard by then and getting dark. They waited until first light to call a tow truck. The shift commander knew Ernesto Pedrosa but didn't want to notify the old man right away. He had called Anthony instead.

They saw the flashing lights a couple miles in, police vehicles blocking the left side of the narrow road – Metro squad cars, a couple of vans, a black-and-tan Florida Highway Patrol cruiser. Yellow tape had been strung from tree to tree. Police Line Do Not Cross. A few onlookers had gathered, early-morning fishermen most likely, their pickup trucks and rusty sedans parked on down the road. An ambulance waited to one side, lights off. No hurry.

The back bumper of the silver Mercedes had been unhooked from the wrecker. The trunk was open. Police leaned in, looking.

Anthony drove slowly past, found a place to park. He turned off the engine. 'Wait in the car.'

'Why?'

He looked at her. 'Stay out of the way, then. I don't want anybody to ask what Gail Connor is doing here.'

They got out, mist turning to drizzle. Gail stayed on her side of the yellow tape. Anthony ducked under it, then spoke to the cop who came to see what he wanted. They went over to the Mercedes, behind the open trunk lid. Gail noticed the headlamps. One of the little gold wipers was twisted back, the light smashed. Dirt and leaves stuck to the heavy chrome grill. The windows were foggy with grit.

She glanced toward the road. A dark blue sedan with a small rooftop antenna had just come to a stop. Frank Britton got out, closed the door. Gail ducked behind a heavy man in boots and overalls.

A couple of men rolled a gurney over to the Mercedes. The cops moved back. She could see Anthony now, his face grim. He came toward her. She went under the tape, met him halfway, took his arm. They stood next to a green-and-white, the chatter of a police radio coming through the half-open window.

Raindrops silvered Anthony's hair. He said, 'It's Carlos. He was shot. Twice. Once in the back of the neck, once in the temple. His hands were tied.'

'My God,' Gail breathed. 'Are you okay?'

Anthony nodded. His color wasn't good. He hadn't shaved and he looked tired.

They waited. The men with the gurney rolled it to the back door of the ambulance. There was a black body bag on the gurney. When it was loaded the attendant slammed the door, got in. The lights went on, but not the siren. The ambulance pulled up on the road, crunching gravel, heading to wherever they would take Carlos Pedrosa's body. Gail didn't know how she felt about this.

Frank Britton ended his conversation with a state trooper in a yellow rain slicker. He lifted his hand, then turned and walked toward Gail and Anthony.

Anthony said, 'Frank.'

'Hell of a thing, buddy. Sorry as can be.' Britton looked at Gail, sizing up the situation. 'Ms Connor, it's kind of a surprise to see you out here. Did you know Mr Pedrosa?'

Anthony said, 'Frank. She's not talking to the police.'

Britton's glasses had drops of water on them. He was wearing a tan windbreaker, shirt and tie underneath. The rain was beading up on the shoulders. He said, 'Is there something I should know about?'

Gail said, 'Sergeant, I have nothing to say to you.'

His eyes lingered on her, then shifted to Anthony. 'You know if Carlos carried a gun?'

'I believe a thirty-eight,' Anthony said. 'Was it in the car?'

Britton shook his head.

'Where are the car keys?'

'Didn't find them either. We've got Recovery coming out, we'll see what's in the water. So what do you think? Any ideas?'

'Not immediately,' Anthony said. 'Carlos had some financial problems. He owed money. Looks like a professional hit.'

'Looks that way,' Britton said.

'How long was he down there?' Anthony asked.

389

'Day and a half? Two?'

Gail glanced around at the half a dozen people standing behind the yellow tape. Britton read her thoughts. He said, 'Tell you about this road. Not too many people out here after dark. And if you happen to pass by, and you see a car like this one parked, with its lights off, you don't stop and ask if the guy needs a ride.'

Gail asked, 'Did it happen here?'

'Don't know yet.' Britton spoke to Anthony. 'How about if we talk for a few minutes?'

Anthony said, 'Ms Connor and I need to get back to Miami.'

'I'll want to speak to you at some point,' Britton said. 'Preferably today.'

Anthony gave a formal nod of his head. 'I'll be with my family. You can reach me at Ernesto Pedrosa's home, Coral Gables.'

He led Gail back to his Cadillac, held the door for her, then went around and got in. He closed his eyes for a few seconds. The interior of the car was silent, only the light rain ticking on the roof.

'How's your grandfather going to take this?' she said.

'Not well.' Anthony put the key in the ignition, turned it. 'I wish I didn't have to be the one to tell him.'

'Is there anything I can do?'

He smiled at her. 'No.'

Anthony turned on the lights and windshield wipers and made a U-turn back toward Miami, gravel kicking up against the underside of the car until they hit the pavement.

She said, 'I wouldn't tell him Carlos was stealing his money. There's no point, is there?'

He shook his head. 'But for your case, Ray Hammell

will need to use that information.'

Gail sat silently for a while, knowing how hollow any attempt at sympathy would sound. She noticed his car phone. 'It's nearly nine,' she said. 'Let me call my office. I'll be late.'

He punched the buttons one-handed, steering with the other. Gail told Gwen at Hartwell Black she had some personal matters to attend to. Then Gail asked Anthony to dial her mother's house. 'I have to let her know you haven't kidnapped me,' she said.

'Not yet.'

When they came out on the Trail again, Anthony glanced to his left for traffic, then turned east, picked up speed. He hung up the phone when she gave it back to him.

Gail said, 'If Carlos is gone, how does that affect my trial?'

Anthony thought for a minute. 'It depends on how Ray handles it. Carlos won't be around to refute the allegations. However, it might look too convenient to blame a dead man. And the jury will wonder about the connection. Why did Carlos die just now? You heard Britton. It was in his mind already.'

'What, did I kill Carlos, too?'

'Not you.' Anthony adjusted the digital control on the AC. 'He thinks I might have done it. When I see him today, that's probably what he'll try to find out.'

'Are you serious?' Gail gave a little laugh. 'Well, Mr Quintana. And where were you on the night in question?'

Anthony smiled at her. 'If it was last night, you know where I was.'

Gail let her eyes go to the road. The windshield wipers moved silently on the glass. She wanted to ask him. The question was sitting in her mouth, pressing on her teeth. *Did you do it? Or did you hire someone? You would know the people to contact. Did you do it?*

She crossed her arms, the knuckles of her left hand against her lips, wondering where the hell she had gotten that idea. Lack of sleep, maybe. General paranoia. But she wanted to hear him say no and make her believe it.

Anthony took her hand, kissed her fingers, then tucked it into his lap with his own hand tightly curled around hers. Gail smiled at him, then looked back at the road.

Chapter Twenty-Four

Gail stood at the bathroom mirror in the skirt to her blue suit and a camisole, putting on her makeup. Irene came in. Gail supposed she wanted to hear about Carlos again.

'More coffee?' Irene asked.

'No, thanks, I'm late as it is.' Gail rummaged through her makeup bag. After a week at Irene's, she had still not unpacked it. She found the right eye shadow, clicked open the box, leaned closer to the mirror.

Irene set her own mug of coffee on the vanity. 'By the way. Jimmy Panther called me last night. I forgot to mention it, with all this about Carlos Pedrosa. Jimmy says Edith Newell has been after him to donate that Tequesta deer mask to the museum. He says he's thinking about it, but he can't just give it away.'

Gail glanced at Irene over her mascara wand, then back at the mirror. 'So why did he call you?'

'He knows me. He trusts my opinion,' Irene said.

'I don't suppose he suggested you buy it.' Gail did the other eye. 'You know, pay him five or ten thousand, give it to the museum, then take the tax deduction?'

Irene looked annoyed. 'Yes, that did come up, but it was my idea.'

'Was it?' Gail tossed the mascara back into the bag.

'You can be so suspicious at times,' Irene said.

On her way out of the bathroom Gail bent to kiss her on the cheek. 'And you're a nice lady. Do whatever you want to, Mother. There, that's my opinion. Just make sure you get a couple of appraisals first.'

Irene followed her down the hall, then into the guest room. The convertible sofa was still folded in, pillows untouched. Irene hadn't complained about Gail's absence last night. She seemed too stunned about Carlos Pedrosa to make a fuss.

Irene said, 'I think I can persuade him to donate the mask.'

'Great. I doubt Jimmy Panther would have a sudden attack of generosity, but you never know.' Gail pulled her black pumps out from under the sewing machine cabinet.

'Yes, I do know,' Irene said. 'He's looking for some land where they can have a retreat for emotionally disturbed boys. A camp. They could go there and live like Indians did before the white man. Jimmy says he wants a place that's not poisoned by modern civilization.'

'Is he making an exception for mosquito repellent?' Gail put on her shoes.

Irene gave her a look. 'For some reason or other they can't use tribal land. Jimmy says it's federal red tape, you know how that goes. Anyway, if he could find some property to rent cheaply, he could save a lot of money, and if he saved money there, he could afford to give the Tequesta mask to the museum.'

Gail took an ivory linen blouse off its hanger, hung the hanger back in the closet.

Irene said, 'We got to talking about what kind of land he needed, the right location and so forth, and I thought of Ben's property. He said it might do, but he wasn't sure.'

'Ben? Renting his property to the Indians?'

'He might, if he were approached the right way,' Irene said.

'So fine. Tell Jimmy to talk to Ben about it.'

'I did.' Irene took a sip from her coffee mug. 'But Ben won't be back from his fishing trip for ten days, so I said maybe I'd call Ben myself before he leaves.'

'Lucky man, ten days vacation with his best buddies.' Gail tucked the blouse into her skirt. At the dresser she put on her earrings, studying her reflection. Neat little suit, conservative jewelry. Her hair looked a bit flat this morning, but she'd had no time to wash it. Makeup hid the circles under her eyes.

She fastened the other earring. 'Maybe Ben has the right idea, leaving Miami. A country law practice with a fishing lake out the back door. Walk downtown. Have lunch at the drugstore. Leave your windows open at night.'

Irene said, 'Do me a favor. Call Ben. Ask him what he thinks of Jimmy's idea. I told Jimmy I'd let him know.'

Grabbing her purse, Gail headed for the den, where she had left her files and briefcase last night. 'I can't, I'm frantically busy today.'

'Five minutes,' Irene said. 'You know how to put things in legalese.'

Gail stacked her files on the desk, tucking papers back inside. 'I'd rather not. The last time Ben and I were together, leaving Ray Hammell's office, we practically yelled at each other. I think he's still mad at me.'

'Whatever for?'

Gail dropped her files into her briefcase and closed the lid. 'It's not worth talking about. Same old thing. He has the answers and wants to make sure I know it.'

'He's done a great deal for you,' Irene said.

'Mother, I'm extremely grateful for Ben's help, I promise you. And yours.' Grateful to Ben, but not comfortable about it. She felt a need to keep her distance for a while. Maybe her reaction was irrational, but she didn't care. It was what it was. In the driveway Gail's car crunched over acorns from the oak tree, then whirled through leaves on Seagrape Lane. Gail had explained once to a friend visiting from Boston, in South Florida the leaves fall off the trees in springtime. *How upside down it is here*, the friend had said.

Gail turned left on Biscayne Boulevard as though her car were on automatic pilot.

Again this morning she had looked at the photo of herself and Renee. She remembered now: Their father hadn't taken it after all. He had been on the porch frying hamburgers, the yard teeming with kids and adults. Ben was the one with the camera, taking pictures of everyone. He told Renee to sit in the swing. Smile real big, honey. *Click*. Gail knew now why she had pushed her way onto the swing. Not to have fun with Renee but because she had been seething with jealousy. She had pumped the swing higher and higher to frighten Renee, secretly hoping she would fall out.

Renee must not have realized it. Or she had forgotten, too. She had kept the photo on her desk in a gold frame. Me and my sis, happy times.

The idea was stunning – Gail's emotions had raged, even as a child. Ben had been an innocent magnet realigning the field between herself and Renee. But Renee had died before Gail could tell her any of this. Before Gail could ask to be forgiven. And how much of that rage was still alive, poisoning her thoughts about Anthony, who had slept with both of them?

She made it to the parking garage in fifteen minutes flat. It was nearly eleven o'clock and the only empty spaces left were on the roof, sixth level. It hadn't rained downtown last night but the sky was mottled gray, the air heavy and hot. Her back was moist with sweat by the time she entered the air-conditioned lobby of the Hartwell Building.

In her office, the telephone rang. Gail dropped her briefcase on the desk. It was Ben.

He had heard about Carlos. His secretary had been listening to the radio in the coffee shop. Prominent Latin developer shot to death, body found in the trunk of his car. Execution-style slaying, no suspects.

'I don't know what to think of it,' Gail said.

Ben said, 'Son of a bitch finally got what he deserved, is what I think. No, better to bring him to trial for Renee, than shoot him. That would've been better. Did you call Ray Hammell yet?'

'I will, but he probably knows already. We have another appointment at four this afternoon. I'm sure we'll talk about it.'

'Lord. I hope this doesn't mess up your defense,' Ben said. 'Maybe I ought to call him myself.'

Gail heard the question: Did she want him to? She said, 'No, Ben, it's okay. Thanks, though. Really.'

'All right,' he said.

'Have a good time fishing,' she said.

'I wonder if I should go.'

'Go,' she said. 'Call me this weekend, I'll let you know what Ray says about Carlos.'

After Ben's goodbye, she realized she had forgotten to pass on Irene's message about Jimmy Panther. She thought of calling him back. 'The hell with it,' she muttered, and dialed Ray Hammell's office.

Alisha came on the line. 'We know! I was just about to call you.' Her voice was breathy with suppressed excitement. 'Ray had to go to court or he'd talk to you himself. He wants me to get the details from the police.'

Gail decided not to say, just then, that she had driven to the scene with Anthony Quintana. That she had seen Carlos's body taken away. It would require more explanation than she wanted to give over the telephone. She confirmed her appointment with Hammell and hung up.

Miriam brought her a sandwich and they worked through lunch.

Anthony called shortly after one o'clock.

'I wanted to hear your voice,' he said.

'Where are you?'

'At my grandfather's house. The place is *un manicomio*. A madhouse. There must be fifty people here.'

'How did he take it?'

'Not well. He's sedated now. The doctor is guarding against another stroke. In fact, I called the doctor before I broke the news.' Gail could hear only silence in the background and supposed Anthony was in Ernesto Pedrosa's study with the heavy door closed, sitting at the big desk that was angled toward Havana.

'And how are you?' she said.

'Frank Britton just left,' he said. 'He didn't stay long. He wants me to come to headquarters Monday.'

Gail forced herself to ask the question. 'Does he think you had something to do with Carlos's death?'

'He asked me where I was for the last two days. He said he had heard relations between me and Carlos were bad. He asked me about my grandfather's properties. He even asked me if it was true Renee had left me to start an affair with Carlos. Where did he get that idea?'

'Probably from looking into my case,' she said. 'He talked to a lot of people.'

Anthony said, 'It's strange. I have never been in this position. Frank apologized for having to question me.'

'Here's some advice given to me by an excellent criminal attorney,' Gail said. 'Don't talk to the police. They'll hang you with your words.'

398

She heard the chuckle. 'Ah, but I have nothing to hide,' he said. Then another sigh. 'Gail, I wish I could leave here and go back to sleep with you. We didn't sleep much last night.'

Gail closed her eyes, desire surprising her, flowing through her like a sudden throb of pain, and this for a man who could have tied his cousin's hands and shot him through the head.

She said, 'I'm tired, too. Trying to get some work done, but the gears are slipping.'

'You're seeing Ray Hammell this afternoon?'

'At four.'

'I might call him before that and tell him what's going on,' Anthony said.

'If you even know,' Gail said. 'This is so complicated. But what did you tell me once? Murder is a simple act of passion?'

'An intimate act with a simple motive based on passion,' Anthony said. 'Not always true, but more often than not. And the answer isn't always easy to find. But when we do see it, we say, ah yes, of course. I should have known.'

Gail swiveled her chair around to face the window. The sky was still gray, the clouds unmoving. 'What if the right answer is the simplest of all?' she said. 'What if Renee really did commit suicide? And one of Carlos's questionable friends got rid of him, just like you read all the time in the *Herald*? And we're all going crazy trying to see motives and meanings where there aren't any.'

'Ah, Gail.' Anthony sounded exhausted.

'I'm sorry,' she said. 'You called me for some solace and I haven't helped a bit.'

'I don't need solace,' he said. 'I need two or three drinks and a pillow. And you.'

Anthony's pillow. He had put it under her hips last

night. Lifted her up to him, open. She blinked to clear the image.

He said, 'Unfortunately, I will be here for the next two or three nights, until the funeral. Have you been to a Cuban funeral? We stay up all night with the casket before the graveside services, drinking *café* to stay awake. I'll call you when it's over.'

'All right.'

The sound of a soft kiss came over the line. '*Cuídate, mi amor.*' Take care, my love.

'You, too.' Gail closed her eyes and heard the click of a disconnect.

Her thoughts were on a silver Mercedes with its trunk open, dripping stagnant water. A gurney and a black body bag.

Anthony had to be innocent. A weird correlation occurred to her: His innocence was linked to Carlos's. If Anthony was fair enough to have read Carlos right, then how could he have been vicious enough to kill him? Anthony had never said Carlos was guilty. He had said it was a plausible theory, useful to her acquittal. At his house last week he had said Carlos might be capable of petty violence, but not murder.

Gail had wanted Carlos Pedrosa to be guilty. Now he was dead, and that awful event made him seem helpless to her, worthy of pity. His death wasn't what she had wanted.

But if Carlos had not killed Renee, who had? Someone close. Close enough to know she had tried to commit suicide with a razor blade.

Loan sharks could have killed Carlos. A business rival. Drug dealers. Maybe a jealous boyfriend. Anyone.

Frank Britton had looked at Gail, standing there in the drizzling rain behind the yellow police tape. She had seen the speculation in his eyes. What is the connection here?

Now Gail felt as though her mind were a computer screen, lines of data flashing past. Combinations, recombinations. Constructing theories out of air, out of scraps, looking for patterns. No conclusions, only the steady flow of bits of information.

Gail jumped a little and turned her chair around when she heard a thud on her desk.

Miriam had come in with a banker's box full of deposition transcripts and a folder crammed with photocopies. She made a little panting noise, her tongue sticking out like a tired dog.

Gail managed a smile.

There was a handwritten letter on top of one box and Miriam handed it to Gail. 'This came in the mail a couple days ago from Harold Irving, the client you did the condominium class action thing for last year.'

Gail glanced at it. 'Well, give it to Bob Wilcox.'

'I did already.' Miriam began unpacking the depositions. 'And then Mr Irving called a little while ago and wanted to speak to you. He said he didn't want anybody else to handle his cases and he didn't care if you had shot the president, he wouldn't believe it anyway.'

'What a guy.' Gail remembered him. Bald, plaid pants, cane, running shoes, an expression like someone had just stolen his baby blue 1973 Chrysler Imperial.

'He said if you didn't do his case he'd go somewhere else, and screw Hartwell Black.'

'Miriam.'

'He said that, *te juro*. I swear he did.'

Gail blew a breath through pursed lips and scanned the lousy handwriting. Harold wanted her to write an option to purchase an ape on Mi Beach? An ape?

Miriam said, 'Why don't you open your own office?'

Gail didn't look up. 'What?'

'I mean it. I'd go with you. You wouldn't even have

to pay me that much to start. I bet you could get lots of clients.'

Apartment, Gail realized. Apt on Miami Beach. He wasn't sure he liked the building with all the guys – gays? – around but maybe an option would be OK so he wouldn't have to rash – rush – making a decision.

Miriam said, 'I know you can't leave right now, with the trial and everything, but maybe afterward.'

Gail slowly lifted her eyes.

'Ms Connor?'

'Option.'

'What?'

'Shh, be quiet a minute.' Gail stood up, paced to the window. 'Option. Carlos wanted an option.'

'What—' Miriam cut herself off, but crossed the room to stand next to Gail, looking intently at her.

Gail continued to stare through the window. 'Carlos wanted an option on Ben's property. Ben changed his mind and the deal was off. Now Jimmy Panther wants to rent the property. Or so he says.' Gail turned to Miriam, who looked worried.

'Are you okay?' she asked.

'I don't know. Yes.' Gail took a deep breath. 'My God. This is crazy. But I think there's something here. I think there is.'

Miriam's eyes widened. 'You're scaring me.'

Gail grasped her hands. 'No, everything's fine. Really. I want you to call Ray Hammell's office for me and cancel my appointment. Tell them – Just say I had to leave the office on a personal emergency. Then get Edith Newell at the historical museum.'

Gail picked up her phone and dialed Ben's office. She had the clear, cold sense that she was getting down to solid truth.

Chapter Twenty-Five

Ben was waiting on the cabin steps when Gail turned off her engine. His three dogs ran back and forth growling. Flicking his cigarette away, he told them to shut up. The look on his face said he had better things to do than go hiking in the woods at three o'clock in the afternoon, temperature pushing ninety, sky threatening rain.

'Hi, Ben.' Gail watched the dogs warily as she got out of the car. One of them sniffed at her blue jeans.

'Barney, cut it out,' Ben said. The dog wandered into the sparse grass beside the cabin and flopped down in the shade, tongue pink against black fur. The others went to the water dish.

Ben said, 'Okay. Tell me about this Indian mound.'

Gail unfolded an aerial photo on the edge of the porch, two legal-size photocopies taped together. They bent over it. Edith Newell had it waiting for her when Gail had dashed into the museum.

'I can't recognize a damn thing.' Ben leaned closer. 'What's that line, Krome Avenue?' He traced it with his forefinger.

'Yes. The yellow is the parcel Carlos wanted. The circles inside it are where Edith said we should start looking.'

She explained what Edith had told her. Look for a patch of trees higher than the others; the ground under them will be slightly elevated. Edith had cross-checked the map with the 1878 geological survey. She had begged to come along. Gail had dissuaded her. There were only a few hours of daylight left.

Ben turned the pages around the other way. 'This dark strip here is probably the slough that runs along the old pasture. I guess we could drive out, save some steps.' He folded the map and handed it to Gail.

'Is there a road?' she asked.

'More or less.' He finally smiled. 'We'll take your car.' He went over and opened the trunk of his Lincoln, took out a canteen, a box of shells, and his shotgun.

Gail grinned at it. 'Oh, good. Your snake repellent.' She unlocked her trunk and he stowed them inside.

The dogs followed them for a while, barking at the tires.

She guided the Buick between potholes and rocks. 'Thank you, Ben.'

'For what?'

'For meeting me here. I had to do it today. You're leaving tomorrow and I'm too nervous to wait until you get back.'

'You going to tell me what this is about?' He was looking at her, expecting more than he had gotten over the telephone.

She had kept the details sketchy. Carlos Pedrosa and Jimmy Panther working together. An Indian mound on Ben's land. The Tequesta mask.

Gail said, 'Okay. A lot of this is theory, but let's see how it hangs together. Jimmy Panther and Renee meet at the historical museum. Not by accident. He knows her reputation and knows she is related to you. What he really wants is access to this property because of what is buried on it. What I *think* is buried on it.'

The dirt road narrowed, curving through melaleuca trees and tangled pepper bushes with glossy red berries.

'Jimmy has the Tequesta mask. He either knows his

404

family found it here, years ago, or he found it himself, trespassing to look for artifacts. Where there's one, he figures there must be others. And this one is worth ten to fifteen thousand dollars. Jimmy couldn't take his time exploring because you showed up too often. And the dogs were a problem. It takes months to excavate a mound properly. Jimmy knew this from working on other sites with the Dade County archaeologist.'

The car bounced into a deep rut, weeds scraping the underside. Gail felt the tires spin on wet ground, then grab. The tracks twisted into a clearing.

She said, 'Then Renee becomes romantically involved with Carlos Pedrosa, a land developer. Renee introduces him to you. Carlos wants an option on this property. Not a coincidence. I believe it was Jimmy Panther's idea. Edith saw them all in the museum together. Renee, Jimmy, and Carlos.' Gail glanced over at Ben. 'Okay so far?'

'Go on,' he said.

Gail swerved to avoid a broken soda bottle. 'How does Jimmy persuade Carlos to risk ten thousand dollars of his grandfather's money? He shows him the Tequesta mask, but that wouldn't have done it. Jimmy tells Carlos a story – which happens to be true, by the way. In 1732 a Spanish ship coming from Havana docked at the mouth of the Miami River to take the Tequestas to Cuba, those that wanted to go. They were under attack by some other tribe. But they stole the gold on board and supposedly hid out in the Everglades with it. Edith Newell showed me government documents referring to this, dated around 1835. The maps take in this part of the county. Think of what Jimmy must have told Carlos. The last descendant of the Tequestas. Buried treasure. The connection with Cuba.'

Ben laughed. 'Was Carlos that feeble-minded?'

'Remember, he was desperate to cover up his

embezzlement from Pedrosa Development. And you have to admit, Jimmy Panther has a way about him.'

'I told you he was a con man.'

'Yes,' Gail admitted. 'Anyway, Carlos takes the risk and if it turns out there's no gold, well – There are artifacts in the Indian mound to sell. Masks, pots, whatever. Not a bad return on ten thousand dollars. But Jimmy might have gotten away with most of them while Carlos was still grubbing in the dirt for pieces of eight.'

Ben pointed through the windshield. 'Head toward those trees.'

'Then the deal goes sour,' Gail said. 'You change your mind about giving Carlos the option. Now Jimmy has no use for him anymore. In fact, Carlos is a distinct liability. And something else. When I spoke to Jimmy, I pointed the finger at Carlos for Renee's murder. Renee and Jimmy were close, I'm sure of it. Very close. He was her . . . spiritual father, you might say. This morning Carlos was found dead in the trunk of his Mercedes, dumped in a canal off the Loop Road.'

Ben was squinting at her, waiting for her to say it.

'I think Jimmy Panther shot him with his own gun. Got him alone on some pretext and killed him for what he did to Renee.'

After a few seconds, Ben said, 'Possibly. So tell me. What are we doing out here, running around in the woods instead of going to the cops?'

'Because I haven't got any proof. Not yet.' That wasn't the only reason. The rest of it was, she wanted to find evidence that Anthony had nothing to do with Carlos's death. Gail kept her eyes on the narrow, rutted road ahead of them.

She said, 'This morning Mother told me Jimmy called her. He wants her to talk to you about renting some property to him.'

'Renting property? Why?'

'A camp for emotionally disturbed children. So he says. Get them away from modern urban society, let them play in the fresh air.'

'Christ almighty.' Ben shook his head. 'Irene bought that?'

'It's obvious what he's doing, once you see the relationships involved. He's trying to get onto your property so he can look for artifacts. If we find an Indian mound where I think it might be, I can tie him to Carlos.'

'And tie Carlos to Renee.'

'Yes.'

The tracks ended and Gail stopped the car. They got out. The land was flat and scrubby, open to the left, with tangled woods further on to the right. The rain last night had left sheets of standing water that reflected clouds and treetops. A flock of white egrets flapped overhead, long necks tucked close to their bodies.

She opened the trunk, took out two pointed shovels and an old book bag of Karen's. Inside the bag were a spray can of Off, two tightly folded plastic rain ponchos, a trowel and garden gloves from her garage, a plastic grocery sack in case they found something, newspaper to wrap it in, two liters of Evian, and a bag of trail mix.

Ben swung his canteen across his chest and the shotgun over his shoulder on its leather strap, then stepped away from the car and did a slow three-sixty. 'We'll use this as a base point and branch out from here. Say a couple hundred yards in each direction. I hope to hell you know what you're looking for.'

'So do I.' Gail folded the map into eighths and tucked it into her back pocket. 'All right. We're not far from Krome. I can hear the traffic.'

'A little Sunday stroll,' he muttered, easing the strap on his shoulder.

They set out north, each of them carrying a shovel. Insects buzzed in the hot, unmoving air.

'As long as we're speculating,' Ben said, 'what if someone besides Carlos killed Renee?'

Gail jumped over a rut filled with greenish water and the bag bounced on her back. 'Such as who?'

'Panther.'

'Why would he do that? They were friends.'

'Let's say she found out the gold was a hoax and threatened to tell. Or maybe she and Carlos decided to cut Jimmy out. Say he made Renee's death look like suicide because if it was murder, Carlos would have suspected him.' Ben scanned the line of trees. 'Renee could have driven out to see him after Irene's birthday party. If they were friends. If they were doing a con on Carlos together. Did Panther have an alibi for that night?'

Gail had slowed her pace and Ben turned around to look at her. 'Well?'

'No. I asked him.'

'If they were friends,' Ben said, 'he would have known how she liked to go out to that park. And how she tried to commit suicide before. He was the one who called the police, wasn't he? A nice touch. He even had witnesses with him when he found her body.' Ben shrugged. 'It's a theory. Talk it over with Ray Hammell next time. He could use it at your trial.'

'I don't know. I'm afraid if we start confusing the jury with too many alternatives, they might wind up pointing their fingers right back at me.'

'Well, you let Ray handle it. I didn't pay him all that money for nothing.'

She had nothing to say to that, only fell into step behind him, weeds slapping against her pant legs.

* * *

Two hours later, Ben leaned back against a palmetto palm, hands resting on his shovel, shirt soaked with sweat. He lifted his canteen. Letting her own shovel clang to the ground, Gail took off her garden gloves. Cotton, with little yellow daisies. Filthy now. Her hands stiff and burning from abrasion, she unscrewed the cap on a bottle of water and drank.

Ben laughed, pointed at Gail. 'Little girl, your face is about as dirty as mine feels.'

Gail wiped her cheeks on the neck of her T-shirt.

They had made almost a complete circle around the area outlined on the map, digging in eleven likely places, most of them in the woods or scrub, occasionally pulling up broken glass, cans, animal bones, brass cartridges, rotting wood.

Grunting a little, Ben let himself down on a fallen tree trunk and pulled a cigarette out of the pack in his shirt pocket. He took off his gloves.

Gail asked, 'What time is it?'

He checked his watch. 'Six-twenty.'

'How much daylight do we have, an hour?'

'Less.' He cupped his hands around his cigarette to light it.

Gunfire crackled from the south, as it had occasionally during the afternoon. Target shooters, aiming at bottles and cans. Gail remembered the last family picnic at the ranch. They had sat around the table and heard bursts of automatic weapons fire. Good citizens, bearing arms. Or middle-aged Cubans, dreaming of going home again.

'I'm beginning to feel sorry I made you do this,' Gail said.

Ben blew out a stream of smoke. His white hair was stringy, sticking to his forehead.

She said, 'It all seemed to fit together at the time.'

Cigarette between his teeth, he put his gloves back on. 'Okay. Let's finish here. Then we'll do that area by the slough, and that's it.'

Gail picked up her shovel and dragged it to a spot about ten yards away, where there was a gentle rise in the ground. She put her foot on the blade and wiggled it between loose rocks. A hole eighteen inches deep would be enough. Edith had told her what to look for.

To fill the silence she spoke her thoughts out loud. 'Carlos Pedrosa and Jimmy Panther were the least likely pair to be working together. They'd never have gotten together without Renee. She was the common denominator.' Gail tossed a shovelful of dirt aside, then bent to snap off a root. 'My theory about Renee is, she was fragmented. Different people filled different needs for her.'

Ben pulled something oblong out of the hole he had dug, looked at it, pitched it away. A brown bottle. It clanked on a rock.

Gail said, 'Jimmy Panther was her spiritual guide. Carlos was dark sexuality. From Dave she got innocent romance. Valentine's Day cards and flowers.'

Ben said, 'Is that what happened to you two? Renee turned his head?'

'No. It wasn't Renee's fault. If Dave and I were still married, it was only force of habit. But as I told Ray Hammell, there was nothing physical between them.'

The knees of her jeans already crusted with muck, Gail got down to look into the hole. Nothing but roots and rocks. With a little groan she stood up, looking around for another place to dig.

Ben was scraping back a layer of dried, brittle palm fronds. 'And what was I? Her patsy?'

'Her protector,' Gail said. 'She might have gone to prison without you.'

'Big mistake, covering up what she did.' Ben grunted

as he lifted a shovelful of rocks. 'Should have made her say it was Carlos who put her on the boat. Made some kind of exchange with the prosecution.'

'I don't think he knew she went on that trip.'

'Of course he knew. It was his deal.'

'It wasn't his boat,' Gail said. 'Ray Hammell's office found out who it belonged to. Nelson Restrepo, a client of Anthony Quintana's.'

'Quintana was involved in that?'

'No. He wasn't. He explained to me how it happened.' Gail paused, wishing she hadn't said this much. 'Renee knew how to get access to the boat, because she and Anthony had taken a trip on it together.'

'Renee and Quintana?' Ben looked puzzled for a second, then laughed, stepping on the blade of his shovel. 'Christ. Doing both of them. That must have been cozy.'

'Ben, come on. It wasn't like that. Her affair with Anthony was over by then.'

'And how do you know so much about him?'

Gail hesitated, trying to think of how to word it.

He gave a half smile. 'Don't tell me. You and Quintana.'

She felt her face growing hot, knew he could see it.

'And still married to Dave.'

'Don't. I mean it, Ben. I'm not discussing this.'

He levered the handle, ripping out a root. 'As long as we're playing what if – What if Quintana was the one who planned the drug run? He borrowed the boat from his client, Restrepo. Say he needed a young white American girl to act as a shield. Like hiding cocaine in a baby's diaper. But uh-oh. They got busted.'

Gail stood still, holding her shovel. 'No. It was Carlos's idea.'

'You're sure of that.'

'Yes.'

411

Ben went on. 'Say Renee can't let go of Quintana. He's a slick-looking guy, plenty of money, smart. But for Quintana she's a major headache. She's unstable. She might let it slip what kind of business he does on the side. He fakes her suicide. Then when it begins to appear that Carlos killed Renee, Quintana gets rid of him, too, so he can't deny it.'

Gail was shaking her head. 'Renee didn't cause problems for Anthony after their affair was over. She was still in love with him, but she accepted it.'

'Who told you that, your boyfriend?' Ben waited, his eyebrows raised. 'Honey, I told you. Back when he was giving you legal advice, I said, Gail, don't get involved. Didn't I say that?'

'This is none of your business, Ben.'

He went back to work. 'You know best. What is it with you girls and the Cubanos, anyway? I didn't think you'd get led around by your—' he made a vague gesture toward her crotch '—like your sister did.'

She stared at him.

After a few seconds he let his shovel fall, then threw his gloves down after it, one then the other. 'Oh, lord, Gail. I'm tired. Is that any excuse? Maybe we've been out here too long. I didn't mean to compare you to Renee.'

'She wasn't a slut either.'

He smiled, making an effort, deep creases in his cheeks. 'What do you say we sink a couple more holes, then call it quits? I'll take you and Irene out to dinner.'

'No. I want to leave now,' she said. 'There's no point to this.'

He snapped his Zippo open, shut, open, then lit another cigarette. 'You get me out here sweating all afternoon and then tell me there's no point.'

Two gunshots cracked into the still evening air, echoing among the trees.

Ben said, 'That was pretty close.'

Gail shrugged. 'Somebody shooting at a road sign on Krome Avenue.'

'Wrong direction.'

'Why don't we just go?'

He listened for a few more seconds, then went back for his gloves and shovel. 'Not yet. You dragged me here, we're going to finish. I'm not doing this again. We'll get this one other area, then go.'

She exhaled. 'Fine.'

They walked fifty yards or so, making their way through the scrubby underbrush. Already the light was fading. Gail heard the whine of mosquitoes in her ears, swatted at them. She watched Ben walk, a tall, solid man, the plaid shirt sticking to his back, the shotgun slung over his shoulder, barrel extending past his head. His neck was creased with deep wrinkles. She smelled cigarette smoke and sweat.

He glanced around, laughing. 'You keeping up, little girl?'

It had always been like this. Gail turning sullen, Ben teasing her for it, making her churn with anger. Renee had known how to play him to get what she wanted. Acting like a ninny, chewing on her thumb, looking at him sideways, giggling. When he got mad, her mouth would tremble and tears would well up in those incredibly blue eyes and spill down her cheeks. Gail had never mastered that little trick. But now she remembered despising Renee for it. Or despising Renee for succeeding at it.

At the point where the ground seemed to rise again, they stopped. The slope ran twenty yards or more on either side.

Gail dropped the book bag, put her gloves on again.

Ben tossed his cigarette away and kicked aside the thick covering of leaves and ferns. He said, 'We find

413

anything, I'm going to buy me a couple thousand acres of forest up the state.'

He was in a good humor again, she noticed.

He laughed. 'I bet Irene will try to make me donate it all to the museum.'

Gail shoved a fallen branch out of the way with her foot and began to dig. 'I doubt you could buy much land with a few pots and clay masks. Assuming they're even here.'

'Hell, I'm not talking about a bunch of trinkets. I mean a big wooden chest of Spanish treasure. Gold bars. Pearl necklaces. Emeralds and diamonds.'

'Right.' Gail stamped on the shovel.

'Yo-ho, and up she rises.' Laughing, Ben held up a gray, pitted jawbone. 'Elsie the Cow,' he said, then sent it spinning into the brush. He walked a few paces and started another hole. 'My granddaddy – your great-grand – told me he'd pay the Indians to come out here and salt this ground.'

'Salt the ground?' Gail wiped her forehead on her sleeve.

'Way back. Turn of the century.' Ben's words punctuated his efforts with the shovel. 'They'd bury beads, arrowheads. Couple inches down. Cheap stuff. Granddaddy would bring tourists in a wagon. Sell tickets. He had this half-Chinese, half-negro guy that would dress up like a Miccosukee. Patchwork jacket, turban with an egret feather.'

'The same upstanding Benjamin Strickland whose immortal, life-size photograph appears in the historical museum?'

'The same.'

And the same, Gail remembered, who had looked on while Renee and Carlos Pedrosa were making the streetcar rock. Renee had said she always wanted to do it in front of Benjamin Strickland. But now Gail didn't think she had meant the man in the photograph. She had probably meant Ben. Flesh and blood and resentment.

Ben said, 'Kind of funny there might have been real artifacts buried here all along, and I'm the last to know it. Your sister didn't see fit to tell me. I'd have given her what she wanted of them. She'd rather go behind my back.'

'I think she was trying to be independent.'

'Nice word for sneaky,' Ben said. 'For stealing from your family. She's no better than Carlos Pedrosa. Two of a kind.' He glanced at Gail. 'What's the matter?' When she didn't answer, he set his shovel against a tree trunk. 'Lord have mercy.' He puffed out a breath, then tried a smile. 'You got any more water in that bag of yours? My canteen's dry.'

She bent over, took hers out. When she stood up, Ben put his hand on her shoulder. She shied away.

He took off the cap. 'We never got along, you and me. I tried. I'm still trying.'

'It's not your fault,' she mumbled. Her head was beginning to pulse from the heat.

He finished off the water, the muscles in his throat working, sweat making shiny lines down his neck. She took the empty bottle from him, put it back in her bag.

When she turned around he said, 'You're still mad at me for what I said about Renee, aren't you? I guess I shouldn't have disturbed these romantic notions you're getting about your sister.' He picked up his shovel. 'Girl was sick. You don't want to see it. She had some very serious problems.'

'What are you talking about?'

'You know what I'm talking about,' he said.

'Because she touched you the night of Irene's party?' Gail went to stand beside him. 'Is that it?' Ben slid the shovel point into the ground, twisted it back, threw the

415

dirt to one side. Gail said, 'She was drunk. Or maybe she was making a joke and you took it wrong.'

'A joke?' He glanced at her. 'You weren't out there with us. Don't tell me what it was like.'

'You said you dragged her out there to yell at her—'

'I didn't yell at her.'

'Talk to her, then. Whatever. She was almost thirty years old. Maybe she didn't want to be treated like a child anymore. That's what you and Mother did, both of you.'

Ben's shovel rang on the stones. 'Are we going to finish here or not?'

'I remember when she broke Daddy's new radio. He wanted to spank her but you wouldn't let him. I remember how she clung to you, crying, and you told Daddy to let her be, you'd buy him another one. Don't you see? She learned that you would always take care of her. My little flower. I heard you tell her, "Don't you worry, Ben's going to take good care of his little flower."'

Ben swatted a mosquito off his cheek. 'She's dead and you keep talking about her, talk talk talk. You're still so jealous you can't see straight.'

'No.' Gail's mouth was dry. 'That isn't – No. Not because of that. It was—'

He gave her a long, quizzical look, then pulled off his gloves, crammed them into a back pocket. 'That's it. We're done here. Pick up your stuff.'

Gail didn't move. 'The other night. When you came in to say good night to Karen. In Renee's old room. You kissed her. My little flower. That's what you used to call Renee.' The patch of sky above the trees dimmed and Gail squeezed her eyes shut. 'It wasn't right. I didn't want you to touch her.'

She sucked in a breath through her nose and sat down hard on the ground, leaning over one knee to keep from passing out. Ben's lace-up boots moved closer to her. He asked her what the hell was the matter, but his words seemed to come through a long, hollow pipe.

Gail swallowed and her throat ached. 'I woke up one night. It was . . . after Daddy died. I woke up and went to her room. Mother was gone, I don't know where. I wanted to go inside, but I couldn't. I heard you. I heard you . . . saying things to her. You smell so sweet. Like a flower. So pretty.'

'That never happened! You don't know what you're talking about.'

She laughed, more a moan. 'Yes, I do know. I knew it without knowing, and I hated her for it.'

'Filthy-minded bitch. I would never do anything like that. Never. You're as sick as your damn sister.'

'Renee. Oh, God.' She rocked back and forth. 'Maybe I am. Maybe. You could tell me.' Behind her eyes, Renee's face. She could see her clearly now. Renee's blue eyes. The small mouth, going into a lopsided smile. The single dimple. Perfect skin. Gail opened her eyes, made them focus on a snail shell, then a scrap of leaf. The woods were darker, the colors going gray.

Ben muttered, 'Crazy,' and his boot tapped her thigh. 'Get up, we're leaving.'

Then she heard the dogs baying. Barks, then deep snarls. A gun fired, one sharp crack. A yelp. Then two more, quickly. More yelps. Another shot. Then silence.

'Somebody's shooting my damn dogs,' Ben said. 'Somebody's out there.'

Gail stood up on her knees, still dizzy. Ben was listening, head turned to one side. A blackbird flapped away from a pine tree, gave a rasping caw.

Ben grabbed Gail by the arm and dragged her behind some tangled bushes, then went back out for his shotgun. Crouching low, he slid down beside her, pumped a shell into the chamber. He whispered, 'Who did you tell we're here? What do they want?'

'I don't know.' Her breath stopped, then started. 'Edith. I told her.' She felt an urge to laugh. 'I don't think Edith carries a gun.'

'Shut up, let me listen.'

Far overhead came the faint rumble of a jet. Birds twittered in the gathering dusk. Then she could hear the shifting of palm fronds, footsteps. Careful, slow.

'I told Mother,' Gail whispered, her heart leaping in her chest. 'I told her I was coming here with you. Jimmy Panther was going to call her this afternoon.'

'Panther.' Ben dug two more shells out of his jeans and put them in his shirt pocket. He motioned her toward the ground.

Gail crawled on her stomach to the other side of the bush, then peered through the thick leaves.

A man. Dark hair. White shirt, drawn pistol.

'Anthony?' She scrambled to her feet.

'Gail! Where are you?'

Ben yelled, 'Drop it!'

Anthony turned. Ben fired. The impact of the shotgun blast spun Anthony into the trunk of a pine tree. He held on, then dropped.

Her ears still ringing, Gail screamed, tore through the underbrush. Ben grabbed the back of her shirt.

'Gail, stop. He's got a gun.'

'Why? Why did you shoot him?'

'Listen to me. I had to.' Ben dropped the shotgun, gripped her arms. 'He was going to kill us. He had a gun.'

'No!' Blood was spreading on Anthony's white shirt.

Ben shook her. 'He killed Carlos. We were next. Gail, honey. I had to.'

'Let go!' Gail pulled away, stumbled a few paces.

Ben swung her to the ground, straddled her hips and pinned her shoulders. She flailed her arms at him.

'Gail, listen. Listen. He did Renee, too. It was him. She wanted him, he had to get rid of her. We'll say – Damn it, hold still. We'll say Quintana admitted doing both of them. They'll drop the charges against you.'

'Get off! Ben—'

'We're family. We can stick together, Gail. We'll all go to Arcadia. It's going to be all right. I swear.'

His shirt was ripped, gaping open. Then she saw it, swinging low on his chest. Gold. A heart. A thin outline of diamonds.

She whispered, 'Where . . . did you get that?'

He glanced down.

Gail screamed and tried to roll away.

Ben's weight was on her, bearing down hard. He was reaching for her hands. 'Gail, don't. Don't. You don't know how it was. She gave it to me. Out in the yard. She threw it at me, said take it back.'

'Liar! She had it when Dave drove her home!' Gail sobbed. 'My God. Mother didn't buy it for her. You did. She wanted it and it cost too much. You gave Mother the money. Renee told me that night, her birthday. She knew where it came from. Said don't tell. Don't tell mamma. She was twelve years old!'

'You don't know how it was. You don't know. Gail, she came after me.'

'She was a baby!' Gail hit him in the mouth with her fist. 'Bastard! You killed her! You killed my sister! You did that to her!'

He pinned her wrists beside her head. His mouth was dark with blood. 'Listen to me. You don't know how it was. Please. She knew what she was doing. She wanted me to give her things. Gail, please. I wasn't her father, not her uncle. It was okay. She let me. She wanted it. And I kept her out of trouble. I took care of her and she used me. For years. Years.'

'All right.' Gail let her body go slack and gasped for

419

breath. Her chest burned. 'Yes. I know how she was.'

Ben was weeping openly now. 'She shut me out. I saved her from prison and she shut me out. That night in the backyard she said she was going to tell. Ruin me if I touched her again. As if it was my fault, what she did. Gail, please. She was bad. Bad.'

'Yes. I know.' Gail watched him. 'We're family. I can't tell. I won't.'

He sat back on his heels, his cheeks wet. 'Honey, we'll get through this.'

'Yes.' She slid her legs out from under him. 'And Carlos. He deserved it.'

Ben nodded, wiping his eyes on the heels of his hands. 'I had to. He said I better change my mind back about the property. He said Renee told him things. She told him what we did. Then he said I killed her. He didn't know I had to. I had to.'

Trembling, Gail rose to her feet. Ben looked up. And his face slowly changed.

He leaped for her.

She staggered toward his shotgun, grabbed it by the barrel and swung. She heard the crack of wood on bone, felt the impact up her arms. He fell slowly, twisting.

Gail slung the shotgun away and raced to Anthony. In the twilight the stain on his shirt looked black. He moaned when she touched him.

'Anthony! Get up!' She took his face in her hands, saw the blood on it. He opened his eyes. 'Get up! Anthony, please.'

'Where is he?'

'Over there. I knocked him out.'

'Kill him.'

'What?'

Anthony grimaced. 'Find my gun. Kill him. Do it.'

Gail looked back at Ben. 'I – It's all right, he's not

420

moving. Come on, it's getting dark. We have to get out of here.' She put his arm around her neck, grabbed his wrist, and made him stand.

'*¡Ay, coño carajo!*' His knees buckled.

'Dammit, get up!'

His face was sweaty. His right arm hung by his side, blood dripping off the fingers. He leaned on her. '*Bueno.*'

They walked. Slowly around trees, his feet shuffling. She felt the blood on her shirt. Warm, sticky. Her back trembled with the strain of his weight.

'How did you know?'

'Carlos . . . couldn't have. I knew him.' Anthony was breathing in shallow gasps. 'You were right. Dave didn't. Panther . . . no motive. It had to be someone . . . who knew her . . . intimately. I considered the judge . . . days ago. Because I knew Renee. What she was like.'

'You didn't tell me.'

'I didn't know. Until . . . Carlos. And I thought . . . he could have. When I knew you were alone with him—'

'Who told you?'

'Edith Newell. I called your office . . . your secretary. You cancelled your appointment. Ray didn't know why.' Anthony stumbled and she steadied him.

'Why didn't you call the police?'

'I wasn't sure. But you were here—' Anthony sank to his knees.

'Get up!'

Gail could see open ground now. Her car. And Anthony's. Two dark mounds lay beside it. Dogs. Anthony must have shot them. And the third one earlier, closer to the cabin.

'*Si me muero antes de—*'

'Shut up! You're not going to die!'

'Gail . . . *preciosa. Tú sabes que te amo.*'

421

'Yes, yes, I love you too. Now please get up. The car is right there, I promise.'

He murmured things to her in Spanish as they stumbled along the last few yards. She leaned Anthony against the side of her car, held him up with a shoulder in his chest, felt in her pocket. Nothing. 'Oh, God. My keys are in the book bag!'

Gail slid her hand down Anthony's thigh and felt the bump of a key chain. She reached inside.

'We're taking your car,' she said, putting his arm over her shoulder. 'I really didn't want to get blood on mine anyway. You're making such a mess.'

'Tengo sueño.'

'Forget it. You're not going to sleep here,' she said. 'Move.'

She walked him the ten feet or so to the right door of his Cadillac. When she let him go to unlock the car, he dropped like a stone. She flung open the door and popped the locks. The interior lights went on, illuminating soft gray leather. She found the seat adjustment and laid it back.

'Get up!' She pulled Anthony's arms. He groaned. 'I know, baby, I don't want to hurt you. Get in the car. Come on.'

She heard Ben's voice. 'Gail!' He was weeping. 'Gail, don't.'

For an instant she froze, then shoved Anthony into the seat. He pitched over. She lifted in his legs.

'Gail!'

She slammed the door, ran around the back end of the car. She could see him now, a movement in the darkness. Nearly there.

She opened the door. The lights came on and she saw Ben's face. Bloody. Renee's necklace on his chest, in the matted gray hair. He reached for her.

'Gail, honey. Don't.'

She screamed, pushed against him. He staggered backward. She got in, slammed the door, hit the lock.

'Nobody will believe you! You've got no proof!' Ben's hands were leaving streaks on the glass.

She fumbled with the keys, finding the right one, her fingers slick and red. 'Come on, come on.' She put the key in the ignition, turned.

'I didn't do anything!' He pounded on the window. 'Nobody will believe you!'

Gail slammed it into gear and gunned the engine.

Chapter Twenty-Six

Standing at the door to Anthony's room, Gail recognized one of the two women at the foot of his bed. Elena, his cousin.

'Come in, he's awake.'

His bed was cranked up and he smiled at her. Gail crossed the room. He looked better than the day before, she thought. They had taken the breathing tube off and unhooked the intravenous. His right shoulder, arm, and chest were still heavily bandaged. He had a gauze patch on his cheek. She leaned over and kissed him lightly on the other one.

'You smell delicious,' she said.

'Elena just shaved me,' he said. 'Elenita, I think you nicked my chin.'

She made a face at him, then introduced Gail to the other woman – her mother – and to the older couple sitting in armchairs by the window – more relatives.

Gail put her purse down on the bedside table. The hospital room looked more like a well-appointed bedroom, except for the raised bed and the dials and outlets in the wall behind him. Flowers took up every square inch of the dresser and window ledge.

'Elenita, mi amor, danos unos minutos solos.'

The older couple got up and the women followed out the door.

'You didn't have to ask them to leave,' Gail said.

'It's all right. Anyway, they've been here all day.'

425

'When I came yesterday you were asleep.'

'I missed you,' he said.

Gail kissed his mouth.

He sighed. 'Yes. Better.' He took her hand. 'You're here in the middle of the afternoon?'

'Karen has a play at school tonight I want to go to. We're moving back home this weekend. Trying to get our lives back to normal.'

Anthony looked at her for a few moments, then asked, 'How far back to normal?'

She smiled. 'Dave's living at the marina, if that's what you mean.'

He raised her hand to his lips. 'Have you told Karen about Ben?'

'As much as she'll understand right now. She asked where he was. I had to tell her we don't know.'

Anthony said, 'I hope you don't drive anywhere by yourself at night.'

'I'm not worried.'

'I worry for you,' he said.

Gail moved a magazine so she could sit on the edge of his bed. 'I was looking at a vacant office just now,' she said. 'It's on Sunset Drive, not too far from my house. Tempting.'

'Oh? You've decided, then?'

She shook her head. 'Not completely. It's too big a move to decide so quickly. I'm just window shopping for now.'

'George Sanchez's office is empty,' Anthony said.

She laughed. 'No. I wouldn't get anything done with you around.'

Someone rapped at the open door. 'Hey, buddy.' It was Frank Britton. He nodded at Gail. 'Ms Connor.' She had seen Britton three times since last Friday, twice in Ray Hammell's presence.

He nodded at Anthony's bandages. 'Looks like

you're going to make it, *amigo*.'

'So it appears.'

Britton said, 'Ms Connor, I might as well give you the latest. The State Attorney's considering whether to drop your case. Ray Hammell has talked to the prosecutors already about what we found in Judge Strickland's house, which you probably know.'

'Yes. He told me.'

Ben had apparently come home to bind up his wounds and take what he needed. There was blood on the carpets and stairs, kitchen cabinets open, clothes strewn about. In the little study adjoining his bedroom, desk drawers were upside down, the contents gone. He had missed a file box on a shelf. The police had found old bank statements, among them checks totalling thousands of dollars to Renee. And he had forgotten the photographs in his closet. Under a stack of dreary magazines, a hundred or more photos in a cardboard box. Polaroids. Some showed the two of them, a remote shutter cord trailing from Ben's fingers. Most were of Renee alone. Various ages, mostly young.

Ray Hammell had not told Gail precisely what the pictures contained, but his reticence had told her enough. She had not asked to see them.

She said to Frank Britton, 'Ray expects to hear something in a week or two.'

'We hope to find Strickland and get him to talk. If not, maybe Anthony can give us a statement as to what he heard Strickland say to you. That might help.'

Gail said, 'He was unconscious. What kind of statement—'

His expression stopped her in midsentence. Anthony said, 'Yes. I'm sure it will come back to me.'

Britton pulled a chair closer and sat down. 'I spoke to that Indian, Jimmy Panther. He confirms he and Carlos and Renee were going to take the artifacts from

427

the burial mound. He says it was out there, you just didn't find it.'

'What about Ben Strickland?' Anthony asked. 'I assume you have an arrest warrant.'

Britton knitted his fingers across his stomach. 'Well, as to attempted murder, no.'

'No?' Anthony laughed, then winced. 'They took twenty-six shotgun pellets out of my body and no?'

Frank Britton grinned. 'Okay, put on your defense attorney hat for a minute. Ben Strickland hears his dogs shot to death. Then he hears somebody coming through the woods. It's getting dark. The guy's carrying a gun. Strickland tells him to drop it, the guy aims, and Strickland shoots. What would you call it?'

'Frank, it is not your job to argue for the defendant,' Anthony said. 'It is mine, and I do not wish to argue for this one.'

'Well, we do have a warrant out on the other charges. Two counts of murder. Renee Connor and Carlos Pedrosa.' Britton's shoulders rose and fell under his brown jacket. 'We'll do our best.'

Gail said, 'He admitted killing them, Sergeant. Renee and Carlos. What's the problem?'

'With no other hard evidence?' Britton looked at Anthony. 'Counselor, you want to take this one?'

Anthony's eyes drifted shut for a moment. 'Frank—'

'Tell her.'

The eyes came open, dark brown, and fixed on Gail. 'If the prosecution has only the exculpatory statement of the person herself charged with the same crime—'

'This is crazy. What about the photographs? The money he gave her?'

'Enough to create a reasonable doubt in your case,' Anthony said. 'That has to be what Ray Hammell is arguing to the State Attorney. But would a jury find Ben Strickland guilty on that same evidence? No, a lawyer just out of law school could win an acquittal on what we have. A pedophile is not necessarily a murderer. In the absence of anything to connect him with the deaths of Renee or Carlos – Do we still assume that, Frank?'

Britton shrugged again. 'We're doing what we can. Checking for alibis. Examining his records. We've gone through every cubic inch of his house and office. We might find something in his Winnebago, if we could find his Winnebago.'

Gail said, 'He's in it. Parked in the woods somewhere, that's my guess.'

'We've got a three-state BOLO out on him. He can't hide forever.'

Gail turned around and stared out the window. The bay glittered. Sailboats skimmed over the water, white sails tilting with the wind. She said, 'So he gets off. Is that what you're telling me?'

'No. We find him, we'll arrest him. The State's going to file a case. Then it's up to the jury.'

'He could claim Carlos killed Renee,' she said. 'We've been making a great case for that.' Ray Hammell had told her just yesterday that Betty Diaz had admitted giving Carlos a false alibi the night Renee was murdered.

She watched a sloop unfurl its spinnaker, a sudden blossoming of bright yellow, small and silent at this distance. She pressed lightly on the glass as if to make sure it was still there.

'I hope you find him. I hope he resists arrest and you have to shoot him.'

When she turned back from the window, both men were looking at her. She said, 'Sergeant, don't tell my mother what happened years ago. What he did to my sister then.' Britton nodded. 'I've told her they had an adult affair and he was jealous about Carlos. That was hard enough for her to accept. She never suspected the rest. It would kill her if she knew.'

Gail glanced toward the door. Elena had knocked lightly, several people behind her.

Britton got up. 'Well, family time. I'd better be going. Take care of yourself.'

Anthony said, 'Thanks, Frank.'

Ernesto Pedrosa came in, his wife Digna with him. Others followed, speaking Spanish so fast Gail couldn't pick out a word of it.

Leaning on his cane, the old man went over to Anthony. He kissed both his cheeks, embraced him. Gail saw Anthony suck in his breath.

Digna Pedrosa tugged her husband away. '*¡Cuidado! Lo dueles.*'

Gail picked up her purse, gave Anthony a little wave, mouthed a see-you-later.

'Gail, don't leave.'

His grandfather turned and bowed slightly. '*Buenas tardes, doctora.*'

She came closer. '*Señor Pedrosa, ¿cómo está?*'

'Anthony has told me that you saved his life.' He took her hand in both of his and looked at her through his heavy glasses. 'I am indebted forever.'

A woman about sixty pushed through with a casserole dish, which she held out to Anthony. She lifted the lid. '*Mira, Antonio, lo que te traigo. Masitas de puerco, moros, plátanos maduros . . .*'

He sighed. '*Gracias, tía. No puedo. Ordenes del médico.*' Such a liar, Gail thought. A doctor ordering him not to eat Cuban food.

The woman – his aunt – turned to Gail. '*¿Tiene hambre, señora? Parece que te falta comer.*'

Anthony translated. 'She says eat, you look a little thin.'

'Do *you* think so?'

'Ask me later.'

Someone uncorked a bottle.

The nurse looked in, started to object. She shook her head, then closed the door.

Gail held out her glass and the old man filled it.

Epilogue

Jimmy found Gail Connor where Irene had said, out at Bayview Memorial Gardens. But she wasn't alone, he could see that as he pulled his pickup truck in behind her car.

There was a little girl with her and a man in a suit. Jimmy waited for a minute or two, watching, his arms draped across the top of the steering wheel. Then he got out.

He didn't like cemeteries. Too much death in one place. When he died, he wanted to be laid out in the Everglades. His grandparents had been done like that, and his father. It was better. He wanted his bones to sink into the earth, not be put in a box.

He could see the headstone now, some flowers. Renee Michelle Connor. Beloved daughter and sister.

The little girl saw him first, staring the way kids do. Jimmy smiled at her. The girl smiled back, said something to Gail Connor, who looked around. So did the man. He had his right arm in a sling. Spanish-looking guy. Cuban, maybe.

Jimmy motioned for Gail Connor to come over. The man spoke to her. She touched his hand, must have told him it was okay, to wait there.

She walked across the grass. Nice-looking woman. The breeze making her hair move. She pushed it back and stood in front of him on the sidewalk, looking at him. Waiting. She reminded him a little of Renee.

'Your mother said you would be out here.' Jimmy glanced back at the man, who hadn't taken his eyes off them. 'I just gave that Tequesta deer mask to her.'

Her mouth opened, surprised. 'Did you?'

'Donated in Renee's name to the museum.'

Gail Connor was smiling now. 'Thanks. That was a good thing you did.' Then she asked what Jimmy had known she was going to ask. 'Where did that mask come from? Really.'

'My grandmother gave it to me.' He shrugged. 'That's true. One of our people found it, years ago. It took me a while, but I figured it came from that property your cousin owned and there were probably more out there.'

'I see. And you asked Renee to help you.' When Jimmy nodded, she said, 'And Carlos.'

'He told me he was doing it as a favor for Renee. Like I'd believe that.'

'Did he believe you about the gold?'

Jimmy was about to ask her what gold, but stopped. You could tell she was a smart woman, ready to pick out a lie. He only shrugged. 'I never said it was there. He let himself think so. People do that. Anyway, I did tell him he couldn't have what was in the burial mound. It was sacred. Not for personal gain.'

She might have been a little skeptical. Let her think what she wanted.

Jimmy said, 'Your mother told me the property goes to Ben Strickland's two sons in New York.'

'Yes, according to his will.'

'I asked her if maybe they'd let the county archaeologist in there to excavate. Better than letting the ground get bulldozed for houses or whatever.' After a pause, he added, 'Irene said I ought to be there. You

434

know. Make sure the things are handled with respect. And nothing gets broken.'

Gail Connor smiled again. 'Of course.'

For a while Jimmy watched a squirrel skitter up an oak tree, run out on one of the branches.

'I heard they found Ben Strickland.' He looked back at Gail to see her reaction.

She nodded, didn't seem sorry.

'Where was that?' he asked, already knowing the answer.

'In a camper about ten miles outside of Arcadia, in the woods. He had been dead for a couple weeks. He must have known they would find him, sooner or later. He wrote a letter confessing what he did. And then he killed himself.'

'How'd he do it?'

'With a knife.' Her mouth tightened before she said, 'He cut his wrists. Appropriate, wouldn't you say?'

Jimmy nodded. 'I'd say so.' He glanced at the man again. Still watching, like if Jimmy made a wrong move he'd come on over and see what was going on. Or take out his gun. Cubans, they carried guns. They were crazy like that.

Jimmy faced away from him. 'I've got something for you.' He reached in his shirt pocket. 'And don't ask me any questions about it.' He took her hand, opened it, let go of what he had.

Her eyes flew up to his, back down again. The color went out of her face. 'Oh—'

The gold chain looped through her fingers. The diamonds around the heart sparkled in the sunlight.

Her breath rushed out. 'Where did you get this?'

But Jimmy was already backing up.

In his pickup, he looked through the side window. The man and Gail Connor were talking. The girl was on tiptoe, trying to see what she was holding. The man started to come to the truck, but Jimmy put it in gear and let out the clutch.

In the rearview mirror, he saw her show the necklace to the little girl.

More Thrilling Fiction from Headline:

—— STEVE MARTINI ——
PRIME WITNESS

THE STUNNING NEW COURTROOM DRAMA
FROM THE AUTHOR OF *COMPELLING EVIDENCE*

'MR MARTINI WRITES WITH THE AGILE EPISODIC
STYLE OF A LAWYER QUICK ON HIS FEET' JOHN GRISHAM

'Steve Martini seems to have hit the nail right on the head' *Irish Times*
'A real page turner' *Sunday Telegraph*

PRIME WITNESS

In the space of five days the rural college town of Davenport is
rocked by four brutal murders: two couples – undergraduates – their
bodies are found tied and staked out on the banks of Putah Creek.
Then two more bodies are discovered. This time the victims are
Abbott Scofield, a distinguished member of the university faculty,
and his former wife Karen.

The police suspect Andre Iganovich, a Russian immigrant and part-
time security guard, but Paul Madriani, hot-shot Capitol City lawyer,
thinks there is more to the case than meets the eye.

Forensic reports on the physical evidence suggest lingering questions
about the Russian's involvement in the Scofield killings, and Paul
becomes increasingly convinced that the second murders are the
product of some copy-cat killer – a cold and calculating murderer
who has taken the lives of the Scofields for reasons that Paul is
determined to uncover...

'Prime is indeed the word for this involving read' *Publishers Weekly*

'Nice insider touches, and a hard-punching climax' *The Times*

Don't miss COMPELLING EVIDENCE and THE SIMEON CHAMBER
also available from Headline Feature
'The best debut, in my opinion, is *Compelling Evidence*' John Grisham
'Compelling indeed. This is a terrific debut' *Sunday Telegraph*
'A tense and gripping story, which held me to the end' *Books*
'A sensationally good courtroom thriller' *Los Angeles Times*

FICTION/THRILLER 0 7472 4164 3

More Thrilling Fiction from Headline:

TELL ME NO SECRETS

THE TERRIFYING PSYCHOLOGICAL THRILLER

JOY FIELDING

BESTSELLING AUTHOR OF *SEE JANE RUN*

'People who annoy me have a way of... disappearing'

Jess Koster thinks she has conquered the crippling panic attacks that have plagued her since the unexplained disappearance of her mother, eight years ago. But they are back with a vengeance. And not without reason. Being a chief prosecutor in the State's Attorney's office exposes Jess to some decidedly lowlife types. Like Rick Ferguson, about to be tried for rape – until his victim goes missing. Another inexplicable disappearance.

If only Jess didn't feel so alone. Her father is about to re-marry; her sister is busy being the perfect wife and mother; her ex-husband has a new girlfriend. And besides, he's Rick Ferguson's defence lawyer...

Battling with a legal system that all too often judges women by appalling double standards; living under the constant threat of physical danger; fighting to overcome the emotional legacy of her mother's disappearance, Jess is in danger of going under. And it looks as though someone is determined that she should disappear, too...

'Joy Fielding tightens suspense like a noose round your neck and keeps one shattering surprise for the very last page. Whew!' *Annabel*

'The story she has to tell this time is a corker that runs rings round Mary Higgins Clark. Don't even think of starting this anywhere near bedtime' *Kirkus Reviews*

Don't miss Joy Fielding's *See Jane Run* ('Compulsive reading' *Company*), also from Headline Feature

FICTION/GENERAL   0 7472 4163 5

More Thrilling Fiction from Headline:

ABOVE THE EARTH, BELOW THE EARTH, THERE'S NO DEATH MORE HORRIFYING

GARY GOTTESFELD
ILL WIND

When a massive earthquake uncovers a large Indian graveyard in Beverly Hills, forensic expert Wilhelm Van Deer – known as 'the Dutchman' – is confronted by more bones than he can cope with. But he soon realises that some of the remains are not as old as they should be, nor the manner of death as straightforward as first appears.

Digging deeper, he comes across weird underground passages and strange paintings of giant centipedes. Somehow these discoveries are linked to mysterious deaths that occurred over twenty years earlier, but there are powerful anonymous people now determined to keep their dark secrets buried for ever.

When the chilling murders begin anew, the Dutchman sets out to catch a maniac – an elusive psychopath obsessed with a grotesquely unusual method of killing...

FICTION/THRILLER   0 7472 4168 6

A selection of bestsellers
from Headline

NIGHT OF THE DEAD	Mike Bond	£4.99 ☐
SPEAK NO EVIL	Philip Caveney	£4.99 ☐
GONE	Kit Craig	£4.99 ☐
INADMISSIBLE EVIDENCE	Philip Friedman	£5.99 ☐
QUILLER SOLITAIRE	Adam Hall	£4.99 ☐
HORSES OF VENGEANCE	Michael Hartmann	£4.99 ☐
CIRCUMSTANCES UNKNOWN	Jonellen Heckler	£4.99 ☐
THE ASCENT	Jeff Long	£4.99 ☐
BRING ME CHILDREN	David Martin	£4.99 ☐
THE SIMEON CHAMBER	Steve Martini	£4.99 ☐
A CALCULATED RISK	Katherine Neville	£4.99 ☐
STATE V. JUSTICE	Gallatin Warfield	£5.99 ☐

All Headline books are available at your local bookshop or newsagent, or can be ordered direct from the publisher. Just tick the titles you want and fill in the form below. Prices and availability subject to change without notice.

Headline Book Publishing PLC, Cash Sales Department, Bookpoint, 39 Milton Park, Abingdon, OXON, OX14 4TD, UK. If you have a credit card you may order by telephone – 0235 831700.

Please enclose a cheque or postal order made payable to Bookpoint Ltd to the value of the cover price and allow the following for postage and packing:
UK & BFPO: £1.00 for the first book, 50p for the second book and 30p for each additional book ordered up to a maximum charge of £3.00.
OVERSEAS & EIRE: £2.00 for the first book, £1.00 for the second book and 50p for each additional book.

Name ....

Address ....

....

....

If you would prefer to pay by credit card, please complete:
Please debit my Visa/Access/Diner's Card/American Express (delete as applicable) card no:

Signature .... Expiry Date ....